"This emotional family saga and thriller explores PTSD and childhood trauma in a narrative blending psychological suspense with hard-won emotional breakthroughs. Kain has crafted a fast-paced contemporary thriller that delves with insight into themes of mental health. Readers who enjoy unreliable narrators and jolting plot twists will enjoy this."

— All-A's from *BookLife*

"Vivid descriptions of the character's CPTSD episodes help readers understand the disorder on a deeper level. Good writing is conversational yet clever; Kain nails it. Artfully written, entertaining, and intriguing. This one is a must-read."

— RECOMMENDED by *US Review*

"What Lies Buried is a dramatic story about taking the hardest steps forward to confront the scars of our past. A thought-provoking sequel that dives deep into the way our histories shape us."

— 5 Stars from *Indies Today*

"Kain really knows how to focus a dramatic and engaging lens on ... trauma's enduring impact on individuals and relationships. [She] beautifully juxtaposes Gavin's journey with Katie's self-discovery, painting a vivid picture of resilience in the face of adversity. ... Exploration of art as a means of coping and healing ... a powerful narrative ... highly recommended for fans of deeply psychological, cathartic, honest storytelling."

— 5 Stars from *Readers' Favorite*

"The explosive sequel to the psychological thriller *Secrets In The Mirror*, *What Lies Buried* continues the story of Gavin and Katie as he struggles with Complex PTSD and Katie struggles to save her family. Kain is not afraid to dig deep into the dark side of life, and her courage in telling this story is reflected on every page, right up to the jaw-dropping end."

—Barbara Conrey, *USA Today* Bestselling author of *Nowhere Near Goodbye*

"Fasten your seatbelts, readers; this novel is a tumultuous ride. In this psychological thriller, Gavin is a tortured soul, plagued by Complex PTSD that exacerbates his flight and fight responses to the point of endangering others and himself. His wife Katie, an artist and mother, must balance the well-being of herself and their child against the needs of her psychiatrically disabled husband. This searing look at how mental illness can impact a family is at times disturbing, but readers will root for Katie as she struggles to do what is right."

—Carla Damron, award-winning author of *The Orchid Tattoo* and *Justice Be Done*

WHAT LIES BURIED

A NOVEL

LESLIE KAIN

atmosphere press

© 2024 Leslie Kain

Published by Atmosphere Press

ISBN 979-8891321816

Cover design by Matthew Fielder

No part of this book may be reproduced without permission from the author except in brief quotations and in reviews. This is a work of fiction, and any resemblance to real places, persons, or events is entirely coincidental.

Atmospherepress.com

CONTENT WARNING

One of the characters in this story suffers from trauma experienced during childhood and early adulthood. He has now been diagnosed with Complex PTSD (C-PTSD) and exhibits reactions to flashbacks and triggers that some readers may find disturbing.

If you or anyone you know is having difficulty managing their emotions, is a trauma survivor, has been diagnosed with PTSD, or is feeling suicidal, please reach out for help:

- PTSD Foundation of America: (877) 717-PTSD (7873)
- NAMI HelpLine | NAMI (National Alliance on Mental Illness): https://www.nami.org › help
  Call 1-800-950-6264, or chat, or text "Friend" to 62640, or email helpline@nami.org
- National Suicide Prevention Lifeline: (800) 273-TALK (8255)
- Crisis Text Line: Text HOME to 741741

"Though each night he cried out, each night no angels came, no ministers of grace to save the son from the spotlight glare of grief."
—Mairead Small Staid

1

PRE-DAWN SHADOWS SUSPEND TIME AND SPACE as Gavin peers through his kitchen window, scooping coffee beans into the grinder. Something feels unfinished, like a song cut off mid-coda, notes pulsating in the void, a preamble to uncertainty.

It is Monday, the one day of the week he and Katie close 'Ono Kūloko, their Kauai restaurant, so they can manage the weekly deep-clean, pay bills, order supplies, and deal with unanticipated problems. Except he has been AWOL for the last few months. *He* was the unanticipated problem, after his twin brother...was gone.

But today Gavin is convinced he's put all that behind him. Getting back to being the successful chef and business owner before it all happened, before his world imploded. Before *he* imploded. Now he's determined to resume responsibility, resume life, after being a useless invalid for almost three months while Katie carried the full burden of managing the restaurant, her *Makakū* gallery, their daughter Maggie, and their home—doing everything *he* was supposed to do, while also supporting her traumatized husband.

He had gone into a tailspin—his own virtual death spiral—after Devon passed. But guilt, his lifelong curse, now digs its claws into his neck, nagging shame for his impotence, his failure to support, take care of, save—first Mom, then Dad, and finally his identical twin—and now these last months he has also failed Katie and Maggie. Echoes of Devon's taunts ring in his ears. *Dad was right. You're a wimp, a loser. Can't even take care of your wife and kid. You just can't live without me, Twinkie.*

Gavin tries to shake off the torment, pushes his shoulders back, takes a deep breath, and stretches his lanky frame up to its full height. His self-talk takes over the microphone. *Okay, man. Time to prove you're not a loser. Better get this show on the road.*

He reaches over to touch the button on the grinder. Instantly its loud piercing assault throws him into a terrified huddle on the floor, arms protecting his head, his body jammed into the corner cabinet, pain gripping his chest. He doesn't hear the delighted squeal of little Maggie running down the hall, or Katie's laughter in the chase.

Katie comes into the kitchen carrying her giggling captive and turns on the overhead light. "Coffee smells good, Tiger, but making it by braille might not be the best method."

Maggie wriggles down from her arms and starts running to Gavin, who is still hunched in the corner. Katie quickly intercepts her; touching someone mid-trigger can be dangerous. Precocious almost-two-year-old Maggie loves playing games and cheers, "Find Da-dee!"

Katie eyes Gavin's curled back and forces a weary smile. "You can come out now, sweetie, it's safe," she says, as Maggie claps her chubby hands. "Thanks for grinding the beans. Do you want me to finish making the coffee?"

Gavin begins to stir. Arms first, releasing his turtled head, then unwrapping his tightly wound body as he mumbles, "I'll make it."

"You sure you're okay now, babe?" Katie swallows hard,

forcing tension from her voice. These episodes—Gavin's random reactions to whatever triggers his traumatic memories—have been occurring more frequently, forcing her into a daily dance around eggshells. And confusing Maggie.

"Thanks for rescuing me. Again."

"Maggie did it. She found you." Katie offers her hand to Gavin as he stands. "And you know it's okay if you haven't totally recovered. It's a process, remember? What you've gone through can take time. A lot more than a couple months and a tattoo." She stretches on tiptoes to peck a kiss onto his cheek.

Katie releases Maggie to the floor and watches as her daughter opens a cabinet door and begins pulling out every pot and pan, handing each to her daddy. "Bekfass," she says.

"Are you hungry, Mags? Is that why you didn't let Mommy sleep in this morning?" Gavin lifts her into her high chair, while their dog Patches jumps up to help.

"You were doing a lot of that tossing and turning thing again last night, Gav." Katie studies him while smoothing Maggie's strawberry curls off her face and putting on her bib.

Gavin turns away to put the grounds into the coffeemaker basket. "I was having those dreams again," he murmurs, glancing down at the ink on his bicep holding the name of his twin.

"The same ones?" Katie asks. "Y'know, I was going to suggest maybe it might help if we had a formal service to bury Devon's ashes," she turns to open a drawer, "and then this letter came last week while you were on your hike with Tray." She hands him an envelope.

Gavin doesn't take it. He stares at the return address: *Levine, McDermott & Lombardi, LLP.* Lombardi was his father's attorney. "What do they want?"

"Open it, Gav."

"Just tell me."

Katie pulls a letter from the envelope. "I opened it while you were gone with Tray, in case it was bad news. Which you don't need any more of right now." She looks at him, then unfolds the letter. "They just need you to contact them to settle your dad's estate, now that…"

"Now that Devon is *dead*," he spits out the word, which feels like a knife to his heart when he has to say it.

Gavin glances out to the living room, strewn with Maggie's toys. A black marble box sits almost touching the ceiling, high atop the bookshelves that dominate the room. He hadn't thought about that box since Trayvon dragged him out of his dark hole to hike the Kalalau Trail along the NaPali coastline. The "retreat" that was supposed to help him. Maybe he'd just repressed the thought of the box, the reminder.

Now the weight of his brother's suicide…seeing him hanging there…in front of the taunting message he left…comes crashing down on him all over again, after he thought he'd finally put it behind him. That message had felt to him like Devon was gaslighting him one last time, one final put-down. But when Dr. Pedersen, Gavin's loyal counselor since high school, visited Kauai a few weeks after Devon's death, he explained that for someone like Devon, who had Narcissistic Personality Disorder, the greatest fear is to be discovered as a fraud—not superior as he claims. So with NPD, suicide can seem to be the only way to divert people from one's shame of being an imposter. Rather than the wish to die, the need is to hide from the truth.

Gavin isn't sure that's true. He just blames himself for failing to save his brother. But Katie is right; it's going to take time for him to recover. Yet those dreams are right, too. It may never really be over.

"Bekfass!" Maggie sings, slapping her hands on her empty high chair tray.

"We can talk about it later, Gav." Katie puts a sippy cup of juice on Maggie's tray. "Here, Mags, have some orange juice while we make your oatmeal."

Nina Simone's low windup to *"I'm feelin' good"* rolls out from Gavin's cell phone next to the coffeemaker. He stares at it. Who was he kidding—besides himself—when he installed that as his ringtone? Blood drains from his already pale face. He seems to know exactly who is calling.

Katie pauses her task to hand the phone to him, watching closely in case he's triggered.

"Hello?" Gavin's voice cracks. He hesitates. "Yes, this is he." His body contorts into a knot as he listens to the caller. His hands begin to shake, an almost imperceptible tremor. "Can't you just do all that stuff? You can send me all the papers to sign..."

Katie's attention goes on full alert as she sees her tall husband shrivel into a fearful little boy. She comes close to place her hand tentatively, gently, on his shoulder.

"Yeah, I guess so," he mumbles. "Might not be for a week or two. I'll let you know when I can be there."

Gavin's face twists, his mouth grim under his red stubble, his brow in a deep scowl as he throws his cell phone onto the table, narrowly missing his coffee.

"I have to go back." His head droops like a wilted flower. "They want me to get whatever's important from the house so they can sell it, and deal with the building commissioner on what to do with the Prince Street building. It's been boarded up for more than three years now, and the City says it's a hazard and they're going to put it up on the abandoned properties auction, where the proceeds go to the City." Gavin snorts. "It's probably more like some buzzards want the property."

His entire body begins shivering with increasing amplitude and frequency, like a man lost in sub-zero temperatures.

"I'm sorry, Gav," Katie eyes him warily, watching for the now-familiar signs of his all-too-frequent flashbacks, the triggers, his unpredictable reactions—freeze, flight, or...fight.

He struggles to stay afloat, above all the memories flooding him now. "Going back will be like replaying all of it, all over again. Even though Rizzo said I'm safe now."

"Well, no way can you go there now," Katie sets her jaw in fierce determination.

"Then what do you think I can do, just hand over my family's assets?" Gavin challenges.

Katie sits down beside him at the kitchen table. "Gavin, you're the guy I've loved since high school, the father of our daughter. I don't want anything or anyone to hurt you at this vulnerable time in your recovery." She peers into his face, speaking softly. "If you really *have* to go, then I'm coming with you."

His teeth chatter as he mumbles, "No fucking way! You really don't think I can handle it, do you?" Gavin clenches his jaw now, glaring at her. "Besides, you have to manage the restaurant, and your gallery, and Maggie! We sure can't bring her to Boston and drag her into that cesspool. That danger." His voice ekes out of his constricted throat like a man being hanged.

Dueling emotions face off inside Katie. Fears that Gavin might lose his grip altogether in the environment where it all started, where she couldn't be there to pull him back. Versus relief that she could be free of her husband's unpredictable ups and downs—his frightening roller coaster—for a few days. She had been the sole caretaker for her mother since she was nine, but that was because of a medical illness that affected her mother's body, not her mind. This thing with Gavin is different, and it's beginning to wear her down. The result of his lifetime of emotional abuse topped by violent deaths in his family, she hopes it won't require another lifetime to resolve.

"Maybe we could get Pedersen to write a medical waiver so they'll delay the auction?"

Now Gavin slams his fist on the table and stands abruptly, shouting, "Bullshit! That sounds like you want to commit me to a mental institution or something!"

Maggie begins whimpering, and Katie thrusts out her hands, palms down, signaling for calm. "Not at all, sweetie... just trying to avoid anything *like* that." She recalls Pedersen warning her after Devon's death that the impact of Gavin's grief might occasionally cause him to distrust or feel paranoid. Maybe this is it?

"Well, I *do* have to go, without dragging you into all that shit." Gavin exhales a lungful of angst and drops back down onto his chair. "I have to face it anyway, like vomiting all the poison that's crippling me. I'll let Pedersen and my O'Malley grandparents know I'm coming, and get all that business with the lawyers over with, once and for all."

"Okay then, I guess...," Katie sighs. "If you're sure. But you have to stay in touch with me every day, just so I won't worry. Maybe that stuff won't take too long. You might be out and back in a week or so. Just make the decisions and leave the paperwork to the lawyers." She mentally crosses her fingers, hoping it won't be more complicated than that. Or risky. "You could even bury Devon's ashes beside your parents while you're there. Have Father Decker do a little ceremony."

"I don't think any amount of Decker's mojo will help Devon. Or me."

Katie rubs his back with comforting strokes. "I'll be as close as your phone."

Gavin stares at the cracked tile floor as if some profound message were written there.

"You can probably stay in your grandparents' house while you're there," Katie murmurs.

"Well, I sure don't want to spend too much time at the scene of the crime."

———

Gavin walks into *'Ono Kūloko*, the restaurant he and Katie designed and crafted together, yet now that he has committed to break his months-long fast and return to work, he feels like a stranger. An imposter. Nothing has changed during his absence, but everything seems different, alien. Even the smells. He stands, staring at it all anew. Upside-down chairs rest atop gray faux granite tables from last night's clean-up. Clusters of differently shaped and sized Edison lightbulbs hang from the vaulted corrugated steel ceiling, giving a hip glow to the rough unfinished wood walls and bar. Colorful paintings by local artists from Katie's gallery punctuate the cool tones of the space. He isn't sure what to do, where to begin.

Maggie runs past him, squealing "dumper," jolting Gavin from his reverie. He laughs and follows her into the restaurant's office, where she begins pulling out toys from a deep box and dropping each onto the floor until she finds her prize: a bright yellow dump truck. She holds it up to Gavin and manipulates the truck bed with a satisfied giggle. Katie comes in carrying a heavy briefcase, plops into the desk chair, plugs in her laptop, and straightens everything on her desktop. "Maggie, you can't have all those trucks on the floor, we'll trip on them. Put some of them back now. Maybe Patches will help."

Gavin suddenly realizes that life has gone on without him. Even Katie seems different. Still pert and petite with untamed blonde curls, but somehow changed. The former Salutatorian and Phi Beta Kappa, she's now focused yet distracted, moving faster, like she's in a race to get everything done. Then he turns toward the sound of unfamiliar voices at the rear door of the restaurant. "Who's that?" he asks Katie, flicking his head toward the sound.

"Staff. Here for Monday deep-clean duty," Katie says. "You know Koni and Bill, but I've had to replace a couple staffers with new people. C'mon, I'll introduce you."

The awkward sense of feeling out of place begins to wane in Gavin as the day goes on. Under Katie's direction, he keeps busy, soon forgetting the worst and remembering what was good. The certificate in the window declaring their restaurant Number One on the island. His passion for cuisine, for business, for people. He inches back into the rhythm of life before. Even the smells become familiar, reminiscent, as he attaches full kegs of microbrew to the lines in the cooler behind the bar.

Maggie has the run of the restaurant, her playground every Monday. Everyone, including the staff, seems to enjoy tending Maggie, who plays with her trucks or "writes" in Katie's office one minute then tries to engage people in hide and seek the next. "Don't let her get away with any nonsense," Katie calls out to the staff. "She seems to think the cuter and more fun she is, she can get what she wants. Right, Gav?"

Around lunchtime, a short muscled delivery guy comes with their meat order from the abattoir, hoisting cuts of beef bigger than he is. Koni ushers him into the walk-in cooler and helps unload everything onto the heavy steel shelves that have just been cleaned and sanitized. After that's done, Gavin goes out into the dining area, stepping around an agitated Patches, to tell the staff it's break time. He sticks his head into the office and tells Katie he's going to walk the dog. "Take Maggie with you," Katie says, not looking up from a pile of bills. "She needs the exercise so she'll be tired enough to take a nap after lunch."

Gavin calls out, "Hey Mags! Where are you? We have to go walk Patches!" When Maggie doesn't respond, he begins looking for her, heads into the kitchen, and nearly trips over their one-eyed, one-eared rescue pup scratching at the door of the cooler and whining. "C'mon Patches, let's find Maggie," he says, rubbing the mutt's good ear before continuing on.

Then it hits him, like a runaway freight train, a howl erupting from him louder than any three trains could blare. For a suspended moment he is paralyzed, unable to breathe, memories of being stuck in the cooler, trapped there by his brother, fire crackling in the restaurant, with Patches scratching outside the thick insulated door. He spins around, falls to his knees, sobbing, frantically scrambling to the cooler on all fours, just as Katie and several staff rush in response.

In an instant, the memory of what happened to Gavin seven months ago flashes back to Katie. She grabs the heavy lever and opens the door to find a bewildered toddler standing there. Gavin lunges to smother his daughter in his arms while escalating his howls, which frightens little Maggie into her own shrieking and crying, muffled in the grip of her equally hysterical father.

Katie quickly pries Gavin's arms from their baby before he can cause her greater trauma. "It's okay now, Mags. Daddy was just scared that you could have been hurt," she whispers, kissing Maggie's head. "Please promise you won't go into the cooler again, sweetie. That's not a good place for hide 'n' seek."

Four staff members look down and shift awkwardly, having witnessed this widely beloved man, known as the epitome of cool and calm, just devolve into an overwrought lunatic.

Katie reaches her hand down to Gavin, beckoning him to his feet, then turns to the speechless staff. An apologetic smile won't pretend the scene away; she's direct. "Hey guys, thanks for coming in today. I think our family has other stuff we need to do right now. Can you all just finish up the usual Monday tasks? Koni, remember there's a couple deliveries today—produce and fish. And you know where to find me if you need anything."

Unnatural quiet sucks every molecule of air from the car as Katie drives home. Even Maggie doesn't make a peep. When they finally pull into their carport, Gavin mumbles, "I guess we need to talk."

Once inside the house, Gavin drops onto the sofa with an exhausted sigh, heavy with remorse and embarrassment. Katie hands a glass of iced tea to him, then puts Maggie into her high chair and gives her lunch. There have been several of these incidents over the past months, like the one that just happened. Dr. Pedersen had cautioned that Devon's suicide would likely bring all Gavin's past traumas to the surface and certain things might trigger reactions he had previously repressed. And that Katie would need to be patient and supportive, but also protect herself and Maggie. That weighs on her every day.

Katie perches on the arm of the sofa beside Gavin, worry creasing her face. "So talk to me."

"I'm not sure what happened," Gavin says. "Maggie must have gone into the cooler when Hector and Koni were putting away the meat. They probably didn't see a short little person there and just closed the door behind them when they were done."

"I get that," she nods. "We need to understand your reaction. Where that's coming from."

"Kinda over the top, right?" Gavin hangs his head low, then takes a sip of tea.

"I'm guessing the idea of Maggie being in danger brought up the responsibility your family always expected of you, to take care of everyone, save everyone."

"Which I failed at doing. Miserably. Mom, Dad, Devon. And now I just *cannot* fail with you and Mags!"

"Bad things can happen to good people, and you can do everything in your power to prevent that, but sometimes it might be out of your hands. Today you realized where Maggie was, but freaking out from that old guilt trip actually blocked your ability to act quickly." Katie leans forward to see whether any of her words are getting through to Gavin, who is silent.

Although she, Dr. Pedersen, and even Tray, have presented this logic to him numerous times, it hasn't changed Gavin's reactions. She recalls Pedersen saying that if Gavin's life were fiction, his behavior would self-correct after one explanation. But words can't rewire the neurological damage from his lifetime of traumatic assaults.

"I know all that logically," Gavin sighs. "But something just takes over. Old memories, old feelings, fears, just put me back there, totally outside logic. Outside reality."

"I know. Like the noise of the coffee grinder this morning

took you back to gunshots."

"Yeah. My shootout defending Devon. And the shot Dad took for him."

"Y'know, Pedersen always said you can't let other people define you—who and what you are. You took your dad's assignment to save everyone as the definition of who you are, but it's impossible to save everyone all the time. You're not a failure if you can't do that—whether it's Maggie when stuff happens out of your control, or other people when they cause their own problems. You are *not* responsible for cleaning up everyone else's shit."

Gavin snorts irony. "I hope I can just slip in and out of Boston before any of that old shit even knows I'm there."

Katie smiles in the pretending way of mothers encouraging their kid's belief in Santa Claus, trying to quell her worry. "Have you made your travel arrangements yet?"

"No." Gavin squirms. "Maybe next week."

Katie chuckles. "Next week you'll travel, or next week you'll make the arrangements?"

"I guess I'll book a flight for next week," Gavin says with an eye-roll.

"Make sure your grandparents are going to be in town then, and Pedersen too."

"You think I'm gonna fall apart, so I'll need them?"

"Think of them as your support, your fan base." Katie rumples Gavin's curly red mop. "They can be your just-in-case safety net. And *promise* me you'll call me at least once a day! I'm still not comfortable with you insisting on going there without me. Remember what Pedersen said."

"He said a lot of things..."

"Oh, definitely," Katie smiles. "He's a treasure trove of wisdom. You were even writing some stuff down while he was here. I'm thinking now about two things in particular: Surround yourself with people who love and understand you. And breathe. Like meditation."

"I've never been able to meditate. All those voices..." He shakes his head at the mystery of the voices that take over his thoughts, going down trapdoors into darkness. He takes a long gulp of tea.

Katie nods. "Nalani told me that after Puna went through several traumatic events back-to-back, both professionally and personally, he did one-on-one guided TM with a trained expert here on the island."

"TM?"

"Transcendental Meditation. Nalani said it really helped at the time, and Puna still uses the techniques he learned, almost every day."

"Wow. He never told me that! It's hard to picture big burly super-cop Puna doing meditation." Gavin grins. "Maybe that's why he's so chill."

"So I've got a deal for you, babe." Katie snuggles down close to him and drapes her arm on his thigh. "I can handle the restaurant a couple more weeks while you get your Boston mission out of the way. Spend the time before then to learn a few techniques to survive it, take the trip, then come back to us, and the restaurant. I'll call Nalani for a referral to the TM guide, and you may want to talk with Puna about it, too."

"It kills me to see you working your ass off because of me, sweetheart."

"You'll be much stronger after you get all that Boston stuff out of the way." She hopes. She misses the Gavin she loves. The steady, compassionate guy she married.

Gavin nods. But a foreboding sense of disaster lurks deep within his amygdala.

"Freedom of the will is a psychological fiction."
—*Louis Berkhof*

2

GAVIN AND KATIE HAD FIRST FLOWN TO KAUAI IN July 2002. More than three years ago, after his father stepped in front of a bullet meant for Devon. But as a couple of newlyweds, the trip had seemed quick then, making it easier to put behind them the tragedy and danger that forced them to flee. The reasons they fled then are the same reasons he shouldn't be returning now. Old memories and fear claw at him like a vulture, accompanied by hallucinations and mirages of danger distorting reality all around him.

The trip seems like endless torture. Two flights—one a red-eye—then sitting in an airport during his layover, drag on, plunging him into emotional catatonia unassuaged by the app on his phone the meditation guide gave him. Katie's supportive text overnight didn't help much either, and the two vodkas from the flight attendant only seem to have heightened his fears about what awaits him in Boston.

Landing in Logan Airport during early morning rush, he is simultaneously eager to get off the plane, while fighting the urge to immediately return to Kauai. It's three in the morning in Kauai, so he can't even call to hear Katie's voice.

Now his long legs plod, stiff, through the crowded baggage area. As if he is equipped with radar, he instantly spots a likely suspect from the past at the outside fringe of the crowd. The posture...hands in pockets, ultra-cool; the attire...leather jacket with suspicious bulge, sunglasses indoors; the body language...gaze darting around, macho strut. Gavin tells himself it's probably just his paranoid imagination, but regrets having informed the lawyer of his travel itinerary.

He quickens his pace to get away from the crowd; he has no checked baggage. The din of disorganized activity in the busy area clatters against hard surfaces, assaulting his mind, signaling his body to run, escape. Then just beyond the partitioned baggage area, standing among another crowd, he sees his maternal grandparents scanning arriving passengers. They wave at him now, with smiles on faces that seem more weary and aged since he last saw them three years ago. He'd always thought of them as the epitome of wisdom, quiet dignity, and virtue. Today they are his lifeline.

Gavin rushes through an obstacle course of people, luggage, and carts to reach his grandparents, and spreads his arms to wordlessly embrace both of them together.

"We're so happy to see you, Gavin. You must be exhausted," Grandpa O'Malley says.

"I slept a little during the last flight. I think."

"Well, you look like you could use a little more, son. And are you hungry?"

Relief and comfort surround Gavin like a warm hug when Grandpa's car pulls up to their "cottage Victorian" house on the periphery of the Wellesley College campus. After a cup of tea and half a blueberry scone in his grandparents' kitchen, Gavin excuses himself to retreat upstairs to the guest room. But sleep eludes him as he lies awake on the same antique bed he and Katie slept in after his father's murder. It's also where he and his twin brother, as kids, were put when their parents' fighting became prolonged and extreme.

Although his body is drained of all energy, his mind races

in tormented circles, from the practical to-do list *(first off: rent a car)* to the worries. What will it feel like when he goes back to the house of his childhood torment? Then back in the place of his darkest deed? What if some guys in the mob are still after him? What if Rizzo no longer has the power to prevent that? Gavin just spent months in the sub-basement of his soul trying to recover from...seeing...and failing to save...his identical twin. He isn't sure he's prepared to deal with reminders of his childhood mistreatment. And he definitely doesn't want to deal with the mob.

But now he remembers what Dr. Pedersen explained to him. That he can't get past his crippling condition—PTSD—without facing all that he has buried. So here he is in Boston now, where it started, where it's all buried. He'd fled to Kauai to get away from it, but it followed him there. He could go to Mars and it would follow him there. It controls him. Maybe the only way he can get rid of it is to face it here. Kill it off here.

He is soothed by the glow of maple trees outside the window, dazzling gold and red of autumn in New England. Brilliant sun reflects their radiance into the bedroom, and the lusty fragrance of decaying spores permeates the room, trumping his grandmother's lavender potpourri. A garbage truck rumbles down the street outside, its hydraulic maw opening to masticate trash, then closing with a satisfied belch. Children chattering on their way to school prompt thoughts of Maggie. As he anticipates the tasks ahead, and the concomitant risks, every muscle in him wants to flee, back to Kauai, away from what nearly destroyed him.

Finally giving up on sleep, Gavin gets off the bed and goes downstairs. The house is late nineteenth century, a small Victorian that hasn't been extensively updated and remodeled, retaining its vintage charm. His grandmother is Assistant Dean at Wellesley College, which merits this quaint faculty house on the outer edge of campus. Grandma has office hours this time of day, so Gavin fixes himself a cup of tea and browses through the thousands of books in the library. Although his grandfather had offered to adjust his schedule at Harvard to accompany him to the house across town, Gavin declined and is expecting Hertz to deliver his rental car within the hour. Tackling the task of sorting through everything in his childhood home is something he must do, by himself. And for himself.

When his car arrives, he is eager to begin, to get it all over with. But first he stops by Whole Foods to buy a bouquet, then to Woodlawn to place the flowers on his parents' graves. He thought it would be a simple gesture, but when he stands in front of the headstone, emotions overtake him. The last time he was here, the day his father was buried, there was only his mother's headstone. After Tony was buried beside her, he sees that someone replaced her headstone with a joint one. *Who did this? Who authorized it?*

Antony Umberto DiMasi, Husband   Colleen O'Malley DiMasi, Wife
October 28, 1951   April 13, 1962
July 15, 2002   December 25, 2001
Together in Love

Bitter choked cries overcome Gavin's derisive laughter. Memories of their fights, his mother's bruises, her assuring him of their mutual love. Although Gavin had given Tony forgiveness as he lay dying in his arms, it was an act of charity, granting grace. He had never forgotten the sound of the blow that preceded his mother sailing down the stairs to her death at his feet. *No fucking way am I going to bury Devon's ashes here with them. The root cause.*

Still protecting his twin, even in death.

Gavin pivots on his heel and leaves, letting the bouquet fall from his hand onto a stranger's grave as he sprints to his rental car.

It's lucky there are no policemen near, nor in the short distance to the house where he and his twin grew up, where he now spins and screeches to a halt in the driveway. He throws the shift into park with a hard grind that could strip the transmission, and sits, gripping the wheel, out of breath like he'd just run a 10K. A group of teenagers stare, having been narrowly missed by his speeding car; one mouths a "Holy shit."

Finally Gavin takes a deep breath, pounds the steering wheel with his fist, gathers the notepad, Post-Its and pen he got from his grandmother, and gets out of the car with grim determination.

He looks around the yard. Whoever had been hired to maintain the landscaping hasn't been doing a good job. Weeds have overtaken the flower beds, and the grass is beginning to poke through the unraked fall leaves. But outward appearances are a credit to Wellesley's upscale culture for the lack of apparent vandalism to the house, a 1910 white clapboard gambrel-roof Georgian Colonial with black shutters and attic dormers.

Which doesn't guarantee all is rosy inside.

No one has lived in the house since his father died more than three years ago. Gavin doesn't think his brother ever visited their childhood home after that, but if he did, it wouldn't have been more recently than a year ago, when Devon moved to Kauai. To encroach on Gavin's safe place and resume torturing his twin, "up close and personal."

Gavin walks up the four steps to the front porch slowly, one at a time. As if ghosts of the past may accost him at any moment. Then he remembers an exchange with Dr. Pedersen when his dad died, a year after his mom died. Gavin had asked, "With half the family gone, does the dysfunction go down by half?" To which Pedersen had replied, "The ghost of past dysfunction remains."

Those ghosts still linger, lurking here today.

He squints through the oval pane of decorative leaded

glass in the front door. He sees nothing amiss. And the key still works.

The door creaks as Gavin opens it with caution, wary of the unknown. He moves in slow motion, as if suspended inches above the floor by invisible cords. He realizes he isn't breathing. The purpose of his being there is lost to him in that moment; he feels as if he is a museum visitor viewing a diorama of a bygone civilization. A violent one.

Now the diorama of his life rises renascent, assaulting his memories, throbbing his heart, reigniting the pernicious debasement that suffocated him here, replaying the lethal trauma, as all of it now chokes his breath, blurs his vision. His gut wrenches in excruciating pain, his entire body tenses, and he is overcome with the conflicting urge to flee—get the hell out—or destroy—tear the place apart, knock it all down...

He is roused from his cowered clump by the smell of worn leather, bourbon, and toxic masculinity. He slowly opens his eyes, peering up from his father's brown recliner to sun-sparkled dust motes streaming through sliding doors badly in need of cleaning.

He sighs, unwraps his tightly coiled limbs, and stands. *This PTSD thing sure makes me do some crazy shit.* He looks around the family room, now rationally weighing whether to simply have someone empty out the place and sell it, or if he should bother trying to retrieve anything of value before doing so. He may find things that revive good memories among all the bad, or things he should save for Maggie. Or something that could help him understand and exorcise the family's dysfunction from him, so he won't pass *that* along to Maggie. Exactly what Katie has long feared, what he promised wouldn't happen.

He looks down at Tony's recliner chair and wonders why he tried to find refuge there. Consorting with the enemy. Although Gavin had come to realize, two weeks before his father died in his arms, that Tony's asserted masculinity had been a defense against his feelings of inferiority, that he was actually a misfit for the "winner" role he imposed on Devon. At the expense of Gavin, Tony's putative "loser."

Gavin takes a big breath and expels it, preparing to do the work.

Seeing nothing amiss save for lots of random clutter, dust, and indescribable smells in the airless house, he goes into the kitchen. Ah, the smells: dirty dishes, empty pizza boxes, unemptied trash baskets. He opens the refrigerator. It is stocked with a large quantity of beer and hard liquor. And one carton of milk, with an expiration date of November 2004, almost a year ago.

Gavin's love of cooking, even as a teenager, is apparent in all the special kitchen tools and appliances he'd acquired at the time. His mother had retained them all, even though she rarely used them; she wasn't really into cooking or baking.

But now his innate compulsion to clean up takes over. He first opens windows to air the place out, then loads the dishes into the dishwasher, pours out the old milk and all the alcohol, collects all the debris, stuffs it into the overflowing trash basket and carries it out to the garage, where he is greeted by two large trash barrels overflowing with garbage, trash, and empty bottles. Lots of them. He is unsure how much of the trash—specifically the empty bottles—belonged to his father and was left behind after he died, or was the detritus from Devon crashing (or hiding) here after Tony was killed.

Gavin surveys the garage, then returns to the kitchen. He makes a note to have a dumpster delivered to the driveway to facilitate tossing trash and unwanted or unusable items. He pulls out the Post-Its and walks into the dining room. That room and the living room are virtually untouched, as they had always been. He notices a few choice items in the china cabinet that had belonged to one or the other of his grandmothers. He sticks Post-Its on the few he wants to save for Maggie. The small silver servant bell that Devon used to summon him after he returned from the hospital all those years ago...*well, that can just rot.*

It begins to dawn on him that this might take more time than he anticipated. More rooms, more stuff, and likely more discoveries. He plans to hire people to go through everything and decide what can go in an estate sale and what can be given to charity, the rest to the dump. But first he must stick Post-Its on anything he may want to keep for himself and his little family.

When he returns to the family room, he spots just such items. His mother's watercolor paintings. He recalls her taking him and Devon to Wellesley College's Child Study Center when they were little, while she took classes for her degree, and the few times she had picked them up with a painting in her hands, still fresh and fragrant. He recognizes at least one of those here now, framed and hanging. He isn't sure if he can or should keep them all. He'd always thought of them as the thoughtful, tender representation of his mother, a counterpoint to the dark oppressive family in which she struggled to raise him and Devon. Now he studies all six of them with a new perspective, in order to decide which one—or more—he'll keep. There are three landscapes, two still lifes, one abstract. All of them light, transient, translucent, airy, as if the artist were not really of this world. One in particular now catches his attention. A virtual hole in the paper draws him in, a dark, scrambled gnarl of angst left of center at the end of a rocky precipitous path diverting from an otherwise tranquil landscape. It is almost as if he is pulled into the painting, to disappear and never return. He wonders what his mother's frame of mind had been when she painted it.

He affixes a Post-It to it.

Anxiety begins crawling up his skin like a den of snakes as he realizes the enormity of this task. And the potential for triggers embedded in what he may find. With a deep breath attempting calm, he steps into the library before going upstairs. None of the family had often spent time in this room, which is still lined on three sides with tall overstuffed bookshelves.

His mother had always been a voracious reader, which peaked during her time in college and then during postgrad for her doctorate. The room is also where Devon's hospital bed was set up when he first returned from the hospital. *If only getting drunk, stealing my friend's car and crashing it on our sixteenth birthday had been the extent of Devon's asshole moves...*

Gavin glides his fingers across a dusty shelf, then pauses in a section holding his mother's psychology textbooks. There are also several old-fashioned vertical "banker's box" files with cryptic hand-written labels and stuffed with papers. Curious, he pulls one out. Inside, there is a collection of research papers, all focused on domestic abuse. Causes, bullying, violence, impact on mental health of victims, impact on children in a family, lasting effects, and variations on the theme. The papers include notes in his mother's distinct handwriting. On the shelf next to this box there's a book titled *Trauma and Recovery*. He opens it and sees underlining and more of his mother's notes in the margins. Although he's eager to read his mother's notes, he lacks both the time and emotional strength now. He puts Post-Its on the box and book, and returns them to the shelf.

But there are other such box files with different labels. His eagerness to understand, to know, trumps his reluctance to be pulled into a time-consuming and potentially stressful "rat-hole." He pulls another from the shelf. Inside are papers and notes on narcissism and Narcissistic Personality Disorder. His rapid breaths suspend in his tightened chest. Another box holds papers on substance use. Another on identical twins. He exhales and slaps Post-Its on all of them, suspecting that collectively they hold a map to his family's tragic journey. Their path of dysfunction and death.

His anxiety escalates. He turns to rush out of the room. But then he notices outside the library window a large black SUV with tinted windows parked across the street. Afternoon sun pierces its tinting enough to reveal the silhouettes of two men in the front seat. Exhaust from the tailpipe indicates the engine is running.

Gavin tries to tell himself it's nothing, not what he fears. But he regrets pouring out the alcohol.

Casting a glance through the kitchen toward the rear stairwell, he recalls again the image of his mother plummeting to her death. He spins around on his heels and rushes away. He walks into the foyer, pausing at the base of the front stairs, and parks his butt on the third step, practicing the slow, measured breathing he learned in his TM sessions. Deep, imagining toxins being expelled, then taking in fresh life, cleansing every nook and cranny of his lungs, coursing through blood vessels to reach every cell of his body, calming his over-stimulated amygdala. He looks up the curving stairs, along the graceful line of the wooden banister, leading to rooms hiding ghosts. Everything in him wants to leave. Run out. But he thinks of Katie. The faster he can complete this task, the sooner he can be back with her and Maggie.

Two o'clock. Eight o'clock in the morning in Kauai. He calls Katie.

"Hey Tiger," Katie's energetic voice answers.

Gavin lets out a lungful of breath he doesn't realize he'd been holding.

"I'm glad you caught me before I head over to check on *Makakū*." Clearly in a hurry to her gallery of local and indigenous art, before going to manage their restaurant, her words tumble out in a rush. "How were your flights?"

"Long. But everything was on time."

"You get any sleep?" She sounds organized, like she's going down a checklist of symptoms. Trying to remain clinically objective, not get pulled into Gavin's dark sub-basement. Which wouldn't be helpful for her or for him.

"Not much."

"Sorry, babe. You'll adjust to the time difference in a day or two. How are your grandparents?" Next down the list.

"Good, I guess. They picked me up at the airport. They're both off to their offices now, but we'll have more time to talk over dinner. They do seem to have aged, or lost some of their vigor, since we last saw them."

"That'll be us in a few years, Tiger! Where are you now?" She homes in on the critical issue.

"In my parents' house. I've done the first floor. Sort of. I think Devon must have been here at some point, judging from the mountain of empty liquor bottles and mostly empty pizza boxes."

"You doing okay so far?"

"So far. But I haven't gone upstairs yet."

"You could wait," she says, her compassionate voice touching him through the phone. "Give yourself a break."

"I have to go to Prince Street tomorrow, meet with the city building inspector."

"So the upstairs can wait 'til after that. Could one of your grandparents be with you in your dad's house?"

"They've offered, but I...maybe I need some privacy to digest this stuff. And freak out in private, if it comes to that. And I really want to get this over and done with, as fast as possible, and get the hell out of Boston." He hears Maggie screeching in the background.

"Uh-oh, meltdown time," Katie laughs. "She insisted on trying to dress herself. I'd better go rescue her; she's got her head stuck in her shirt. Let's talk tonight, okay? Love you!"

God, I love her. Always so positive, no matter if the world's falling down on her head.

Gavin stands up to face the ghosts in those bedrooms. He turns, slowly taking one step at a time. When he reaches the top of the stairs, he sees the open door of Devon's bedroom. Stale odors of dirty socks and weed now cloud the room that he and his twin had shared until he'd finally convinced their father to let him have his own room. Oh, how he'd hated this room! The imprisonment, the ever-present demeaning domination by his brother. Now he doesn't have the courage to face it, as if he might be captured and tortured all over again. Even though he knows he may encounter truths hidden there, he isn't sure he wants truth. Yet.

He turns and runs down the hall, to what had been *his* bedroom. He opens the door and immediately falls to his knees, as if he's been sucker-punched. The handsome Prussian blue walls he'd painted in his junior year of high school are covered, on all four walls, with writing, frenetic scrawls in white paint, streaks down the walls, onto the hardwood floor.

YOU'RE A LOSER, WIMP
I LOVE YOU. I ALWAYS HAVE
DON'T YOU LOVE ME?
I'M THE BEST – THE WINNER
DON'T YOU FORGET IT
YOU CAN'T LIVE WITHOUT ME, TWINKIE

It goes on. And on. Much of it indecipherable, mad scribbles. But that last line stops Gavin cold...exactly what his twin had written in blood on the wall behind his suspended body, swaying, mocking his brother, his lips curled in a sneer and eyes bulging, staring...

Gavin rises and begins throwing lamps, books, chairs, anything he can get his hands on, crashing it all against the walls, against those taunts, with a fury and rage, a war cry erupting from his chest. Finally out of breath, he runs out of the room, slamming the door behind him, back down the hall, staggering with contorted sobs, running for his life, lurching down the stairs and out the front door. He doesn't bother to lock it.

He notices the black SUV is gone as he reaches his car.

> "Cooking, therefore,
> can keep a person who tries hard sane."
> —*John Irving*, The World According to Garp

3

GAVIN STOPS AT WHOLE FOODS TO BUY A FEW ingredients for dinner. But forty-five minutes later, he walks out with a shopping cart overflowing with more than an entire army could eat in a week. Stuffing it all into his grandmother's fridge, cabinets, and pantry is a feat for a magician.

He fully escapes into his zone, the dimension in which he is in charge, in control. He cooks. And bakes. Eventually the entire house is full of savory fragrances of his favorite comfort food. Tomato-basil salad, sourdough rolls, meatloaf, three-mushroom gravy, roasted potatoes, garlicky sauteed spinach, charred squash. And apple pie. He will do fine cuisine tomorrow night; he needs comfort now.

After cleaning up the kitchen, he sets the dining room table, opens one of the bottles of Syrah he selected at Whole Foods, and decants it just as Grandma O'Malley comes into the foyer.

"Oh my goodness!" she shrieks. "Gavin, what have you done? I could even smell it from outside, and there's a whole pack of dogs trying to get in!"

Gavin laughs. Which feels good, a relief. "Would you like a glass of wine, Grandma? I stuffed endive leaves with herbed goat cheese to have with it."

"Oh dear, I'm already salivating. Let me get out of these

shoes first, then put my feet up."

Gavin takes the decanter and three glasses to the glass-topped coffee table in the living room—or, more appropriately, the "front parlor." He pours all three glasses, then takes one and settles into a dark emerald-green overstuffed chair. He sips it and inhales deeply, taking in the homey clutter of the house. Subtly patterned wallpaper, lace curtains in the windows, white crocheted doilies on side tables crowded with family photos, a Tiffany lamp in the corner, a well-worn sofa with cratered seat cushions (obviously pre-foam core, maybe even feather stuffed). Definitely a grandparents' home.

But he avoids scrutinizing the photos on the side table. He doesn't need the reminders.

Grandma comes downstairs in slippers. "I had wanted to be here earlier, but I had late-running meetings." She picks up a glass of wine, turns to Gavin and clinks her glass to his, then sits in a floral side chair opposite him and rests her feet on a dainty footstool. "We had intended to take you out for dinner, dear boy."

"Thanks, Grandma. I appreciate that, but I wanted to do something for you. And I needed to do it, for me."

"It's like therapy for you, I suppose."

Gavin chuckles. "You suppose correctly, Grandma," he says, lifting his glass in an air toast toward her. He loves how his grandparents are so proper, stiff-upper-lip, camouflaging their very human warmth underneath.

Just then Grandpa comes home, walking into the foyer, making noise to announce his arrival, as grandfathers tend to do. He pokes his head into the living room and says, "Everyone ready for sushi?" Then laughs uproariously at his own joke. He sets his briefcase down in the library, then turns to pick up the third glass from the coffee table in front of the sofa. He lifts his glass in a toasting gesture to Gavin, clinks his wife's glass, and sits on the sofa. "It's so good to have you here, Gavin."

"Thanks for letting me stay with you. I won't be here too

long, I promise. I want to get this business with the lawyers wrapped up quickly and get back to Katie and Maggie."

Their catching-up small talk continues through hors d'oeuvres and into dinner. And another glass of wine.

Then gets a little more serious.

"We miss your mother every day, son," Grandpa says, his eyes locked on Gavin's and his voice an open invitation for Gavin to talk about that trauma.

Gavin looks down and sips his wine. "As do I," he murmurs, his lips terse. A constricted pain builds in his chest. "But I know how hard her death must have been on you, especially given *how* she died."

"Yes, although it was doubly so for you," Grandma murmurs. "You witnessed it, and that must be indelible in your memory." The age lines in her face droop in mournful anguish.

Gavin is silent, then takes another sip. "Yep," he nods with a grim set to his jaw.

Grandpa adds, "You've endured so much, Gavin. We wanted to support you after your father's death—that was such bitter irony—and be with you at your marriage ceremony, but we just couldn't bear to come to Kauai after Devon..."

The unspoken words hang like dirty linen in soured suspension.

"Well, yeah, you didn't miss anything after the fact. But I'm left with 'yet another' indelible memory."

"How are you coping with all that, Gavin?" Grandma asks with genuine concern in her voice.

"Not too well. I haven't been myself for the last few months. And Pedersen warned me that some memories might trigger some out-of-control responses. He was right."

"We're so sorry, son," Grandpa says. "Funny—we just saw Dr. Pedersen last Sunday after the UU services. He tore the meniscus in his left leg while jogging, and he's using a cane 'til it heals. You should get together with him while you're here—I know he'd be thrilled to see you."

"Yeah, Katie said the same thing." Gavin cracks a wry grin and empties his glass—his fourth—in a single gulp. He's slurring a bit, and with an angry edge asks, "By the way, do you know who replaced Mom's headstone with a joint one after Dad died?"

"No, Gavin," Grandma stiffens at Gavin's tone. "We thought you may have done that." She directs a concerned look toward her husband.

Grandpa inserts a cork into the half-empty third bottle of wine and stows it in a corner of the kitchen counter. "Have you called Katie, Gavin? I'm sure she'd love to hear from you."

Gavin can't finish his piece of pie, and gratefully accepts Grandma's offer to clean up after dinner. He's exhausted, and a little tipsy. Well, maybe more than a little. He climbs up the stairs and flops onto the guest bed, his head spinning. He looks at the clock: a little after nine. Three o'clock in Kauai; Katie will be in full swing at the restaurant. He hits speed-dial. It rings several times before she answers.

"Hi, sweetheart," Katie greets him, frenetic energy in her voice. Lots of noise reverberates in the background, sounding like the restaurant is busier than usual at this between-meal time of day. "How's everything going? You doing okay?"

She always gets to the point right away. Because she knows. Gavin takes a deep breath. "I'm all right. But it's going to be a bigger job, and take longer, than I thought."

"Do you need any help?"

Although what he found in his old room still weighs on him, he can't bear to talk about it. And also doesn't want to bring down her positive mood. "I'll be able to get it done, but it'll just take more time than I thought. How's Maggie?"

"Oh, she's determined. Wouldn't let me help her get dressed this morning, insisted on doing everything herself!"

"I love it. Stubborn, persistent little girl."

"Well, she's a redhead!" Katie laughs. "Takes after her daddy."

"Remember I'm going into Boston tomorrow," Gavin grumbles, as if the prospect of that task is more daunting and perilous than walking through a wall of fire.

"Yes, to meet with the building inspector." Katie's matter-of-fact tone skirts his implication, avoiding his angst and its potential for triggers. Which she has no way to counteract, more than five thousand miles away. Instead she deflects to his more predictable routine task, "The lawyers too?"

"Uh-huh. Should be interesting." But his tone anticipates contention.

The background noise from the restaurant increases several decibels. "Well, I can hear you're tired," Katie says. "Probably had drinks with dinner, too. So you need to get some sleep if you want to be on top of your game tomorrow."

"Right..." Sometimes he fears sleep, which often serves as a movie screen for his frightening dreams.

"I know this is hard, sweetie, and some reminders of bad stuff may come up, but keep telling yourself it's all in the past, over. Just hang in there—you can do this."

"Yeah, I think I'll turn in now," Gavin sighs.

"Good night, Gav. Sleep tight—love you!"

Gavin mumbles, "Uh...I think they're followin' me..."

But the phone in Kauai has already hung up before those words come through.

Gavin falls back onto the bed, asleep before he lands. As if he's instantly sucked into a deep slow-wave-sleep cycle.

But he doesn't have a good night's sleep. Disturbing dreams of humiliation, transforming into an insect, then danger, being tortured, trapped, fires, gunshots—nightmares that hadn't visited him in three years impose upon him now, thwarting restful sleep, locking him in violent REM.

"The original, shimmering self gets buried so deep that most of us end up hardly living out of it at all. Instead we live out all the other selves, which we are constantly putting on and taking off like coats and hats against the world's weather."
—Frederick Buechner

4

IT'S ONLY BEEN A FEW DAYS SINCE GAVIN LEFT, BUT already Katie feels more rested, more relaxed, than she's been in months. She left *'Ono Kūloko's* sous chef Koni and Henry, the restaurant's host-cum-manager, in charge for the day so she could be here at *Makakū's* one-year anniversary celebration, delayed by a month, now that life is a bit less tense.

The place is crowded with artists, customers, and friends enjoying wine, Mai Tais, pupus, and the gallery's newest collections of local and indigenous art—paintings, sculpture, carvings, and textiles. There are even representatives from *Garden Island News*, *This Week* magazine, and *Hawaii Magazine* interviewing the artists and Kalea, the gallery's manager.

Katie has been surrounded by well-wishers most of the afternoon, and now stands in front of a large abstract oil painting that oddly strikes a chord in her. There's something primal about it, and at the same time familiar in a way she doesn't understand. An unfamiliar familiarity, she mocks her contradiction as she considers the energy of its forms, pulsating and alive, drawing her in with a feeling of urgency, as if there's something unspoken inside that must be spoken, answers revealed. Its artistry speaks the universal language of human history, executed in a strident dark-versus-light tempo of angst. It's a bit unsettling, making her feel like she's forgotten something important. She scrutinizes the artist's name. Aliana Ka'uhane, a local. Katie recalls meeting her—an exceptionally probing, insightful young woman. Katie turns to see if she's in the gallery now, instead bumping into a young man standing to her right.

"Katie DiMasi?" he asks.

"Oh, I'm sorry, sir," Katie apologizes. "I'm always bumping into people."

"That's okay," he smiles. "I'm glad you did. I wanted to talk with you. I'm Jeremy Māhoe from *Hawaii Magazine*."

Katie smiles, knowing that "Māhoe" is Hawaiian—originally Polynesian—for "twin." "How can I help you, Jeremy?"

"You're the owner of this gallery, right?" he asks, pulling out his cell phone. "I was wondering if I could ask you a few questions for the feature I'm writing on the art scene on Kauai?"

"Have you talked with Kalea Hokulani, our manager?" Katie asks. "And some of the artists we feature, several of whom are here now?"

"Yes, I have. But I'd like to include your perspective as well."

"Well, okay, but keep in mind that I'm not an artist myself. I'm just a businesswoman. Although I certainly enjoy art; it was one half of my double major in college. Can we step aside, where it's not quite so noisy?" She grabs a glass of iced kava from a passing server.

Jeremy turns on the recorder in his phone, first recording a brief notation of the date, Katie's name, title, business name, and location of the gallery. He then proceeds to pose a few warm-up questions, such as how long she's lived on Kauai, does she have a family here, what inspired her to move here (of course she doesn't include fleeing Devon and the mob in her answer), and so forth.

Then Jeremy asks how she chooses the artists that display in her gallery.

"That's a good question," Katie responds with a thoughtful smile. "There's a lot of interesting art, and many hard-working artists on Kauai. But Amy Beach, the first female U.S. symphonic composer said, back in the late nineteenth century, 'Technique is valuable only as a means to an end. You must first have something to say, something that demands expression from the depths of your soul. If you feel deeply and know how to express what you feel, you make others feel.'" Katie pauses to cast a penetrating glance at Jeremy. He snaps her picture, and she goes on. "That's true of all art forms. We bring in artists who have something meaningful to say, those who can make us feel."

"Wow." Jeremy catches his breath. Then he asks something bigger: "What do you see as the future of the arts on Kauai?"

"That's a big question, Jeremy," Katie smiles. "I believe that all art forms must reflect and preserve culture—human culture. Although," she jokes, "the case could be made for representing the cultures of other life forms, I suppose," she laughs and sips her kava. "But most importantly, we need to ensure the historical cultures that preceded our current one are honored and preserved. The history of humans in Hawaii, and specifically on this island, are grounded in allegedly primitive cultures traveling across vast oceans in crude vessels from Polynesia and other lands, but it is arrogant to assume that peoples who managed that nearly impossible feat were primitive and ignorant. They have much to teach us, and we must not lose their perspectives, the threads of their wisdom."

"So you believe that the cultural beliefs and practices of prior generations should be embraced and proliferated?" Jeremy prods.

Katie now thinks of the DiMasi macho culture of violence and misogyny. "Every culture includes both good and bad practices. We need to honor the good and eschew the bad."

"One final question," Jeremy says. "You say you aren't an artist, but art was one half of your double major, you have a critical, discerning eye for art in many forms and genres, you select an outstanding collection of the best in art, you own an award-winning gallery, and act as a visionary spokesperson for the art community here on Kauai. That sure sounds to me like you're an artist, at least at heart."

Katie laughs. "Is there a question in there somewhere, Jeremy?"

"Yes," he smiles. "What are you hiding?"

They both laugh now, just as Nalani walks in with her children and Maggie, who runs to Katie with her arms up.

Katie picks up Maggie and greets Nalani. "Hey Mags! Did you have fun with Nalani and Anela today?"

Maggie looks over Katie's shoulder and points to the painting Katie was immersed in before her interview. "Mommy." She wriggles to get down from Katie's arms, and runs over to the painting, pointing up at it. "Mommy!"

"Armon stared into the wild darkness of his opponent and saw a reflection of his own fall."
—Wayne Gerard Trotman, *Veterans of the Psychic Wars*

5

GAVIN HADN'T BEEN TO THE NORTH END SINCE HIS father's funeral, and had never seen the traffic as bad as it is today. Finding a parking space sets him on edge and proves impossible. He finally gives up and leaves his car in a parking garage on Hanover Street, several blocks south of Prince Street.

He hadn't ever spent much time in the North End, unlike Devon, who got a condo there after college so he could be near all the "action." Which just got him in deep with the mob. But today the sun is shining and the streets are mobbed with tourists.

Now he observes all the local shops and restaurants on Hanover Street like a tourist. Sections of the street are included in Boston's famous Freedom Trail, so it's jammed with people and cars, along with entire fleets of delivery and service trucks. There are no chains or fast-food places. Most of the shops have deep, colorful awnings hanging over the sidewalks in front of them, and the restaurants and cafés have tables, chairs, and umbrellas completely crowding the limited sidewalk space.

As he continues across Parmenter Street, he spots the lush greenery of St. Leonard's Peace Garden up the next block. The church where his father grew up and was buried. He slows, then walks past another storefront and stops, frozen, his chest tight and painful as if a giant fist has gripped his lungs. He stands unmoving on the sidewalk, seeing the understated name of the Café Pompeii restaurant. People bump him impatiently as they pass by, weaving past tables and umbrellas. A logjam of pedestrians builds up around him, annoyance expressing in sighs and muttered complaints.

Gavin remains frozen, fear cementing him in place. His mind, his memories, all swirl in dangerous, throbbing flashes. Back three-plus years to that July day...the guy Dom in a stained T-shirt, the set-up, Jimbo's gun aimed at Devon, Dad stepping in, falling into Gavin's arms, Devon running...Dom cooly watching while Dad bleeds out and cops bang on the locked doors of Café Pompeii...

Nausea rises in Gavin and his head spins. His eyes open. He looks up from the concrete, into the sun, seeing the outline of a guy he doesn't recognize.

"You better watch out, Red," comes the voice.

That name jolts him. Gavin jumps up and lunges at the guy, who is long gone in the crowd. All he knows for sure is that he's no longer in Café Pompeii with the cop seeing Dad's blood and assuming he was Devon, barking "Red," his twin who was well known for trouble in the North End.

"Sorry," Gavin says to a few people looking at him strangely, and takes a deep breath. "Guess I just freaked out for a minute. I'm okay." He swerves around bodies, walking fast, almost running if it weren't for so many people and tables in his way. At the next corner he turns left onto Prince Street and slows, resuming his deep breaths. Who was that guy?

Deep breath in, and out. *That shit happened in the past. This is now. It can't hurt me any longer.*

Mantras help keep him in the present, in control. Unless he spins out of control.

He sees the boarded-up three-story brick building ahead in the next block, on the left. He smirks at the irony that his grandfather had decided to open his liquor business diagonally from St. Leonard's, as if being within spitting distance of God would help protect him. There's a guy in a dark suit standing in front. All window and door openings are closed with crude slabs of thick plywood, grayed after all this time. The makeshift padlocked door is plastered with weathered notices from the City declaring the building unsafe, and another one prohibiting entry. Blackened evidence of the fire adorns the brick outlines of vacant windows. Surprisingly, only a few graffiti tags are on the front, mostly confined to the plywood.

Gavin stands rooted to the sidewalk, staring at the building where he'd done the unthinkable, what seems like a lifetime ago. It looms like a gaunt, blinded spirit, belching the stench of decomposing flesh. He can't breathe it in. His lungs constrict. The words of his mantra whisper in his ear. *All that happened in the past. It can't hurt me now. That happened in the past, it can't hurt me now,* he repeats. He coughs, shakes his head, and sucks in air. *Tell that to whoever's directing my nightmares.*

"Are you Gavin?" the thirty-something guy in the suit asks.

Gavin continues trying to expel the building's toxicity.

"Gavin DiMasi?" the man repeats, walking toward him with his hand out. "I'm Jake Lombardi, your attorney."

Gavin jumps back, fear wrenching his face.

"Oh, you must have been expecting my dad, Vincent." He smiles in the way people do when they're trying to soothe a frightened child. "Dad knew your father well, but he retired last month. Health issues. Do you want to go in and check out the building?"

Gavin exhales and thuds back to Earth. "What am I going to see in there? What's the condition of the building?"

"Well, there was a fire in most of it. It's still standing, even though it's about eighty years old. I haven't seen inside, but the Building Inspector will show you when she comes in a few minutes."

"So theoretically, I could just tell the city to go ahead and tear it down and then sell the lot, right?"

"Sure, but you'd have to pay for the demolition, and it definitely won't be cheap," he warns. "Or we could put it on the market as-is and whoever buys it can decide whether to do restoration, or tear it down and re-build from the ground up. We might know some people who could be interested…"

Just then a sleek black SUV pulls up close and lets out a heavy-set forty-something woman. She's carrying three yellow hard hats and joins them on the sidewalk. As the SUV pulls away slowly, Gavin wonders why the driver is staring at him.

"Hi, you must be Gavin DiMasi. I'm Marge O'Connor from the City," she says all business-like, dignifying an unmistakable Boston accent. "Sorry for running late." She flashes her City ID and hands each of the men her card.

"We haven't been here too long, ma'am," Gavin says, extending his hand to her. Her face reminds him a bit of an older version of his mother, although O'Connor is heavier and clearly "enhances" the redness of her hair.

"You guys want to go in and look around? I'll explain everything we know about the building's condition." She hands each man a hard hat. "Regulations," she says as she puts on hers, then goes to the doorway in the center of the building with a large overly full key ring.

For the first time, Gavin notices what seems like another boarded-up doorway on the left. "What's that—another entrance?" he asks.

"That goes to the floors above, the residential area," O'Connor says. "Not quite so much damage there, except the fire did do a job on the ceiling of the ground floor, which impacted the floor of the second. The stairs are gone, so we can't go up there without ladders."

"Was anyone living there when the fire broke out?" Gavin asks, wondering why he'd never thought to ask that question.

"Not according to our records," she says, finally identifying the right key to open the padlock on the plywood doorway to the store's entry.

The warped plywood "door" is stuck from lack of use, squealing its objection as Gavin pushes it open. Words of his meditation guide begin humming in his ears, anticipating what's inside.

As he expected, the inside is dark and littered with debris. Odors of charred wood and different materials combine with other smells he can't identify. Rat dung? Mold? Dust motes sparkle in narrow beams of sunlight through gaps in the poorly boarded-up windows. Broken glass from liquor bottles crunches under his feet. Metal shelves that had displayed the bottles now lie on the floor like the bones of fallen soldiers. The entire hollow space pulsates in a clouded visual aura.

Memories of what happened here after his father died now take a back seat to Gavin's analytic mind, as he inspects walls, beams, ceilings, floors. The ideal distraction for him at the moment.

"As you can see," Ms. O'Connor takes a flashlight and scans the interior, "the building was originally built very well, with two layers of brick on the outside of a concrete core, and one brick layer on the inside. Despite its age—it was built right before the Great Depression—the fire did minimal damage to the frame. The concern is with the flooring. What you're walking on right now—be careful where you step—has been damaged in several places from the fire and the water to put it out. And also, what's above your heads. The wood beams that separate the floors. And finally, the support structures holding up those beams have been compromised in places."

Gavin carefully steps through the space, trying to identify where certain features Devon had shown him are now, or had been. The rough-hewn wall covering his twin was so proud of is mostly gone. The temperature-controlled wine storage area's glass doors all shattered, leaving only partial frames. The tasting area, where only the marble top of the bar remains, lying atop the residue of burnt wood. And all the way to the back, where the "VIP Room" was, that Devon had bragged about when he took over the business five years ago... Gavin's breathing stops. This was a crime scene three years ago. Now he sees and feels that pivotal scene all over again, the event that made him question who he really is, what's inside him, what he's capable of.

He struggles to get ahead of his triggered response, hoping Lombardi doesn't notice, consciously forcing deep breaths and intensifying his mantra, with a vague wish that he could just push a pre-programmed button to engage those two defenses automatically, moments before the memories descend upon him.

He realizes this "room" must have been upgraded after the building's original construction, but doesn't know whether Devon or his father had been responsible. For some reason, instead of installing wood-framed walls, as the partitioning of any interior walls would have been, the wall separating this room from the rest of the first-floor space had been structured like a brick fortress, and now with a few bricks fallen out, Gavin sees a concrete core that's much younger than the building. He remembers Devon showing off the room to him as his "safe room," where he conducted "serious business with important people." That was in 2002, the morning before they met Tony for lunch that day their father was killed. By a bullet meant for Devon.

Gavin takes in a deep gulp of stale air and expels it, shaking off those memories and refocusing on his analytic task.

Although the entrance to this room now lacks a door, most of the wall that separates it from the main store still stands. But to the right of that entrance, over against the building's perimeter, there's a place in the wall where the fortress is broken through, destroyed. *So much for "safe," Devon.*

Gavin hesitates, then cautiously ventures through the entry into the room. Directly on his left he spots the notch in the brick where Devon stored his gun, accessible by touching a button to open the secret panel. He turns on his heel to leave, before that memory can overtake him.

He collides with Ms. O'Connor, who is leading the junior Lombardi into the room. "Oh, Gavin, come look in he-ah!" Her voice is excited, her Boston accent breaking out into high gear. "The walls in this room are still standing, even though everything in it is chahed beyond recognition," now dropping Rs and expanding words from one syllable to two. "We'ahd."

Gavin stands just outside the doorway, as if there's a dangerous animal inside. Which there had been, back then. Two of them—Jimbo and Spucky, waiting to kill Devon. But Gavin had instinctively grabbed the gun from his twin's secret nook and fired back, miraculously hitting the men who'd just shot at him. Now he runs from that memory as if it's chasing him, wrenching it from the jaws of those animals.

Lombardi eyes Gavin's fearful tension with a conniving smirk, as if that's the reaction he hoped for, to ensure his—or someone's—desired outcome.

Gavin repeats his mantra now and focuses on the present, forcing himself back to his analytic task, a distraction from panic.

He notices that the room doesn't seem as wide as the rest of the building. It looks like the left wall protrudes maybe three or more feet into the room, compared to the left side of the building. The main part, where the store was, appears wider than this room because of that protrusion. Maybe there's storage or equipment behind that brick wall? But he doesn't see a doorway anywhere in it, for accessing the space.

Then he sees an empty beer bottle on the floor ahead, intact, not shattered like every other bit of glass strewn about. The bottle's label isn't discolored by age or by fire. *Someone has been in here recently.*

"Ms. O'Connor, is there another entry to the building?" Gavin asks.

"Not really," she says. "The doorway you saw on the left outside opens to stairs up to the floors above, but there's no access from those floors to this one, or vice versa. Front door's the only way into or out from this floor. Only way the upper floors can exit is either that boarded-up stairwell or the metal fire ladders on the outside of the building. There's also no access on the sides or back because all the buildings in this area are jammed cheek-to-jowl against each other, on all sides. So if it wasn't for the fire station being so close, the fire coulda took the whole street."

"And it's been boarded up and locked since shortly after the fire?"

"According to our records, yeah. I wasn't with the City at the time." She turns to the right, scrutinizing the safe room's inner wall. "Too bad about the fire. It was a good solid building. No defense against that gas blast, though."

Gavin's head whips around. "Gas blast?"

"Yeah, some asshole's bullet hit a gas line and it blew. See that part of this here wall it knocked out? Must not've been a primary line, or just residual gas in a line that'd been turned off already, else it'd been a lot worse."

"And *that's* what caused the fire?" He had been blaming himself for the fire. Everything about that night had been a blur. It still is, even now. The shots, running out, the fire. He had always believed he had been responsible for everything. Turns out, maybe not all of it.

O'Connor seems impatient, checking her cell phone, clearly eager to get out of here.

Lombardi breaks in. "So what do you think, Gavin," he says, not as a question. "Our advice is to sell the place and leave the headaches to someone else. That would be the smartest thing to do. We can draw up the papers, get you back to your wife and kid."

Gavin's bullshit detector buzzes. *This guy is too eager. And why is O'Connor wanting to duck out before showing the rest of the building? Something isn't quite right.*

"I'll be in town a few more days, Jake. Let me think about it and get back to you." He turns to the inspector. "Thank you for the guided tour, Ms. O'Connor. I need to leave right now, but I may want to return with a structural engineer and lights—oh, and a ladder, to get a detailed risk assessment. Is there maybe an extra key to that padlock? As the owner now, I should probably have one."

O'Connor pulls back with a quizzical look, then shrugs and fishes in her large handbag, pulling out the ring that must hold keys to every property in the area currently under City management. "Well, can you help me look through all these keys?"

Lombardi scowls and turns away.

Gavin eventually spots one key that appears to have the same lines and notches as the one O'Connor used to open the padlock. "We can test it on the way out," he says.

Miraculously, the key does work. Lombardi abruptly turns to Gavin with his hand out to shake. "I'm sure you'll make the right decision, Gavin," he says, looking pointedly into Gavin's eyes.

Gavin does not proffer his hand. *"The right decision" for who? I just survived this trip down memory lane, so don't think I'm blind to your game.*

As Lombardi walks away, O'Connor purses her lips in his direction, which is not lost on Gavin. He turns to her and says, "Can I treat you to a cup of coffee?"

The woman smiles in a knowing way. "I'd like that, Gavin, but I can see that my colleague is here." She nods toward a man standing across the street, the same one who had stared so intently at Gavin earlier. "You have my card. Can I have a rain check?"

As O'Connor crosses the street, Gavin scrutinizes the man. There's something familiar about him, someone he encountered recently.

Was he the guy leaning over him in front of Café Pompeii, telling him he'd better watch out?

"Instead of worrying about what you cannot control, shift your energy to what you can create."
—*Roy T. Bennett*, The Light in the Heart

6

WHY HAVEN'T I HEARD FROM GAVIN?

Katie paces their restaurant in Kauai, holding her cell phone, willing it to ring. It's almost eleven in the morning, time to open the place for lunch. She left Gavin a message early this morning, which was two in the afternoon for him. Now she frets, her worry generating imagined disasters in Boston and anguished internal dialogue in her.

Gavin said he was going to meet with the building inspector and the lawyer at eleven, so Katie thinks that *has* to be all over at this point. It's almost five o'clock there now, while anxiety chokes off her air supply here. She worries what may have happened to him, fear exacerbating her nausea.

She knows it's got to be really hard on him, being back in that place. When he finally confessed it all to her months afterward—about confronting his dad's killers before they could get to Devon—it tore him up with guilt. Having to defend himself, resulting in killing *them*. Going against his entire nature, making him doubt who or what he really is.

Yet she's had doubts about that too. With all the dysfunction in generations of DiMasis—the abuse, the deaths, the crime—she has wondered how much of that is genetic. Whether it runs in the family. She loves Gavin so much—the good-hearted Gavin she's always known—but she's also worried whether the crazy stuff in his family might come out in him at some point. Whether her sweet Jekyll might become a dangerous Hyde.

It's been a roller coaster ride these past months. It's given her whiplash, constantly on edge, sick with worry, never knowing how to help him, how to deal with his ups and downs, what to do. She's decided she doesn't like roller coasters.

After Gavin found Devon, his identical twin—*how much closer could any two people be?*—hanging, with a threatening taunt on the wall in his own blood, Gavin buried himself in grief. She remembers that he virtually buried himself, staying in bed, hiding under the sheets, for a straight week, then emerging as a walking zombie for another week, then picking up and going on, sort of delusional, like it never happened. As if Devon was still doing all his usual shit, stalking and harassing his twin. The ultimate gaslighting postmortem.

She had to call in the rescue squad. Pedersen and Tray.

It's good that she did. Tray came as quickly as he could, given his nonstop travel with the FBI. Then when Dr. Pedersen arrived, he explained how all Gavin's family trauma is affecting him, even years after most of it happened. Why he's reacting the way he is, what to expect, how to deal with it. He said that Gavin has PTSD—Post Traumatic Stress Disorder. Katie had read about it in war veterans, but Pedersen said that Gavin's traumas had been spread out over many years, starting with emotional abuse when he was a kid, and then the violent deaths of his mother, father, and his twin all happened "in his lap"—literally in his arms. So the final death, Devon's, could release *all* the traumas and abuses, going back to childhood.

Pedersen cautioned them that Gavin had probably buried all the psychological abuses from his childhood in order to survive, and now it all might come out in ways that are totally antithetical to the Gavin everyone has known and loved. And now Gavin's recent behavior shows that Pedersen was right.

Pedersen also explained the best ways for Katie to deal

with Gavin's PTSD, and how she needs to take care of herself, to guard against the stress and trauma that Gavin's condition will put on *her*. Like it already is now. But the roots of Gavin's PTSD developed over many years, so it won't go away overnight. She'll have to deal with it for a long time to come.

She's been reading stuff Dr. Pedersen sent her after he left. And she bought a book, *Trauma and Recovery*, by some woman doctor at Harvard. All that and what he explained won't stop the roller coaster, but at least she sort of understands, in the abstract, what's going on, and what more might be in the future. But she rarely knows the right way to deal with it, what's best for Gavin, what's best for Maggie. And for herself.

By the time Pedersen left Kauai, Gavin had stopped thinking Devon was still around and taunting him, but the anxiety and jumpiness were still there, constant. Hiking with Tray out on the NaPali coast for three days seemed to divert Gavin onto the next curve of the roller coaster, in which he declared he's "all better," and "back to normal," whatever that is. But his behavior—his reactions to triggers—clearly shows that he's not "better." Unless this is his new normal.

Katie has no illusions that "all better" will happen anytime soon. She tries to separate her own feelings from what Gavin is going through, to be there for him without losing herself. Showing her love and support, without allowing herself to be worried or fearful about something she can't change or control. At least not *showing* her worry, because that only makes Gavin feel guilty. It's hard, though, like she's separating herself into different parts. Clinical cool versus worried wife.

She had walked that tightrope, taking care of her mother all those years. Now she has to take care of Gavin. He needs to trust her in that, but Pedersen warned that because of Gavin's memories of family members failing him, he may go through periods of questioning whether people—even her, whom he loves—can be trusted.

Regardless of how hard it is, she's determined to support Gavin through his recovery. Especially now that...

> "However greatly we distrust the sincerity
> of those we converse with, yet still we think
> they tell more truth to us than to anyone else."
> —François de la Rochefoucauld

7

GAVIN CALLS MARGE O'CONNOR JUST AS SHE'S finishing her last inspection of the day in the West End, a neighborhood Gavin thinks probably doesn't include the sort of characters he wants to avoid. She suggests something stronger than coffee, so they meet at a little pub on Charles Street, at the bottom of Beacon Hill. It looks like something out of *Cheers*—narrow, rustic, wide pine floors, walls covered in funky signs, a dartboard, and crowded with people engaged in lively conversation, even at two in the afternoon. Clearly a local hangout, where no one looks like an Italian mobster and "everyone knows your name."

The only open seats are at the far end of the bar. They settle on the barstools, order their beers, and begin with small talk intended to make each other comfortable—*where do you live, do you have kids, call me Marge,* etc.—while carefully dancing around the real purpose of their meeting.

A cheer erupts from the crowd watching what is likely the last double-header of the Red Sox season, before the World Series.

"That's one thing I do miss on Kauai," Gavin says with a sheepish grin.

Marge smiles and nods. "Once a Sox fan, always a Sox fan."

"Say, I wanted to ask you about your colleague today. He looks vaguely familiar."

"Richard Salvatti?" Marge says. "Yeah, he covers East Boston, Charlestown, and Chelsea territories. Rick's a Townie. I have North End, West End, and Southie, where I live. Rick was on his way to East Boston when he drove me this morning."

"Any relation to Joe Salvatti who hung around with Pete Limone?"

Marge almost spits out her mouthful of beer. "You've done your homework, kid."

"Is he Joe's son?"

"As a matter of fact, yes. Joe's youngest. But he's clean as a whistle," Marge says. "After what happened with his dad, he doesn't want anything to do with the business. Which is more'n I can say about your lawyer."

"Lombardi. I guess I shouldn't be surprised."

"And I noticed you don't trust him."

"Right," Gavin nods. "So why was Rick staring at me?"

"He knew your twin, didn't like him. Thought you were him."

Gavin is becoming hyper-skeptical of people, unsure of what's truth or lie. He knows that the Irish mob is still alive and well in Southie and Somerville. So he's reluctant to trust anyone, even Marge. Clearly Irish, she appears to be open and honest, but he still harbors doubts. "Yeah, I don't know what Lombardi's game is, but I'm not willing to just go along with what he's pushing without bringing in a 'second opinion' on the Prince Street building. Including checking the basement, which you didn't even show me. It's gotta have a basement, right?"

"Sure, but the report doesn't say anything about a basement. You know I wasn't responsible for the original inspection and verdict on your building, right?" Marge asks. "I wasn't with the department three years ago, so today I just covered what the report says."

"So what reason would Lombardi have for pushing so hard for me to sell 'as-is'?"

Marge takes a gulp of beer and pauses. "Just pushing to sell could mean they have a buyer in mind. Pushing to sell 'as-is'—well, that's another kettle of fish." She chews on her lower lip, as if she's being careful of what to say and how to say it. "If Lombardi, or his firm, has a 'benefactor,'" she air-quotes, "who really wants the building but doesn't want you or anyone else to demolish it, the only logical reason would be if they think there might be something inside or under the building they don't want to be discovered or destroyed, something they want for themselves."

That jibes with one possibility Gavin had considered. "So can you recommend an unbiased structural engineer I can bring in? Someone who isn't corrupt, and not connected to the mob?"

Groans come from the crowd as the Sox strike out with bases full.

Marge laughs. "That eliminates more'n half the city." She pulls out her phone and begins scrolling through her contacts. "Hmm... Well, you might try either Christine Simmons—I know her—or...Mark Solomon—someone told me he's good too. I'll send you their contact info. Tell them I sent you."

Gavin smiles. Marge passed the test. He had called Grandpa O'Malley at noon, after he left Prince Street, to ask whether he knew anyone who could do this sort of inspection. Grandpa recommended Solomon. Maybe O'Connor *can* be trusted. Maybe.

Gavin fidgets and paces while the phone rings in Kauai. He's so excited to tell Katie about his survival today.

"Gavin!" Katie whoops in relief above a chattering din in the background. "Are you okay?"

"I'm just great, sweetheart—wait'll you hear all about it!

What's that noise? Where are you?" He rattles on in rapid-fire, not waiting for a response. Just like his father always did.

"I'm at the restaurant, Tiger—it's almost noon here. We're hosting a lunch meeting for the local women's club—what a kick-ass group of strong women they are! They want me to join, and I think I will! So tell me all about it—I was so worried when I didn't hear from you."

"Worried about what, Katie?" he challenges angrily, pulling back, distancing, wary of scrutiny or criticism, dissection of his actions and motives. "You think I can't handle this stuff? You think you're Wonder Woman, managing my restaurant and your *gallery*," he goads derisively. "I survived two major triggers, Kat—I don't need your condescension."

Katie recoils from Gavin's outburst, which is probably driven by the distrust issues Pedersen warned of. Nothing she might say in this moment is likely to mollify him, and risks triggering him.

Just as quickly as his anger flared, he clams up and shifts to disconnected mode. "I'm preparing dinner for Grandma and Grandpa now, so I can't talk much longer. I'm doing fresh schrod wrapped in romano-layered phyllo with a white wine reduction, wild rice pilaf, carrot pennies, and grilled asparagus. With spinach and fig salad. How's Maggie?"

> "Numbing the pain for a while
> will make it worse when you finally feel it."
> —J.K. Rowling

8

THE LAST THING GAVIN REMEMBERS BEFORE FALLING into bed is Grandma suggesting that he invite Dr. Pedersen over to join them for dinner the next evening. He falls asleep without calling Katie.

In the morning he wakes up in a tangle of sheets so twisted he has difficulty extricating himself from the bed. With the worst hangover he's ever experienced, from a couple glasses of Sancerre. Well, maybe it was more than a couple; he can't remember. He shuffles to the guest bathroom down the hall, the sound of each footstep assaulting his head. He's afraid he's going to heave, but he feels nothing in his throat except putrid bile. As he's peeing, he braces one hand against the wall and catches a glimpse of himself in the mirror, instantly recoiling as if he's seen a cobra about to strike. He throws himself over the toilet and wretches his insides out until every muscle in his body is reduced to flaccid dross.

He grips the toilet, then pulls himself up to the sink and cautiously peers into the mirror. The face staring back looks exactly like his brother's, the last time he saw him alive. On that day, his identical mirror twin's body appeared desiccated by the psychosis that consumed him, leaving his face a hollowed-out shell, an apparition.

NO! Not like Devon!

A sudden urge to punch the mirror rises in him, but a woozy swoon overtakes him. He takes a deep breath to avoid passing out and flings open the medicine cabinet, looking for Excedrin or some other painkiller. Nothing. His hands are shaking like he's got *delirium tremens*. It's too soon for the DTs to come on, so he turns on the shower, extra hot, then climbs into the vintage claw-foot tub and stands directly under the spray of the shower ring so long he imagines he has shrunk by several inches. Or at least his head has shrunk, because the pain has receded to a dull bruise by the time he gets out.

Hot steam has fogged the mirror—a good thing, so he can't see himself. He needs coffee.

In the kitchen downstairs, he sees three "dead soldiers"—empty bottles. Two Sancerre and one bourbon, sitting beside the sink piled high with dishes, pots, and pans. Now he remembers the pub yesterday, drinking with Marge O'Connor. He realizes he must have started there, and then didn't stop.

"Your grandmother wasn't feeling too well last night," Grandpa says as he comes into the kitchen. "So we thought the dishes could wait 'til this morning when you got up."

"Sure," Gavin mumbles. "I'll do them after I have some coffee."

"The pot's empty, but you can make another pot," Grandpa says, sitting down at the kitchen table and opening his *Boston Globe* with a decisive rustle. "You look like shit, Gavin. Do you usually drink so much every night?"

Gavin stops, paralyzed, unmoving. He stares into infinity through the kitchen window, withered under shame. "I should leave," he blurts, then runs out the front door and jumps into his car.

He doesn't remember exactly where he has driven for the last hour and a half, but now his car sits in the driveway of his childhood house. Which never felt like a home and feels like a house of horrors now. The Post-Its and pen are still on the passenger seat. He knows he has to make progress on the tortuous task he began two days ago, so he gets out and heads toward the front door, remembering he hadn't locked it when he rushed out before.

But the door is locked. Either a Good Samaritan from the neighborhood reached in to turn the button on the knob, then closed it, or he really did lock it after all. He's confused.

Inside, everything looks undisturbed, at least on the first floor. He hopes his grandfather is still home, and dials the number.

"Hello—Grandpa? This is Gavin. I'm sorry I ran out without doing the dishes." He pauses while Grandpa speaks. "Yes, you're right. I'm under a lot of stress right now. I never drink much at all back home. I can't, really, working ridiculous hours in the restaurant, so I guess I can't hold my liquor." He pauses again. "Yeah, yeah, that'd be okay. What time did you say—six-thirty? All right. I'm over at the house now to do more sorting, and I'll clean the kitchen when I get home this afternoon. Enjoy your day off, and tell Grandma I'm so sorry."

Gavin's shoulders slump, deflated, and he drops onto the family room sofa. *I'm a total shit. A loser, like Devon and Dad always said. So now Grandpa is bringing Pedersen in to talk some sense into me, I guess. Good luck with that.*

Suddenly he pops up and goes to the front stairs with a determined stride, like he's headed for a fight. Taking the steps two at a time, he barges into Devon's room and screeches to a halt as if he has seen a ghost. No one else would be able to see it, but he does. His brother, standing in front of him, arms crossed with a smirk on his face. "See, Twinkie, you can't live without me," the derisive nasally voice taunts him.

A lifetime of conflicting memories converges on him in the same devastating moment, waging war in his mind, scenes and images battling simultaneously in hologram. He and Devon bonded and floating *in utero*, playing and dreaming together as children, their bond corroded to a winner-versus-loser dichotomy by their father's bullying, Devon's demeaning abuse of Gavin that robbed him of his selfhood, Gavin's fruitless efforts to save his brother, that which cannot be salvaged...

An uncontrollable fury overtakes Gavin like a rampaging tornado, thrashing and assaulting him from all sides. Regardless of whether his father or his twin is at the heart of the storm, he now lunges for Devon but lands on the bed in front of him, pounding and punching with a rage unlike anything he's ever experienced.

Eventually his animal roars give way to helpless sobs. For all he has lost.

He lies on the bed, limp and spent, he has no idea for how long. Finally rousing, he looks at his watch—it's already after eleven. With a deep breath and long sigh, he rises, determined to finish the job he began, recognizing that finishing what you start is a requirement in every dimension of his life. *I've got to get my act together, dammit.*

As he walks around Devon's bedroom, a picture of his brother's state of mind begins to form. The room is in complete disarray. Junk—tchotchkes from various bars; trash—empty cans, bottle tops, half-empty takeout containers, crumpled wads of paper; stains—spills, vomit, urine; piles of dirty clothing; dirty dishes, magazines, shoes, all scattered in piles and random disorder among haphazardly positioned furniture, all the trash continuing into the closet. Indecipherable scribbles adorn two walls. Curtains and blinds have been ripped from the windows; there are two panes of glass broken in one window. It looks like Devon may have been throwing stuff in a rage of his own.

Gavin doubts there is anything worth saving in all this, but he begins digging around. On Devon's desk, under disorganized piles of paper, he finds several photos of him and Devon together as children. They seemed so happy, so connected then. He sets them aside to take home and opens a few drawers, where he finds more junk and trash. And then he unearths his brother's beloved wooden chess case beneath wrinkled, ripped shreds of paper in the bottom drawer. When he opens the case, residual smells of the drugs he'd always stored there escape. The drugs are gone now, but there's a well-worn brown leather-bound journal inside, with a note clipped to the outside:

> Dear Twinkie — If you find this it's because I'm gone. Probably a good thing for you, since I've made your life miserable. So the truth is that I've always been the loser, not you. I love you more than anything. Happy reading inside. Kisses from the real DUD.

Everything Gavin thought he knew has just turned upside down. Devon claiming to be the loser, not him. He's torn between crying and laughing. And he'd never noticed that his twin's initials—for Devon Umberto DiMasi—spelled "DUD."

Devon had been clinically diagnosed as having Narcissistic Personality Disorder, fostered by their father's pressure on his "favorite son," which drove Devon to claim he was superior even when he knew he was not. It was always a show for other people, to convince *them* of his superiority, and to reassure himself.

Now Gavin sees that Devon must have known, before he moved to Kauai to torture his twin, that he would die. Either by someone else's hand or his own. As Devon anticipated the end of his life, he became stripped of all his pretensions, finally being honest with himself and Gavin. That realization takes Gavin's breath away and knocks him on his ass, onto the desk chair. He chokes back sobs of regret... That he'd had so little understanding of the anguish and pain his brother had been carrying. That he had failed to save his twin.

He looks down at the journal. He's reluctant—perhaps fearful—to begin reading it. At least not yet. He extracts it from the case and pictures fall out, fluttering to the floor. He picks them up one at a time. Each one is a photo of him. Gavin winning a cross-country race, Gavin giving his valedictorian speech, Gavin accepting honors at his Culinary Institute graduation, Gavin at their father's burial, Gavin at the opening of his Kauai restaurant, and so on. He has no idea how Devon got all of them, these pictures of Gavin at events where his brother wasn't present—as far as Gavin knew. And now as he riffles the pages of the journal, he catches the passing blurs of red hearts.

Gavin has a sense of what those hearts are all about, and he definitely doesn't have the stomach to begin reading his brother's confessional now. It could either be another of Devon's narcissistic mind fucks, or a peek into an obsession Gavin isn't sure he wants to know about. With some trepidation, he gathers it up with all the photos and turns to leave the room.

As an afterthought, Gavin pulls out his cell phone and takes pictures of his brother's writing on the walls. He wants to capture Devon's deranged rants before it's all covered over, buried down the cesspool of DiMasi family dysfunction. And before the house goes on the market, someone has to put a coat of Kilz over all the writing and then paint the whole place. That goes on his to-do list.

It is now after noon. He can't deal with more archeological digging into the ruins of his fucked-up family at this point. One room a day seems all he can handle. Besides, he has to clean up his grandparents' kitchen, call the structural engineer for an appointment, and call Katie.

On the way out of the house, he steps into the library and pulls down one of the banker's boxes stuffed with his mother's research papers. The one focusing on domestic abuse. He glances out the window and sees what looks like the same black SUV he saw last time he was here. He writes down the license plate number and gathers his booty to leave, then sees something on the Persian runner in the foyer he hadn't noticed before.

He picks it up: A receipt from McCarthy Brothers Liquors in Charlestown, dated yesterday morning at 9:45. Unless one of his neighbors likes to buy their booze in Charlestown, the Good Samaritan who locked the front door wasn't a neighbor.

A chill shudders his spine and he rushes out the front door as the SUV across the street peels out, wheels spinning dust in its wake.

As he locks the deadbolt, he makes a mental note to have a security system installed. And to check out Rick Salvatti.

> "Never awake me when you have good news to announce, because with good news nothing presses; but when you have bad news, arouse me immediately, for then there is not an instant to be lost."
> —Napoleon Bonaparte

9

DESPITE BEING SO EXHAUSTED AT THE END OF EACH day that she can't see straight, sleep often doesn't come for Katie. She'd just drifted off to sleep when the phone rings. At three in the morning. Katie shoots up from bed to grab it. "Hello?!"

A deep, proper voice says, "Hello, Katie. This is James Pedersen."

She'd only ever thought of him as Doctor Pedersen. She isn't sure if she ever actually knew his first name. And now he's apparently forgotten about the six-hour time difference.

"Oh, Dr. Pedersen!" Katie clears her throat. "It's so good to hear your voice."

"I'm calling because Gavin seems to be having some difficulty now that he's back here—"

"At the scene of the crime." Katie sighs.

"Yes," Pedersen pauses with a reciprocal sigh. "I got a call from his grandfather this morning," he begins in an apologetic tone. "Professionally, I hesitate to disclose this to you. But as a friend—by the way, after all this time, please call me Jim—and knowing that Gavin is in a precarious and potentially dangerous state, I believe I must share—"

"Please don't apologize, Dr. Pedersen," Katie almost snaps at him, impatience and fear vying for space within her. This is clearly urgent—"potentially dangerous"? This is about the man she loves. "Just tell me."

"We know he's been through a lot since his twin brother died, which has exposed a lifetime of trauma and abuse he's buried and hasn't acknowledged, much less dealt with. So now it appears to be coming out, in a way that suggests it may be just the beginning."

"Just spit it out, *Jim*. What happened?" Katie is in a full-blown panic but tries to keep her voice down so she doesn't wake Maggie or Patches, both of whom can always sense when something is wrong.

"His grandfather Gerald—my longtime friend, you know—is concerned about Gavin," Pedersen says.

A fear tucked away inside Katie heaves its curdled dread as if she'd expected this, and more, all along but tried to deny it. "What has he done?" she asks, afraid of the answer.

Pedersen continues in his usual professional manner, yet his voice is warm and caring, laced with regret and sadness, as if describing the loss of something good, something deeply cherished. "Gerry tells me that Gavin seems extremely tense and on edge, rather distant and disconnected, not like his usual self. And he significantly overindulged in alcohol two nights in a row."

Now Katie's morning nausea threatens to erupt earlier than usual. "I remember you warned us, when you came to visit in July, that excess alcohol or drugs can often be a way of coping with triggers and flashbacks when someone has PTSD."

"Yes. Also—as we discussed, the victim may pull back from people he's always been close with, as if he can no longer trust them. He may either turn off or flatten his emotions, or may become more impulsive and extreme. For example, he could become angry or lose his temper for little reason, sometimes to the point of violence."

For years, Katie has worried whether the dysfunction in Gavin's family could be genetic, that its code may be embedded in his DNA to someday manifest its toxicity in him. Although Pedersen has assured her that the behaviors in the DiMasi family were not likely genetic, those latent fears have primed her for bad news, which immediately sent her imagination into orbit when the phone rang at three this morning, assuming Gavin was in trouble. And now she knows. He *is* in trouble.

"I'm seeing a lot of that already, Dr.—*Jim*," Katie groans, like admitting a fatal diagnosis. "In the phone conversations we've had while he's been gone, he's been pushing me away, not sharing, not trusting. He's reacted to trivial things with belligerent anger, and now there's excessive alcohol. On top of the nightmares, flashbacks, and outsized reactions to triggers." Katie feels sick. She's afraid all that is just for starters.

"I think I explained, when I visited you in July, that Gavin's response to things that trigger his trauma will fall into either freeze, flight, or fight patterns. You're seeing 'flight' firsthand—"

"When he doesn't call, doesn't trust, breaks off conversations and retreats..." Katie confirms. "And 'fight' is when he gets defensive, angry, or worse."

"Yes, and there's another possible response mode. 'Fawn'—cozying up to the abuser to avoid being a target of their offenses—in this case, the criminal types his brother, father, and paternal grandfather consorted with. That's a self-defense maneuver we haven't seen Gavin engage in yet, but if he begins aligning himself with them, taking on their tactics himself—that's when we'll really have to worry."

"That's why I have to be with him, to keep him from going over that line." Katie's voice tremors with fear, laced with fierce determination.

"That could be dangerous for you, Katie," Pedersen emphasizes. "That's why Gavin will need *all* of us."

"What can we do now, so it doesn't come to that?" she pleads.

"Well for starters, Gerry and Carla have invited me to dinner at their home this evening. Of course Gavin will be chef. So I'll do an informal assessment and then hope to pull him off for a private conversation."

"Do you think I should fly back to be with him? He was adamantly opposed to that."

"I think he'd appreciate it, Katie, despite his protestations, and it might help." Pedersen's voice sounds like he's carefully choosing which rock to step on, to cross a raging stream. "But you could also get caught in the crossfire."

"What do you mean, Jim? That sounds ominous."

"It is, Katie." Pedersen takes a long inhale. "Remember I told you that Gavin's symptoms during his long-term recovery process can end up affecting you and Maggie in a similar way? It's called 'vicarious PTSD,' traumatizing *you*." His tone seems unfinished, hinting of more on the matter.

She thinks she might be able to deal with that, but definitely doesn't want Maggie to be traumatized. "So that's the 'crossfire' you're talking about?"

"One aspect of it, Katie." Pedersen hesitates and gentles his voice. "Keep in mind that Gavin is dealing with the building in the North End, which carries his family's history with the mob. So he might be poking a sleeping monster that could endanger him, as well as you and Maggie."

"Oh, jeez," Katie moans. "I hadn't thought of that. But I can't just abandon him!"

"Yes, I understand. Regardless of what you decide, you're caught either remotely or up close, in various levels of Gavin's trauma."

"Caught in the crossfire. It's already been pretty hard on me. If I weren't so tired all the time from handling the restaurant, my gallery, Maggie, and worrying about Gavin, I might feel stressed!" She snorts at the irony.

Pedersen chuckles. "You're remarkable, Katie. You've spent almost your entire life taking care of others, people you love.

You have every right to be stressed, so don't be afraid to admit that. Own it. Because you've had to be strong and responsible most of your life, you tend to deny your own vulnerability. Which does no one—Gavin, Maggie, or yourself—any good."

Katie is silent for a moment. "But if I let Gavin see that I'm stressed, he feels guilty that he's hurting me, not saving me. And recently, he's even reacted to my worry about him by being angry and resentful." She pauses, considering the contradictions in Gavin's unpredictable reactions. "So I've tried to detach my emotions from what's going on with him, to keep from being pulled into his emotional chaos. Protect myself. But sometimes he can see when I'm detaching, and concludes that I don't care, don't love him, that I'm turning my back on him. It can devolve into a self-fulfilling spiral."

"And you risk being pulled down into that no-win spiral yourself," Pedersen agrees. "You can verbalize to him what he's feeling in that moment, confirm and affirm it so he feels heard, understood, without attempting to find a solution—which ultimately has to come from within him, anyway."

"Yes, and he takes his responsibility for me and Maggie so seriously that he feels guilty that I have to help pick up the slack while he recovers. But that's now shifting to resentment."

"Well, you understand that no one gets over PTSD quickly. It takes time, with minor steps of progress, as well as major setbacks. But Gavin's family abuse all during his childhood adds other symptoms to those created by the trauma of family deaths, effectively multiplying how long and hard he'll have to struggle with it. A protracted and uncertain journey lies ahead of him."

Katie fights back hopeless despair. "Gavin is everything to me. I've never loved anyone like I love him. He's such a good and wonderful person—husband, father, *human!* So kind, generous, and thoughtful. But now I'm watching him turn into a different person. I want my husband back," she moans, grieving. "It just breaks my heart."

There is painful, doleful silence on the line.

Then, abruptly, "Excuse me—don't hang up—" and Katie runs to the bathroom. She hopes the sounds don't come through on the phone.

"Are you okay, Katie?" Pedersen asks when she returns. "Does Gavin know yet?"

Katie isn't surprised that Pedersen got it. "Not yet." She clears her throat and thinks about the irony of her pregnancy at this time. Her and Gavin's last intimacy was the morning of his birthday. They'd shared their love on the same day he later found Devon hanging. The tragic day when one life was destroyed, while another life was created. One their union may not be ready for.

A mournful silence settles over them. Then Pedersen speaks, "Katie, I promise I will be here for you and Gavin all the way."

"So if I venture into the lion's den and go to Boston to be with Gavin, you'll be there?"

"Absolutely. Right in that den with you."

Katie looks into Maggie's room after Pedersen hangs up. Poor Maggie. During the last few months, she's become so confused. She loves her Daddy, and can't figure out why he's been so different. And now that he isn't here, she's been crying, wanting to know when he's coming home.

Katie realizes that Gavin's grandparents can't be expected to deal with his erratic behavior, even though they really care about him. He's the last thread they have of their only daughter, and they want him to survive. And thrive. But for Gavin, getting there—becoming whole again—may be a lot more complicated and stressful than they're prepared to handle.

She's now convinced she must go be with Gavin, despite

his objections and the potential dangers. He can't be alone, left to deal with everything in Boston, plus his PTSD, by himself.

But she's read that a high percentage of spouses of war veterans with PTSD develop a version of it while coping with their spouse's recovery. And marriages don't survive the strain.

I am not going to let our marriage break up, not if I can help it!

She decides she must take Maggie with her to be with Gavin, and Patches too. Before Gavin left for Boston, Patches had become like his service animal, following him around. That smart mutt seems to sense Gavin's moods, moving in on him and leaning his weight against his leg whenever Gavin starts to freak out. After all, Gavin's the one who rescued him and nursed him back to health. Minus an eye and ear. So Patches has to help rescue his hero now.

Katie begins making a list. She must do a crash training course for their staff manager Henry, and Koni for managing inventory. And Kalea her gallery manager, too, so they can all take the reins while she's gone. She can also do some of the work remotely: paying bills, doing payroll, and a myriad of other "executive level" tasks. As for living arrangements back in Massachusetts, the Babson professor renting her mother's Wellesley house transferred to Dartmouth and broke the lease earlier this month, so their family can stay there—get their drama out of the grandparents' hair—while Gavin straightens everything out with the lawyers on the estate stuff. That could take a few weeks, unless some surprises pop up.

Who am I kidding? There will be surprises. Possibly not good ones.

"All men should strive to learn before they die,
what they are running from, and to, and why."
—James Thurber

10

GAVIN IS IN THE MIDDLE OF WASHING THE LAST, biggest pot from last night's dinner when his phone rings. Katie beat him to the call. It's seven in the morning in Kauai. He wipes his hands on the dishtowel. "Hey, beautiful! How's my favorite wife?"

"Glad I caught you!" Katie chirps. "How's your day going?" Like nothing is amiss, as if Gavin's angry outburst yesterday never happened.

Gavin hears Maggie babbling in the background. He aches with missing her, and Katie, and life the way it was before it all imploded. "Good. Busy doing dishes right now."

"You didn't get a chance to tell me about your trigger survival yesterday—I want to hear all about it!"

"It wasn't such a big deal. I did my breathing and mantra in the Prince Street building. Found out I didn't set the fire after all; a bullet hit a gas line during..." He trails off before saying the fatal words. "Oh, yeah, and I did my TM stuff in front of Café Pompeii too. After I passed out on the sidewalk. So getting me to work with the meditation guide was a lifesaver, babe."

"You passed out," Katie repeats, trying to keep worry out of her voice. "On the sidewalk. You want to talk about that?"

"No big deal. People just stepped over me," he scoffs. "Today's another day. You know what they say—a trigger a day, or two or three, keeps the doctor away."

"Okay, smart-ass," Katie giggles. "When you're ready, I'm all ears. Oh, by the way, how did your dinner turn out last night? Sounded delicious."

"It was good! I wish we could get schrod on Kauai."

"Me too, but by definition—'young fresh cod or haddock catch of the day'—that wouldn't be feasible. But I do miss it," she sighs. "What are you fixing tonight?"

"I haven't thought about it yet. Pedersen's joining us for dinner this evening."

Katie wouldn't be a very good spy, or poker player either. "Oh, that's nice," she says in the flat tone of she-who-already-knows. "What prompted that?"

"Grandpa invited him."

"That's thoughtful of him."

"He and Grandma think I'm spinning out of control, I guess."

"Are you?"

"Maybe. I had way too much to drink last night."

"Um-hmm..."

"Yeah, yeah. Pedersen said that might be one way of handling triggers, right?"

"Yes, he said excess alcohol or drugs are sometimes a coping reaction to the discomfort of triggers, a way of dealing with the feelings they evoke. But of course triggers aren't really *handled* or prevented with alcohol or drugs..."

Gavin's defenses go up. "Well, maybe I just celebrated surviving those two major triggers." He feels himself being backed into a corner, trapped, threatened.

Katie's voice goes soft. "And I'm so proud of you, Tiger. But I've never known you to celebrate victories that way before, so—" she stops herself before "worry," or "concern" escape her tongue, "this is something new."

Gavin's self-defense shifts to offense. "I've never had a victory like this!" he snaps, belligerent anger rising in his voice as he punches his way out of the corner.

"Yes, sweetheart, I know, and I'm so sorry. You've never had challenges like these, so winning a round or two is something you can be proud of. Does a liquid celebration increase the joy, or bury the problem?" she asks in a loving near-whisper.

Maggie begins crying in the background.

Gavin throws his phone across the room.

Gavin decides to keep it simple and make lasagna and salad for dinner. Of course, his version of lasagna—with ground turkey instead of beef—is never really simple, and it's loaded with vegetables. The usual garlic, onion, and fresh herbs in his homemade slow-cooked fresh tomato sauce, plus spinach, zucchini, eggplant, red bell peppers, and three kinds of mushrooms, held together with three unique cheeses between layers of pasta. It takes hours to prepare, bake, and set.

Gavin can always quell his anxiety or stress by cooking. And he is definitely anxious today. Regretting his anger at Katie, and worried that he has failed not only his grandparents but also Dr. Pedersen, his former high school counselor who has stuck by him since he was sixteen. More than eleven years. When Pedersen flew out to Kauai two weeks after Devon died to support and counsel Gavin, he thought he understood the words, but those words are insufficient to quell the emotions, nightmares, and flashbacks assaulting him daily. And now the people who care about him are concerned he's losing it. His lifelong feelings of guilt, shame, and inadequacy cling to him like dirt.

But now the aromas comfort him. The entire house—and possibly the entire neighborhood and campus—is awash in delicious smells by the time Dr. Pedersen arrives.

Grandpa hears the doorbell and opens the front door to greet him joined by Grandma, while Gavin wipes his hands on his apron to welcome Pedersen, who walks in with the assistance of a fancy hand-carved hickory wood cane. Gavin is overcome with the urge to apologize to the man who has stuck with him, helping him overcome the damage inflicted by his dysfunctional family, for more than a decade. *And still I can't get it right. Guess I'm just a slow learner.*

Pedersen's face lights up with a broad smile as he stretches out his free arm. "Gavin! I've come to see if you'd like to go jogging with me!"

All four of them laugh in response, immediately relieving awkwardness and tension. Gavin comes to Pedersen for the man-hug. "Good to see you, sir."

And it is. Gavin feels relief, like he's just found someone who understands his language in the middle of a foreign country. Dr. Pedersen has stood by him, understanding, supporting, and helping him for more than eleven years—since his junior year in high school. He'd always struck Gavin as so proper and professional that he should have a British accent, wear a tweed jacket and smoke a pipe.

"Come sit down, Jim," Grandma says.

"I haven't eaten all day, saving up for Gavin's meal," Pedersen says as he settles into the green armchair. "And judging from the aroma, I'd say the wait is certain to be well rewarded."

Gavin sets a tray of grapes, figs, and apple wedges on the coffee table. "I've made lasagna, a heavy meal, so we can just nibble on a little fruit first. We have chianti if you'd like me to pour some for you now."

Almost in unison, the grandparents and Pedersen decline. "That'll be perfect when we dig into the lasagna, Gavin," Grandpa says.

Gavin gets the message.

Once they've gathered at the dining room table, the four of them drink only one bottle of chianti that evening over lively conversation.

"Are you still counseling at the high school, Dr. Pedersen?"

Gavin asks as he distributes plates of arugula and grapefruit salad to each place.

"No, I resigned that, and I've returned to private practice," Pedersen says. "My schedule can be more flexible this way. And it's about time you start calling me 'Jim.'"

Gavin smiles, a bit flustered. "So now, *Jim*, you don't have to be surrounded by out-of-control teenage hormones."

"Well, those hormones provided a much-needed change after..."

Grandma interjects, "After you lost Marilyn and Todd."

That feels like a jolt of lightning to Gavin. He casts inquiring glances toward Grandma and then Pedersen.

"My wife and son both died fifteen years ago, Gavin."

"Oh, I'm so sorry, sir," Gavin says, his voice heavy with genuine grief. And guilt that he had been so consumed with his own problems, leaning on Pedersen, without considering that his savior might have problems of his own. Although he'd often sensed there was a tinge of unexpressed sadness, of loss, in Pedersen.

"I took more than a year before I felt strong enough to return to work, helping other people," Pedersen smiles. "I couldn't very well help others if I couldn't help myself. Then I made the mistake of assuming that being a counselor to high school kids would involve 'no heavy lifting,'" he laughs.

Gavin does a quick mental calculation. So four years before Pedersen came to his rescue after Devon's accident, he'd had his own double loss. The wall between counselor and patient prohibits knowing anything personal about the doctor. He has so many questions now, which would be inconsiderate to ask. How did his wife and son die? How old were they? Does Pedersen have more children? Has he remarried? And Gavin wonders whether his counselor's ardent devotion to his well-being has in some way been compensation for Pedersen's failure to save his own son and wife. Questions that will likely never be answered.

Grandma reaches over to Pedersen and pats his hand. "I know their anniversary was earlier this week, Jim."

Pedersen smiles. "Were you the one who left the flowers on their grave, Carla?"

"No! I'm sorry I didn't think of it," Grandma apologizes.

"Well, some thoughtful person laid a beautiful bouquet from Whole Foods, but I don't know whom to thank."

Gavin remembers dropping the bouquet he'd intended for his parents somewhere on his way out of the cemetery, and wonders about the coincidence, but doesn't say anything. He gets up to clear the salad plates before serving the lasagna.

Grandpa changes the subject. "So tell us all about your mission here, Gavin."

Gavin busies himself cutting the lasagna into serving sizes. "Not much to tell," he mumbles, not taking his eyes off the lasagna. "Just settling Dad's estate with his lawyers."

"And you may not have known that part of that estate was what your mother inherited from her uncle," Grandpa says. "Unless Tony or Devon depleted it."

Gavin is both surprised and confused. "I—I—"

"My brother Mark," Grandma explains. "He never married or had kids, but he did become very wealthy," she laughs. "And he adored your mother."

"As we all did," Grandpa adds, and eyes the large serving of lasagna Gavin puts in front of him. "So what else needs to be decided, Gavin?"

Gavin sits down and begins toying with his food. "The properties. I have to go through everything at the house and decide what we should keep, then turn the rest over to a liquidator to sell or give away before a crew comes to clean and paint, then put the house on the market." He takes a deep breath and holds it.

Grandpa casts a glance over to Pedersen, who nods almost imperceptibly.

"Anything good there you want to keep?" Pedersen asks casually.

"One of Mom's watercolors. Grandpa and Grandma, you may want to come over to get some of those, and maybe some of the antiques you gave her, in the dining room cabinet."

"That would be lovely, Gavin—thank you," Grandma smiles.

"Before I turn everything over to the liquidators, you should come get what you want," Gavin urges. "And Dr. Pedersen—*Jim*, Mom kept a ton of research papers from her postgrad work and after, all organized by topic in these vertical boxes that sit on the bookshelf. If you're interested."

"Banker's boxes?" Pedersen asks. "Sure, I'd be curious to check them out. But you may want them, too."

Gavin looks down, sheepish. "Um, I just brought one back this morning, to look over," he shrugs, immediately regretting it, hoping Pedersen wouldn't ask the topic of the contents.

"Are there other properties?" Grandma asks.

"Just the building in the North End," Gavin shrugs again. "Dad leased the stores in all the other locations, so that makes it a little easier. Just have to sell the business. Which will no doubt attract all the vultures."

"That's the building where the fire was?" Grandpa asks.

As far as Gavin knows, no one had ever made public what happened in that building. He certainly didn't, but now he becomes tense and defensive, fearing that his grandparents, or Pedersen, may have learned the truth. His sin. "Yeah, yeah," he snaps with a frown, clenching his fists. He's beginning to feel threatened, backed into a corner again. "The City wants to know if I want to salvage it or sell it," he snarls. "And Dad's crooked lawyer is pressuring me to sell it 'as is,' like someone wants something that's in there," he spits and slams his fist down on the table, releasing a cloud of tension into the room with a chilling effect on those gathered around the table.

Grandpa looks to Pedersen with concern. "And that's why you need the structural engineer," he says in a soothing tone. "Smart of you, son."

"Right," Gavin grunts, then exhales the breath he'd been

holding. "Anyone want seconds?"

"Oh my goodness," Grandma says. "It was so delicious, but I'm so full I couldn't eat another bite. We'll enjoy leftovers tomorrow!"

"Same here," Pedersen and Grandpa agree in unison.

"But a spoonful of the pineapple-ginger-mint sherbet I made will help you digest the lasagna," Gavin says with excess cheer, in an attempt to expunge his angry outburst from the room. As he collects all the dinner plates and utensils, he adds, "With chamomile tea," and nods to Pedersen, recalling the special cups of chamomile his old counselor used to serve him when he came, despondent, to his office in high school.

After sherbet and tea, Pedersen announces that he's up past his bedtime. "Thank you so much for including me here this evening, Gerry and Carla, and Gavin for the amazing dinner. But I really must be going, before I overstay my welcome."

"You're always welcome here anytime, Jim," Grandpa says, while Grandma smiles in agreement.

"If it weren't for this bum knee, I would ordinarily have walked here," Pedersen says. "I found a parking place around the corner. Gavin, would you mind walking me to my car?"

"I'll begin cleaning up while you do that, Gavin," Grandma says.

As Gavin escorts his counselor out of the house and down the sidewalk, he senses that Pedersen wants to tell him something. *Probably wants to tell me I'm out of control, getting pissed for no reason. Like I don't know that. I don't need him to tell me.*

"I'm disappointed that I have this meniscus tear, Gavin," Pedersen says. "It would be fun to go running with you. I'm not a cross-country champ like you, but I can usually hold my own."

Gavin wonders what Pedersen's intentions are with this topic. "Sorry about your knee," he mumbles, holding Pedersen's elbow as they negotiate a broken curb.

"I go to the gym twice a week to rebuild strength in my leg, Gavin, if you'd like to join me."

Gavin thinks about that. "I haven't been running for the past few months. I'm so out of shape, having pains I've never had. I'd probably embarrass myself."

"No more than I embarrass myself," Pedersen chuckles. "I'll text you the next time I go."

They reach Pedersen's car. "Thanks for coming tonight, Dr. Pedersen—Jim. It was good to see you."

"How are you dealing with all this, Gavin?"

Gavin doesn't respond. He looks away and begins turning around.

"Being confronted with all you're finding at your house," Pedersen notes, "and having to confront what happened in the North End must have triggered some powerful memories."

Gavin whirled back around. "You know?"

"You told me, when I spent time with you in Kauai after Devon died."

"Well, I was wrong. I didn't set the fire," Gavin growls. "It was a gas explosion."

"That must provide some consolation."

"Doesn't change the shooting though," he mutters. "The killing."

"In self-defense, Gavin."

"Defending Devon. My lifelong curse."

"That too," Pedersen says softly. "How are you handling the triggers? The flashbacks? How can I help?"

"They're following me, Dr. Pedersen," Gavin moans.

As he says this, the ubiquitous black SUV rolls by.

> "Three things cannot long stay hidden:
> the sun, the moon and the truth."
> —Buddha

11

THE SUV SLOWS, THEN STOPS IN FRONT OF HIM. THE *darkly tinted window on the passenger side rolls down. A long gun emerges from it, pointing at him. The back door flings open and a clean-shaven guy with slicked-back hair and sunglasses steps out, holding a Glock pointed at him.* Get in, Red, he says.

Gavin doesn't move. The guy waves his gun. Don't make me hurt you, kid. Get the fuck in, or you'll be sorry. *Gavin knows running would be fatal. He doesn't move. The man in the passenger seat opens the door and walks toward him. A muffled shot penetrates Gavin's knee. He goes down. Warm blood bathes his leg. The shooter motions for Back Seat Guy to drag Gavin into the vehicle.* You're an idiot, kid. We just want to talk about what's in that burnt-out building of yours. We might even cut a deal with you if you're good. *Front Seat and Back Seat Guy laugh in morbid harmony.*

Gavin's flailing arms finally vault him up out of bed, a shout struggling to erupt from his breathless lungs. It takes a minute for him to realize where he is. And where he is not.

He realizes that dream was probably the product of his planned investigation into the Prince Street building today, but it felt ominous, prescient. His nightmares have become more vivid, and more disturbing, since he's been back in Wellesley. He dismisses it as being a function of different bed, different time zone. And missing Katie and Maggie.

It's six-thirty. The eastern sky is beginning to lighten, although the sun won't appear for another ten minutes or so. He won't be able to get back to sleep, so he doesn't bother to try. Solomon the structural engineer can't meet with him on Prince Street until ten, so Gavin decides to go over to the house to sort through another room.

He opts for coffee first. At least he doesn't have a hangover this morning. He heads toward the stairs, but as an afterthought turns back to get Devon's journal. *A little light reading with coffee—ha!*

He's glad Grandpa and Grandma aren't up yet. He relishes the quiet and solitude as he settles into the big green chair with his coffee and Devon's journal. The handwriting ranges from legible—although deeply pressed into and often through the paper—to frenetic illegible scrawls. Gavin can easily discern what his brother's mood probably was at the time he wrote each entry, most of which focus on Gavin, and now elicit a range of diverse emotions in him as he reads his twin's version of their shared history. It's as if he's in one of those amusement park rides through a dark tunnel, barreling at high speed, violently jerking in every twisted turn, then up, then down, defying every law of physics.

> Gav beat me in a race today — he can't do that! Dad says I'm the winner — so I got him in the shower — always wanted to do that — what a turn-on! He freaked
>
> Gav has a girlfriend — he can't do that! — he has to love ME
>
> Gav saved my life last night — wish he didn't
>
> Dad's so tough — killed Mom. yeah, real tough — she's the only person he can beat
>
> I'm in trouble. I need Gavin. He's supposed to save me
>
> Spucky's stooge Jimbo tried to kill me — asshole missed — got Dad — good riddance — deserved it
>
> **TWINKIE LEFT ME!!! HE CAN'T DO THAT! HE'S MINE**

Gavin's head goes dizzy as he flips pages rapidly, rushing through the distress, the calls for help from his twin, when one line prompts him to go back to it.

Found stuff from Grandpa D's time!

He jumps up, almost spilling his coffee. In the Prince Street building? Something hidden? Dad said Grandpa DiMasi played ball with the mob back when he first opened his store. Is that why those black SUVs have been following him? He has to talk with Rizzo. How can he find him? Assuming he's still alive, it's not like he can Google him, or find him in the Yellow Pages. Who would know where he is? Someone who won't re-up his membership on the mob's hit list.

Gavin buzzes, thrilled by the possibility of finding secrets in the building, evidence of what his father and DiMasi grandfather may have done. The idea that the building his father's lawyer is pressuring him to sell may still hold mob secrets and maybe even money—why else would those SUVs be following him?—has sparked his curiosity and reignited his desire to understand his family's toxicity. But it also raises his fear that he might now be caught in the mob's crosshairs. He weighs those conflicting ideas and decides to go to the building—before Solomon gets there, to do a little investigation himself. But he'll need tools to poke around, and he knows the local Ace Hardware doesn't open until eight in the morning. Maybe Grandpa has something he can use. Just as he's headed to the garage, Grandpa comes into the kitchen.

"Good morning, Gavin," Grandpa says, pouring himself a cup of coffee. "Thanks for making the pot—you're up early!"

"Grandpa, do you have any tools? Like maybe a hammer, crowbar, screwdriver...?" Gavin grabs a cinnamon-apple muffin from the batch he made yesterday and bites into it, then has an afterthought. "Oh, and a flashlight too!"

"I'm not very handy," Grandpa chuckles. "But the faculty that lived here before us left some tools in the garage—apparently the professor's husband was some sort of craftsman before he died—so you can check. Are you doing some work over at your dad's house? Maybe there are some tools there, too."

"Dad wasn't very handy either." Gavin laughs, takes another bite of muffin, and goes to the garage. Ten minutes later he emerges, victoriously brandishing a bulging Home Depot bag of tools and a large flashlight like weapons of war. "Bingo! They left everything I need!"

"What are you planning on doing?" Grandpa asks, clutching his coffee cup and a muffin.

"Oh, just going to conduct an interrogation into secrets," Gavin intones in spy-speak, then laughs and turns to go.

Grandpa pulls back with a puzzled look on his face. "What do you mean, Gavin?"

"I'm going to unravel some mysteries in the Prince Street building, Grandpa," Gavin says with a cryptic smile.

"Now, wait a damn minute!" Grandpa raises his voice. "You could be playing with fire, just asking for trouble. You get crosswise with the mob and Katie'll come running, endangering herself and Maggie. You really want to poke that bear?"

"Ah, it'll be okay. Devon wrote in his journal that he found something in the building from Grandpa DiMasi's time! Maybe it'll help me understand my messed-up family."

The good thing about going into Boston so early in the morning is the lack of traffic. Well, except for the delivery trucks already lining both sides of Hanover Street. But at least Gavin finds a parking place near his building on Prince Street. He doesn't see a black SUV anywhere.

He lugs his bag of hardware to the front door and pulls

out the key Marge O'Connor gave him. It doesn't fit. The same key that fit a couple days ago no longer fits, because someone has changed the lock. He is unsurprised, as if he expected it. He pulls out a screwdriver from his bag and removes both the hasp and its corresponding loop from the weathered plywood, taking the padlock with it, and pockets the screws. Once inside the building, he fishes out the rusty slide-bolt latch set he'd found in Grandpa's garage and uses the screws to install it on the inside of the door. He doesn't want unexpected visitors.

Gavin isn't sure where to start. By this time the sun is up, although there isn't much light in the building. He turns on his flashlight and begins walking slowly through the first floor. He proceeds methodically, slaloming in rows, using his feet to sense variations in surface as well as density, in case he steps on an area that is compromised or unsafe, or an area that's of a different composition than the rest of the floor. Maybe a hatch where something's hidden inside.

Then he needs to investigate the basement—he's sure there must be one—although Marge O'Connor didn't mention it because it wasn't in the report, she said. He wonders why it wouldn't have been.

There's something about this mission that energizes Gavin, like the treasure hunts he and Devon went on when they were kids. He becomes lost in the adventure, the mystery to be solved, an intriguing diversion from the threat of impending triggers and flashbacks weighing upon him at every moment. It seems to raise confidence in himself, that he can do something worthwhile in the place where he had done something destructive, something he never thought he could or should do. Something he'd like to forget but knows he never will.

He has criss-crossed most of the main floor without detecting any areas of concern or interest, and finally enters what once was his brother's VIP room, where earlier in the week he had wondered about an inexplicable protrusion into the footprint of the building. He's eager to investigate that, hastening to complete his row-by-row exploration of the floor, where he discovers nothing of interest except the destroyed gas line.

Gavin inspects the brick wall on the left side of the room to see whether there might be any way to enter or penetrate. A knob behind one of the bricks, camouflaged hinges between bricks, a magic button somewhere, a place for commanding "Open Sesame!"

He pulls a hammer from his bag and taps various spots on the protruded wall, and then does the same on the exterior wall. The protruded wall has a very different sound; there isn't concrete inside. Instead, as he taps along horizontally, he hears the tell-tale pattern of solid, hollow, solid, evidence of regularly spaced wood studs behind the brick. He wonders if this wall was constructed at a different time than the front wall of the VIP room, because their internal composition, behind the brick fascia, is obviously very different. He's convinced *something*—he doesn't know what—is behind this wall that someone wants hidden. The only way to access it is to tear down the wall. Unless there's access from above or below...

A banging sound reverberates through the emptiness of the building. Gavin checks his watch; Solomon is early. He runs to open the door.

A short wiry guy looking like a refugee from an old Andy Capp cartoon stares at him with wary fear clouding his gray eyes. Casting a furtive glance over his shoulder, the guy rushes past Gavin into the building, dragging an extension ladder and a bulky canvas tote almost as big as he is.

"Mr. Solomon?" Gavin asks. "Are you okay?"

"Yeah, yeah," the guy stammers, breathing hard. "Parked my truck up the street. Then thought I saw a guy I used to know. I try to avoid this neighborhood."

"I'm sorry, sir. My grandfather said you're the best structural engineer in town. Honest, too."

"Well, to be *honest*, I've had some bad experiences in the

North End, so let's just get this over with." He takes off his Scally cap, pulls out a headlamp and puts it on his bald head, then sets out a large industrial multi-light lantern. "You need to get NSTAR to set up an electric feed outside the building with a locked cover, so you can plug in extension cords for lights. And see what the hell you're doing."

"Oh, I didn't think that was possible."

"Just need to know the right people." He scans Gavin head-to-toe. "From the looks of it, you've already been pokin' around this dusty place, sonny."

"Uh, yes, sir."

"Okay, let's get this show on the road," Solomon says. "I remember hearing about this fire three years ago. July 2002, if memory serves. A minor gas line got ruptured, but the trucks came faster than for most fires around here. Like there was something special about this place. Dumped a ton of water and foam on it, I gather." He looks all around, assessing the situation. "Two of the clues to extent of damage are how long the fire burned and how hot it got. So," he huffs, as if beginning a lecture, "I understand this was a liquor store. Alcohol has a low flash point, but it doesn't burn as hot as other stuff like paper or some woods. I don't see much exposed concrete to test. The brick walls don't have as much soot as you might expect, and there's limited deterioration to the mortar in most places. There are some brick areas that had been covered with wood, maybe for decorative effect, and because I still see some wood remaining, although charred, that tells me the fire didn't go on too long before it was put out. Looks like it was oak?"

"My brother wanted the inside walls to look like oak wine or whiskey barrels," Gavin offers.

"Um-hmm. Oak takes longer to catch fire, and since the trucks got here so quickly, that's why there's still some wood up against the walls," Solomon says. "Now over there, I see a brass knob layin' on the floor. Looks like it might have been from a door. Front," he points to the plywood entry, "or basement," he points over to a knob-less damaged door on the left wall of the building, behind piles of debris and directly under a slanted area that's apparently the stairs from outside to the upper floors. Gavin doesn't know how he'd missed that obvious entrance downstairs to the basement. Solomon walks over and picks up the knob. "The sort of discoloration and lack of distortion tell me that the fire didn't go on too long, and it didn't burn very hot. So now let's take a look at those overhead beams."

He extends his ladder against the right-hand wall. Taking a flat-head screwdriver from his tote, he climbs up and begins poking it into the beam. "Oh, I see the hole down there on the back wall, must be where the gas blast came through, which sent fire traveling along this side of the building. So I'm checking up next to the ceiling where fire is always hottest, and near the front here first, where oxygen would have fed the fire even hotter." He continues poking, but his screwdriver doesn't penetrate much at all. "Good God, this old place was built solid! Old wood—especially old hardwood—takes longer to catch fire, but they actually used *ironwood* for these beams—un-fuckin'-believable! That wood is super hard, slow to catch fire, and doesn't burn as hot as most. There's very shallow charring on this beam—so it's solid and weight-bearing, just needs cleaning."

Gavin begins to think the damage to the building is much less than what the lawyer implied, and what the City building commission reported. So what's their game?

Solomon climbs down and checks a vertical column supporting the ceiling beam. "Son of a bitch! This is ironwood too. Tough as iron!" He shakes his head, baffled, and walks to the next beam, bouncing his knees with each step to get a feel for the floor. "Fires are always hottest at the ceiling, so this floor incurred less fire damage; it feels solid. We'll confirm that in the basement."

Gavin stiffens. *Uh-oh.* He isn't sure he wants this guy to be poking around in the basement. What if the stuff Devon found is down there? Well, if Devon didn't take it out.

As the engineer proceeds toward the back of the building, every beam, and all their vertical support columns, get the same verdict. When Solomon reaches the entry to the VIP room, he stops, looking puzzled. "This is an interior wall! Why did they construct it of concrete and brick?" he asks, chipping away a bit of mortar to reveal the concrete.

"Yeah, I wondered the same thing," Gavin agrees.

The engineer pokes at other spots along the wall. "The concrete seems to be solid. And that hole down there is where the gas blasted…" He points to the right.

"I guess so. That's what the city building inspector said."

Solomon nods and continues into the VIP room. "Ah, there's where the gas came from." He walks to the right side of the room and points to the damaged line. "They must've had a small gas-fired heater here that they didn't bleed when they turned it off for the summer, just turned off the gas down below. So there was just enough gas left in this section of line to blast when some macho Italian guy starts shootin' something up. Coulda been much worse if it wasn't turned off at the main feed. What did you say the inspector's name was?"

"Marge O'Connor."

"Hmm… Thought I knew 'em all, but not that one."

"She mentioned your name," Gavin says. "You and someone named Christine Simmons, and Grandpa recommended you too."

"I've heard of Simmons. Winter Street girl, over in Somerville."

Gavin knows about the Irish mob, Whitey Bulger's Winter Street gang in Somerville that's now operating in Southie too. His stomach begins to churn. So maybe Marge O'Connor's with Winter Hill too? "I understand, sir. What about Richard Salvatti? Rick—"

"Oh, yeah," Solomon growls, stuffing his hands into his pockets.

"What can you tell me about him?" Gavin prods. Panic slowly crawls up his back.

"Now I realize who I saw outside as I was pounding on your door," the engineer coughs. "Piece of shit. Stay the hell away from him."

"Mob?" Gavin's breath is locked tight in his chest.

"You better believe it. Fuckin' Italians." Solomon shakes his head, then checks his watch. "Hey, kid, much as I dislike being in this neighborhood, I'm gonna have to come back to finish. I didn't figure this would take so long, and I still haven't checked the basement or the floors above."

Although Gavin is eager to learn more from the engineer, he feels somewhat relieved. He will have more time to explore by himself before Solomon returns.

"I'll leave all my stuff here," Solomon says, "so I won't have to lug it both ways, and come back tomorrow. That okay with you?" He hands his headlamp to Gavin.

"Okay, sir. Ten o'clock tomorrow?" Gavin asks.

Solomon nods. "Yeah, I can do that."

"Thanks—I'll see you out."

As Solomon exits, he looks quickly up and down the street—probably checking for Rick Salvatti. But there's only a black SUV with darkly tinted windows.

> "Principle #1: Avoid dangerous
> people and dangerous places.
> Principle #2: Do not defend your property.
> Principle #3: Respond immediately and escape."
> —Sam Harris

12

GAVIN NEEDS MORE SUPPLIES BEFORE HE CAN continue searching the building, but he can't leave without securing it. So he has to remove the screws from the slide-bolt latch and use them for replacing the hasp and loop—along with the attached padlock—on the outside of the plywood door. Of course, that "security" measure won't keep out whoever changed the lock, which he'll replace after he gets supplies at the hardware store.

He looks around for the black SUV, but it's gone. It has become a constant appurtenance to his life, so he sort of misses it when it's not there. Like a steadily dripping faucet that leaves a portentous silence when it stops.

As the crow flies, the closest hardware, Charles Street Supply, is nearby, but in cross-town traffic it's an aggravating twenty-five minutes. While Gavin drives, his mind goes in circles and mazes as he chews over what he knows and doesn't know. Of course the mob must have already searched the building, trying to find whatever it is they think is there. So why are they following him? For what's in the building, because they think he knows, or they think Devon told him where it's hidden? Or for some other reason? Does he still have an active "do-not-touch " protection from Frank Rizzo? He has to find Rizzo. Put that on the growing "to-do" list.

Someone pulls out of a parking spot on Charles Street near the hardware store in the West End, and Gavin pulls in. It's just up the street from the pub where he had beer with Marge O'Connor two days ago. Inside the store, the product selection is almost as varied as Home Depot but concentrated in a much smaller space. High shelves and racks overladen with colorful goods, labels and signs, people with baskets and carts jammed in narrow aisles, a cacophony of multi-pitched voices and other noises. Sensory overload assails him.

He begins feeling claustrophobic and rushes through the aisles to find what he needs, bumping people along the way. A heavy-duty hasp and loop set, pliers, wrench, screws, bolts+nuts, washers, a bigger stronger slide-bolt latch, a weatherproof high-security square padlock that looks like an impenetrable strongbox, a rechargeable drill and bits (although he can't charge it until he plugs it in somewhere), and a hand drill for this afternoon. He knows there will probably be more stuff he needs as his exploration continues. He makes a note to call NSTAR about getting power to the building. And that flimsy plywood joke of a door should be replaced. His "to-do" list is getting longer every day. Katie was always good at lists, schedules, and getting all that shit done.

When he finally checks out of the store and goes outside, _t's raining like there's no tomorrow. He runs with his loot and puts it all in his trunk, then notes the pub three doors beyond his car. He only had half a cinnamon-apple muffin this morning, and it's twelve-thirty now.

When he walks into the pub, the place is bustling in a more harmonious, less frenetic vibe than he just left behind. He finds a stool at the bar and sits, taking in a deep breath. He realizes he hasn't been doing enough of that, and tries to find the flow zone he's been neglecting. The bartender appears and puts a mug of beer in front of him. Gavin looks up at him, puzzled.

"That's the one you like," he says, handing Gavin a menu. "The hazy IPA."

Gavin doesn't remember the guy, but assumes he must be whoever served him when he was here with Marge. He hadn't planned on drinking mid-day, but it does look awfully good. "Thanks, man." He takes a sip. "I'm sorry, I forget your name?"

"Joe. And you're Gavin. Or was it Devon?"

In an instant, the universe closes in on Gavin, attacking on all sides in a life-threatening assault, spinning him out of control, letting all those treacherous voices in: *"Joe" is a dangerous mobster, he knows about Devon, thinks Gavin is like Devon. Gavin is Devon, Gavin is evil and sick, they're out to get him.* He can't breathe, or utter his mantra. There's no place to hide. All in a single motion, he jumps up, knocking the barstool onto the floor, throws the beer against the mirrored wall behind the bar in a cascading crash, lunges over to grab Joe by his hair, pulls him over the bar and starts punching him, kicking him to the floor.

Suddenly Gavin is in a headlock from behind and a fist is pounding his face. He is being dragged through the bar to the entrance and thrown out into the rain onto the sidewalk with a final kick.

"Now you've done it, Red," a familiar voice growls.

Before he passes out, Gavin sees the face of Rick Salvatti.

He is being nudged by someone who then takes his arm, attempting to lift him to his feet. At first he recoils in fear, but quickly sees it's a woman. Blonde hair wet from rain, late twenties. He cooperates and gets up. "I'm sorry."

"Why are you sorry?" she asks. "You're the one with a bloody nose and split lip, flat on the ground. Are you going to be okay?"

"Yeah, sure," Gavin mumbles. "Thanks. My car is just up

the block. I have to get out of here."

"You hit your head pretty hard on the concrete," she says with a cunning grin. "And someone hit your face pretty hard with their fists. Will you be okay to drive?" Saccharine tones undulate from her red lips.

Gavin feels like he's being cornered, triggering his fight response all over again. "What's it to you? Who the hell are you?"

"I'm Christine Simmons, Gavin. I understand you know Mark Solomon?" She smiles in the purring Cheshire-cat manner of one who has the mouse in her clutches. "You know he's not to be trusted, right?"

A pulsating red cloud of rage engulfs Gavin—*I'm trapped, they all know me, setting me up, can't trust anyone, it's a plot, they're all ganging up on me*—as he lunges toward the woman.

She jumps aside and hisses sweetly, "You wouldn't strike a woman now, would you Gavin?"

After a frozen moment, Gavin abruptly shifts from fight to flight response, turns and runs to his car, starts it up and pulls out into traffic, cars barely missing him, honking, as he barrels around pedestrians, through streets and red lights. He drives aimlessly, with no thought of where he's going. Nearly an hour later, he finds himself on Prince Street, with no memory of where he drove all that time.

He sits in his car, clutching the steering wheel, panting like he's been chased by a wild animal. His panting eventually tapers off and he consciously takes in deep breaths followed by long, slow exhales. He looks up through the windshield and sees St. Leonard's Peace Garden. He isn't religious, but it does telegraph a sense of peace for him. Which he really needs now. He gets out of his car and walks to it, wandering slowly among the trees, bushes, and late-season blooms, then sits on one of its white marble benches. He gradually attains an oddly surprising calmness, one that feels undeserved after the altercation he just had in the West End.

Oblivious to the concerned glances at his bloody face and

shirt from other peace-seekers in the garden, Gavin finally rises and returns to his car. He looks all around but doesn't see the black SUV or suspicious characters. He opens the trunk, pulls out the supplies he got at the hardware store, leaving the rechargeable drill, and goes to the plywood door. After removing the old hasp and loop, along with the obtruded lock, he uses the hand drill to make holes through the three-quarter-inch plywood to install the new heavy-duty set via bolts through the door, secured with washers and lock nuts on the inside, while constantly looking over his shoulder. He then goes inside to install his big new slide-bolt latch.

He checks his phone. Almost three o'clock. He doesn't have a lot of time to do much of anything at this point, but at least wants to check out the basement. He dons Solomon's headlamp and lugs his bag of tools, and Solomon's industrial lantern over to the basement door. It's secured with a padlock, so he pounds out the exposed hinge pins and dislodges the hingeless door from one side to lever it out and away.

Gavin peers down the stairwell. The impenetrable darkness is indifferent to his headlamp. Dank and foul smells of sewer and decay assault him in a noxious blend that makes him light-headed. He turns on Solomon's industrial lantern to aim its light down the stairwell, clinging to the wall as he descends to avoid passing out. When he reaches the bottom, he is not surprised to find that the "floor" of the basement is dirt, which would not be unusual for buildings as old as this one. But it also means that layers of history may lie buried beneath his feet. Or what Devon found.

He drags the lantern down to the dirt floor and looks all around as far as the light can penetrate. The basement expanse extends the entire depth of the building, from the street to the rear. Which means that thoroughly investigating the area could take several days, assuming he had a shovel and could effectively light the area. Nothing is burned here; the fire obviously did not breach the basement, although there's some evidence of water damage. There are cardboard boxes from alcohol distributors with empty bottles inside, wooden crates from wineries, metal shelving components, and lots of miscellaneous junk and trash scattered about. Movement in one trash pile tells him there are mice, or rats, down here. With his screwdriver, he makes a few test pokes and prods at the granite and brick perimeter of the foundation to determine how solid it is, toying with the fantasy of what could be hidden behind the bricks, as if there might be a *Cask of Amontillado* redux.

The foundation is constructed primarily of large irregularly shaped, inconsistently sized granite stones-to-boulders, with bricks filling occasional gaps. In the center of the back wall, just below the cross beam, Gavin notices a small rectangular shape underneath the sealer with ridges and indentations that spark his curiosity. He pulls out Solomon's flat-head screwdriver and begins scratching away the paint, trying to avoid scratching whatever the rectangle is. Old-fashioned letters emerge, and finally Gavin can see faint words:

Hutchinson
1687-1765

The small heavily oxidized copper plate is affixed into the wall by what appear to be common cut nails, one through a hole in each end, inserted into the crevice between granite boulders. Although Gavin is surprised, because O'Connor said the building was "built right before the Great Depression," he has read about houses being built atop earlier foundations after a fire or other destruction. He takes a picture of the plaque and wonders whether Grandpa DiMasi knows anything about the history of the building. Another task for the to-do list: Visit Grandpa D.

Gavin suppresses his urge to start poking for buried treasure in the dirt floor; that will have to wait for another day. Now he hurries to inspect the left side of the foundation, where there is a storage area built out from the wall, approximately the same dimensions as the mysteriously protruded area into the VIP room above. A padlock on the door prevents entry.

The acrid smells in this basement burn Gavin's damaged nose. Blood drips on his shirt and onto the dirt floor. He uses the screwdriver to remove the locked hasp on the door, opens it and shines his flashlight in. More boxes—old wooden ones stacked all the way up to the underside of the first floor. He wonders if these boxes hold what Devon found, so begins pulling them down one by one, opening to inspect what's inside, finding nothing but empty bottles and cobwebs.

When he has pulled out and inspected all the boxes, which are now spread out on the dirt floor outside the closet, he sighs in disappointment. As he reaches to pick up the lantern sitting in the closet doorway, its light flashes against the ceiling of the closet—the underside of the first floor—near the rear of the building. The boards of the ceiling between first-floor beams in one area look different than their counterpart boards between other adjacent beams. Lighter in color, less aged.

Gavin pulls two of the sturdiest boxes back into the closet and stacks them, climbing up to see the suspect area, which is confined to the distance between two beams and extends almost the full depth of the closet. He uses the hammer to tap the area and compare its sound to that of the boards between other beams. The area of lighter wood sounds a loose resonance. He pushes up first on one side, then another, and on the third side it lifts slightly. He pushes harder, then slams his hammer up on that side. It loosens sufficiently to lift what is a square hinged hatch, opening into what his flashlight reveals is most likely the mysterious storage area.

When Gavin pulls himself up into the "room," he has to pinch himself. *This is crazy, like cloak and dagger from pulp fiction.* His headlamp illuminates the darkness. The narrow, oblong area is in fact the inaccessible space adjacent to the left side of his brother's VIP room. He takes a moment to scan the area with his headlamp, still incredulous at the whole preposterous concept, way beyond any of his and Devon's fantastic imaginings when they played as kids.

Now he pats his back pockets, making sure his flashlight and cellphone are still there in case his headlamp goes out, and looks around. More boxes. Most are old, with labels he doesn't recognize—Braumeister Beer, Storz Beer, Oshkosh Brewing Co.—made of discolored, tattered cardboard. Inside the first one, he finds sales receipts, accounting records, supply orders, all information a business might save. Sifting randomly through the hundreds of papers—some as old as 1950—he sees many familiar names, populating decades of mob activity in the North End.

One more box, and then he needs to leave. He pulls out what appears to be a fireproof lockbox. He fiddles with the combination dial, trying to channel the safecracking experts he's seen in movies, listening to the clicks with each turn. Giving up after a few tries, he pulls out the flat-head screwdriver and teases it under the edge of the lid, near the center locking mechanism. He taps it with the hammer, jamming it further in, then levers the screwdriver into the widened gap, forcing the lockbox to open. He hoped what Devon found might be in this lockbox, but he only finds a 1950 deed to the property and a ledger in which names, numbers, and dates were recorded.

Gavin flips through the ledger, recognizing many of the names from his research into the Boston Mob, realizing he's uncovered a trail of mob history here. The ledger details how much money who owes whom; the entries begin in 1949 and continue as late as 2000. There are columns for dates of debt, name of debtor, name of creditor, amount of debt, dates and amounts of whole or partial payment, interest levied, and then individual records are struck out with an indication of when a debt has been paid in full. A few debts are struck out with no indication it was paid in full, and Gavin wonders what may have become of the debt. Or the debtor.

Grandpa's name is the first entry in 1949, when he borrowed from someone named Fil Buccola. Then he borrowed a very large amount, in today's money, from J.L. Lombardo in 1950. Gavin remembers that's the year he bought the building.

The entries on these pages span fifty-plus years after that, showing that Grandpa or Tony (after 1976, when he took over the business) borrowed from different people, among other records of more people borrowing money from someone else, as if Grandpa D had been the records-keeper for the mob. He seems to have been precise and almost anal in his organization skills. Or did he do this for other reasons? Protecting himself, or evidence with which to bribe or pressure others?

Gavin recalls many of the names in that "spreadsheet" from the research he conducted when he tried to convince Devon to avoid the mob. Not that it helped.

There are no records involving Devon after he took over the business in 2000, but Gavin doubts that's because he had no debts, only that he declined to acknowledge or record them.

Gavin is fascinated by these clues into his family's history, his mind vacillating between a mystery to be solved and a danger to avoid. On the face of it, it seems that his grandfather had gone into hock with mobsters to buy the building in 1950, and Tony continued the pattern when he took over the store in 1976. Although the records stop after Dad died, Gavin is certain that Devon followed suit when he took over the business, which got him into trouble. Gavin would need more time and research to fully trace and reconstruct the entire picture. For what consequence other than curiosity is not apparent to him. Yet.

Finally, at the bottom of the lockbox is a notebook with names and dates, clearly written at different times by different people over the last fifty-plus years, following no pattern of frequency or regularity. Gavin wonders about the significance of those names—more than twenty—and dates. The notebook and its pages aren't titled or labeled, and there is no suggestion of why those names and dates are recorded. And then he recognizes some of the names in the notebook who were also listed as debtors on the spreadsheets with their entries crossed out, with no indication of their debt having been paid. He makes a note to research the names to see if anything significant occurred around those dates.

The to-do list keeps growing.

Gavin checks the time. It's almost four-thirty—he needs to get out of here! He puts everything back in the boxes and begins descending through the hatch, thinking of all the remaining questions and areas in the building left to investigate. As he is about to close the hatch, his headlamp shines on the underside of the second floor, illuminating a square with wood that looks very similar to the underside of this hatch. Maybe that's an alternate access to and from the second floor? Then he hears a sound up there, like footsteps above the storage space. Maybe it's a homeless squatter that got in by the fire ladder?

Panic courses through his veins, igniting a fire in his brain and in every muscle of his body. Triggered by the fear of being trapped down here, with God knows who they are or what they want. The battle within him swings from fight—go find, confront, and vanquish whoever made the sound, to flight—get the hell out to safety, flee.

Determined less by conscious choice than by a chance flip of his reactions—like flipping a coin—Gavin just takes flight. He turns off the lantern and grabs his flashlight, runs up the stairs to the first floor, takes his new padlock, and goes out the front door, locking the door behind him. He doesn't notice the black SUV down the street.

As Gavin drives to Wellesley, he worries that someone may have observed what he was doing in the building.

> "I've learned to lick
> my own foul wounds
> and prize the taste of ache."
> —Chila Woychik,
> On Being a Rat and Other Observations

13

GAVIN'S LONG HOT SHOWER HASN'T DIMINISHED the bruises and cuts on his face. Nor on his knuckles. But it has returned his breathing to normal and soothed his tension.

He is sitting in what has become his favorite chair—the big green overstuffed one—listening to Katie's messages on his phone, feeling guilty that he hasn't talked with her yet today, and drinking a beer straight from the bottle, when Grandpa O'Malley comes home.

"Say, Gavin," Grandpa calls out as he takes his briefcase into the library, "your grandmother dropped by here between meetings and saw that you must have been working late today, so we thought we'd take you out to dinner tonight!" At this point he turns into the living room and sees Gavin's face. "Oh, Christ, what happened to you?"

Gavin forces a laugh, which puts pressure on his bruised (he hopes not broken) nose and cut lip. He had been so engaged in his "mystery tour" of the Prince Street building that he was oblivious to how much damage he incurred in his West End confrontation. Until he looked in the mirror upstairs. "Who knew that working in an abandoned burned-out building could be so dangerous?" he shrugs.

"It looks like it hurts, so will you be able to eat dinner?" Grandpa asks.

"Oh, sure," Gavin suppresses his laugh into a subdued chuckle. "I was planning on taking you out to dinner, since I dropped the ball on fixing something for us tonight. I may not look pretty, but I've never been known to pass up a good meal."

"Well it's our treat; you've been treating us every evening," Grandpa says. "There've been a few new additions to the culinary options in Wellesley since you lived here. We're big fans of the new Italian restaurant—Northern style, and we love the new Asian fusion restaurant."

"Oh, that's great!" Gavin's split lip constrains his smile. "The closest good Italian used to be Il Capriccio over in Waltham, and the closest fakery to Asian fusion was the PF Chang chain. So can we do your local Asian? I really can't deal with more Italian right now."

"Sounds good," Grandpa agrees. "I'll make reservations. Your grandmother has a late meeting and should be home soon. Have you talked to Katie today?"

"I was just checking her messages before calling her," Gavin says. "I'll go upstairs and call her before we leave for dinner."

"Good. I just need to check my email, then I'll call the restaurant," Grandpa says, going into the library and typing emails as Gavin heads toward the stairs.

"Hello, Katie?" Gavin says when Katie answers her phone. "Sorry I haven't been able to answer your calls."

"Oh, I know you're really busy—you're tackling a lot of stuff, sweetie. But I've missed you! Is everything okay?" Katie tries to make her question light, not laden with worry.

"Oh, yes, absolutely! It's exciting—I've discovered some weird shit in the Prince Street building. It's like a Rubik's Cube of historical mysteries."

"Wow! I can't wait to hear all about it! How long has that building been in your family?"

"Grandpa DiMasi bought it in 1950, and Dad took over the business in 1976," Gavin says. "The building is much older than that, but what I'm finding is my grandfather's and Dad's business dealings since that time."

"It sounds intriguing, Gav. Anything to do with the mob?"

"Well, yeah," his voice inflects with an unspoken *"DUH."*

"How does that affect *you?*"

Does she always have to go there, to my PTSD? "Too soon to tell," Gavin snaps. "So far, it's nothing I can't handle." Gavin is feeling anxious, pressured by Katie's questions. "Just don't worry about me. You take care of the business." He has to shut this down. "I hear a lot of noise in the background—it's lunchtime at the restaurant, so I'll let you go. Give Maggie a kiss for me." And he hangs up.

> "Some of the greatest battles will be fought within the silent chambers of your own soul."
> —Ezra Taft Benson

14

GRANDPA O'MALLEY'S EMAIL PINGS ON KATIE'S CELL phone while she's talking with Gavin. The restaurant is mobbed at the moment, Henry is having a meltdown, Koni has to go out for more tomatoes (how did we run short?), and both dishwashers called in "sick" this morning (of course; it's a beautiful day and the surf's up). She sees who it's from but isn't able to read the message at the moment.

But then there's an email from Dr. Pedersen. Something is undoubtedly serious. Fear turns her into fierce. She grabs Henry. "Henry, I spent the entire day yesterday, and all this morning, preparing you for my absence," she spits, her voice low so the staff can't hear. "Time to buckle up and *manage*, instead of melting down. In fact, a little *leadership* might avert the occurrence of disasters you have to manage."

Henry stands more than a head taller than Katie, but now shrivels to pint-size. "Emergency in Boston?" he mumbles the question, looking down at his shoes.

"Get your act together, we're all counting on you," Katie pleads with her hand on Henry's arm, then rushes into the office to read both messages that just came in.

She learns that Gavin's bruised and bloodied knuckles indicate that he got into a fight, but his denying it is serious—more so than the fight itself. He's scratched up, but okay physically. Pedersen says it's time for her to come to Boston. She goes online to change her flight from two weeks hence to the first flight out—nine o'clock tonight direct to Los Angeles, connecting to an eight-a.m. direct flight to Boston—then calls Kalea to tell her she's in charge of *Makakū* and Nalani to say she'll be picking up Maggie and Patches in an hour. She notifies the manager of her mother's house that her family will be staying there indefinitely, beginning tomorrow night.

Katie is so focused on all the necessary arrangements that she doesn't have the time or bandwidth to feel anything except the pressure to get everything done and get on the plane with her family. She already has the travel certificate for their dog, but she has a myriad of other things to do before she, Maggie, and Patches can get on the plane.

She emails replies to Grandpa and Pedersen, saying she's scheduled to arrive in Logan at four-thirty tomorrow afternoon, their time. She asks them both their opinion on what she should tell Gavin, why she's coming so suddenly. He'll probably think she's questioning his ability to handle things there, which could make things worse or even completely untenable.

Katie's entire body is vibrating, shaking, as if she has stuck two fingers into an electrical outlet. Nervousness, worry, fear, energy to burn, all on an empty stomach.

Koni, who has been with Gavin and her since before they opened the restaurant two years ago, is back from his tomato errand. He taps on the office door then opens it to give her a plate of food and a cup of tea. "Henry told me it's show time, Katie," he says. "You haven't eaten, you need my famous tea to calm your nerves, and you're pregnant. Take a break from taking care of everyone else for a minute. Someone has to take care of *you*, mama."

Katie nearly crumbles with relief, tears wetting her giggles over the idea of someone taking care of her. And now the universe is conspiring to take care of her. Puna calls to ask if there's anything she needs him to pick up from the store for the trip, and that he'll bring Nalani, Maggie, and Patches to Katie's house to help do laundry and pack, then drive her to the Lihue airport this evening. Grandpa sends a message that he'll pick her up from Logan tomorrow. Her mother's house manager texts her that he'll make sure sheets, towels, and everything else are all fresh and ready for her, including a crib and high chair for Maggie.

Katie didn't ask for anyone to help her. She's capable, strong, and tough. So she thinks, as she sips Koni's chamomile-lemon balm tea. But now she feels an overwhelming sense of gratitude. She exhales, finally realizing she's been holding her breath.

Then Pedersen calls. "Tell Gavin you need to be with him because you're pregnant."

"Oh—yes! That will probably work! Make him feel important, needed, and valuable," she says, pausing. She takes the last sip of tea. "Dr. Pedersen—Jim—I'm so scared."

"Don't be afraid to show that to Gavin, Superwoman," Pedersen teases. "It will serve as the reason, the purpose, for your supporting him when you need to intervene. Which—without that—may seem like manipulation or coercion to Gavin. If he realizes that you're scared, which is vastly different from worried—for him, for yourself, for Maggie—he's more likely to understand when you do what's needed to keep him out of trouble. He doesn't want to hurt you."

Katie sighs. It's going to be a long, arduous trip with a baby, dog, and the uncertainty of flight schedules. And the greater uncertainty of what she will encounter in Boston.

"Never surprise any member of a venomous species
with a home visit. It's not only rude,
it's potentially hazardous to your health."
—*Seanan McGuire*, Half-Off Ragnarok

15

GAVIN IS SO INSPIRED BY THE INNOVATIVE CUISINE at Karma, the Asian fusion restaurant, that he can't wait to tell Katie all about it. The menu items conflate world cuisines, serving traditional Japanese à la Paris, Thai with a Mexican twist, Korean Northern Italy style, Chinese from McDonald's, defying even Gavin's imagination.

"Katie, you wouldn't believe it!" he begins babbling as soon as she picks up his call, like he's high on MSG at nine o'clock at night. "Chinese in a burrito with a French aioli straight from Julia Child, sashimi served like a McDonald's burger with phyllo 'bun' and secret sauce—I took pictures! Everything is so beautifully presented. I want to start offering some of these dishes at '*Ono Kūloko*—think about it! Hawaii is already a mishmash of cultures from the Far East—Polynesian, Japanese, Chinese, Indian—oh, and did I tell you they served tuna poke at Karma? Not as good as mine, but good. I'm going to send the menu and pictures to Koni, start experimenting with my own recipes, I'm going to contact Andre to see if there's good Asian Fusion on Maui—I bet there is! Of course, how that cuisine is interpreted can be really varied—I can put my own spin on it—maybe team up with Andre and brand our own chain across all the islands, license it to cruise ships—"

He suddenly stops. "Oh, I'm so sorry, Katie. Hello. How are you?"

Katie is giggling uncontrollably. It's three o'clock in Kauai, and she is in the middle of packing. "I love you, Tiger. I love hearing you so excited about this—that's the Gavin I married! But I think you're having entirely too much fun there! First treasure hunts, and now a whole new business model!"

Gavin's laugh rolls out from deep within him, a just-out-of-prison sense of escape and freedom. Something he hasn't experienced in months. It feels good. "So enough about me and my hare-brained ideas. How's everything going there? The business, you, Maggie—"

"Well," Katie begins, taking a deep breath. "I have a surprise. Two, actually."

"You're pregnant," Gavin deadpans in his signature brand of humor.

"Who told you?" Katie gasps.

Gavin is still in comedy mode. "I saw it written on the men's room wall at Karma. And you're having twins."

"Oh, Gavin!" Katie sighs. "I *am* pregnant, sweetie."

Gavin is speechless. Literally. No words.

"Are you still there, Gav? I thought you'd be happy. And no, it isn't twins."

Gavin finally resumes breathing and finds his voice, which cracks in his own "fusion" of laughing and crying. "Really? And I'm not there with you?"

"Well, that's my other surprise, big guy," Katie says, a coy tease tickling her voice. "I'm going on vacation—in Boston!"

Gavin doesn't know what to say. He instantly suspects Katie is coming to Boston because she doesn't believe in him, thinking he might crash under his PTSD.

"I miss you, Gav, and I need you," Katie says. "So does Maggie."

"When you were pregnant with Mags, you were invincible. Superwoman. What's different now?"

"I had you right by my side then. You're a world away now. And I'm scared," Katie says, pausing to let it sink in for Gavin. "Scared that the mob life your brother, dad, and grandfather were involved in is way too close, and might hurt you in some way. I *need* you by my side, now more than ever. And I need to be *with* you."

"What about the restaurant? Your gallery? Maggie and Patches?"

"I've trained Henry, Koni, and Kalea to take over. And I can do a lot remotely, like paying bills, meeting payroll, and overseeing most of the key decisions," she says. "And Maggie and Patches are going to have their first plane ride!"

Excitement, joy, worry, and fear all jockey for position in Gavin's mind. "When are you coming?"

"Tomorrow, sweetie. Four-thirty your time."

Fear takes the lead position in Gavin—that Katie will judge him, that he won't be able to keep his shit together, that whoever is following him could endanger his family. *Katie's going to see my beat-up face. What if she has to deal with me losing my shit, freaking out? How can I keep her and Maggie safe?* Now he avoids voicing his fears by focusing on logistics. "I'm not sure it's a good idea to foist our whole family onto my grandparents. And I have to do a lot of stuff here, so I can't spend much time with you."

"Got that covered, Tiger," Katie forces a chuckle. Pedersen has prepped her well. "My mother's house isn't rented, so we can stay there, out of Grandma and Grandpa's hair. I've scheduled time for Maggie at Wellesley College's Child Study Center—where your mom used to take you and Devon! And I can help you with any routine or logistical issues you may have."

Gavin's fear recedes a notch. And then he remembers his growing to-do list and starts laughing. "All right, Katie-Kat. You asked for it! I have a to-do list that's longer than your arm, and just keeps growing every day. You're so good with that stuff, you've just won yourself a new job!"

"Can't wait, Tiger," Katie says. "But I'm not cheap! My salary consists of you cooking and giving me backrubs. See you tomorrow?"

"Absolutely, babe—send me your flight itinerary. I love you—and thanks for doing this."

When Gavin gets off the phone, he runs down the stairs with a lip-splitting smile, literally hopping with joy. "Grandpa and Grandma! Guess what? Katie is coming tomorrow, with Maggie and our dog Patches! Isn't that fabulous? I'll be picking them up at Logan at four-thirty!"

The grandparents of course already know, but feign surprise. Grandma pops up and throws her arms around Gavin. "That's so wonderful! We'll finally get to see your beautiful Maggie—our first great-grandchild!"

"You're going to love her! And she's going to have a little brother or sister soon, too—Katie's pregnant! She deserves a break; she's been working so hard. And don't worry. Our little menagerie will stay at Katie's mother's house in town."

Grandpa comes to him and claps him on the back. "I'm really happy for you, son. Katie's so good for you."

Later that night, Gavin has a hard time falling asleep. He can't turn off his mind, thinking about all he must do, all the unanswered questions. He isn't even sure he knows what all the questions are. Then there's the issue of what he should do with the Prince Street building, and why he's being followed, whether he's in danger. And how can he keep his family safe?

Finally, well past one o'clock, he drifts off to sleep.

Maggie walks along the sidewalk with Katie holding her hand. She sees a bright yellow dump truck ahead and breaks away from her mother, running after the truck. "Dumper!" she squeals, her little legs gaining speed. A black SUV pulls up beside her. The back door opens and a goateed man dressed all in black and sunglasses leaps out and grabs Maggie, dragging her into the vehicle. Katie screams and runs after them. The SUV pulls out, tires screeching. Katie falls to her knees, howling, pounding the earth.

> "Was my dream but a mirror of the truth?"
> —Mary Wollstonecraft Shelley, Transformation

16

AFTER ERUPTING FROM HIS NIGHTMARE COVERED IN sweat at one-thirty, Gavin lies awake for hours, fearing sleep. Yet cruel morning light rouses him from troubled slumber before seven o'clock. As he makes a pot of coffee in the kitchen, he is haunted by his dream. He doesn't ascribe to the idea that dreams can be prescient, yet it seemed so real. Ever since returning to the Boston area, he has had vivid dreams that play on the dangers here, and on his fear for his safety, which now extends to the safety of his family.

He hears a shower going upstairs, and takes his coffee outside to sit on the small back porch to pull his thoughts together before Grandpa and Grandma come down for breakfast. The shiny leather-like leaves of the saucer magnolia tree haven't yet begun turning color. Those at the top of the tall sinewy branches catch rays of early morning sun, shimmering in the slight breeze and contrasting with the densely scaled fingers of the stalwart eastern red cedar beside it. Not quite like the peace garden, but calming nevertheless.

Gavin needs to determine what the threat level is. Like storm warnings—hurricane, tornado, lightning—issued by the national weather service, what's the likelihood of danger, when, where, from what direction, level of severity, risk and damage? Where is Frank Rizzo when he needs to know all that and get protection? Then it occurs to him. Tray's father and brothers are all cops in Boston. They might know, or can find out who does know. It's one o'clock in the middle of the night out in Honolulu, but he texts his friend anyway.

Almost immediately, Tray responds:

Shit, Bro, you like to flirt with danger, huh? Last I heard, Rizzo is 'retired' from the business. I'll ask Kyrone; he'll know where to find him. Stay safe & keep me posted.

Gavin texts back:

Thanks — where are you now, world-traveler? And how does Hannah put up with all your travel? So while you're checking on Rizzo, can you or Kyrone tell me anything about Marge O'Connor, Christine Simmons, Mark Solomon, Jake Lombardi or Rick Salvatti?

Tray responds with a thumbs-up emoji. Gavin feels like he's just been thrown a lifeline in the middle of a raging sea. Back to the music, the rhythm he feels around Tray, his friend who always has his shit together, unperturbed and rational even in the face of chaos.

He checks the time. Mark Solomon is supposed to meet him at ten. He remembers seeing a shovel in Grandpa's garage, goes to get that, then grabs a banana and his fully charged power drill and runs out to his car so he can get into Boston before the traffic builds up. He wants to go up to the second floor through the hatch in the ceiling of the "storage room," and also remove some of the documents he found in that room yesterday afternoon, when he'd been too distracted to think of it. And maybe do some digging in the dirt basement.

The SUV isn't there when he parks on Prince Street at eight o'clock; the mob must not be early risers. The lock he installed on the front door looks untouched, but he notices something different about the boarded-up entry to the upper floors. Maybe he just hadn't noticed it before. The screws look too new, and a couple of them seem to be at a slight angle, not straight in. Getting new strong doors, power, and a security system now move to the top of Katie's to-do list.

The key works, so at least no one has changed the padlock. Gavin removes the lock, goes inside and secures the slide bolt. He goes directly to the basement entry with his drill and shovel, placing his padlock on the ledge at the top of the stairwell. He puts on Solomon's headlamp and goes down the stairs.

He goes to the back closet, picks up Solomon's industrial lantern where he left it yesterday and points it toward the front of the building to illuminate the dirt floor. When he inspected the foundation walls yesterday, he hadn't focused on the floor, and now he wonders whether the stuff Devon wrote about is hidden in the dirt. *If it's under here in a metal box, a metal detector would be super helpful.* He makes a few stabs in the dirt with the shovel. It is compact and hard, almost impenetrable. He doesn't have the time or energy to do a methodical digging in the entire floor. *Too bad I can't get a backhoe down here.*

He sets the shovel aside, then loads tools and the Home Depot bag from Grandpa's garage into his Charles Street Supply bag to take with him up to the storage room. In case he decides to take out some of the stuff he found there. He reminds himself that he'll need to get a lantern and headlamp for himself after Solomon leaves today. He climbs up on boxes, wishes he had a ladder, and pulls himself up into the narrow room. He begins opening boxes he hadn't inspected yesterday.

The first one rattles. Inside is a disorganized collection of watches—most engraved and some obviously very expensive, patron saints' medals (Mark, Christopher, Michael, and Matthew seem to be the most popular), engraved wedding bands, initialed money clips, and wallets with family photos, some with identification from several decades past.

Gavin wonders what could have been the purpose of keeping all this stuff that once belonged to other people—none of them a DiMasi. He fingers a few items, slipping on a ring, a watch, as if he might receive some sort of communication from the persons who once wore them. Then a memory of the fat-fingered hand of Dom—the guy who set up Devon at Café Pompeii, instead getting Tony killed—flashes in Gavin's vision, flooding him with a dizzying nausea.

His breathing chokes and his heart pounds faster, fear chasing him across the decades of his family's history. He frantically begins throwing all those trinkets back into the box. But then one name on an ID catches his eye, feeling familiar: William Marfeo, from a 1962 Selective Service Registration card. On a hunch, he opens the strongbox he inspected yesterday and begins flipping through the papers there. On one of the pages of who-owed-who, he spots the name. Willie Marfeo was one of the debtors whose entry had been crossed out, with no indication of his debt having been paid. He digs out the notebook of names and dates, and finds Willie Marfeo there, with a 1962 date.

Gavin suspects there may be more such coincidences in these boxes. What it all means is unclear. All sorts of wild and preposterous speculations pop into his imagination, begging for resolution. He is intrigued by these mysteries—puzzles to solve while cocooned here in an airless little room above a musty old basement via byzantine passageways. Enigmas that serve as diversion from the thoughts and memories that trigger his PTSD—blocking the flashbacks and his unhinged delusional responses. The perfect avoidance, at least in the moment.

He puts the strongbox in a bag and dumps the contents of this box on top of it. He then quickly opens the other boxes, searching for more stuff Devon found. But all he finds are old newspaper clippings and photographs, menus with notes scribbled on them, matches from restaurants with numbers written inside, even a handkerchief with what appears to be old blood on it.

It's all tantalizing, and at the same time mocking, as if there are random puzzle pieces lurking among all these bits, begging to be arranged in the right pattern to create a revealing picture. Gavin has the sense that among all these papers, notes, photos, and memorabilia there are dots he must connect to finally understand the truth of his family. Like what involvement his grandfather, father, and twin had with the mob? Despite what his father said—that Grandpa D didn't play with the mob and made Dad promise to stay away from it, and all the warnings for Devon to stay out of it. But the mob culture imposed its macho onto every boy growing up in the Italian North End—it's what his father struggled to measure up to, but imposed on Devon to fulfill, and on Gavin as the sorry-ass loser. Then Dad imposed the misogynistic culture of the North End on Mom to compensate for his own inadequacy.

Maybe in all this, Gavin might finally understand the truth of himself and how he can finally break the chain of multigenerational family dysfunction.

He checks the time. Only a few minutes before Solomon gets here. Now he stacks a few boxes and climbs up to what he thinks is probably another hatch, pushing it hard until it too opens, and wiggles through it to the second floor, coming out in an empty closet. It's a lot brighter on this floor, where more slits in boarded-up windows permit daylight to sneak through. The floor seems solid, although with water damage from the fire response. Solomon will be able to clarify how safe the floor is. Some old two-by-fours remain, where room partitions once stood, but there's no evidence of fire damage. The third floor above is supported by what look like the same ironwood posts as on the first floor.

He spots the stairway that comes up from the first floor. Despite what Marge O'Connor claimed, the steps do not appear to have been destroyed by the fire. He goes closer and kneels over to inspect them. The treads are made of some kind of stone, either granite or marble. Behind him, a duplicate set of stairs toward the rear of the building goes up to the top floor, where Gavin can see daylight peeking through holes in the roof.

There is debris on this floor, evidence that someone has been here recently. Empty vodka bottles and McDonald's containers, cigarette butts. Either a homeless person squatting, or someone who has a more intentional purpose. He looks all around but doesn't see anything that might hold more of what Devon found. Then his phone buzzes: *"Call me,"* Tray texts.

Gavin hits speed dial and Tray answers.

"Yo, man, don't you sleep?" Gavin teases.

"I'm not in Honolulu. Special duty, weird hours," Tray says.

"Like I said, I don't know how you can stay married with all the traveling you do."

"Yeah, well, that could be a problem," Tray mumbles. "Anyway, I'm on break outside now to talk, but I gotta go back in the SCIF in a few minutes."

"Sorry about your problem. Want Katie or me to reach out to Hannah?"

"Don't think that'll help, man, but thanks," Tray grunts, then rushes on. "So let me tell you what I found out on those names. Rizzo 'retired' because he was hit. Suffered a bad concussion, so has cognitive and memory problems. He's in the North End Rehabilitation Center, same one your Grandpa DiMasi is in. His son Tommy took over and he probably didn't renew your protective order."

"Damn!" Gavin spits. But given all the trolling SUVs, he'd suspected as much. Then he recalls, "Tommy's the one Devon got crosswise with."

"And now he's cozy with your Uncle Marco."

"Oh, that's fucking rich," Gavin groans. "Asshole. You got anything else?"

"You gave me a bunch of names, all bad in one way or another, man."

"Shit," Gavin moans. "Wanna give me details? Any specifics I should know?"

"O'Connor and Simmons are with the Winter Hill gang. Irish mob. Simmons is supposed to be really dangerous, like a Mata Hari or something. O'Connor's too dumb to be much of a risk. She just does what she's told and rats stuff upstairs." Tray takes a breath. "Vince Lombardi's boy Jake took over when Vince was silenced recently for not playing nice with Limone. Jake does the waltz with Limone, and so does Rick Salvatti, and they both play with Marco and Tommy."

"The Italian mob," Gavin concludes.

"Yeah, and Solomon plays with the Jewish mob—his grand-dad was Charles 'King' Solomon, a big bootlegger during Prohibition. But a missing person report just went out on him last night."

"What?" Gavin shouted.

"Yeah, his wife reported him missing yesterday afternoon, and it got elevated to FBI late last night," Tray says. "You know him?"

"He's a structural engineer that came here yesterday morning to assess the building," Gavin says, his voice wavering. "He was supposed to be here today at ten, and if he's still alive, he's late."

"Do you have any reason to think he's in danger?"

"Christine Simmons told me yesterday that he's—quote—'not to be trusted.'"

"Winter Hill hates the Jewish mob. Sworn enemies. And she's evil. Gaslighting's her specialty. She gave you a warning."

Gavin's vision spins and goes foggy, his head dizzy. Before he can focus his breathing, consciousness leaves him.

"Realize that everything connects to everything else."
—Leonardo DaVinci

17

A VISION OF ALL THOSE PEOPLE TRAY REPORTED ON, pouring out of a black SUV like it's some kind of clown car. jolts Gavin up, gasping for air. He takes a minute to recover his orientation in time and space, then checks his phone. Ten thirty-eight. And a text from Tray:

You okay Gav?

Gavin responds with a thumbs-up emoji, although it's pretension. He is not okay. He realizes he could experience the same fate as Solomon, but he still doesn't know why. And if he's in danger, his family might be too. Suddenly desperate to get the hell out of the building, he gives the second-floor area one last glance, and is puzzled by what he sees. Or what he doesn't see. But it's something he has little patience to deal with right now.

Gavin drops down to the storage room, closing the second-floor hatch. He looks around. He should take some of this stuff out of here. With all the mob names on everything, Tray might want it, given FBI's campaigns against various mob families. He begins opening more boxes to check their contents, and is shocked when one has a collection of handguns and knives. Shaking nervously, he retracts his hand into the sleeve of his sweatshirt and carefully picks up the gun on top. He holds it up in the light of his headlamp to inspect it, but it slips out of his grip and falls with a clatter against the wall before hitting the floor.

Ever since Dad was shot and Gavin was forced to use a gun to defend himself against the guys who were after Devon and him, Gavin falls apart even at the mention of guns. Now he gingerly picks up the fallen gun as if it may explode at any moment, to replace it in the box. Then he sees the damage in the wall. A sizable hole. There's something gray behind the damaged plaster. Looks like metal, rusted. He recalls tapping on the other side of this wall, in the VIP room. The solid-hollow-solid sequence. But he didn't tap anything that sounded like metal. He's curious. He pulls out his hammer and begins slamming it onto the wall all around the hole. More plaster falls out. He continues, wishing he had a sledgehammer. Eventually all the plaster from one two-by-four stud to the next has fallen out, revealing more gray metal. It doesn't sound hollow when his hammer hits the metal. He wants to get to the upper and lower boundaries of whatever this gray metal thing is, so continues banging away at the plaster.

Eventually he uncovers the full length and width of the metal. Fourteen-plus inches between studs and probably over five feet tall. It looks like it might be a circuit control box for a multi-unit apartment building. From what he can see, it's almost the full depth of the two-by-four studs—about three and a half inches, wedged between the studs.

The bottom of the box rests on the floor. But he can't dislodge it from its position, so it's obviously anchored or attached in some way. He bangs out the plaster on either side of the two studs holding it in place, and finally finds what he's looking for: bolts holding it in place, three on each side.

Gavin pulls his power drill out of his bag. *Good thing I charged this sucker.* He loads a Phillips head bit into it and flips the drill to reverse. In no time at all he has removed all six bolts, their corresponding nuts probably loose now inside the box. He hesitates, thinking there should be a drum roll or dramatic music. He pushes aside the cardboard boxes in the way, grips the top of the box and tips it forward, easing the entire container toward the floor, but it's taller than the room is wide, so he dislodges it and turns it sideways to lie on the floor. The box has a slide latch on one side for opening its front door to check breakers and electrical connections.

But this wasn't used for checking fuses. His vision swirls dizzily. He's holding his breath, then finally inhales deeply as he opens the door of the box. He almost throws up. There are stacks and stacks of money, precisely fitted into the full depth of the box, extending the full length and nearly the full width. At first glance it appears to all be one-hundred-dollar bills. He counts fifty neat stacks in rows, plus partial stacks stuffed in the gap along one side. And a lottery ticket on top of it all.

Gavin looks closely, focusing his flashlight on the ticket. Some of it is worn away, but he can see "1991" and "South Boston Liquor Mart." He recalls the story from what he read. Whitey Bulger's liquor store in Southie sold a winning lottery ticket that "just happened" to be his. And then he disappeared in 1994, and here it is 2005 and no one has found him eleven years later! But Gavin never understood why Bulger—who wasn't known for his generosity—reportedly shared the four-teen-million-dollar jackpot with another mobster—who was that? That could help figure out who's behind the scratchy calculations on the back of this ticket.

If all these bills are hundreds, he does quick geometric math and calculates there might be around three and a half million dollars in this box. His father was running this store in 1991 when the ticket was sold, and Gavin has no idea how a portion of the money and the ticket ended up in DiMasi possession. How and why? Those original "partners" would be unlikely to relinquish their shares. Nor does he know if this is the full original amount that was stored in his dad's building, or if some of it "disappeared." It's unclear what hand Devon may or may not have had in building this storage room when he took over, so Gavin doesn't know who was responsible for hiding the money in this box. Devon's journal mentions "stuff" he found, but not specifically money. Is there some way of dating this box? With both Dad and Devon dead, he may never know the answers.

The bigger question now is what should he do with the money? As far as he knows, there's no law that's been violated, which would make it the property of police or FBI. If he takes it back to Wellesley, he could put his family at greater risk. If he leaves it here, whoever has been messing with him and this building might find it if they find their way into this little "room." If he takes the money, he definitely won't be able to get it out in this box without someone outside seeing. So then what could he do with the box? Leaving it behind would be a tip-off. And what should he do with this destroyed wall? If someone else finds this storage area, they'll see the wall torn open, making it obvious that he's found something hidden—if they don't already know. And what's the significance of the rest of the stuff in here, the papers and notebook with all those names?

Gavin's head spins with all the unknowns. Panic pounds his chest and chokes his breath as he begins to grasp the enormity of these questions. Part of him says to just leave it for whoever's been stalking him. That would get them off his back. Maybe. Another part of him wants to fight. Keep them from getting what they want.

He texts Tray. He waits impatiently for a response. Then he calls the number. No answer. He checks the time. Noon-thirty. He has to get back to Wellesley, shower, then pick up Katie at Logan at four-thirty. He makes an "executive decision." Or at least the first part of it.

Gavin dumps out all the cash from the metal box into his other bag, then picks up the metal box and angles it through the hatch up to the second floor, then up the next level's stairs to the third floor, where he sees no evidence of squatters or interlopers, nor even evidence of residence before the fire. He sticks the box in what seems meant to be a closet.

As he passes through the second floor on his way back, he realizes what was missing. What he *hadn't* seen. Any evidence of fire having breached this floor, or having traveled from the first floor to the second floor. There's soot, yes, and some charring on the floor in the front corner. But no sign anywhere that the fire broke through the floor. Mostly he just sees water damage. The fire department had simply drowned the building in water and foam, almost immediately after the fire broke out. Solomon was right. There must be something special about this building, something someone did not want incinerated.

Gavin sees some tattered clothing squatters had left behind on the second floor. He grabs two shirts and makes his way quickly down to the storage room. He throws some trash from the room over the cash in the hardware bag, then tucks a dirty shirt over that. He does the same with the Home Depot bag holding the papers, ledger, notebook, and jewelry he'd stuffed in it.

He checks the time. Almost two o'clock. He has to get the hell out. He drops down through the hatch to the basement, pulling his two bags behind him, closes the hatch, then re-stacks all the boxes into the closet and re-attaches the hasp mechanism to secure the door. He finally goes up the stairs to the first floor, reaching for the padlock on the ledge. It isn't where he left it. Maybe all the banging he was doing shook it down onto the floor. He searches all around. He can't find it. What if he can't lock the door when he leaves? No way could he get to the hardware store quickly and back, and still pick up Katie in time. Maybe he could skip Wellesley and his shower, buy and install a new padlock, then go directly to Logan from here?

He grabs his bags and goes to the front door. The slide bolt isn't set, like he left it. He pulls on the door. It doesn't budge. It's locked from the outside. *Fuck! Did those assholes discover where I was and what I was doing when they did this?*

Gavin drops to the floor, caught between despair and fury. The stealthy harassment, gaslighting, and implied and physical threats have gotten to him, exhausted him, bled him dry. Which, he realizes, is probably what they want. *They want me to walk away from this building. That's precisely what tells me I shouldn't back down. They will not win.*

At this point he can either remove the locked exterior hasp and loop by taking out the lock nuts, go out the door then replace it, or he can knock out the plywood on the street door from the second floor, then replace that. The first option will be easier, quicker, and less obvious to people outside. He gets the power drill and his lug nut attachments, and quickly removes the hasp and loop—and finds them connected by his own padlock! His stalkers obviously didn't have an extra padlock with them.

Gavin takes his key and unlocks the padlock in order to re-mount the hasp set, looking all around the street as he does this. Finally he reaches inside to get his two bags before closing the door and padlocking it. Although he can never be certain that anyone—even the little old lady trudging down the street—isn't a threat or a snitch, he doesn't see anyone or anything obviously suspicious.

He hurries to his car with his bags.

It's something short of miraculous that Gavin doesn't have an accident driving to Wellesley. With the cargo he's transporting, the shit he's been through, his nerves, PTSD, and the terrible traffic, all on an empty stomach, he probably shouldn't be driving. He decides that, for now, he should stash his two bags at his parents' house to minimize the risk to his family. When he pulls into the driveway, he's relieved to see no black SUV.

He grabs the bags and goes to the front door. He's relieved to find it still locked. He locks it behind him once he's inside and goes directly upstairs, pulling down the attic stairs and taking the bags up. He doesn't have time to do anything else, but on a cursory glance he spots a few items he wants to investigate next time he comes.

He is frantic when he gets back to his grandparents' house, so fearful he'll be late for Katie's arrival that he's hyperventilating. The fear that he will fail Katie, disappoint her, make her think he's out of control, makes his head pound and spin. He sprints into the house, running past his grandfather in the library, calling out as he passes, "Hi, Grandpa, I'm running behind! I'll be out of the shower and ready to go in five minutes!"

"The future is uncertain...but this uncertainty
is at the very heart of human creativity."
—Ilya Prigogine

18

GAVIN AND KATIE ARE FORTUNATE TO HAVE A friend like Puna in the police force. He brought a surprise for Katie—an old "Service Animal" halter and certificate for Patches, their little beagle-size rescue mutt that often rescues *them*, so their dog can board the airplane and sit on the floor in front of Maggie's seat. Patches has been keeping his good eye close on Maggie, soothing her, even resting his chin on her lap in her car seat all during the first flight. He does everything a service animal is supposed to do, even though he hasn't been trained.

Their trip has gone smoothly so far. The night flight from Kauai to L.A. departed and landed pretty much on time, and now the monitor in L.A. says their connecting flight to Boston is on time. They have just enough time between flights to let everyone have a potty break. Including Patches at the pet relief area, and Katie, who always has to pee so urgently when she's pregnant. Maggie thinks she's ready for big-girl pants, and lets Mommy know *after* she's done something in her Pampers, but not before. She'll probably be totally potty-trained well before her new sibling arrives. Just now he—or she—lands a kick to Katie's abdomen like a karate *mae geri*. This is going to be an active one.

"Yes, Maggie, another plane ride!" Katie says. "Then we

get to see Daddy when we land!"

Maggie looks like she isn't sure if that's a good thing. Katie gives her a kiss and whispers, "Yeah, sweetie. I get it."

Maggie brightens and pats the dog. "Pat-us!"

"And Patches will keep you company. Here, let me buckle your special seat into the airplane seat, so you can see out the window."

Maggie has been good during this trip, but confused. At what probably isn't the ideal time in a kid's life to be confused, but she seems to adapt. So far.

Once Katie has Maggie and Patches all settled in, she leans back and lets her mind wander. She realizes that this super-rushed trip has been a walk in the park compared to what she might have to deal with when they get to Boston. She also realizes that she'll have to teach Maggie that she can't instantly be friends with every stranger she meets, like she does all the time. Life on the mainland isn't as safe as it is on Kauai. It's sad that real life has to burst a child's bubble and break that news. Mags is so open and trusting. If she had some "business cards" with all her contact information, she'd probably have passed them out to hundreds of people during this trip! She can't always have her parents and Patches to keep her out of danger.

But Gavin hasn't been doing much parenting these past few months. And it isn't clear how much longer that will be the case. Pedersen says it could be a long time. Everything Katie has read about PTSD paints a dismal picture of her family's future.

Gavin's condition has necessitated a lot of adjustments.

Although Katie doesn't express her concerns aloud to anyone but Pedersen, she feels like she's effectively the only functioning adult in the family these days. To her, the marital "relationship" feels sort of lopsided. The day Devon died is the last time she and Gavin were intimate, and Gavin frequently pushes her away, like he either doesn't trust her or he's afraid she'll judge him. Or he feels his own truth is too scary to bleed onto people around him. There's very little "partnership" anymore, with Gavin being sort of numb most of the time. Except when he spontaneously combusts in a rage about something. No one knows when that's about to happen. Katie's glad her mother's place has an extra bedroom where she can go when Gavin starts tossing, thrashing, and yelling so badly she can't sleep.

Katie confines her complaints to her inner thoughts, and wishes she had friends who understand even half of what is happening to her family. She is exhausted just thinking about going back into the chaos with Gavin. It makes her sad to admit that it's been a reprieve for her with Gavin away. Even though she's spent most of the time worrying about him. But now that he's in trouble, she can't abandon him. She has to do everything she can to help him and their marriage. She knows they had a good marriage before he got PTSD. Although there was always the threat of dark clouds looming just beyond the horizon, thanks to his messed-up family.

She once confessed to Gavin that she hadn't managed to develop many close friendships growing up, probably because most of her time was devoted to taking care of her mother. And now, all her time is spent taking care of him, the business, and Maggie. So she still hasn't made those close friendships that other people wax poetic about. Although she's certainly friendly with people, and they with her, there's no one to whom she can "pour her heart out." Or even just have a bitching session.

She feels really alone at a time she needs just the opposite.

Maggie has drifted off to sleep. Katie decides to take a nap too.

"Suffering whispers, shouts, and screams the story no one wants to remember: we are not in control."
—K.J. Ramsey, This Too Shall Last

19

GAVIN STANDS UNDER A HOT SHOWER PELTING onto his head. He needs its purge after his tumultuous day from hell. Which will soon extend its chaos, assaulting every member of the family today with its mayhem. As he steps out of the shower, his beat-up face looms in the fogged-up mirror like the bad guy in a horror movie. He hopes Katie and Maggie won't freak out when they see him.

He checks his cell phone from the back seat while Grandpa drives him and Grandma to the airport in their car, big enough for Katie, Maggie, Patches, and all the stuff they've likely brought with them. No message from Solomon, but there is one from Pedersen, asking if Gavin could join him at the gym in the morning. And another from Jake Lombardi, asking if he's ready to sign the paperwork for selling the building.

Gavin lands two punches to the back of the driver-side seat.

"What was that?" Grandpa shouts, startled, and Grandma's head spins around.

Gavin catches his breath, snapping back to the moment. "Sorry, my hand slipped," he mumbles.

Grandpa looks back in the rear-view mirror, then glances over to Grandma. "Well, can you give us a warning next time?"

Gavin goes silent, retreating. Cars and buildings pass by in a blur while his thoughts twist and turn. His excitement about Katie's arrival has sprouted fangs, a snarling three-headed Cerberus lunging toward him as his vision blurs. Taunting laughter like Rick Salvatti's assaults him—he releases his seat belt and pulls the door handle, but it doesn't open. He curls into a tight knot, a quivering pangolin, no sound or breath. He disappears into a dark cave, down into a dirt sub-basement.

Grandma's peripheral glance catches Gavin's contortion in the back seat. She touches Grandpa's shoulder and speaks low. "He's doing it. What Jim warned us about."

"Long as he doesn't lash out, don't intervene. It'll pass."

When the car's speed and trajectory change as Grandpa drives through the Sumner Tunnel to Logan, Gavin slowly rouses. "Almost there?" he mumbles. As soon as the car comes to a stop in the parking garage, Gavin pulls on the door handle with a fearful urgency.

"Oh, I forgot to release the child lock!" Grandpa says. "We're here, with time to spare. Good thing the traffic wasn't too bad." Which contrasts sharply with the swarming crowd in the terminal.

Gavin's hyper-vigilance kicks into overdrive. Threats seem to be everywhere. That guy reminds him of Salvatti, that one looks like a dad being abusive to his son, that woman looks like Marge O'Connor, that guy has a gun, some guy is kidnapping a little girl, conflicting discordant noises amplify... Gavin doesn't know where to hide, where to run, who to punch, who is safe. He's jittery and over the edge. They're coming after him.

"Gavin, are you okay?" Grandpa asks, looking at him askance. "Katie's flight is coming into Terminal B, so let's go to baggage claim there. That's where she'll be exiting."

Gavin seems unresponsive, like he's in a fog, or numb.

"It says her flight's on time," Grandma says. "Have you eaten today, Gavin?"

Gavin's eyes dart rapidly, frenetically. He doesn't look at Grandma.

"At least have some water, Gavin." She pulls a bottle from her bag and hands it toward him. He doesn't respond. She touches it to his arm.

He jumps back in shock, fear electrifying his body, digging monster ruts into his face.

Grandpa steps in, takes the bottle of water from her hand and steers her away. "Don't bother him right now," he says in a low voice. "Wait 'til he comes out of this...whatever it is."

For the next seven minutes, Gavin stands rigid, stiff, his eyes the only part of him that moves. Finally, signs of life appear. His eyes blink rapidly, like flicking away the sands of sleep. Then he smiles sheepishly. "Sorry, guess I zoned out."

Just then, Katie emerges from the passageway. She's wearing her overstuffed backpack carry-on, pushing a stroller with Maggie in it and the car seat piled on top. Patches trots alongside them on his leash. Katie looks tired, but beams when she sees Gavin.

"There's Daddy, Mags!" Katie sings.

Maggie looks up and begins screeching hysterically.

Patches bares his teeth and growls.

Gavin turns and runs.

With a vision of Gavin's bizarre behavior attracting security personnel flashing in Katie's mind, she instantly throws off her backpack beside Maggie's stroller at Grandpa's feet and runs after Gavin with Patches at her heels, his leash dragging behind.

Katie's small agile frame weaves deftly between, around, and through the densely packed obstacle course of travelers, keeping an eye on her husband's curly red hair above the crowd ahead. He is running erratically, not in a direct line, instead rushing forward, turning abruptly, resuming speed, turning again, as if repeatedly spotting something or someone to avoid.

Patches catches up with Gavin ahead of Katie, darting between his legs then immediately halting like a cement bulwark directly in front of Gavin's leading stride, causing him to stumble and fall, bumping several people on his way to the floor.

In that nanosecond, Katie can't tell whether Gavin's flight state will interpret a touch as a threat or danger trigger, so she puts her hand up to wave off Good Samaritans eager to help, then approaches him carefully without touching, crouching beside him and speaking softly. "Hey, Tiger. Everything is safe now, sweetheart. I'm so happy to see you. Sorry you tripped. Do you need help getting up?"

From his face-down position, Gavin grunts and rolls over. "No, I'm okay," he says in a flat tone without looking at her, then stands up.

"Maggie is with your grandparents, waiting for our luggage to come out, Gavin." Katie walks a tightrope, searching his face for some indication of his state of mind. "Would you like to come see her? She's missed you."

Gavin doesn't respond, but his face relaxes a bit, as if he's trying to understand what's happening.

"That was quite a fall, sweetie. Would you like to take my hand while we walk back to see Maggie?"

Gavin turns his head and looks down at Katie with surprise. "Katie! You're finally here!" He spreads his arms and wraps her in a smothering embrace that doesn't end. "And we're having another baby, too. Wow," he squeezes her tighter.

Katie hears his heart pumping and his lungs struggling against emotion. She strokes his back as much as her captured arms allow. "I'm sure Maggie is eager to see you, Gav," she murmurs, her strokes graduating to pats, and begins wriggling to free herself.

As she emerges from Gavin's grip, she sees a dark-haired man staring at them, one who sends a chill through her. He looks to be thirty-something, standing slightly off to the side with his hands in his pockets, an intense gaze and a taunting sneer curling his thin lips. Patches's one ear is back and a growl rumbles from deep within him. Katie stiffens, grabs the dog's leash and links her arm in Gavin's, pulling him close to her body. "Can't wait to get out of this crowd, Gav, and we shouldn't desert your grandparents!" She leads her husband quickly through the crowd.

She wonders if Patches's and Maggie's reactions were in response to Gavin and his bruised face? Or because they saw that guy.

> "You know, when someone has been crying,
> something gets left in the air.
> It's not something you can see or smell, or feel.
> Or draw. But it's there."
> —*Gary D. Schmidt*, Okay for Now

20

GAVIN SNAPS BACK INTO GAVIN MODE, SHOWING Maggie his boo-boos, making her giggle, and now takes charge of logistics, rattling on, non-stop, in his puzzle-solving zone. "Grandpa, can you bring your car around—or would you rather I do it? Katie, not sure what luggage you brought. When you see it on the carousel, let me know and I'll grab it and put it all on this cart. We can't dump all our stuff in Grandma's house, we need to take it over to your mother's. So—"

Katie interrupts him with a lingering kiss to his lips, locking eyes with him. "I love you, Tiger. We'll work it all out."

Thirty minutes later they've all squeezed into the Subaru Outback. Gavin is now sitting in the front passenger seat with Grandpa while Grandma is in the back seat, totally smitten with Maggie, who is telling all about her plane ride, the clouds that look like ice cream, the cookies the flight attendant gave her, Patches is wearing a jacket, Daddy looks like a clown with his boo-boo...

Katie smiles at Grandma. "Maggie's a real chatterbox—two guesses where she got that!"

"Grandpa, let's drop off the suitcases at Katie's mom's house," Gavin says, "then we can put my stuff into my rental car and we'll get out of your hair. You've been so generous to let me stay with you."

Grandma speaks up from the back seat. "Unless Katie and Maggie are too tired from their travel," she turns to Katie, "we've planned a barbeque in the back yard. It's such a nice Indian Summer day."

"Oh, how thoughtful of you!" Katie says. "That will give Maggie more time to get acquainted with you and Grandpa. But you must let us help with the barbeque!"

"We've invited Jim Pedersen to join us," Grandma adds. "I hope that's okay with you."

Gavin crosses his arms tightly and stares out the window to his right.

"That's lovely," Katie says, scrutinizing Gavin's profile. "It'll be good to see him again."

When Grandpa pulls up in front of the small two-story colonial-style house off Weston Road, Gavin immediately jumps out and begins offloading Katie's luggage from the back. "Just hand me the keys, Katie, and I'll put all this in the house," he orders, sounding like a drill sergeant. "You and Maggie stay here and get settled, and I'll be back with my stuff in the rental car."

If it were possible to combine confusion, worry, fear and exhaustion in a single look, it would describe Katie in this moment, her face like a chaotic Jackson Pollock assault. "We can all get settled after we have a relaxing dinner at your grandparents' house, sweetie," she says with saccharine soothing.

"That won't be necessary," he says, each word struggling, one-by-one, to escape his clenched jaw.

Grandpa turns around and whispers to Katie, "Do you need my help?"

Katie shakes her head almost imperceptibly and gets out of the car, taking a few small steps toward Gavin. She wishes Pedersen were here in this moment, and weighs her options, each of which has potential downsides. She rolls the die and goes for confirmation. "I'm guessing you may be feeling a little trapped, sweetheart, like suddenly we're all making plans *for* you, which carries expectations *of* you. Ones you're not sure you're comfortable with."

Gavin stops. He turns his head and looks at Katie with his mouth half open as if caught mid-sentence, with realization in his eyes. "Yes," he exhales.

"If you were preparing a barbeque, what would you serve, Gav?" Katie shifts from confirming Gavin's feelings to empowering him.

Gavin smiles. "Let's see what Grandma has planned, and go to Whole Foods to augment if necessary."

Remembering Pedersen saying that physical activity in fresh air is good therapy for PTSD, Katie says, "That's a great idea. We can take Mags in her stroller and walk!"

When Gavin, Katie, Maggie, and Patches walk down Cliff Road, Gavin smiles as he tells Katie how he and Devon used to race down that hill on their bikes when they were kids, even going airborne at times. "Those were the good times, Kat." He negotiates the stroller around some dog poop on the sidewalk.

"It's always so precious to cherish the good times." She touches his arm.

Gavin nods, the smile still on his face. The quiet feels comfortable.

"Tomorrow morning I'm taking Maggie to the Child Study Center," she says. "What do you have on my to-do list, Tiger?"

"Oh, that's a long conversation. You'll need the backstory. So let's do that tomorrow, when I come back from the gym with Pedersen."

"Perfect." Katie wonders how long it will be until Gavin starts pushing her away again.

"We are all a little schizophrenic.
Each of us has three different people living
inside us every day—who you were,
who you are and who you will become.
The road to sanity is to recognize those identities,
in order to know who you are today."
—*Shannon L. Alder*

21

KATIE IS PLEASED THAT THE MANAGEMENT COMPANY had brought a crib and high chair for Maggie. Although on this first night in a strange house, their daughter sleeps in the king-sized bed with Mommy and Daddy.

When sunlight streams through the bedroom window before seven the next morning, Katie awakens and is overcome with a comforted feeling upon seeing them all together again. At least for now. Gavin didn't do much of his tossing and turning, thrashing, moaning, and screaming during the night. She hopes it's the start of a trend, on a path to wellness.

Maggie was up late the night before, and by Hawaii time it's still the middle of the night, so Katie suspects their little girl will sleep for another few hours.

Katie's mother, in her later years, had used the first-floor den as her bedroom due to her difficulty in navigating stairs. That left the upstairs master bedroom, the guest room (which will now be Maggie's room), and Katie's childhood bedroom unused. Now most of those rooms will be occupied, perhaps indefinitely.

She climbs into her running gear and tiptoes downstairs to the sunny kitchen to make coffee and breakfast, then takes Patches out while the coffee is brewing. It feels strange, being in her childhood house without her mother. Katie hadn't been here since her mother died almost four years ago, and has been renting the house to Wellesley and Babson professors. She reminds herself that she should probably do what Gavin is doing in his childhood home. Identify family things she wants to keep and sell or donate the rest, then sell the house.

As Katie looks around the house now, she recalls how limited the household budget was after her father died. Furnishings are low-budget, worn, and certainly not color-coordinated. Not that her and Gavin's small house on Kauai was any more upscale. She fingers the floral needlepoint pillows on the sofa, which her mother made before her illness worsened. But Katie always liked the "open" floor plan of the house, built in the sixties before "open" was cool, which enabled anyone to see the living room, kitchen, and dining room from a single vantage point.

She's relieved that Gavin is taking a short break from his sleuthing to go to the gym with Dr. Pedersen. She could use a "session" with Pedersen too. She never knows the best way to deal with Gavin's behaviors in any given situation. Although she apparently must have done something right yesterday when she succeeded in talking Gavin down from ditching his grandparents' barbeque. But there'll undoubtedly be a lot more challenging times ahead, and she needs all the help she can get.

She is genuinely scared. It's nearly crippling her, inside and out. Far more than just a ploy to get Gavin to trust her, support her, not shut her out. She's scared she'll lose her husband down the sinkhole of PTSD. And she is terrified she could lose him to the mob, or that Maggie could be at risk, too.

She hopes Gavin's brief openness last night will continue, so she can help save him.

Oh, now I'm beginning to sound like Gavin, the guy who's saddled with the imperative to save everyone. Look how that turned out.

Gavin comes shuffling downstairs carrying Maggie, who's patting Daddy's face with her chubby little hands and giggling. "I figured you'd be up before all of us, Kat," he says, putting Maggie down in the kitchen. "Six-hour time zone gap doesn't faze my Superwoman, eh?" He gives her a quick sideways shoulder hug and a peck on the top of her head.

"Yeah, and Patches is already zonked out on the sofa after we took a walk around the block." Katie points to their white and brown fur bundle in the living room. "I was really surprised to see old Mrs. Gillespie still living down the street, still tending her flowers!" She lifts Maggie into her high chair. "How was your night's sleep? Did Maggie wake you up?"

Gavin smiles. "Mags was great all night," he says, and bends over to kiss their little girl. "Even slept through my tossing and turning. I think I may have awakened her when I got up this morning. Some sort of weird dream gave me a poke. Can't remember it now. Other than that, the night was calm. Coffee smells good. Not like back on the island, though."

But he does recall the images from last night's dreams, and stiffens as the memory returns "in living color." *Skeletal limbs clawing up from the dirt basement floor, rising toward him as he runs toward the stairs to escape, but upstairs is ablaze...*

Now his breath goes rapid and shallow, panting, fear choking off air.

Katie turns at the sound of his panting. "Is it last night's dream you're remembering?" she asks gently. "Or another one?" She doesn't approach, doesn't touch him. Her arms quiver against the urge.

"The one that woke me up this morning," he murmurs, struggling to catch his breath.

"Must have been awful. Breathe deep and catch your breath. Do you want to talk about it?"

"No."

As Katie gives Maggie her sippy cup of juice, she watches Gavin for signs of impending freak-out. "Want me to pour you a cup of coffee? I'm fixing breakfast for Maggie. Anything you'd like?"

"I told Pedersen I'd meet him at the gym this morning, so nothing now."

"I'll put water and a couple power bars in your gym bag before you go, sweetie. Tell Jim I said 'hi'."

A confused look comes over Gavin's face, and now he remembers with a wry smirk. "Yeah, Jim at the gym."

"If I'm not here when you get back, I'll be at the Child Study Center with Maggie. It'll be a nice walk!"

If Gavin were a cat, his hair would be standing straight up on end now, suddenly fearful of what could happen to Katie and Maggie on their walk. He fights an urge to cower in a dark closet. "Be careful, Kat," Gavin ekes out the words, his voice pulsing in his throat. "Maybe I should go with you, or at least drive you there."

"And deprive Mags and me of our beautiful walk?" Katie smiles. "We'll take Patches with us, Tiger. We'll be fine." She detects the all-safe signal returning to Gavin's body and approaches with a hug and kiss. "I love you," she whispers. "Don't worry about us."

It's like every gym he's ever been in, as if there's a room freshener called *eau de body sweat*. Definitely with an emphasis on the testosterone side of the equation. Like all such "health clubs," it sounds hollow, amplifying voices, pop music a la Spotify, and noises of clanging equipment. With bright lights glinting off shiny metal, possibly to minimize the likelihood of amped-up bodies tripping over said equipment.

Gavin spots Dr. Pedersen on a rowing machine. "Morning,

Jim. You been here long?"

"Hi Gavin," Pedersen says between pulls. "Not long. This is my favorite machine. Doesn't stress my knee too much, but good for my thigh—perfect warm-up before I have to go to the ones that work my leg muscles *and* my knee. Join me?"

Gavin fiddles with the settings on the rowing machine next to Pedersen, then straddles and begins pulling. "God, I've been like an inert blob these past few months. Really out of shape. Feels good." He begins rowing faster, racing to some undefined finish line.

"Careful not to push too hard," Pedersen cautions. "Feels good now, but it might not feel so good tomorrow."

They both move on to the exercise bikes after that, each with settings appropriate for their needs. Slow with lower resistance for Pedersen's knee, faster with greater resistance for Gavin's quest to escape whatever demons are chasing him. Later, Pedersen proceeds to resistance bands, squats with a ten-pound weight, and finally to an elliptical just as Gavin is climbing onto the treadmill next to the ellipticals.

"This is my last before cool-down," Pedersen mutters, his workout evident in his raspy syllables.

Gavin sets the controls on his treadmill and begins. Slow at first, gradually increasing the angle as if he's running up Highway 550 to Puʻu O Kila on Kauai. Then he increases his speed, then again even more.

Pedersen looks over to Gavin, at first in awe that an ostensibly out-of-shape man could manage such a feat, then in alarm as Gavin's speed continues to increase to a breakneck level. Which might literally be the case if he were to trip over his own feet that presently lag a split-second behind his upper body, intent on lurching forward to some unknown destination. Or away from some unknown threat.

And then he does trip, in spectacular fashion, initially airborne, followed by the force of his entire body weight knocking against treadmills down the line.

Pedersen hits the button to stop his elliptical, jumps off as it is slowing and rushes to crouch beside Gavin, who's lying spread out across two treadmills askew. Jim avoids touch as he looks for clues to Gavin's emotional state. "You okay, Gav?"

Gavin's eyes open and he jerks back, startled.

"Everything's safe here, son. Although the treadmills might beg to differ."

Gavin looks around at the disruption he caused. "Oh, shit."

By this time, several guys—some buff, others wanna-be—have come to observe, perhaps even to help. Next the manager rushes in to see what's going on, with a look on his face that conveys worry about a potential lawsuit. Or, at best, bad reviews.

"Yeah, I'm okay." Gavin slowly rises, while Pedersen offers his hand to assist. Gavin takes it with an embarrassed grimace, then pulls back at the sight of one buff guy who reminds him of Rick Salvatti. He bolts toward the locker rooms. "I think I've had enough workout for today," he says.

Pedersen catches up with him. "You ready for one of those healthy drinks they have over there in the spa?"

"Any of them have rum in them?" Gavin deadpans, slowing his pace and looking back over his shoulder to where the guy was, but now is not.

"I think the closest to that would be their 'mojito smoothie,'" Pedersen grins. "Lots of mint and other green goodies. I always order their 'purple power.' Beets, blueberries, protein, and other healthy ingredients—how could you go wrong with that?"

There's a completely different vibe and fragrance in the spa than in the gym. Sweet incense, soft music, subtle lighting, plush carpets, awash in potted plants and vases of flowers. The juice bar is empty when they enter. They take two stools at the end and Gavin studies the listed ingredients for each smoothie on the menu. "Holy shit, they put a lot of stuff into these drinks."

"Yes, they're definitely *complex*," Pedersen nods with an

emphasis that hints of an adjacent topic. "Nice workout this morning, Gavin! Great for getting out the kinks, both physical and cognitive, eh?" He pauses. "So... How are you adjusting to Katie and Maggie being here with you?"

"Uh, well," Gavin stalls. The abrupt shift from working out to cognitive kinks...how's he adjusting? He isn't sure...his mind has been so confused these past months, and it's been even worse since he's come back to Boston. And now, having Katie and Maggie with him should be a good thing, but it seems harder, more complicated. More expectations.

He's been immersed—buried, even—these last few weeks in a completely different dimension than that of the incapacitated zombie he was right after his twin's death, and that zombie state was a totally different dimension from the reliable father, husband, chef and business owner in which he'd flourished before Devon died. How many different roles has he been playing? Before Katie and Maggie arrived yesterday, his role had been playing out in a sort of *Twilight Zone* of archaeological history of his family, with all its dysfunction, danger, and risk. Solving puzzles, unraveling mysteries. And now Katie's presence is forcing him back into the responsibilities of husband and father, back to the present, in which a different danger exists. That of falling off the cliff, into the jaws of madness. Can there be crossover between all these roles? Can they co-exist in a single dimension? Everything about his life, and about *him*, has been so different since his identical twin died. He's no longer sure who he is.

"Uh, I slept well last night...," Gavin mumbles. "But I keep having headaches, pains in my gut, backaches. I feel like an old man, for crissake."

Pedersen glances over at him. "Could be a reason for that. Remember we talked about PTSD when I visited you in Kauai this summer?" he asks.

Gavin nods, with a grimace.

"So have you been having flashbacks that trigger bad reactions in you?"

Gavin knew his old counselor recognized his out-of-the-blue, over-the-top reactions to certain things the night he joined him and his grandparents for dinner. And again here at the gym. So that question is a transparent set-up, trying to get him to talk about it. Unload. An entire panoply of options flip through his mind like a deck of cards. He could run out of here, avoid talking about the weird shit he's been experiencing. But he isn't blind to the fact that his mind isn't functioning quite like "normal" lately, and the dark, scary holes he's been tumbling into have held other dangers. So it might feel good to talk about it, unload. Maybe he could get a better understanding of it all, and advice on how to handle it, beat it. But if he were to unload, it could be a trap, providing justification for putting him away, hospitalizing him for intensive treatment, and he'd never get out. Or he might just be paranoid.

He skirts Pedersen's question and its implications, turning the table to his own line of questioning. "So explain what causes PTSD, and how long it takes to get over it."

Pedersen releases a knowing smile, recognizing Gavin's tactic. "You witnessed the violent deaths of each of your family members, literally 'in your lap,'" he says, gazing directly into Gavin's eyes. "Those events have left deep scars of significant trauma that take time to get over, and could cause PTSD in most any person who experienced such events. But there's no consistent timeline for PTSD recovery; it depends on many different factors in each victim's life."

"It depends" is so lame... "So it could be a month, a decade, or never, right?"

"Well, you've experienced complex circumstances, even before those specific events. Conditions in your formative years that've left you with a compromised foundation from which to *deal* with such trauma." Pedersen's voice goes soft. Gentle and caring, as if he is draping a pre-heated towel over Gavin's shoulders. "Which adds an entirely different dimension to your situation. Your challenges."

Gavin groans. "What do you mean?" *How many more dimensions can I deal with?*

"As a child grows up, his brain develops an understanding about the world and his position in it, his ability to control things, based on what he sees and experiences in all aspects of his growing life. His brain is *forming* during that time—that's why it's called 'formative years,' during which he develops the basis for defining the world. Who he is, what in the world is safe and certain, what is risky and uncertain, what he can and can't control, how and why. He develops experiential patterns that define himself and the world around him, embedding those definitions into his brain. So if during his formative years he is told by his family that he's a loser, a wimp, yet as that 'loser' he's nevertheless expected to take care of and save other supposedly superior people, that's not only forming a contradictory understanding of his role in the world, but defining that world as duplicitous and not to be trusted."

Gavin feels like he's fallen into a deep hole while shovels full of dirt and trash rain down on him, burying him alive. Suddenly despondent, he slurps the last bit of his mojito smoothie and stares down into the bottom of his glass. "So what does all that mean now? What does that have to do with my PTSD, and how long it'll take for me to get back to normal?"

Pedersen smiles. "I remember the first time you and I talked, back in your junior year of high school, when your twin was coming home from the hospital after his car crash, and you interpreted his return as 'getting back to normal.' I asked if you liked that definition of 'normal'—whether that's what life *has* been, how you've been experiencing it, or some other version of what life *should* be, what you *want* it to be."

"Uh, yeah. I remember that." Gavin keeps his head down, not looking at Pedersen. "I don't think I ever got that question answered."

"Right. Because only you can answer that question, for yourself. So more than eleven years have passed since then, and your uncertain definition of normal—of what life should be, what you want it to be—has had other complicated layers deposited onto it." Pedersen pauses. "On top of an uncertain foundational core that's wounded, distorted and scarred from years of abuse during the period your brain was forming, you then watched each family member die a violent death."

"Yeah, well, I guess I'm just fucked up. What does that mean for my PTSD?"

"It adds more *complex* symptoms to those that traditionally characterize PTSD." Pedersen looks closely at Gavin, hoping his words are connecting. "You haven't processed the continuous demeaning you experienced as a child, because that was just part of everyday life, not a specific event. So those memories instead live in your body, stored in *somatic* memory, changing your biological stress response. That results in the head, gut, and back pains you're feeling, and in your out-of-control reactions to triggers."

"'Somatic'?" Gavin looks at Pedersen like he's talking crazy. "What do my bodily sensors have to do with my PTSD? I thought it was all in my head, my mind, right?"

Pedersen chuckles and takes a sip of his smoothie. "Your brain *is* part of your body, Gavin. All during your childhood, you were under stresses to which you responded with suppressed frustration, anger, fear, urges to hide or flee, or even to fight. You may not have acted on those urges, but every part of your body was poised to do so, stressing your heart, lungs, gut, muscles, your internal organs. So now when you're triggered, your body 'remembers' and instantly responds the same way, except now it isn't so easily suppressed. That heightened stress also overburdens your adrenal glands, increasing the hormone prolactin, which makes you more sensitive to pain."

"Christ. All this time, I thought seeing everyone in my family die is what caused my PTSD," Gavin deadpans, masking his confusion. And his discouragement. He'd been thinking those discrete events might be something he could manage to get over. But this sounds a lot more complicated.

"Yes," Pedersen nods. "But that's only part of it. Although the violent deaths you witnessed are the events that finally switched on your PTSD symptoms, the systemic emotional abuse during your childhood—which formed an uncertain model of yourself and your world—are the cause of the additional symptoms of *Complex* PTSD: inability to manage emotions, especially reactions to PTSD triggers; negative self-concept—feeling worthless or guilty; and interpersonal problems—feeling disconnected or untrusting. Those are the unique symptoms of *Complex* PTSD, which handicap *everything you need* in order to *deal* with your PTSD symptoms!" Pedersen exclaims, holding his vibrating fist poised over the bar, his eyes wide, his voice intense with urgency.

Gavin slams his palm down on the bar and pulls back. "So if I'm 'handicapped,' I can't even lick this PTSD thing? It's hopeless? What the fuck?"

"Not hopeless. Just a bit more complicated," Pedersen sighs. "The support functions you need to help you deal with your PTSD—closeness and trust in other people, confidence in your self-worth, the ability to manage your emotions—are all more difficult, but not impossible, to access because they've been negated by your childhood abuse. That self-doubt, mistrust, and fear are embedded in your understanding of yourself and whether you can control your own experience."

More people come into the café, noisy and chattering. Gavin begins tensing, feeling cornered and trapped, stiffening with pain. He turns to Pedersen and speaks in a defeated voice. "So I get that I need to address the childhood shit before I can deal with the PTSD. You know that isn't going to sink in, become operational, just by hearing you say it. Same thing happened when you tried to get me to understand what Devon and Dad were doing to me. I'm just a slow fucking learner."

He stands and claps a hand on Pedersen's back. "Thanks

for trying, *Jim*," he says and turns toward the door.

Pedersen's words follow behind him as he leaves: "I know someone who can help."

"Knowing yourself is the beginning of all wisdom."
—Aristotle

22

NO ONE CAN HELP ME. AND I'M NOT WORTH THE effort. I'm fucking useless. I can't even take care of my own wife and kid. And now we're getting another one. I should just disappear.

Gavin drives aimlessly, erratically. At times overly slow, like he's easing toward that dark abyss, simultaneously being drawn to it and fearful of being swallowed up into it. Until horns begin bleating at him. Then he hits the gas pedal, zooming down the street, screeching around corners, onto highways, swerving around cars and trucks, fleeing unknown dangers.

Miraculously, no police or other law enforcement intervene. But he won't always be so lucky.

He's unaware of how long he's been driving or where he's been, but now he looks up and sees his childhood house. Back to the scene of the crime.

His gas gauge reads nearly empty. The time is 1:38. With no particular goal in mind, he goes into the house, into the family room, and plops down on his father's brown leather recliner, neutralizing his old abuser. He lifts the lever and reclines it back all the way, stretching his body out flat. He could almost sleep in this position, if only his mind would quiet down.

The ghost of a smell wafts up to him as he runs his hands along the time-worn arms of the chair. Cigar. His father occasionally broke the house rules—typically after drinking too much—and smoked a cigar in the house while reclining in this chair. Mom would keep all the windows and doors open for days afterward, trying to dispel the odor. Gavin chuckles at the memory of how furious his mother would become, how defiantly his father would react, eventually apologizing like a petulant child, finally getting back into her good graces with affectionate humor.

Mom had often reassured Gavin that despite their epic battles and his father's occasional physical abuse, they really did love each other. Now it occurs to him that the mystery of how his parents had coexisted, and loved, for so many years, with such diametrically different backgrounds and personas, was an enigma even more intriguing than the mystery he'd been unraveling in the Prince Street building. His mother—educated, professional, upper-middle-class—and his father—street-smart, working-class, mob-affiliated—may have had as many "bad days" together as "good days," but in the end Gavin got the impression that those good days must have been more meaningful and treasured than the bad days.

Which now takes him back to his conversation about "life" with Pedersen. What is, or should be, his own "normal"? How much of that is about him, his essential core, and how much is about the role he plays in the world he occupies at any given moment? Is his life, his self-definition, necessarily different in different situations—those *dimensions?* Is Gavin the demeaned, abused twin, the successful chef-husband-father, the traumatized sleuth, all the same person?

He had regarded this mission of extracting "stuff" from his childhood home before selling it as a dreaded chore. Now he thinks it could reveal far more about who he is—who he was meant to be—than the historic fingerprints of generations before him on Prince Street.

Gavin sits on the floor of his childhood room among the destruction he'd unleashed in fury last week. He wonders whether the deep Prussian blue he'd chosen to paint the walls more than ten years ago—although recently defiled by his twin's deranged scrawl—says something about who he was then. He still loves the color, which now feels so right, as if the walls are vibrating in his own frequency, resonating within him. Deep, multi-layered, complex, solid, true. Maybe he should write that down? He enjoys a laugh at himself:

Notes On The Archaeological Exploration of Gavin

He begins opening drawers, looking for clues to himself. A drawing he made of himself riding his first bicycle... on the back is a note—*"Proud of you, Gavin!"* signed by Miss Johnson. That was his teacher in second grade—the last year their father allowed him and Devon to be placed in different classrooms. But now he remembers that he kept this drawing because it's the only one Devon didn't either scribble all over or tear up.

Buried in miscellaneous junk in another drawer, he finds his report card from eighth grade. Each A he'd earned in every subject had been crossed out and changed to a scrawled *F*. By his twin. After that, he finds nothing from childhood. He must have stopped keeping things because they had been either literally or virtually nullified by Devon. Even the trophies he'd won in sports were nowhere. There was nothing that might help him remember who he was. A line from an Emily Dickinson poem chirps from his memory: *"I'm nobody! Who are you?"*

Then Gavin remembers seeing something in the attic when he stuck the bag of money up there. He jumps up from the floor and runs to the hall, pulling down the cord to unfold the attic stairs. He climbs up and finds the pull chain for the attic light. Surprisingly, it hasn't burnt out.

Although it's a crisp October day, the attic is stifling, hot and airless. The bag of money is still there. Gavin chuckles. *I guess the mob goons trolling me are slipping.*

And then he sees them. Two large shopping bags from Filene's, where his mother shopped for most of her clothes. Even though Tony made good money in his liquor business, Colleen always preferred foraging the bargains in Filene's Basement. Both bulging bags are full now, but not with clothing.

Gavin starts pulling out papers, photographs, envelopes, report cards, his drawings, notebooks, his trophies! Delirious laughter bubbles up from deep within him, then tears begin streaming down his cheeks. Everything he thought he hadn't saved is here, rescued by his mother. This is quite literally his mother lode.

Under all his treasures he sees four or five slim journals. Nothing leather or fancy. A couple are just tattered old black and white school-type ledgers, the rest are plain brown. He opens one and sees his mother's handwriting, beautiful, flowing script, so lyrical it could evoke a melody, like works of art:

My brave little Gavin, one day you will read this and know who you are.

> "Have you seen my childhood? I'm searching for the world I came from 'cause I've been looking around in the lost and found of my heart."
> —Michael Jackson

23

KATIE FEELS MAGGIE'S FOREHEAD. IT DOESN'T FEEL like she has a fever. "Why are you so fussy, Mags? Do you want to go back to 'school'?"

Maggie loved her time at the Child Study Center; after a two-hour introductory trial, she didn't want to leave. There was a senior instructor who remembered when the DiMasi twins had been regulars there, and remarked on Maggie's resemblance to the twins' mother, daughter of the college's current Assistant Dean. So old Mrs. Anders quickly declared Maggie her favorite.

But now, back in her mother's house, Katie doesn't understand why Maggie—always so happy—is whining, crying, and generally throwing fits. She's had her mid-morning snack. It isn't time for lunch, or for a nap. Maybe it's the time zone change.

Even Patches is being unusually anxious, which seems almost like a continuation of his strange behavior during their walk. As if that black SUV he kept barking at—and tried to chase—was some sort of dangerous monster.

She's surprised Gavin isn't back from his gym time with Dr. Pedersen. How long can two guys sweat it out on treadmills? Maybe Pedersen is having a helpful discussion with Gavin? At least she can hope. He sure as hell needs it.

She could use Pedersen time, too. But if she were to insert herself into Gavin's sacrosanct relationship with him—that special window into his broken soul—Gavin might see that as a betrayal, and it would likely damage his unique bond with his old high school counselor. She needs to tread carefully.

Katie has so many questions. What's the most helpful way to react to Gavin's freak-outs? If he doesn't want to talk about it, is that okay? Should she try to get him to talk, and if so, how? Is it possible to anticipate, before an implosion, what's going to trigger him and how he'll react? How can she help Gavin, while also protecting herself and Maggie? How can she know when it's better to get out of his way, rather than trying to help?

Katie made the decision to come to Boston to be by her husband's side, to help him in any way she can. But she doesn't know how.

And she's very much aware that she and Maggie could be collateral damage.

Maggie comes to Katie, holding her favorite yellow truck. "Da-dee?"

"Daddy isn't here right now, Mags, but he'll be back soon. Would you like to help me look for things in Mommy's old closet?"

Katie stares at the state of the closet, thinking she really should have taken the time to clean it out before now. It's cluttered and crowded so badly; good thing her childhood bedroom had always been locked and closed off to renters.

Digging through boxes and bags of school memorabilia, photos, clothing, and all the paraphernalia of a girl growing up in Wellesley serves to distract Katie temporarily from her worry about Gavin. She pulls down a large dusty box with no markings or labels from the top shelf. She hadn't seen this in so long, she can't even remember what it was—probably so trivial and meaningless she can just toss it, not even bother to check it out.

It's surprising what useless stuff kids hold onto, and then life passes by and it's all irrelevant. Just insignificant stages of a life that naturally evolves...exploring, discovering, reacting, and adapting to circumstances. Real, actual life. She moves it to the pile she's accumulating of stuff to be thrown out with the trash, then begins sorting through the clothes hanging on the rod, and laughs. A short, slinky, low-cut sequined dress she wouldn't be caught dead in now. It must have been during the brief phase in her early teens when she thought she would become a famous movie star, after she got the lead role in *Cat on a Hot Tin Roof*.

Katie has become lost in yesterday, and now turns abruptly at the sound of Maggie doing her version of "singing"—what she occasionally does when Katie spends too long in the shower, perhaps mimicking Mommy's humming? At least Katie doesn't *think* she actually sings in the shower. That would be so cliché, she laughs at herself.

Maggie has opened the discarded box and pulled out several thick papers with colorful—and in some cases dark and gloomy—drawings and paintings, along with small jars of dried-up paints, which she has now arranged in teetering stacks like Towers of Pisa. It takes Katie a few moments to understand what she's looking at, to recall the puzzle into which these pieces of a former life belong. There was a phase, a time...one during which Katie was quite seriously devoted to art. How old was she then? She digs into the box, pulling out sketchbooks, pencils, and a small canvas with what is even now, to her experienced eye, a remarkably powerful abstract that could rival Kandinsky. There's a blue ribbon award affixed to it.

She drops to the floor beside the box. Who was the talented person who created this? What had been in her mind, in her imagination, in her heart? Present-day Katie now struggles to remember, to retrieve what it must have felt like to have the freedom, the bravery, the talent, to create all this.

Where did that child go? What had happened to her dreams?

Now she digs further into the box past certificates of merit, hand-decorated miniature boxes, brushes, and pulls out a large envelope. There are many small photographs inside, along with a bigger one the same size as the envelope. It's of Katie, with wildly untamed snowy blonde curls encircling her delicate face like an aura. She's perhaps nine years old, standing in front of a boldly brushed painting bigger than she was, on an easel. It takes a moment to recognize the woman standing on the other side of the easel—Miss Nelson, her fourth grade teacher. There's a man standing behind Katie, with the smile of someone who just learned he'd won a ticket to heaven. Her father.

Maggie now stands beside her, holding a brush from the box, stroking Katie's cheek. Her tears.

Katie's posture melts into liquid memory. She surrenders to thoughts and feelings she'd put away so long ago that now it all seems new, foreign. She had barely remembered her father five minutes ago, and now...now it all comes back to her like a loving embrace. His warmth, his laughter, his joy. Silly, teasing, chasing her, he was freedom embodied in callused hands and muscled arms. He gave her permission to dream outrageous futures.

It all died with him in that car accident the summer before fifth grade. She had been away at a summer camp for budding artists. She came home to a new role. Taking care of a sick mother. Managing a household. Preparing for a responsible adulthood alone.

She struggles to retrieve memories of him, and now as she sees more pictures, with his arms around Katie and her mother, things she'd completely forgotten are triggered. He gave her that first set of watercolors and considered everything she did to be prize-worthy. He helped her learn to ride a bicycle and claimed that she'd break the sound barrier. He taught her to play hopscotch and checkers, only occasionally letting her win. He let her operate his ham radio, listened intently to her terrible piano melodies, predicting she'd go to Carnegie Hall. All those things she'd forgotten, buried. She found a hand-made birthday card he had given her. He had drawn a caricature of her shooting a bow and arrow into a dragon, with the caption, *"All my love to my brave daughter, the dragon-slayer Princess!"*

But after her father died, she never again felt brave, much less a princess or a dragon-slayer. She felt responsible for his death, because she left him and went off to art camp. After that, she focused on doing whatever was necessary to please her mother and take care of her during her illness.

Now Katie wonders how her life may have been different if her father had lived.

Katie looks at her watch and stands. She'll finish this later—identify what to take back to Kauai, to save for Maggie. Just then a kick nudges her belly. *Oh yes, and for you too.*

It's now noon and Gavin still hasn't returned. Katie's stomach churns. Where could he be? Is he in trouble?

Nearly paralyzed with worry, she feeds Maggie her lunch, but like Katie, Mags won't eat much, just plays with her food. Katie puts her down for her nap, but she fusses and screams for Daddy.

Katie calls Gavin's cell phone, but there's no answer. She paces aimlessly around the house, then finally calls Pedersen.

"Hello?" Her voice wavers. "It's Katie. Do you know where Gavin is?" She is shaking.

"Hi, Katie," Pedersen says. "I was with him this morning, but we parted shortly after ten. He hasn't called?"

"No, he hasn't. And he isn't answering his phone. What was his mood when you saw him?"

"He had an incident at the gym. Not too bad, though. Then we sat and talked for maybe a half-hour after that, and he left in a thoughtful mood."

"I'm worried, Jim."

"Of course you are, Katie. What can I do?"

"It's almost three o'clock. I'm scared. I called his grandparents, but they haven't seen him. Maybe he went to his parents' house? I hope he didn't go to the North End."

"Would you like me to pick you up and we can go check the house? It's a little too far for you to walk with Maggie."

Katie's knees buckle. "Yes, thank you." Her words come out as a moan.

The distance from Katie's mother's house to Gavin's parents' house is only a few miles across town, but it feels like a thousand. Anxious and on edge, Katie sits in the back seat of Pedersen's car holding Maggie, who is squirming and unhappy, mirroring her mommy's mood. Patches nuzzles Mags in an attempt to soothe his charge. When Pedersen pulls his car into the DiMasi driveway, Katie exclaims, "There's Gavin's car!" and gets out with Maggie the moment the car stops. "And the front door is open!"

Pedersen understands the potential for danger in that, but can't catch Katie before she runs into the house carrying Maggie, with Patches already ahead, yapping.

"Gavin!" Katie calls out frantically.

"Da-dee!" Maggie shrieks.

Patches runs upstairs, barking.

Gavin pokes his head down from the attic. "Katie?"

"Man is not what he thinks he is, he is what he hides."
—André Malraux

24

IN THICK STAGNANT AIR LADEN WITH TENSION, THE three of them stand awkwardly around the kitchen island while Maggie clings to Patches in the family room.

Gavin is feeling cornered. And guilty for not contacting Katie. And embarrassed that Pedersen had to come to her rescue. "Sorry I can't offer you a drink," he jokes with a forced smile. "And sorry I didn't get your call, Katie. I was sorting out stuff in the attic and didn't hear my phone down here in the kitchen."

"I understand, Gavin," Katie says. "And I know you understand my worry when I hadn't heard from you." She isn't sure if there's any significance to the front door having been open, but decides not to mention it now. There's no likely resolution at the moment, and it might trigger him.

"Yeah, sure." Gavin nods his head too vigorously, too long. "And thanks, Jim, for giving my family a ride over here. I think I'm done for today, though, so I'll take them back now."

"My pleasure, Gavin," Pedersen says, then discards pretension and calls out the elephant in the room. "Did you find anything interesting up in the attic?"

"You mean anything that triggered me?" Gavin flashes a smile that verges on sneer. "No triggers in this house except a couple on the first day I began my sorting mission. I'm used to it now," he obfuscates and shrugs with a self-deprecating chortle.

"Well, it's to be expected. You're bound to encounter things in this house that remind you of unpleasant—or even hurtful—events and conditions during your childhood."

"But I've also come across some interesting, even helpful, things." Gavin's smile is genuine now. "Like did you know that some Harvard researcher conducted a study, in which Devon and I were subjects when we were little, at the Child Study Center here?"

"That's good news, Gavin!" Pedersen says. "I'd love to read it—who was the researcher? I know quite a few at Harvard."

"I haven't read it beyond the abstract yet," Gavin says. "I found it in Mom's banker's box that's focused on identical twins." He doesn't mention that his mother's journal in the attic is what pointed him to find it. For some reason he doesn't understand, he wants to keep the existence of those journals to himself, as if guarding his innermost secrets. Now he goes on, "But it also has tags in Mom's handwriting, about narcissism. So it must have been a multimodal study of some sort."

"Whether or not intended from the outset," Pedersen confirms. "Sometimes predictive variables that were not included in an initial hypothesis become evident during the research."

"I'll let you have it when I'm done reading it."

"Thank you, Gavin. I'm especially curious to learn who the researcher was. I know quite a few who conducted research with Judith Herman both before and after she wrote her seminal book, *Trauma and Recovery*—"

Both Katie and Gavin simultaneously interject: "I have that book!"

"I bought it after you came to see us in Kauai, Jim," Katie explains. "I'm reading it now."

"A copy was also next to Mom's banker's box on domestic abuse," Gavin adds.

"Well, that book, first published in 1992, was the result of many years of research by Dr. Herman and others, beginning even before you and Devon were born, Gavin," Pedersen says. "Her research is what convinced the World Health Organization to *consider* the inclusion of Complex PTSD in their International Statistical Classification of Diseases—ICD."

"What you told me about this morning?" Gavin asks.

"Yes, that's it. But codifying new conditions requires lengthy processes that can sometimes drag on for ten or more years before becoming official. Meantime, some practitioners are calling it C-PTSD. When a disorder gets reduced to an acronym, you know it's official!" Pedersen laughs. "Regardless, there are a number of well-respected practicing clinicians both in Europe and the U.S. who have been treating patients whose symptoms and causal etiology align precisely with what Dr. Herman identified. I know one of them right here in town—she's the one I was referring to when I said I know someone who can help you."

Katie's face brightens. "That's wonderful, Jim," she gushes.

"I don't suppose she provides references?" Gavin asks with a wry grin.

"Well of course not. Patient confidentiality." Pedersen smiles. "But I can vouch for her."

"Then I guess that's as good as it gets, Jim. Of course it assumes that I *can* be helped, by anyone or anything."

"Now that's your disorder talking, son. Feeling worthless, helpless, beyond help. Of course it's going to take time, *and* your commitment to do the work," Pedersen says, leveling his gaze at Gavin. "Which can't realistically happen, or hold, if you continue to believe you're hopeless and worthless. It's a vicious circle. You incurred damage in your childhood, at a time when a child's sense of self and his relationship to the world is forming. Your injuries can't be wiped away or painted over; there's a gaping hole in the development of your perception of self. You can only re-build yourself—who you are, who you want to be—beyond those scars. But you must truly want to build that person, *because* you believe you aren't hopeless or worthless."

All those words, all those concepts, seem like a swirling blur to Gavin now. "So I guess the big hurdle is to kill the hopeless, worthless shit," he jokes, unconvinced.

"Because it's a myth, Gavin. I can assure you that I, and Katie, and your grandparents, will all be your cheerleaders, consistently reminding you that you *are* valuable and worthwhile."

"You can bet on it," Katie adds.

"Oh, by the way, Katie, I have information on a group for you," Pedersen says. "You don't have to do this alone."

Gavin pulls up short. "Do what?" There's an edge to his voice, like he's getting ready to strike. Whether defensively or offensively is unclear.

Pedersen steps back with a glance to Katie. Maggie runs in from the family room, crying, and wraps her arms around her mommy's legs.

"It's hard for anyone to always know," Pedersen begins, "what's the best or right way to help and support someone with PTSD under different circumstances. This is a professionally led group that can help provide information and recommendations for how Katie can best support you."

Katie is relieved that Pedersen doesn't mention the research about spouses developing symptoms and marriages breaking up. That would definitely trigger Gavin around his failed responsibilities to take care of her. "Well thank you, Dr. Pedersen," she says, careful not to call him "Jim" at this point, which Gavin might interpret as the two of them ganging up on him. "Gavin and I are working together on this. Right, sweetie?"

Gavin un-tenses a bit. "Yeah. Right." He looks over his shoulder toward the stairs. "Hey, like I said, I'm done here for the day. Why don't we just go home now?" He turns to Pedersen. "Thanks, Jim, for bringing my family here. Send me the contact info on that shrink you mentioned."

"Of course," Pedersen says, reservation in his voice. "I think you would like her." With a glance toward Katie, he turns to leave.

As the front door closes behind Pedersen, Gavin turns to Katie with an angry scowl and vitriol in his voice. "Did you really have to call him, Katie? Couldn't you wait? Or don't you trust me?"

Katie recoils, flooded by a tsunami of shock, hurt, and anger. This is the first time Gavin has ever spoken to her like this. She takes a deep breath, stands tall, and suppresses her initial instinct to turn and leave. She assumes a soft and steady voice, hoping her emotions won't be evident to her husband. "I trust the man I married, Gavin, but there are times when you're not that guy. And you're also messing with dangerous people in the North End. So I was literally worried sick."

She swallows what is caught in her throat: *If you'd like me to not care enough to worry, or take Maggie and go back to Kauai, just say so.*

Katie watches Gavin closely, hoping her words won't trigger fight or flight in him.

With a grimace and an eye-roll, Gavin mutters, "Let's just get out of here. Now." He turns to the door without waiting for his family, who trail behind him. But once Katie, Maggie and Patches are in the car, he says, "Forgot something. Back in a minute."

Maggie begins crying in her car seat the moment Gavin leaves.

"Maggie, would you like to sing the song you learned in school today?" Katie asks and begins singing, walking her fingers up Maggie's leg. "Itsy-bitsy spider climbs up the waterspout. Down come the rains—"

She is interrupted by Patches growling deep with his nose pressed against the back seat window. He suddenly jumps over into the driver seat to poke his head through the partial opening of the window and barks a frenzy.

Katie looks through the windshield and sees a black SUV parked across the street, idling, with two men inside. "Patches, what's the fuss? It's just a car." She pulls the dog away from the window, grateful it isn't open enough for him to jump out. But she is nevertheless curious, verging on suspicious. The SUV pulls out and leaves, in the same moment Katie commits its license plate number to memory.

When Gavin returns, he has nothing in his hands.

"What did you forget?" Katie asks.

"I just had to close up the stairs to the attic. And lock the door."

By the time Gavin pulls the car into the driveway of Katie's mother's house, he has been transformed, back to his usual kindness. It's as if leaving the house of his childhood trauma has also left its toxicity behind. "What would you like me to make you for dinner tonight? Or would you rather go out?"

"Oh, I'm sure Maggie would love a night at Chuck E. Cheese," Katie laughs. "But no thanks, Tiger. I prefer relaxing here with you—even a bowl of cereal would be enough, as long as I don't have to fix it!"

Gavin inventories what's in the fridge, pulling out ingredients to inspire the evening menu, while Katie takes Maggie with her to walk Patches.

Maggie perks up as they walk down the street, running down the sidewalk with uninhibited energy despite having had only a short nap today. When she spots a cluster of deep blue asters—their final bloom of fall—in a neighbor's yard, she rushes forward with her hands out to grab them.

"Oh no, Mags," Katie intercepts her. "Those flowers belong to the people who live in that house, so you can't pick them. Just enjoy how pretty they are."

Just then an elderly man walks out of the house with a creased smile. He appears to be perhaps in his eighties, but he stands straight and wiry, with a spry step. "Well hello, young lady." He leans over to Maggie. "You like my flowers?" he asks in an old-world accent Katie can't quite place. Maggie responds with a silent, solemn nod. "Do you know what color they are?"

Maggie looks at him, very serious. "Boo," she says.

"That's right!" the man says, as if declaring the winner of the lottery. "So if you tell me your name, you can have a few to take home and put in a vase."

Katie had coached and practiced Maggie on her name, in case she ever got separated from her parents or got lost. So now the toddler pulls herself up to her full inherited-from-Daddy height and firmly states in fractured pronunciation, "Mag-gie! Ma-gret Cah-yeen Dee-Masi."

"Oh, my goodness!" the man says. "What a smart *bambina* you are!" He lifts a chain attached to his belt to pull out from his pocket a key ring with a large retractable knife on the end. In a single seamless motion, the blade pops out, with which he cuts several aster stems and hands them to Maggie with a grand flourish. "For you, Princess!"

"What do you say, Maggie?" Katie prompts.

"Tank you," Maggie squeaks, suddenly wrapping her arms around the man's leg.

The man laughs with a look of surprise. His facial wrinkles dissolve into joy.

"Thank you so much, sir," Katie says. "I'm Katie. My husband and I are staying for a while in a house up the street. My mother Margaret Goodwin's house. What is your name?"

"I am Luca. Luca Benedetti," he says with a slight bow. "I knew your mother. Wonderful woman. I'm so sorry for your loss."

"Thank you. I miss her every day," Katie nods. "Well, we need to be getting back to the house. My husband is fixing dinner."

"Your husband is cooking?"

"Yes, he's a chef."

"Ah, a noble profession indeed!"

"I hope to see you around the neighborhood, Luca," Katie

smiles. "Maggie, time to go put those pretty flowers in a vase!"

As they turn back to the house, Patches begins his low growl again. Katie tightens her grip on his leash and looks up the street in the direction the dog is facing. The black SUV again. What's that about? The same license plate as the one outside Gavin's parents' house. Maybe Tray can find out. She picks up Maggie with her other arm and hurries to the house.

> "Distrust is like a vicious fire that keeps going and going. Even put out, it will reignite itself, devouring the good with the bad, still feeding on empty."
> —*Anthony Liccione*

25

MAGGIE IS IN BED FOR THE NIGHT AND GAVIN IS sipping his chianti while he and Katie sit at the kitchen table over plates of what had been eggplant parmesan. Warm layered fragrances of garlic and herbs linger throughout the house. Gavin looks down into his wine glass, swirls the inky liquid and watches its legs slither down the sides of the glass. He mumbles into its depths, "Sorry I was a shit when Pedersen brought you to my parents' house." He doesn't look at Katie as he says it, his head hanging low.

"Thank you for saying that, sweetie." Katie reaches over and puts her hand on Gavin's, then pulls him up. "Let's go sit on Mom's sofa, where we used to cuddle."

Gavin sits on one end of the beige tweed sofa and drapes his arm over Katie as she sits close beside him. He looks down at her and kisses the top of her head. "Kat, I know the way I treated you in front of Pedersen really hurt, and I can't tell you how sorry I am." He lifts her chin with one finger and looks into her eyes. "That's the last thing in the world I want. You're too important to me. I love you so much, and really appreciate your standing by me and putting up with my craziness for the last few months."

"Thank you, Gav. So now you probably realize that your

reaction today was an example of the untrust and pushing-away that Pedersen said is a symptom of C-PTSD, right?"

"Yeah, I got that. Afterwards. Didn't stop me in the moment, though. Sorry."

"Well Gav, I'm sorry too." Katie looks at him and gently strokes his cheek. "Sorry PTSD has such power to so completely overtake your good nature."

"It sucks." Gavin shakes his head. "But I got that doctor's contact info from Jim while you were out walking Patches. I'll call tomorrow."

Katie doesn't want to worry or trigger Gavin, so doesn't mention the SUV she saw during her walk. The same one that was outside his parents' house, where the front door was open. She decides to withhold her suspicions until she can find and confirm more details. "Oh, didn't you say there's a to-do list you want me to tackle?"

Her questions shift Gavin into solutions-focused task mode, which is proving to be a good diversion from his crippling triggers. He sits up with the eagerness of a child on Christmas morning. "Oh, yes! Well, at my parents' house, we need to get one of those big dumpsters outside—the long ones that get lifted onto a flatbed. And a security system, cleaning and painting crews, and I'm sure there'll be more I haven't thought of yet." He takes a breath and rushes on. "At Prince Street, we need new strong doors and windows for security—most urgently on the ground floor—it's all just boarded up with flimsy plywood now; we need to get NSTAR to put in a temporary external electric feed, then install a security system, then..." Gavin trails off and looks over to Katie with that sheepish expression she always finds completely disarming.

Katie smiles. "I love you, Tiger." She reminds herself that this glimpse of the former Gavin may only be temporary. "What are the first priorities?"

"Well, NSTAR should be just a call to the right department, so let's hope that's pretty straightforward. But all the other stuff means finding and vetting people to do the work, getting bids and so forth, not so easy."

Now his helpless little-boy expression makes Katie wonder if she's being manipulated. But then she kicks herself for her cynicism, and laments how the DiMasi family has corrupted her thinking, making her question and doubt. "Okay, give me the address on Prince Street and the exact name or trust account NSTAR might have in their records, and I'll get started."

"Oh, Kat, that will be so great!" Gavin says, crushing her in his embrace.

"So, are you taking the day off tomorrow?" Katie teases.

"Nah. First thing in the morning before traffic gets impossible, I should go to Prince Street, get some stuff I left there, and check to see if anyone has broken in again," Gavin sighs.

Katie perks up at that, wondering what the threat level might be. From whom, why, how serious? Seems to be a trend... Does Tray know this?

Gavin prattles on. "Did I tell you? I'm pretty sure the damage from the fire is not so major. It doesn't appear to have even damaged the beams and supports between floors, the upper floors are virtually unscathed except for water from the fire hoses, and the outside walls are built like Fort Knox. So it doesn't look like it needs to be demolished—just totally rehabbed."

"So why do you think your lawyers—and the City—are recommending selling and demolishing it?" Katie asks.

"I'm not sure, but I suspect some shark really wants the building," Gavin says with a shrug. "It's prime real estate in the North End, and corruption is the air they all breathe."

"And of course there's the mob."

"Yeah. The mob. But the North End doesn't hold exclusive rights to that racket."

"Have they been hassling you?"

Gavin jumps up from the sofa and grabs the bottle of wine.

"Naw," he says with his back to her, truth stuck in his throat. "Then after I check out Prince Street, I need to make progress at Dad's house, too."

Later that night, as Katie works on her laptop to manage her six-hours-behind businesses in Kauai, a text comes in from Tray: *"Got it. I'll let you know who owns the SUV by tomorrow."*

Katie feels crushed by the half-truths, secrets, and unspoken words hanging in the air, thick and quietly toxic, all in the name of avoiding hurt or worry or fear. Yet feeding distrust, and threatening to dissolve the bonds of love between her and Gavin.

"If you shut up truth and bury it under the ground,
it will but grow, and gather to itself such
explosive power that the day it bursts through
it will blow up everything in its way."
—Émile Zola

26

GAVIN AWAKENS FROM A DREAM WHILE IT'S STILL dark out. It's that same dream again—skeletons coming up from deep below. From the sub-basement of his soul.

Probably a metaphor for all the buried history in that building. He stirs slightly, not wanting to wake Katie. But as he recalls his plan to go to Prince Street today, a revulsion, a visceral fear, overcomes him. He tries to inhale, but breath won't come. His heart pounds against his chest.

Now Patches is licking Gavin's face, which is partially submerged under his tightly wound arms clutching his shuddering body. He is curled on the floor, in the far corner of the open closet. Early-morning light glimmers in the window beyond the closet. He doesn't know how he got here or how long ago.

He uncurls one arm and pulls Patches to him. "Thanks, buddy," he whispers. "Not going to that place today. Not 'til I learn more about what I'm getting into." He stands, tiptoes to grab his sweatpants, and goes downstairs to make coffee. He breathes in the aroma of the beans, clearing his head.

His thoughts grope and slide through the labyrinthine mass of surprises, curiosities, and puzzles he's unearthed since returning to Boston. He realizes now that he's only been skimming each surface, uncovering many threads he hasn't pulled, hasn't unraveled. In the Prince Street building and the names he encountered there. In his parents' house and what he found there. And there's likely more threads to discover. But he doesn't know why he hasn't unraveled those threads, dug deeper to understand where they lead, what's under the surface. Is it because he's so eager to complete his task and get out of here, or because there's something he fears? Fear of those SUVs following him, or fear of the truth? What would those truths mean? Would any of it make any difference to anyone? To him and his PTSD?

He's weary of saying "PTSD" and even more so because he may have to include yet another letter in the acronym. He thinks he should just give it a simple name. It may be with him for a long time into the future, perhaps even a permanent fixture in his house of horrors, this curse. If he invites it in for a beer and gives it a name, like maybe "Fred," he might turn foe to friend, right?

He is lost down a dead-end of his labyrinth as Katie comes into the kitchen. She knows the look, and that any sudden sound may startle or even trigger him. She begins softly singing one of their favorite love songs, "A Moment Like This."

It takes several long seconds for Gavin to wriggle out of his maze and return to the present. "Oh, hi Katie. Sorry if I woke you. Where's Mags?"

"Good morning, Tiger." She stretches up to give him a kiss, then pulls out her favorite mug. "I smelled the coffee! Maggie's in her crib, still sleeping—she had an exciting day yesterday."

"Well, I hope she has good dreams." Gavin smiles and goes in for a longer kiss, then pulls back to pat her belly. "When are you going to start showing, Momma?"

"I'm only a little more than three months now," she smiles. "So probably not for a month or two. At least I'm over the worst of the morning sickness. Oh, I forgot—are you getting ready to leave for Boston?"

"Change of plans, babe." Gavin pours coffee into Katie's mug. "How would you and Maggie like to go see my DiMasi grandfather this afternoon?"

"Really?" Katie raises her right eyebrow. "What prompted that?"

"I want to see if he knows anything about the history of the Prince Street building." Gavin turns away and puts a muffin into the toaster oven. "You want one of these?"

"No thanks. Don't want to test the morning sickness." She pats her stomach.

"Yeah, so I'll go over to Dad's house this morning to make some progress while you and Maggie are at the Child Study Center. Then we can drive to the nursing home in Boston after that."

The first strains of Maggie's morning aria waft down from upstairs.

"I'll go get her." Katie puts her hand on Gavin's arm. "That sounds like a wonderful plan, Tiger."

"Thanks. Maybe seeing a little person might help him remember," Gavin chuckles. "Based on the last time I saw him three years ago, I suspect he may have the beginnings of dementia, or Alzheimer's."

As Katie turns to the stairs, she says, "Well, long-term memory is usually more available than short-term for people with those cognitive issues, so he might be able to help you."

Gavin pulls down the stairs to his parents' attic and unfolds them. Warm stale air surrounds him as he climbs up. He looks around and doesn't notice anything that's been disturbed since he was here yesterday.

He checks under the dirty shirt and trash in the Charles

Street Supply bag. The money is still there. He has no idea what he's going to do with it, and again questions his rationale in bothering to take it out of the building. Other than wanting to keep it from whoever is probably looking for it, it doesn't make much sense now. Maybe he'll just drop it off anonymously at a shelter somewhere. A battered women's shelter would make sense. He could attach a note: "*In memory of Colleen O'Malley DiMasi, beloved mother.*" But what if whoever's after him for it, later threatens him or his family? He wouldn't have it to give them. But even if he handed over the money, it probably wouldn't appease them anyway. Shit. He should've just let them find it. His head is spinning, dizzy. He forces a deep breath and an even deeper exhale. Maybe he can put it back in the building tomorrow. A peace offering.

But first he needs to find out more about that building. He stuffs the bag of money way in the back of the attic near the eaves, under a few large plastic bags of stuff he hasn't investigated yet, which just feel like old clothes inside. Then he opens the Home Depot bag and pulls out the ledger, notebook and jewelry from under the soiled clothing. They must be important—why else would Dad—or whoever hid the money—have constructed that weird little storage area to hide it all?

He pulls out the notepad and pen he brought with him and opens the old notebook. The dates of recorded names began in 1950 in a handwriting he doesn't recognize, but assumes was his grandfather's, since he bought the store in that year. But then he recognizes his father's handwriting in entries beginning in the late seventies, when he took over the store, with his last entry in March 2001. Gavin remembers that as the time he had to visit Devon in rehab. His twin had taken over their father's business in the fall of 2000, then almost immediately got himself into trouble, in more ways than one. So many dirty footprints of history.

Now Gavin writes down a few names that were recorded in what was probably his grandfather's handwriting:

Vincent Mangano	April 1951
Fredrick Tenuto	June 1952
James Squillante	September 1960
Anthony Strollo	April 1962
Freddy Tameleo	November 1968

Next he copies some of the names written in his father's handwriting:

Dom Cucchiara	October 1976
Salvatore Annunziato	June 1979
Nicolo Zannino	August 1983
Rudy Grasso	May 1987
Michael Linskey	August 1991
Joe Salvatti	March 2001

Gavin's attention perks up as he writes down those last two entries.

He did some research last night after Katie was in bed, and learned that Michael Linskey was the guy who owned the liquor store in Southie, which Whitey Bulger muscled him out of, then when Linskey won a $14 million lottery ticket, Bulger coerced him and his brother Patrick to sell him the ticket for more than $3 million—a number that rings Gavin's bell—the same as what he found in the wall of the secret storage area. Probably not a coincidence...

And Joe Salvatti! Rick's father? *Is this somehow related to why Rick Salvatti is creeping me out?* The 2001 date... Whatever happened on that date must have been recorded by Dad, because Devon was sidelined then.

Next Gavin pulls out the ledger that shows who owes how much to whom, then checks to see whether there are any matches between the entries that were crossed out with no indication of the debt being paid, and the names in the notebook. Of the twenty or so names in the notebook, only eleven—five from his grandfather's era and six from his father's—are a match to unrecorded loan paybacks. So there isn't a direct correlation, although he might find more connections when he has time to scrutinize the jewelry and IDs.

Gavin gathers up the loan ledger, notebook and jewelry, stuffs it all into the Home Depot bag, and moves the bag to the far corner of the attic. With his notes, he now has what he needs to help prompt his grandfather's memory.

"In the end you don't so much find yourself
as you find someone who knows who you are."
—Robert Brault

27

"HAVE FUN, MAGS!" KATIE KISSES HER LITTLE GIRL. "I'LL be back to get you when you're done."

Maggie doesn't seem to care; she's already running for the Center's collection of trucks.

Katie waves to Mrs. Anders as she leaves, then heads into the sprawling campus, past the sleek modern structures of the science center to the gothic revival buildings at the heart of Wellesley College's academic quad, where Pendleton West houses the college art studios. She arranged to meet a former classmate from her first year at Wellesley, who is now an artist-in-residence here. Katie is excited but nervous. She has little notion of what she will do—or how, what she *can* do, or what she wants, whether she can somehow reconnect to the apparent passion and talent she once had all those years ago. Before she put it away, buried it with her father, and smothered it all with daughterly duty and devotion.

"Oh my god, it's *Katie*," shrieks Destiny Abara. "And look at you, how beautiful you are, with that magnificent baby inside!"

Katie gasps. At three months along, she knows her pregnancy isn't showing yet. She can still wear her skinny jeans. What sort of magical perception does Destiny possess?

The tall, lithe artist, a native of Niger, with a graceful

posture reminiscent of a dancer who floats in air, embraces Katie with a warmth she didn't know she's been missing. "Darling, your child just spoke," she whispers, pulling back to survey the whole of Katie. "Have you listened to him, have you heard him, my dear?"

Katie doesn't know what to say. She has suspected the occasional slight movement in her belly may be her baby rather than gas; it's been considerably more than she'd felt from Maggie at this stage of pregnancy. She smiles, embarrassed, and puts her hand on her relatively flat belly. "This baby communicates to me physically, Destiny."

"Oh, my dearest Katie," Destiny says, wrapping her arm around her much shorter friend and guiding her into the studio. "He is communicating *with* you, if you will listen and hear. Just as you will listen and hear your heart and translate that to your hands." She takes Katie's hand in hers, kisses her palm, then places it flat onto a mid-sized pre-primed canvas. "Feel it, my friend. And listen. Here are all your acrylics and brushes, for your adventure into you."

Destiny begins to walk away, then turns back. "My dear. He is distressed." And then she is gone.

Katie is stunned. Her palm remains on the canvas, as if she is receiving communications through electrical signals, tingling her skin and coursing up her arm. To her heart. Her belly moves, a slight nudge, or perhaps a somersault. For the first time she considers the human inside her to be male. *What is he distressed about? The same thing that distresses me?*

She moves her palm from the canvas and cups its warmth against her cheek, as if transmitting the longing of its white void to her imagination. Now she dips each of her fingers into five pots of acrylic, then walks her fingers slowly across the canvas before ending in a downward curving arc. She picks up a wide brush; she used to know what the numbers on the side of each meant, but she's forgotten all that. She tracks the arc on the canvas with a broad stroke of black, then...

Nearly an hour later, her canvas is full, with an overwhelming force of darkness punctuated by brilliant light. Living, breathing, dynamic, abstract movement, energy coursing through it like the pulse of a thousand ancient gods battling evil. Katie is perspiring. Her breathing is labored. Her hands are shaking. Her baby is rocking.

Destiny has come to stand behind her, observing her work. Tears moisten the woman's face and she doubles over, a soundless cry gripping her. "O ya," she finally coughs, standing to wrap Katie in her long arms, merging spirit and love. "It is you. You have heard yourself."

If it is possible to be reborn, it would feel like Katie does now. Simultaneously exciting, daunting, and humbling, she is overcome with an awakening, a freedom she doesn't recall ever having felt. Perhaps she may have, as a child, believing a world of possibilities before her, so long ago she doesn't remember. Freedom that vaporized when she assumed the weight of endless responsibility after her father's death. She wants that freedom now. Desperately. That feeling, where doors within her will open, to unknown unexplored dimensions of a buried life, waiting to be exhumed and reclaimed.

"May I come back tomorrow?" Katie whispers into Destiny's chest.

"Of course, my dear."

There's a vitality and purpose in Katie's step as she walks across campus to the faculty house where the group for PTSD spouses that Pedersen recommended is meeting. Her thoughts dwell on this new feeling, a thrilling sense of nascent self-discovery, her determination to unearth the person she was meant to be. Which then prompts her to realize the parallel to Gavin. Like her, his life was diverted into something he was never meant to be. A scapegoat for the toxic dysfunction that rippled down through generations of his family, suffocating, nullifying, and burying any hope of his own personhood. Like her, his hope—his identity—must be unearthed and freed.

But I cannot, I must not, do that for him.

Before she goes into the meeting, she checks her phone. Nothing from Kauai nor from Gavin, but there's a text from Tray:

> The SUV is owned by Michael Salvatti, son of Joe Salvatti and brother of Rick Salvatti, a guy Gavin has seen a few times. Definitely mob. Not the good guys.

Katie's knees buckle. Now she must tell Gavin. When she joins the group inside, the joy she'd experienced moments before is clouded over. That taste of freedom and possibilities goes stale on her tongue.

But the kind welcoming face of a tall forty-ish man with thick salt-and-pepper hair instantly soothes her nerves with his mellifluous greeting. "Hello, Katie. I'm Dr. Theodore Fisher, but everyone just calls me Dr. Ted. Come in. Jim Pedersen tells me you're a remarkable woman who could use our support." He ushers her into a large living room where a group of a dozen people sit in a circle on sofas and chairs. "Hey group, please welcome Katie," he booms, all the way up from his diaphragm.

Twelve open-smile faces beam "Welcome, Katie!" in unison.

Katie feels like she's just come in out of the cold.

Her baby moves again.

> "If you can't get rid of the family skeletons,
> you may as well make them dance."
> —George Bernard Shaw

28

WHEN GAVIN, KATIE AND MAGGIE ARRIVE AT THE nursing home, there is already a crowd of visitors waiting in the lobby. To Gavin's paranoid eye, many of them look suspicious. But security in the North End Rehabilitation Center is scrupulous, and each visitor must provide identification before being escorted past the reception area to meet their loved one—whether that resident is in the common room or their private room.

Maggie attracts the attention of many of the surrounding visitors with her outgoing nature. Her joyful chatter and singing bring a vibrancy to the room and its occupants as she becomes friends with everyone in the lobby, which concerns Katie about their daughter's safety. She keeps a close eye on Mags, but the vision of her little social butterfly being too friendly with the wrong stranger nags at her imagination.

Gavin paces restlessly, his anxiety rising. Now his pocket vibrates with an incoming message. He pulls out his cell phone and sees a text from Tray:

Solomon's partially burned car was found up in Gloucester. He wasn't in it, but forensics found evidence of gunshots and his blood. Watch your back.

Gavin spins around, wide-eyed, fear radiating from him, scanning the crowd, then abruptly hurtles toward the restrooms, bumping people on the way, like a man running for his life. Katie views it all with alarm, then releases her paralyzed breath when he enters the men's room. She picks up Maggie and rushes to position herself outside the restroom door in order to intercept any man who might open the door into the multi-stall facility. She doesn't know what triggered Gavin, but fears whatever reactionary state he may be in.

Maggie strains in Katie's arms, reaching toward the door. "Oh no, sweetie," Katie pulls her away. "You can't go in there, that bathroom is just for big grown-up men like Daddy. He'll be done and come out in a few minutes." She hears banging and slamming inside, but at least no sounds of things being broken, like glass or mirrors.

Just as the front desk calls out "DiMasi!" Gavin emerges, looking like he'd had a wrestling match with a gorilla.

"You okay, Gav?" Katie carefully scrutinizes him, looking for some indication of his mental state.

"Bad news," Gavin mumbles, "Tell you later."

A muscular young man in scrubs leads them into the activity room, which is bright with sunlight streaming through multiple windows. Most of the apparent residents in the room sit in wheelchairs at various levels of attention from near catatonia to snoring or staring blankly out into space; only a few are interacting with other people, whether visitors or staff. In the far corner of the room, hunched over in his wheelchair, Gavin sees Umberto DiMasi, his grandfather. Grandpa had always hated it when someone called him Bert, and now an attendant is urging "Bert" to eat.

Gavin approaches cautiously. "Hello, Nonno. I hope you remember me, your grandson Gavin?"

The old man doesn't look up, although a nearly inaudible grunt rumbles in his throat.

Gavin addresses the attendant. "Maybe I can help my

grandfather eat some of that fruit, ma'am?"

The young woman looks up at him, then to Katie holding Maggie. "Well, sir, you can try, but I warn you that Bert can be pretty stubborn. He's perfectly capable of eating, he just refuses to do it. But I have other residents I need to deal with, so go ahead. And good luck with that," she snorts.

Maggie waves to the woman as she walks by, then squirms to get down from Katie's arms.

"Mags, this is your other great-grandfather," Katie says quietly as she crouches beside Maggie. "You've met Grandma and Grandpa O'Malley; now this is Grandpa DiMasi."

"Bert?" Maggie lights up. "Ses-me Steet!"

Gavin quickly interjects, "Oh no, Mags. Not Bert! Grandpa D," he laughs. Now he and Katie sit on chairs flanking the old man.

Maggie toddles over to pick a grape off the tray of fruit the attendant was trying to feed Grandpa and holds it out, close to his mouth. "Mmm," she hums, a sound Katie always makes when urging her to eat.

His eyes open in surprise, looking at Maggie, and a reluctant smile tugs at one side of his lips. He opens his mouth and takes the grape.

"Yay!" Maggie claps her hands, gets another grape, and brings it to his mouth. His smile grows wider as he eats it.

Maggie is smiling too, with a mischievous look in her eyes. She loves games. Now she takes another grape and brings it close to his lips, but just as he opens his mouth to eat it, she pulls it back and pops it into her mouth, laughing and doing a gleeful hoppity dance.

Grandpa D erupts in laughter. "What's your name, you little prankster?"

"Mag-gie. Ma-gret Cah-yeen Dee-Masi," she states in her toddler-impaired pronunciation, emphatically nodding her head with every syllable.

Her words are sufficiently coherent for Grandpa to understand. "May I have another grape, Maggie?"

She beams as she picks up a grape and brings it to his mouth.

"Now your turn, Maggie," he smiles.

Maggie takes a grape and pops it in her mouth, then takes another to him.

But Grandpa D shakes his head and says, "Give that one to your daddy, *bambina*."

Maggie's face lights up, whether from enjoying the game or remembering neighbor Luca calling her that name, and redirects the grape to Gavin.

"Thank you, Maggie," Gavin says, then eats the grape. "Grandpa D and I are going to talk now, sweetie."

Maggie nods, all solemn and serious, and stands beside the old man like a guardian sentinel. She looks up to him and pats his cheek with her little hand that a moment ago had fed him grapes.

Gavin hopes this conversation will yield answers to some of his questions. He begins with what he thinks will be an easy one. "So Grandpa, I've been asked by my father's attorney, Lombardi, to come settle Dad's estate, now that my brother Devon has…" he hesitates then takes a breath, "died."

Grandpa's head pops up and he stares at Gavin. "What the fuck did that stupid *stronzo* do this time?"

Gavin struggles to regulate his breathing. He doesn't want to say the truth. "It's very sad, Nonno, and it hurts me deeply. He was my twin brother. So I'd rather not talk about that. I've come here to see you, to be sure you're well, and also to get some information about your liquor store on Prince Street so I can settle all Dad's affairs."

Grandpa won't look at Gavin. "Lombardi is—" he hesitates, "*incapacitated*. And if you mean Junior, *fuck him*," he ends emphatically, crosses his arms tightly and sets his jaw.

Maggie leans her head against his arm.

Gavin isn't quite sure what that implies, but takes a deep breath and plunges forward. He needs to first get Grandpa talking about something he finds interesting, something non-threatening, not directly related to the mob. "I'm curious about the history of your building, Grandpa. I found a small plaque on the foundation wall down in the basement that has the name 'Hutchinson,' and some dates. Do you know anything about that?"

That's a "soft-ball" question, so Grandpa visibly transforms. His face brightens with a glow of authoritative confidence as he leans back, sits up straight and takes a deep breath like he's about to pontificate on an important topic. "Ah, well. Parts of that building are very old. I looked into it, years ago when I found that little plaque after I bought the building—that was 1950. Some guy named Elisha Hutchinson—born here in the North End, and his papa Edward and his wife were born here too, but Edward's dad William and *his* wife Ann—she was almost hanged—came here from England. Well, Elisha built a big-ass mansion in 1687 on Prince Street. That was considered 'out in the country' back then. That foundation you saw is only a small part of what the mansion was then. Elisha's first wife died and he remarried, ending up with a total of something like a dozen kids, but back then not many of them lived very long. One of his kids was named Thomas, and he *did* grow up, and went through two wives too—lotta women died in childbirth back then—and between his two wives *they* had a dozen kids. One of them was named Thomas. Like Junior."

Grandpa is rattling on, in his own world. Gavin's question gave him the opportunity to reveal his knowledge about an arcane topic that probably few among his friends and family had ever cared about. Other residents sitting near them are paying no attention, due either to hearing issues, they've heard it all before, or they find it unimportant. But Katie notices one visitor a few tables away who's intensely eyeing Gavin, raising her suspicions. But then she fears she's becoming paranoid, like Gavin, and hopes that isn't a precursor to "vicarious PTSD."

At this moment Gavin isn't focused on keeping track of all the generations and names Grandpa is rattling off. He's intent on figuring out how to make his next move, and hoping Grandpa will have enough energy and patience left to talk about the most important questions. "So what's the significance of the second date on the plaque—1765," he asks, trying to move Grandpa along to the end of his story.

"Well, multiple generations of Hutchinsons lived in that mansion," Grandpa goes on, apparently in no mood to be rushed. "They all had a lot of money, and this *second* Thomas ended up being the *Governor* of Massachusetts. But when England started taxing and cheating the people—*colonists* they were, because England considered this land their *colony*—Governor Thomas Hutchinson thought it was his duty to support England, even though he'd disagreed with such high taxes, and, well, the people finally started to riot. And in August of 1765 they broke into Hutchinson's mansion while his family was having dinner, chased them all out, and ransacked and destroyed everything in the mansion!"

"Ah-ha!" Gavin declares.

By this time, Maggie's eyelids are drooping, fighting sleep as her head lays on Grandpa's arm.

"Yes," he nods and strokes Maggie's cheek, clearly not ready to move on. "So that big old mansion sat there, empty, through the war with England and for years after. When poor people started coming in from all over—Russia, Poland, Ireland—some of them just took over abandoned places, breaking up those big houses into smaller ones—like mine had been part of Hutchinson's—to fit all those families into the neighborhood. Then in the late 1800s and early 1900s, people from Italy started coming in. Like some of your ancestors from Sicily and Campania. A lot of those guys brought their business from Italy with them, the kind of business no one—especially not your brother—should ever get involved with..."

The implication of Grandpa's final comment hangs in the

air like a bad smell. It may have been exactly what he intended, and *he* was playing Gavin instead of the reverse.

"That's why you're here, isn't it?" Grandpa says, his voice low. "I suppose you got other questions, right?"

Now Gavin realizes that the old man is in this facility solely for physical issues. There is nothing cognitively deficient about him.

Katie reaches over to pick up Maggie before she falls over asleep. She holds Mags on her lap and eyes Gavin, watching for signs of trigger reactions.

Grandpa calls out to an attendant. "Giovanni, I'm gettin' a little tired. Would ya wheel me down to my room so I can finish up with my family before they hafta leave?" Then he turns to Katie with a smile. "You got a smart little girl there, Mama. Hope she can hold out a little longer while I get all your husband's questions. You an artist?" he asks, nodding toward her hands. "So was my wife, God rest her soul."

Katie looks down and notices the paint she missed under her nails and on two fingers. Her cheeks flush red. "Well," she hesitates. Then she stands tall. "Yes, I am," she smiles.

Giovanni wheels Grandpa down the featureless hall, with Gavin beside them. That doesn't leave much more room in the corridor, because Giovanni is very wide. So Katie walks behind them, which satisfies her current need for distance. Maggie slumbers in her arms.

Partway down the hall, Grandpa points to an open door on his left. "There's your old friend Frank Rizzo," he says.

Gavin perks up. "Oh, really? Maybe I can stop in and see him on our way out." He's intrigued and perhaps a bit worried over how Grandpa knows about his relationship with Rizzo, who had been a powerful mob capo.

Grandpa shakes his head. "You ain't gonna get much response from him," he says low and sideways, with a warning look that speaks volumes. "There's a couple more like him in these rooms. Vince Lombardi, for one."

Katie discerns Grandpa's meaning. She can see from Gavin's sudden stiffening that he gets it too. And now she sees his chest expand and contract in a slow rhythm, as he takes in, then exhales, deep breaths.

When the group gets into Grandpa's room, Giovanni says someone will be back later to help him get settled, then leaves. Grandpa motions for Katie and Gavin to sit in the only two chairs in the room, which is as nondescript and depressing as a hospital room. Grandpa turns to Gavin, cracking a self-satisfied smile and says, "Hope you liked that headstone I ordered for Tony and your ma. He was crazy over her."

Gavin sputters in surprise, "Oh! Yes, yes, sir! That was very thoughtful of you."

Now the old man flicks his hand impatiently in Gavin's direction and says, "Okay, whaddaya wanna know? I ain't got all day." The somewhat proper speech of his Hutchinson dissertation now slides into street talk. He lowers his voice to a raspy near-whisper. "You should close the door, kid."

Gavin does as he's told, and re-thinks his plan. He doesn't know if his grandfather can be trusted. Grandpa might be tied to the mob, or at least fearful of them, so he needs to be very careful in the way he proceeds now. He has suspected that some of those names in the notebook—or their families—might be behind the SUVs following him, so he wants to get Grandpa's reaction to some of the names. Indirectly, through casual conversation. Naïve, innocent chat. Although Gavin wonders whether Grandpa is too smart to be naïve. Who's outfoxing whom?

Gavin proceeds carefully. "Thanks for that fascinating history of your building, Grandpa," he begins. "But the lawyers want me to demolish or sell it after the fire damage, so I'm checking it out now—"

"Hold up right there." Grandpa puts up his hand up like a traffic cop. "Don't even waste your time checking it out. And don't demolish it. It'll go down hard 'cause it's built like

Gibraltar and there's only cosmetic damage anyway. If anyone says it's unsafe, they're bull-shittin' you. If you're smarter than your twin, you'll just sell it. Business properties in that area are in high demand. Sell it and move on, put it all behind you."

Gavin takes that as the lead-in to his questions. "So why would they do that? Why say it's unsafe, and should be demolished? Even the City building inspector said the same thing."

"How should I know?" Grandpa shrugs. "Over-cautious or just stupid."

"Well, there's someone—I don't know who—that's been following me. I don't think it's my imagination. I have no idea why anyone would do that. Maybe someone wants me to put the building on the market and get out of town?"

Grandpa scoffs with an eye-roll. "Well, that wouldn't be such a bad idea, y'know."

"But I'd really like to know who's been following me. It feels threatening."

"Well, just get that business over with and go back to your restaurant in Kauai."

Gavin pulls back, almost imperceptibly. He doesn't recall ever telling Grandpa where he lives or that he has a restaurant there.

"Or wherever it is," Grandpa quickly adds.

"Yes, you're right, Grandpa. We need to get back home to our business," Gavin says, resuming his cat-and-mouse charade. "I'm so impressed by how much you know about the history of the North End—you should write a book!"

Grandpa releases a genuine laugh. "Okay, kid, I'll dictate it and you can write it."

"That would be awesome. I know so little about the North End, even though Dad grew up here. I'm pretty naïve about the culture here." Now Gavin escalates the intensity of this kabuki dance. "I've heard there are some dangerous people around here. Should I be worried about that?"

Grandpa stiffens. "Nah. The City cleaned up all that shit years ago."

"I've heard about the old organized crime stuff." Gavin leans forward toward Grandpa. "Was that stuff going on when you first opened your liquor store?"

Grandpa fidgets and looks toward the closed door. "A little. But I didn't want to have anything to do with it."

"Yeah, that's what Dad told me. That's really smart," Gavin nods. "But you probably know all about it anyway, like you know all about the history of your building. I bet you have some amazing stories! I've read about some guys back then with weird nicknames," he chuckles and goes on, "Even better than that *Godfather* movie—'Cue Ball,' 'Cheeseman'—you just can't make that stuff up," he laughs, slapping his thigh.

Grandpa's mouth puckers a constipated smile. "Yeah. Real funny."

"Did you know any of those guys? They must have been real characters."

"Some real oddballs," Grandpa murmurs. As if he's wondering how he can divert Gavin from where he seems to be headed.

"And everyone's heard about Whitey Bulger of course—I love a good mystery!" Gavin jiggles like an excited kid. "Did he really win that lottery ticket, or did he take it from the guy who did?"

"Well, Linskey dropped out after that, so he musta took the money and left town. Nobody seen him since. Probably livin' in luxury on some island." Grandpa's mouth twitches.

"Did he have any family that know where he is?"

"Uh, a brother, I think. But even he might not know."

"But Bulger disappeared too, didn't he? Maybe he took the ticket and cashed it?"

"Nah, he didn't drop out 'til three years after the lottery. He probably doesn't have as much money as people think he does. That's what they call an urban legend."

"Sounds like there's a lot of that here," Gavin laughs, pleased that Grandpa lobbed an easy setup for him. "Like, I've read about other guys doing that, dropping out and no one knows where they are. Maybe they wanted to get out of the 'business,' as you called it? You probably know some of them—or their family, like Jimmy Squillante, Anthony Strollo..."

"Nah, it's been so long," Grandpa sputters. "My memory ain't as good as it used to be. I mighta heard those names before, back in the day. But I have no idea where they are now, or their families."

Grandpa's "poker face" is unwavering, but other parts of his body are beginning to crack. His gaze pierces through and beyond Gavin while his leg twitches.

Gavin rushes in for the score: "Or Salvatore Annunziato, Joe Salvatti..."

Katie's eyes flit toward Gavin upon hearing the last name. She pulls Maggie closer.

If Grandpa were able to stand and walk away, he probably would. Instead, his annoyance—or perhaps fear—broadcasts in his voice. "I don't know any of those guys, so I can't tell you nothin' 'cept what everyone else knows. Like Salvatti—I think I heard a few years ago he just dropped outta sight, who the hell knows where he is now." He slams his palms on the arms of his wheelchair and pronounces, "That's it, kids. Enough. I told you everything I know, which ain't much."

"Well, thank you, sir," Katie says and stands, sensing the old man's escalating tension—either impatience, or anger. "Would you like us to wheel you to the common room, or the dining area?"

"Nah," Grandpa mutters, touching the device hanging on a lanyard around his neck. "I'll just call for someone to get me settled here. I *am* tired, y'know." He looks up at Katie and whispers, "But you can come back with your *bambina* any time. And maybe one of your paintings to perk up this barren little hole." He reaches for her hand.

She squeezes his hand and smiles just as Maggie begins to stir in her arms. "It would be my pleasure, sir."

Then as Gavin heads toward the door, Grandpa stops him with an intense gaze. "Be careful. Some things are best left buried."

> "Life can only be understood backwards;
> but it must be lived forwards."
> —Søren Kierkegaard

29

GAVIN SITS FROZEN IN THE NURSING HOME PARKING lot, gripping the steering wheel. No one has spoken a word since they left Grandpa. He hasn't started up the car yet. He just sits now, staring without seeing, his face pointed toward the odometer with his eyes unfocused, to another universe.

Katie is in the front passenger seat with her arm reaching into the back, touching Maggie's leg in her car seat. She eyes Gavin and hopes Mags won't awaken. This isn't a good moment.

Finally Gavin moves. He reaches into his pocket to pull out his paper and pen. Next to Michael Linskey and Joe Salvatti's names, he writes "*missing*." He starts up the car and turns onto Fulton Street.

"You okay, Gav?" Katie asks softly.

"Grandpa didn't tell us even half of what he knows," Gavin grumbles, bitterness curdling his words. "But his body language and silence told us a whole lot more."

"Um-hmm," Katie nods. "Which suggests there's a reason he didn't divulge anything."

"Maybe you and Maggie can do a re-match with him and find out more," Gavin says. "You and Mags really softened him up. That's why I wanted you there today." He merges into heavy traffic on I-93.

"I don't trust him, Gavin." Katie pulls her arm back to the front and speaks softly. "We need to consider why he didn't tell us much of anything. Was it for our sake, or his?"

Gavin's face is tight and grim. "Who the fuck knows?"

"But Tray found out who owns that SUV that's been following you," Katie says. "Someone named Michael Salvatti."

Gavin's eyes instantly pivot to her, then quickly back to traffic. "How did you know about that?" he snaps.

Katie doesn't respond immediately. She takes a breath then forces a placid tone. "When Maggie and I were in the car outside your parents' house yesterday, waiting for you to lock up, I noticed a black SUV sitting across the street." She watches as Gavin clenches his jaw and tightens his grip on the steering wheel. "And then when I walked Patches and Mags while you were making dinner last evening, I saw the same SUV sitting on our street. It seemed odd, so before alarming you, I texted Tray to check out the license number. He texted me right before we went in to see your grandfather."

"Well, Michael Salvatti might be related to either Joe, who disappeared, or Rick, who's been hassling me."

"Yes, Tray says he's Joe's son and Rick's brother. But that's who owns the SUV, not who was driving it or who else was in it."

"You should've told me about the SUV last night." He turns a scowl toward Katie, as if she has violated his sovereign territory.

"I didn't want to worry you if it wasn't anything to worry about."

"You should just let me deal with this shit." Anger and resentment punctuate his words.

"Yet you want my help," Katie utters a flat, calm statement. She doesn't want a confrontation, but she does need clarity on where Gavin has drawn his seemingly mutable line.

Gavin is silent, staring at the traffic ahead.

"We aren't competing, Gav. We're on the same side. Because it affects all of us."

"But I want to protect you and Maggie from all this." His tone is plaintive, anguished, like a child being deprived of his Superman costume.

Katie remembers what Pedersen explained, that Gavin's purpose—to save and take care of family—had been branded into him all his life. It is his identity, the justification for his existence. Failing his purpose threatens to expose the empty place within him. Understanding that saddens Katie, and also worries her, because life can't always be controlled. Gavin must define his own self-worth, minus any guilt for not being able to save everyone. Katie reminds herself now that she must do the same—define her own self-worth. In a way, that's exciting, but it also frightens her. Like exploring foreign domains where there may be land mines.

"The best way for us to be safe is to be fully aware of all the facts and dangers, Gav." Katie rubs two fingers on the furrow creasing her brow. "You're still thinking you're solely responsible for protecting everyone, but anyone who might be at risk has a share in that, so they need to be prepared—armed with the facts—to anticipate, avoid, and defend against it."

"All right, all right," Gavin shouts. "How about this 'fact'? Tray told me that the structural engineer I used, who didn't show up on the second day as he agreed to, is missing and presumed dead."

Katie's breath holds for a moment. Then she lowers her voice, "So are you thinking there may be some connection between his work for you and his disappearance?"

"Bingo." Gavin slams his foot on the gas pedal and zooms around the car in front of him. "Those names I asked Grandpa about—and almost twenty more—were all written in a notebook I found in a hidden storage closet in Prince Street. From what I could find online, about half of those names have been reported as missing and presumed dead, and the other half have been confirmed dead. And they're all in a notebook in what is now *my* building." He spits out his words like angry punches, as though he resents having to say them, enraged to be caught "holding the bag" in this morass of secrets and danger, thanks to his grandfather, father, and brother.

"Jesus." Katie catches her breath, fear clawing at the edge of her thoughts. "Thanks for sharing that. But maybe you should back away from it, leave it to someone else to investigate, like the police? It might be too dangerous, a threat to you. Or our family."

"Yeah, I'm going to talk to Tray about it. FBI might be interested in the notebook. A lot of those names were at one time connected to FBI's investigation into organized crime."

"That's a smart idea. Gav. And I'm going to keep Maggie very close to me at all times. Unfortunately, we'll have to tell her not to talk to strangers unless we're right there with her."

"Yeah. Sad, isn't it?"

"This also has got to be an extra challenge to your PTSD, which you do *not* need."

"No shit," Gavin says, exiting the Pike. "Double whammy. So, as soon as I drop you and Mags off at the house, I'm going over to that shrink's place. Her office is in her home over on Forest Street."

"She's the one Pedersen recommended?"

"Yeah, but it's just an initial meeting." Gavin shrugs off hope. "I think she needs to evaluate me, figure out whether I need to be in McLean or jail."

"You're doing it again, Gav. Belittling yourself," Katie chides with an eye-roll. "But you also need to evaluate *her*, see if she gets you, whether you like her style and her approach."

"Yeah, yeah." He screeches around a curve in the road. "I'll pick up some pizza for dinner on my way back."

"Oh, Maggie will love that."

Patches jumps and does an aerial somersault when Katie and Maggie come home. "Just a minute, Patches." Katie pats him and rubs his good ear. "I have to change Maggie's training pants and give her some juice before we go for a walk."

Maggie may have snoozed at Grandpa DiMasi's place, and on the ride home, but now *Katie* would love to have a nap. This day has gone from an energizing journey through her painting to excruciating tension in the last few hours—inside what felt like a morgue—digging into death and the threat of it. Continually on high alert, tiptoeing on eggshells, trying to avoid landmines, coping with implosions and eruptions. She feels like her life has become a mixed metaphor for madness. She is overcome with the visceral need to be held in someone's arms. Arms of comfort, safety, reassurance.

An image of that feeling forms in her mind, pulling her in. One she will try to create the next time she sees Destiny. Warmth and shelter in the midst of darkness and danger...

"All-l-l-l done!" Maggie declares, stretching on tiptoes to deposit her sippy cup in the kitchen sink.

Patches drags his leash to Katie and drops it at her feet with a little woof. "Okay, guys, I get the hint," she says. October afternoons in New England can be chilly, so she puts a sweater on Maggie and one on herself.

Fluorescent pink-bottomed white clouds suspend languidly against infinitely blue skies, as if angels had a pillow fight. The air is crisp and cool, like a cleansing breath. It is four o'clock in the afternoon and the sun is low in the sky, twinkling through bare deciduous branches and feathery evergreens. Fall in New England has always made Katie feel like secrets are whispering on the breeze while gypsies dance to music foretelling the future. Indian corn decorates many houses on the street, with pumpkins heralding the approach of Halloween.

Maggie trots and runs down the sidewalk, getting too far ahead for Katie's comfort.

"Slow down, Mags, I want to show you something!" Katie explains about the Indian corn hanging on a neighbor's door, then shows her the carved pumpkin sitting next to a neighbor's mailbox. "Does that look scary to you, Maggie?"

"Toos!" Maggie says, pointing to the pumpkin's teeth.

"Yes, that mouth has some sharp teeth, doesn't it, Mags?"

Maggie nods, her eyes wide.

"But it won't bite you, sweetie, it's just pretend. It's for a game called Halloween, when kids dress up in silly clothes and fancy costumes, then go to people's houses and get candy. Would you like to dress up in a costume next week on Halloween and get candy?"

Maggie claps her hands and sings "Yay!" while doing her little dance.

"Okay, we'll find you a costume, and Mommy and Daddy will take you to houses down our street next week during Halloween." Katie crouches down next to Maggie. "That will be fun, won't it?"

Maggie giggles and squeezes Katie's cheeks between her hands.

"But you will have to stay with us when we do that, Mags, and not run ahead. Okay?"

Maggie nods with a big smile. "O-kay, do-key!"

"And you must *never* go anywhere with anyone but Mommy or Daddy, or Grandma or our good friends, do you understand?"

Maggie protrudes her lower lip, looking confused.

"Do you see that pumpkin with the scary face, Mags?"

She nods, now a bit sober.

"That's just pretend, but there are some real people we don't know, who might be scary or bad. Because we don't know, we must be careful. So stay with Mommy and Daddy or people we know, not just on Halloween, but other times too. Okay?"

Maggie wraps her arms around Katie's neck. "O-kay."

Just then Luca comes out of his house and waves to them. "Will you come to my house next week to get candy, little Maggie?"

Maggie becomes very serious and takes Katie's hand. "Yes."

"You can talk to Luca, sweetie," Katie whispers.

Maggie brightens and claps her hands. "How-ween!"

Katie turns to him. "How have you been, Luca?"

"Good, good. My knee bothered me earlier during the rain, so I'm glad for the dry weather now." He pulls out his big pocketknife to cut one remaining yellow chrysanthemum and hands it to Maggie. "For the pretty little *bambina*."

Maggie is fascinated with Luca's knife, and reaches out for it.

"Oh no, Mags," Katie intervenes. "Luca's knife could cut you."

"I always keep it handy," Luca says. "By the way, have you noticed a big black car with dark windows here? It doesn't belong to anyone on this street, and it just sits across from your house for a long time. The windows in the front aren't so dark, so I can see two guys sitting there. And then they leave."

Katie tenses. "Are you talking about a black SUV?"

"I guess that's what it's called." Luca puts his knife back in his pocket. "It's not a regular car. They used to call them station wagons."

Katie doesn't want to alarm him, or Maggie. "Well, if you think it seems suspicious, maybe you could write down its license plate number for me?"

"I can do that," Luca nods. "I have good eyesight, but my hearing isn't that good. And then my knee..."

"I really appreciate it, Luca!" Katie smiles and touches his hand. "Well, we need to get going, don't we, Maggie?"

When they get to their house, Katie points to their house number. "Do you remember what number that is, Maggie?"

"Seb-un!" Mags cheers.

"Good job! Do you know the name of our street?"

Maggie lights up. "Ses-mee!"

Katie laughs. "*Sesame Street* is what you watch on television, sweetie. The street where we *live* is this street," she points up and down the blacktop. "Marshall Street. Can you say 'Marshall Street'?" Katie puts her face in front of Maggie's and exaggerates her mouth movement, separating the syllables.

Maggie concentrates, toying her lips. Then she finally attempts, "Ma...sul Steet."

"Very good, Mags! We live at seven," she points to the number, then clearly enunciates, "Mar-shall Street." Katie hugs her little girl, then takes her hand. "Let's dance to that, okay?" And in a drumbeat dance, they mount the stairs together, chanting, "Sev-en Mar-shall Street" all the way into their house, finishing with a grand flourish.

"Would you like to look at pictures with me now, Maggie?" Katie asks. "I'll get some carrot sticks for you and we can go upstairs."

"Yay!" Maggie claps.

As they sit poring over boxes of pictures from Katie's childhood, she explains to Maggie who's in each picture and tells stories about them. The same way her father used to hold her on his lap and tell her stories about his childhood in England, which makes her feel that aching emptiness again, that need to be held, to be sheltered. She pulls out her phone and looks up the number for the leader of the PTSD spouse group she met with that morning.

"Doctor Ted? Hi, it's Katie. The new member of your group from this morning."

> "One of the most courageous decisions you'll ever make is to finally let go of what is hurting your heart and soul."
> —*Brigitte Nicole*

30

GAVIN DRIVES UP FOREST STREET LOOKING FOR THE doctor's house number. This tree-lined two-lane street is more like a road, heavily traveled with cars going to and from Babson College, Wellesley Country Club, the town of Needham, and I-95. Although there's a solid double yellow line in the middle, cars frequently disregard its no-passing designation.

He sees the number and pulls left into the house's driveway. It's about the same vintage as his parents' house—a stately two-story colonial with a slate roof, attic dormers, and a circular driveway, set far back from the street and surrounded by mature trees. There's an entrance to a one-story wing on the right side of the house, where he was directed to go for his appointment.

If anyone were to ask him to describe what he's feeling now, he wouldn't be able to find the words. Fear, dread, resentment—all that and more doing battle within the confusion inside him. More than anything, he just wants to run.

Just then, a teenage boy comes out of the garage on the left side of the house. The garage door closes behind him as he begins dribbling a basketball and shooting hoops. As Gavin watches him, a calmness creeps over him. The regular beats of the dribbling ball, the swish through the basket, the reverberating bounce against the backboard. His breaths rise and fall in steady rhythm.

Gavin walks to the intricately carved hardwood door. It opens on his first knock.

"You must be Gavin," a gray-haired woman greets him and gestures for him to enter. She moves like someone with too much energy to contain in one slender body.

"And I'm Dr. Eva Skokou. Please sit," she points him to a black leather armchair.

Gavin sits and looks at the woman inquisitively.

"You're trying to place my accent," she smiles, as she sits erect in a straight-backed wood chair opposite him. "I'm from Greece. You may not know that although Dr. Herman was the researcher at Harvard who first identified the unique condition of Complex PTSD, most of the early practitioners treating it were European."

"Oh, Dr. Pedersen didn't tell me that—thanks." Gavin begins to relax somewhat. The chair is comfortable, the leather soft and broken in, the sort of chair that invites sinking into it. Muted lighting complements the smell of polished wood and old Persian carpets.

"Well, I'm so glad you could come, Gavin. Would it be all right with you if we use this first meeting to get to know each other?"

"Uh, sure," Gavin mumbles, tensing again. Dr. Skokou's intention to "get to know" him has caused him to throw up his protective wall.

"So how are you feeling today?"

Gavin chuckles, looks down at his hands and shakes his head.

The doctor smiles, "You find that question amusing?"

"Well, I was just thinking, before I came in, that you'd probably ask me that to start out, and I wouldn't be able to come up with an answer. Like, I have no idea how I feel. No words to describe it."

"So I guess I'm somewhat predictable, eh?" she chuckles. "Is that indescribable feeling true for your entire day?"

"Oh hell, no. Just when I was anticipating coming in here."

"So your entire day today was different? Could you describe your feelings during the day?"

"Uh, sure." Gavin takes a deep breath, thinking. "Mixed."

"That's it? Your description of how you feel, or felt, today?"

"It's been a long day."

"And what are the ingredients of that mixture?"

Gavin sighs a long exhale. Something in him wants to throw it all at her, like a slap, an assault, all the tormented emotions his roller-coaster day has taken him through. It's even too much for him to begin enumerating everything he's felt today. Fear, anger, pain, distrust, detachment, withdrawal, guilt, shame, self-loathing... "How long do we have?" Gavin finally speaks, in his defensive language of sarcasm. "Like I said, it's been a long day."

"A lot to unpack?"

"Yeah." He's thinking this is just another cat-and-mouse charade. He needs to find a way out of it. "But what can be gained by that unpacking?" His defenses verge on offense.

"Each event of your day may have triggered a plethora of stressful, painful, or dangerous feelings, each of which needs to be unpacked in order for you to understand *why* they have such control over you and your reactions." She looks at Gavin, checking to see if he's still tuned in.

He blinks.

She resumes, "The ultimate goal is for you to manage those feelings and control your reactions. Initially that unpacking—peeling away layers—may expose and dredge up old feelings you'd rather keep buried. But when they're buried, they're dangerous! They exercise remote control over you and your reactions. Like the unseen guy behind the curtain, pulling your strings."

"So how do you deal with my reactions *during* that 'unpacking' process?" Gavin sneers, his voice and everything about him challenging, poised to strike.

Skokou pulls back, softening her posture and voice. "In a 'safe environment,'" she air-quotes, "with professional support, we will gradually un-bury, confront and neutralize the origins, the root causes, of those feelings. We'll not only disarm and disempower what has been triggering, taunting and torturing you. We'll debunk the untruths that drive them, the falsehoods you were fed in childhood, thereby de-sensitizing you to their effects on your reactions."

"It all sounds abstract at this point." Gavin feels overwhelmed.

"It sort of does, until we roll up our sleeves and actually do the work," Skokou smiles. "As we dissect and understand the events and conditions of those origins, we unmask their fallacy—sort of de-fang them. Those fallacies are usually based in the distorted manipulative untruths of an abusive childhood, which deformed your concept of who you are."

Gavin pulls back, concerned, like he just realized something. In a near-whisper, he says, "Wait a minute. I don't know what I'll be left with if you dismantle everything I grew up believing, everything I thought I was. What I am."

"When we expose, and you reject, the manipulative untruths on which your beliefs have been built, then you can rebuild on truth. Your true self, your real self, your essential identity."

"I don't know what that means. Or who my real self is."

"Complex PTSD is the result of continuous abuse or neglect that occurs during childhood, when your brain is in the process of developing." Dr. Skokou locks her eyes with Gavin's. "So you may be missing, or have some flawed, pieces in the way your brain interprets and understands the world, and yourself. By challenging old assumptions, revisiting and re-understanding the world, you will establish a firm foundation of truth on which to rebuild what's missing, and in the process develop your own healthy selfhood."

"Sounds like a fantasy. Complicated, risky and uncertain."

"Gavin," Dr. Skokou leans toward him and gazes intensely into his eyes. "You're here because you're having problems that are out of your control, problems that need to be fixed in order for you to be back in control of your life. Your success will depend, first of all, on accepting that fact. Secondly on your willingness to do the work required to fix it, and finally on your willingness to trust the process, and trust an experienced professional like me to help you with that work."

Gavin is rigid and silent. His eyes stare through and beyond the doctor.

She resumes, "I can see all of that frightens you." She leans toward him and gazes intensely into his eyes. "Whenever you feel unsafe, Gavin, in any situation—here or elsewhere—focus your thoughts on connecting to the good of the here and now. People who love you. The natural world around you. Not the memories, the illusions, or even the real threat in front of you. Connecting to what's good will empower you to overcome whatever is threatening you in the moment."

Gavin shakes his head, grim. "Trust—even toward people I know and love, like Katie—has become really hard. I often shoot myself in the foot with my distrust."

"Distrust is one of the most self-defeating symptoms of Complex PTSD," Skokou nods with grim regret. "Even under normal circumstances it can be scary to expose your vulnerability, secrets, and wounds. But the paranoia and distrust of C-PTSD can make you resist the help that Katie and professionals are offering in order to help you deal with those secrets and wounds—which constitute the root cause of what you're struggling with. If that stuff isn't addressed and resolved, nothing can be fixed."

Gavin feels completely exposed. The doctor sees him. There's no cat-and-mouse game in any of this. He thinks of all the twisted family history he's trying to unearth in the Prince Street building—"un-bury," in the doctor's term—and how it's dredging up the overwhelming feelings that are almost destroying him. And he thinks of his family. The stress his PTSD is imposing on Katie and Maggie. And Patches! Brave resilient Patches. He wishes he could be like that fierce little dog, brave enough to face and overcome the past.

"But if it took a whole lifetime to fuck me up, how long will it take to 'rebuild'?"

"It's not an overnight miracle, but if you can trust, and commit unreservedly to the work, it isn't a lifelong project either."

"If I can trust, if I do the work, right?" *If, if, depends, blah, blah.* "Well, your *theory* sounds good, but..." Gavin mumbles.

"I invite you to work with me to test that theory, Gavin. We can go at whatever pace you can handle. Are you willing to commit to it? Trust the process, trust me?"

"Uh, yeah, I guess... Yes. I promised Katie I'd do it."

"Like AA, I can tell you that you will only stick with this program if you value yourself enough to want to do it for yourself. Because *you* want to be whole."

"Maybe I'll start valuing myself if I can make some progress on this 'work.'"

"Then we need to begin. This may help," Skokou says, handing him a plain brown journal. "I want you to record whenever you're triggered by anything, even at night, in your dreams or nightmares. What went before, what your reaction was, how you felt. That will help us understand what triggers you, how it relates to your past, and work to desensitize your reactions."

Gavin looks down at the journal. It's similar to some of the ones his mother had written in. He reminds himself that he wants to read more of what she wrote. Maybe it will help him understand.

"Gavin, you love your wife, and care about her and your little girl, right?"

"Yes, of course! Why would you ask that?"

"Because your condition is undoubtedly affecting both of

them. Marriages often can't survive one partner having Complex PTSD, particularly if it's untreated. It's so hard on the spouse who's trying to help, support, and survive their partner's behavior."

"Katie and Maggie mean everything to me." Gavin's head droops mournfully, as if he's already lost them. "And we're having another baby, too."

"Then let's get to work. Will you trust enough to meet again?" Dr. Skokou prods.

Gavin vaults out of the chair and almost runs out the door. "I'll see you Monday at four o'clock," he barks over his shoulder.

When he gets in his car, he sits for a minute, catching his breath. The teenager is still shooting hoops. *Focus on connecting to what's good. That kid's dogged practicing brings up good memories. I think I can do this. I hope.*

Before he drives off to get pizza, he calls Tray to set the hook.

"Hey man," Tray picks up. "I was just thinking about you. Get my text about Solomon?"

"Yeah, and I have something else you might want."

"Yeah? Spill."

"I found a long list of names and dates in a notebook, and a bag of watches, jewelry, and IDs belonging to some of those names, in a hidden place in Prince Street. Guess some of the names?"

"Probably some old mobsters, I bet."

"Yep. Going back as far as the fifties, and I looked them up. From what I could find online, a lot of them had been declared missing or presumed dead."

"You're shittin' me."

"Nope. And I also found more than three million dollars in a wall, with a lottery ticket from Whitey Bulger's liquor store in Southie."

"Holy shit, man!"

"You think FBI might be interested in any of that?"

"Damn straight. Hold tight—I'm in New York now, but I'll run it up the ladder and get back to you."

"I figured there had to be a way to get you back here in Boston."

A wide smug grin broadens Gavin's face as he puts his car in gear and turns right onto Forest Street. The idea of having Tray with him, and closing in on the mysteries in Prince Street, make him almost giddy.

And then he sees the SUV. Again. Sitting over on the right side of the road just beyond the doctor's driveway. An animal rage overcomes him, voiding logic, safety, and reality. Fury burns and boils within him, shaking him uncontrollably, as he pounds his fists on the steering wheel, dashboard, and the inside of his car door. He imagines himself running up and beating on their front windows to see who's inside, or gunning his car into them. He slams his foot on the gas pedal and his car accelerates, fishtailing, just as the SUV does the same. Gavin's car has a micro-second head start and nearly crashes into the SUV's tail, but he manages to pull abreast of it to look into their driver-side window. He sees two guys inside just before the SUV shifts gears and pulls ahead.

As he speeds along on the left side of the road, an oncoming car comes toward him, veering defensively onto the shoulder as Gavin swerves back to the right, grazing the back bumper of the fleeing SUV. He loses control and goes off the road, crashing head-first into a tree.

The image of the two guys in the SUV imprint on his memory. It's the first thing he recalls when basketball boy pulls him out of his car.

> "When there is no enemy within,
> the enemies outside cannot hurt you."
> —*African Proverb*

31

WHEN GAVIN GRADUALLY OPENS HIS EYES, WHAT he sees is a nightmarish blur, initially popping him up into fight mode, accompanied by the IV feeds and monitors attached to him. Several people surround him now, and two men rush forward to restrain him. It takes a few minutes for him to recover his orientation to reality and realize who they are.

"If this is some kind of party," Gavin mumbles through a swollen lip and broken nose, "I want to know where the Mai Tais are."

Witnesses—including Dr. Skokou's basketball-playing teenager and the driver Gavin swerved to avoid—had described to police Gavin's reckless driving, as well as his belligerent behavior and incoherent rant when he was pulled from his car. So extreme that the paramedics had to restrain him on the gurney in the ambulance.

Now, despite her growing concern that this accident might signal a worsening of her husband's C-PTSD, Katie forces a weak smile and comes near to touch him. "You're okay now, Gav. But the tree? Not so much."

The image of the two guys in the SUV flashes in Gavin's memory. He's certain one of them is Rick Salvatti, and he knows he could identify the other in a lineup. He needs to tell Tray! Now he looks around him and realizes he's in a hospital room. "So why am I here?" he asks. He assesses the crowd. Pedersen, Grandpa O'Malley, Katie, Dr. Skokou, and a guy in a white coat—must be a doctor or resident.

That doctor speaks up now. "Gavin, I'm Dr. Chapman from ER. Although you weren't wearing your seat belt, your airbag prevented you from going through the windshield head-first. We took an MRI, which revealed no internal damage to the brain or cervical spine. We manipulated your nose back into alignment," he smiled, "so it'll heal—and we're just keeping you here overnight for observation."

Gavin becomes agitated and pulls at his attachments. "I have to get out of here! I have to talk to Tray!"

Katie lays her hand on his, where his IV is inserted. "Tray is on his way from New York, Gav. He'll be here in the morning when we bring you home."

"Where's Maggie?" Gavin is still frantic, in panic mode.

"She's with Grandma O'Malley, Gav. Just breathe."

"What's all this?" Gavin says, pointing at the wires and tubes attached to him, as memories of his twin's car accident eleven years ago taunt him. When Devon had been in this same hospital.

"Monitors collecting data on your heart, blood pressure, oxygenation and other bodily functions," Dr. Chapman says. "And an IV feeding saline, anti-inflammatory and pain medication, and—"

"And that Mai Tai!" Pedersen laughs, interrupting before Chapman can mention the anti-anxiety meds being fed through the IV. That knowledge could trigger Gavin's defensiveness, his feelings of shame and guilt.

Katie adds, "They'll give you some delicious hospital food soon," she says, attempting to further distract and calm him, "and we'll have that pizza tomorrow evening. Maggie can't wait!"

Dr. Chapman holds up his hand. "I believe the patient needs to rest now. Visiting hours aren't over yet, but it would be best for Gavin if you all say your goodbyes so he can be fully rested to go home in the morning."

Gavin's visitors have been informed of the circumstances of his accident, so now the room virtually sighs in palpable relief. Pedersen, Grandpa and Dr. Skokou each touch Gavin's shoulder and give him their good wishes, then embrace Katie with hugs and encouragement. Dr. Skokou takes her hand and whispers, "We're all here to support you, Katie, and to help Gavin. Call me if you need anything."

Katie feels like she's drowning in all the conflicting emotions assaulting her now like a blast of sewer gas. Love for Gavin. Relief that he's okay, didn't kill anyone, and he's in this room tonight, giving her a brief respite from worry. Fear of the future and its impact on her and their children. Resentment and anger that his condition and his needs are superseding her own selfhood and well-being for the foreseeable future. Grief over the loss of their dreams as a couple, as well as her own dreams. Both physical and psychological exhaustion from dealing with it all. Defeat from its apparent hopelessness. Determination to save her family...and herself.

Altogether, Hieronymus Bosch, Edvard Munch, Jackson Pollock, Van Gogh and Picasso couldn't create an image that accurately depicts the tormented nightmare of her life.

But she stifles all that, like holding back a volcanic eruption, and steels herself for the job, her duty. Amid the uncertainty that lies ahead, she knows she must set aside her own newly unearthed passions and do whatever it takes to protect her child. She leans over and kisses Gavin's forehead. "Goodnight, Gav. See you in the morning." She turns to go.

"I'm sorry I've gotten you into all this, babe." Gavin leans back against the raised head of the hospital bed with his eyes closed. "I know you didn't ask for this, and you don't deserve it." If his face weren't so swollen, an expression of his own bitter sadness would be obvious. A gurgled sob chokes inside him.

Katie turns around before exiting. A mournful grief overwhelms her, as if something has died, which vies with her desperate desire to help, fix, and save her husband and the love they've shared. But she restrains herself from giving in to her urge to rush in and act on those desires. It takes all she has to resist, but she understands the stakes. She knows she can't fix him; only he can do that, with hard work over time.

"I know you're sorry, Gav, and that all this is not your intention. In some ways, but not all, it's out of your control." She crosses her arms, holding herself back. "But you can't allow your disorder to confirm your guilt, your shame, or feelings of worthlessness. That would feed on itself, making you feel like you're helpless to do anything about it. You're strong enough to help everyone else, so now commit to helping yourself. *Work* with Dr. Skokou and Dr. Pedersen. Do the hard work, and don't give up. Because if you give up, you're giving up on us. On me, on Maggie, on yourself, and on our marriage."

With that, Katie leaves. And Gavin weeps.

During the ten-minute drive home from Newton-Wellesley hospital, Katie explains to Grandpa the different types of reactions to triggers for someone with PTSD. Freeze, flight, fight, or fawn, depending on the trigger and what memories and feelings the victim experiences.

"So Gavin reacted in fight mode to seeing that SUV again?" Grandpa asks as he pulls into the driveway of Katie's mother's house, where Grandma is taking care of Maggie. "Before we go in, let me ask you what you're going to do, to protect yourself and Maggie?"

Katie's resolve deflates with that question. "That's my big dilemma, Grandpa. I've been dealing with Gavin's disorder now for several months. It's taking a real toll on me, and I can see it impacting Maggie too." She pauses to look out the window. For the SUV, which isn't there.

"You can't let that happen, Katie," Grandpa says with a fierce urgency, laying his hand on her shoulder.

Katie pulls a tissue from her bag to wipe her eyes, then goes on. "Research shows that spouses of people with PTSD, and especially with C-PTSD, develop mental health conditions themselves while trying to deal with their spouse's disorder. And a lot of marriages don't survive the ordeal. I've begun going to a group for PTSD spouses that Jim recommended. I don't know how long it will take for Gavin to beat this thing, or how long I will be able to deal with it, either."

"Well, you can't make the same mistake our daughter made. Gavin's mother," Grandpa pleads. "She hung in there, stuck by her husband. She loved him and tried to save their marriage. But it caused damage to her sons, and she paid for it too, with her life."

"I don't intend to, Grandpa." As Katie says this, she feels imbued with an intense resolve within her.

"Always know that we will be there to help you in any way you need."

"Thank you, Grandpa."

"You haven't eaten, have you?" Grandpa smiles. "I think I smell pizza."

There's something that feels familiar to Katie as she sees Grandma and Grandpa playing with Maggie in what had been her mother's house. Something warm and...*normal*. She misses normal.

Grandma and Maggie have already eaten their share of pizza, so now Grandpa and Katie sit at the kitchen table to finish it off. But Katie just picks mushrooms off her pizza and eats them, leaving the rest. Maggie comes to stand beside her, picks up a slice of mushroom-less pizza and urges Mommy to eat. Katie takes a nibble then prompts Maggie, "Hey Mags, can you tell Grandma and Grandpa where we live?"

Maggie concentrates, chews on her lower lip, finally takes a deep breath and blurts, "Sebun Ma-shul Steet!" Then she beams proudly while Grandma and Grandpa cheer and clap for her.

"That is wonderful, Maggie," Grandma says. "Is it your bedtime now?"

"Weed," Maggie says, runs to get her favorite book, *Goodnight Moon,* and gives it to Grandma.

"Would you like me to read that to you, Maggie?" Grandma takes the little girl on her lap and reads, while Maggie keeps pace with Grandma's reading by putting her finger on each word and saying it. When Grandma kisses her great-grandchild and says good-night, she turns to Katie with a glowing smile.

"Thank you, Katie, for letting me do that. It means so much to me."

"Of course, Grandma. I'm so glad you could do it. It's a precious experience, isn't it?" Katie thinks of how her father used to read to her when she was a little girl, and doubles her determination to protect her daughter, while hoping it won't come to sacrificing her marriage.

After the grandparents leave, although Katie is glad to be away from the tension Gavin brings with him, she doesn't want to be alone. She calls Destiny.

"Destiny, thank you so much for allowing me to paint in your studio this morning."

"The honor is mine, my dear. You have remarkable innate talent, which I believe you are only beginning to realize. And I can see that you are dealing with tragic, dangerous circumstances."

Katie's breath catches. Dangerous? How could this woman, whom she saw today for the first time in almost nine years, see all that in her? During Katie's first year in Wellesley College, there had been an impression among her classmates that Destiny had some sort of unique instinct. Some classmates were intrigued by that, but others were skeptical and joked that she must be a witch. But Katie always simply took Destiny for what she is. Warm, kind, caring and insightful. Katie believes she can trust her with anything.

"Are you coming to the studio tomorrow?" Destiny asks.

"I wish I could. My husband had a car accident. He's okay, but they've kept him in the hospital overnight for observation and I need to bring him home tomorrow morning."

"You're dreading that, Katie. Why?"

Again, Katie marvels that Destiny can see inside her, even over the phone. Maybe she is a witch. A good one. "Gavin suffers with Complex PTSD."

"And you suffer trying to cope with his unpredictable highs and lows, my dear."

"Yes."

"Katie, I will bring paint, brushes and canvases to your home early tomorrow morning before you leave. You need to *express* the turmoil within you, to retrieve your essence." Destiny pauses and takes a deep breath. "And the next time you come to Pendleton, I'd like to hear all about your successful gallery in Hawaii. I could use your help—I know nothing about business. Now you need to go to bed and sleep. Have cleansing dreams."

After Destiny hangs up, Katie feels like she's been sprinkled with magic dust from a fly-by angel and kissed by a shaman.

Later, as she lay in bed reading old letters her father had sent her mother, her phone rings.

"Hey, 'Katie-did,'" Tray's deep voice greets her with his old nickname for her.

"Tray!" Katie squeals. "It's so good to hear your voice. How are you? And how's Hannah?"

"I'm good," Tray says, answering only one of Katie's questions. "When I got your message, no way I'm gonna let you down, girl. Had a hard time getting a flight, but I'm here now. What time are they discharging my man tomorrow?"

"Ten o'clock, but you know that process is always drawn out."

"I'll be there at ten, girl—oh, you need a ride?"

"Grandpa O'Malley is driving me, thanks."

"How's our boy doing?"

"Up and down. He saw that SUV again, waiting for him outside his doctor's office, and it pushed his crazy button, full-on into fight mode. Tried to race his car to overtake the SUV, almost front-ended another car coming toward him, swerved and hit a tree."

"Shit. All this must be doin' a job on you."

"Um...yeah, it's hard."

"Well, it might get worse. He's messing with some bad dudes. They be messin' with him."

Katie groans. "Tray, there've been several unexplained break-ins. Gavin's house, Prince Street..."

"Shit," Tray groans. "I'll look into it. And you need to be careful. Keep the Magster close."

"Now you're really scaring me, Tray." Katie shudders and pulls in tight, remembering she needs to have security systems installed at the DiMasi house and Prince Street. Maybe here too. "So if I see that SUV again, should I call the police?"

"There's nothing they could be charged with if they're just sittin' there."

"But when they start doing something, it'd be too late to call the police."

"Right. I'll see tomorrow what our boy has found, and then I'll bring in FBI if it looks t'be what I think it is."

"Then you'll put me on speed dial to the FBI, right?"

"In the Tarot deck, the Fool is depicted as a young man about to step off a cliff into empty air. Most people assume that the Fool will fall. But a Fool doesn't know he's subject to the laws of gravity."
—Richard Kadrey

32

WHEN KATIE, GRANDPA AND TRAY ARRIVE AT GAVIN'S hospital room, there are two white-coated doctors outside his door conferring with Skokou and Pedersen. They are leaning in, speaking in a hushed manner, with serious expressions. Katie's imagination goes into high gear. Something is wrong. Is it physical or mental? His injury or PTSD? She steels herself for bad news and approaches the group. Each step she takes feels like lurching closer toward a dangerous precipice.

"Excuse me, I'm Katie DiMasi, Gavin's wife." She looks to the white coats, then turns to Pedersen. "Is there some sort of problem, Dr. Pedersen?"

"Good morning, Katie," Pedersen nods to her with as much warmth as his professional demeanor allows. "This is Dr. Adler, Chief of Psychiatry here. He's an old colleague of mine. You met Dr. Chapman last evening, and you know Dr. Skokou."

"And the reason for this confab?" Katie's worry is quickly becoming impatient.

Dr. Adler speaks up. "The nurse is taking Gavin's vitals and disconnecting his IV and monitors now, Mrs. DiMasi, so why don't we go down to the office and talk? It's just right down the hall."

Katie turns to Grandpa and Tray. "I have to go talk with the docs. If the nurse finishes, can you go in and keep Gavin company? Keep him chill, Tray."

The room is small and spare, probably not Adler's main office for seeing patients. There aren't enough chairs for the group. Katie stands, hoping the discussion will be quick. Pedersen insists she sit in the chair opposite Adler's desk, then Dr. Skokou insists he sit beside Katie, likely deferring to his age and cane, while she stands. It's all sort of awkward, and Katie's impatience edges toward annoyance.

Dr. Adler gets straight to the point. "We are concerned about your husband's well-being."

Katie mumbles an inaudible *"Join the club."*

Dr. Adler continues, "Gavin had a very...*disrupted* night. He seemed to go from one nightmare to the next, at times becoming emotional, other times belligerent. Is that a normal occurrence for him?"

Katie's annoyance escalates. She doesn't need to be told what she already knows, and just wants to get out of here. "He has nightmares frequently, and reacts accordingly. I guess I'm used to it." *Tell me something I don't know.*

Seeing Katie's agitation, Pedersen turns to her and asks quietly, "Are you okay, Katie?"

Katie shakes him off and turns to Adler. "What else can you tell me?"

"These episodes occurred despite the medication we gave him, and—"

Katie pops to attention. "What did you give him?"

"We administered a low drip of clonazepam—"

"What is that?"

"It's a safe, fast-acting medication to assuage anxiety."

"Well, as far as I know, Gavin has never had multiple nightmares all night long. Is there empirical research on the use of clonazepam for patients with Complex PTSD? And is it standard practice to get consent from the patient and the family before administering it?"

"Your husband was out of control when he arrived, Mrs. DiMasi, a potential danger to himself and to others." Adler leans his elbows on his desk and steeples his fingers. "In such cases, consent is not required. And yes, clonazepam's use with PTSD has been fully researched and approved."

"He was fairly calm when I saw him last evening."

"Not when he arrived—before his MRI. And not after you left..." The doctor pauses, eyeing Katie.

She wonders whether Gavin's obsession with saving others—in this case her, and his fixation on being "good," may have suppressed his unhinged behaviors while she was with him. Whether intended or not.

Dr. Adler looks to the other two doctors. "We—all of us," he circles his hand to include Pedersen and Skokou, "are recommending that your husband enter intensive residential care at McLean Hospital for a month, possibly more if he doesn't make progress."

"Have you discussed that with Gavin?" There's a sharp edge to Katie's voice.

Adler pulls back and clears his throat. "Yes, we have."

"And he vehemently objects, right?"

"Yes, and—"

"And how did he react?" Katie challenges. "Freeze, flight, fight...?"

"He tried to run out of the room. We had to restrain him." Adler looks down sheepishly, as if he now expects Katie's wrath.

"Which I'm sure flipped him to fight mode, right?"

"We were hoping you could convince him..."

Katie tries, unsuccessfully, to stifle a sarcastic laugh. "I *don't. Think*. That's a good idea." She turns to Pedersen, trying to control her anger. "Were you there when Dr. Adler made this *suggestion?*"

"No Katie, I wasn't," Pedersen almost whispers, his eyes downcast.

"I didn't think so. You and I know Gavin better than that."

Now she turns to Adler, "If you're convinced that McLean is the best thing for Gavin, you should have *first* consulted with the people who've known him for more than ten years. *If* we agreed, we might have been able to convince him without a huge blowback, but now you've set it off in the wrong direction. That bruise will have to heal first. Hospitalization may ultimately be necessary, but right now he's too raw. Your 'suggestion' obviously got him totally triggered. You have no idea what you've done." She grinds her teeth on the last sentence, stands up and turns to leave.

Pedersen and Skokou follow her. As Katie nears Gavin's room, she sees the door is open, with Tray and Gavin inside. She turns to Pedersen. "Jim, I'm sorry I lost my cool with Dr. Adler, but—"

"Don't apologize, Katie—"

Dr. Skokou breaks in, "Yes, Katie. It takes working with a patient a lot longer than a few minutes to know what's right for him, and how to present options."

"Well, I put Gavin on notice last evening that unless he works seriously and consistently with both of you, he's giving up on himself, and on *us*," Katie says, her jaw set in determination, then brightens. "At this particular moment, he has a solid anchor—his best friend Trayvon flew in last night. Tray has always been a steadying influence on Gavin. And he can also help him solve the puzzle of his family history. That logical analytic process seems to divert Gavin's triggers. So now let's get my man home."

"Let us know if you need help, Katie." Pedersen says. "And if you think you can convince him to take the medication, I'll prescribe it. Clonazepam has been shown to help quiet the patient's hyperactive amygdala, begins acting almost immediately, and increases effectiveness over time."

"Didn't help last night though, did it?" Katie scoffs.

Pedersen makes a face and looks down. "There are other options when and if necessary, Katie. It isn't an exact science."

Before Katie goes into Gavin's room, she sees a guy down the hall who looks familiar. Someone who prompts an uncomfortable feeling in her, although she can't place him... Wait! The nursing home, where they visited Grandpa DiMasi. Is he the guy she noticed staring at Gavin that day, or just someone who looks like him? Or maybe she *is* becoming paranoid.

> "True friendship comes when the silence between two people is comfortable."
> —*David Tyson*

33

GAVIN'S ACCIDENT WAS TREATED AS JUST THAT—AN accident, for which local police issued him a ticket for reckless driving. And now, despite the hospital and Dr. Pedersen's urging, Gavin rejects continuing medication and is simply overjoyed to have Tray with him. He can't seem to wipe the smile off his injured face. With Tray, he feels so grounded and safe. And free, like someone just removed his handcuffs. Now as Tray pulls up to his parents' house, Gavin can't wait to show his best friend what he found in the Prince Street building.

"The place hasn't changed much, has it?" Tray says. "You just gonna sell it?"

"Yeah, no way would I ever think of living here. That wasn't living," Gavin laments. "But first I have to go through the painful process of getting rid of everything, except the few things I want to keep—which isn't much, for sure."

When Gavin and Tray get to the front door, Gavin finds it unlocked. He's certain he locked it when he left yesterday morning. It seems so long ago. So much has happened since then. "I'm positive I locked it when I left," he mutters.

Tray pushes him aside, pats the bulge under his jacket and goes into the front foyer. "Has it always been this messy?"

"Not on this floor. My brother's room, for sure."

Tray locks the front door then checks out the entire first

floor. "Not random trashing, like kids," he concludes. "Just stuff sort of systematically pulled out of all the places that might have something stored or hidden."

Gavin looks around and sees kitchen cabinets, bookshelves in the library, liquor cabinet and every storage space standing empty with their contents dumped out onto the floors. "So the intruders are methodical, I guess," he mumbles. "So far, I don't notice anything missing that's valuable, so it isn't robbery."

"You need a security system and better locks, though." Tray continues checking every room.

"That's on Katie's to-do list. But the only good stuff is in the attic." Gavin leads the way upstairs. He opens the door to Devon's old room for Tray to check. "Nice and neat, eh?"

"Shit, you weren't kidding about your twin's room," Tray says. "And what's with the writing on the walls?"

"That's not the only place he left his handiwork," Gavin grumbles.

Next, Tray goes into Gavin's parents' room. Gavin hasn't had the courage to go in there yet. The memories are painful. He leaves Tray, turns around and goes down the hall.

"They had the same M.O. in your mom and dad's room," Tray says, then follows Gavin down the hall and into his friend's old bedroom. "Oh, shit, what'd he do, write a novel and then tear it up?"

"I tore it up."

"Gotcha."

Gavin loved the comfort of communicating in shorthand with his friend. They didn't need many words. They understood each other. "So we have to get a repair and painting crew after we get all the shit out of here. We'll need one of those big dumpsters for that."

"Yep. So where's the attic?"

"I cut off the pull-down rope last time I was here, so it wouldn't be so obvious to 'intruders,'" Gavin says. He grabs his desk chair and takes it out into the hall, under the attic stair panel. He climbs on the chair and catches the edge of the panel, then pulls it down. "Your stairway to heaven, sir."

"All-right!" Tray smiles and goes up ahead of Gavin. "Okay, lots of bags and boxes up here, but nothing dumped out."

"That's good," Gavin says. "Shows they haven't been here to find what's really valuable—the stuff I pulled out of a hidden storage area in Prince Street. You're gonna want to take most of it back to Chelsea."

"Well, FBI's Northeast HQ in Chelsea handles a lot of mob cases. They're near the airport and harbor for contraband, *and* near all the mob hot spots." Tray starts rummaging through bags. "So what do we have?"

"I stuck the important bags way back under the eaves. I'll pull them out."

When Tray sees the notebook with all the names and the bag of IDs, watches, and jewelry—much of it engraved with some of the names in the notebook—his intensity rises. Focused, serious, grunts, nods, ughs, hmms... "Okay, we gotta take this shit outta here. These names are all familiar. All mob, some of 'em from way back. Question is, why are these names here, all in one notebook, what's the significance of the dates, and why was it in your Prince Street building?"

"That's why you're here, genius."

"Well, no way am I gonna take this stuff home with me. I'm calling HQ." Tray pulls out his cell phone and makes a call. "Yo, Hank. Trayvon Harris here. I need a car to transport evidence back to HQ. What case number? We'll have to re-open a couple dozen old, cold cases. Yeah. 17 Bradford Road, Wellesley Hills. ... Don't make me wait forever, man. And tell him to give me a heads up when he's near." He hangs up then turns to Gavin, "It'll take almost an hour for someone to get here from Chelsea, unless there's a car nearby. Ya got anything else?"

"You missed the ledger on the bottom of that bag. It has notes on who-owes-who how much money, with dates. Interesting cross-reference between names there and some of the names in the notebook. But you're really gonna love this." Gavin brings his friend the other bulging bag. "Check this out." He pulls off the top layer of dirty clothes.

"Ho-ly shit, motherfucker!" Tray yells, digging through the bundles of bills.

Gavin fishes out the lottery ticket and hands it to Tray. "Whitey Bulger's liquor store. Why haven't you guys found him after all these years, man?" Gavin lands a playful backhand to Tray's bicep. "Well, maybe you can learn something from the serial numbers on these bills, anyway. I estimate about three and a half mil."

"Good thing I called for a driver." He re-dials the number. "Hank? There's more. Cash. Lots of it. I recommend two armed personnel. Pronto."

Tray turns to Gavin with a grin like a kid who just found a stash of candy. "You been holdin' out on me, boy. You have anything else up your sleeve?"

"I didn't have enough bags to haul other stuff, like a bunch of invoices and receipts, *and* a box of firearms I didn't want to touch. Not with a ten-foot pole, man. And there's a couple boxes there that I haven't opened yet. We can go to Prince Street tomorrow and get all that if you want."

"Definitely. While we wait for the car, we should take this stuff somewhere where there's better lighting. I'd like to check all the names, make notes."

"Well, okay I guess…" Gavin screws up his mouth. "I kept it up here in case someone comes into the house. Y'know, for quick cover-up."

"Good point. This place isn't too secure, and neighbors are far enough away, surrounded by trees, that anything could go down and no one would notice." Tray thinks a minute. "Okay, let's leave the cash and jewelry here and close up the attic, but take the notebook down to the light."

"Too bad we don't have anything to eat or drink here while we wait."

"Just call in for pizza, dude."

When the doorbell rings, Tray goes to the front door. A teenager in a shirt with the pizza shop's logo stands outside the door's window, and his motorbike is on the driveway. Tray opens the door to take the pizza, then nods toward a black sedan with tinted windows across the street, exhaust coming out the tailpipe. "You see that car across the street?" he asks the kid.

"Uh, yeah," the kid says. "Why? Someone you know?"

"Did you notice if there's anyone in it?"

"Just some guy."

"One guy, or two?"

"I just saw one, but I didn't really pay much attention. You want that pizza, or just wanna talk?"

Tray pays the kid, takes the box and locks the door.

"Someone must have figured out you called in the FBI posse, Gav. We have a welcoming committee across the street." Tray puts the box on the kitchen counter. "And he might have a friend in the bushes. Go make sure all doors and windows are locked. I'm going to check whether the license plate is visible from the far end of the upstairs."

Tray turns and races up, then runs to the bathroom opposite Devon's room, opens the window and leans out. His view of the car is at an oblique angle, with trees partially blocking what little is visible from this position. But they're deciduous, so most of the leaves are off. A breeze sways the empty branches back and forth. He gets a couple numbers. Then a couple more when the branches sway in the opposite direction. He waits for a few more sways, then calls Hank again.

"Hank, we have visitors outside, so you need to send two cars, one for evidence, one for a passenger. Or two. And they better get their ass here fast." He rattles off as much of the license number as he was able to see. "No, only my service weapon."

Tray calls out to Gavin. No answer. Tray yells. No response.

He turns and rushes down the stairs, running from room to room, and finds Gavin cowering in the powder room, frozen into a tight ball. Instead of taking the time to slowly rouse his friend from his triggered reaction, Tray first goes all around the first floor and basement to secure all doors and windows.

Then he returns to Gavin and crouches down close to him, careful to avoid touching. "Gavin, we're safe now. I've locked everything up, and the FBI car is almost here. Let's go have pizza. I'm hungry." He stands up and extends his hand down to Gavin, who slowly rouses, takes Tray's hand and stands.

"What now?" Gavin whispers.

"We're taking the pizza and the notebook upstairs. You're going to keep watch out back from your parents' room, and I'll keep watch out front from your room. While we're having our pizza."

The next thirty minutes are the longest of Gavin's life. He tries to do what Dr. Skokou told him to do—focus on what's good in the present, connect with that. He looks out the window into the back yard and connects with the tree where he had once built a treehouse, where he had often escaped and hid when he was a kid. It's a graceful tree, with branches that reach out like comforting arms. He recalls the safety he had found there, and tries to avoid thinking about what he'd been seeking respite from so long ago. Which he has never been able to escape, even after all these years. At the same time, his peripheral vision continuously scans for movement in the yard.

Tray keeps watch out the window in Gavin's old room while tearing into the pizza. Now his cell phone vibrates with an incoming text:

Heads up, one street away.

And then another one:

The car you called in is registered to Patrick Linskey. Lives in Southie.

Tray sees the rescue car coming up the street, and another one behind it. He runs down the hall and flies down the stairs just in time to hear the sound of someone trying to jimmy the basement door. He pulls out his service weapon, carefully turns the button on the knob and stands back. The guy bursts through the door, straight into Tray's gun pointed at him. "Down on the floor!"

Tray holds the intruder down with his foot and calls up the stairs with a playful voice. "Hey Gav, can you think about a cool fun adventure while you open the front door down here?"

Gavin comes to the top of the stairs. "What?"

"And bring me a belt, or shoelaces, something to tie with? We're playing a little game here."

Gavin comes down the stairs with fearful hesitation, carrying the tie from his mother's old robe.

"Good job, Gav. Say hello to Patrick here, then open the door. My friends outside are waiting for him."

Gavin enjoys a feeling of victory over his trigger reactions as Tray drives him home after all the FBI squad has left. "I can't believe I actually held my shit together."

"You did good, man."

"So all that stuff, including the money, is now going to FBI in Chelsea?"

"Yep, and they had to hand over the two guys to the local police for B&E, but we'll be securing authority to hold and charge them as soon as we can sort out the evidence to make the case."

"So it's over?"

Tray looks at Gavin with a chuckle. "It's just beginning, my friend. Thanks to you."

When Tray pulls up to Katie's house, Gavin says, "Come on in and meet Maggie before you go, Tray. She's grown so much since you saw her in Kauai."

"Okay, but then I have to hurry back to Chelsea."

Maggie squeals and Patches wags his tail when Gavin walks in. "Da-dee! Make sketti!"

"I can smell it, Mags! Did you help Mommy make the sauce?"

"Yes!" Maggie beams.

Katie walks in from the kitchen. "You two must have made progress over at your parents' place. You were there longer than you expected." She gives Gavin a kiss and Tray a hug, then turns to Maggie. "Maggie, do you remember Tray? He came to visit us on Kauai?"

Maggie looks like she's trying to figure it out, then smiles. "May-be."

Tray laughs. "Well, I remember you, Maggie, and you've grown a lot since I saw you last."

Maggie stretches her arms up and dances on her tiptoes. "Yay!"

"Can you stay for dinner, Tray?" Katie asks.

"I'm sorry, Katie. Another time, please. I need to get back to the office now."

"Well, I'll hold you to that. And I'll walk you out while Gavin puts the pasta on and adds his final magic to the sauce."

Katie links her arm into Tray's and walks out the front door with him. "I need to tell you that someone came to the door this morning while Grandma O'Malley was taking care of Maggie."

"Oh?"

"Yes, it really scared her. He asked where Gavin was, and tried to wedge his way in through the door. But Patches went after him, jumped up and clamped the guy's arm in his jaws!" Katie's eyes widen. "The guy pulled away from our little furball and Grandma slammed the door in his face, then locked it. She saw a long black sedan across the street with dark tinted windows. The guy ran and got into the car; there was another guy driving, and they took off. Grandma called the police, but they were gone by the time the police arrived."

"Did she get their license number?"

"No, she didn't."

"Well, we may have encountered the same car and guys over at Gavin's old house."

Katie's jaw pops open. "Wha—?"

"They're in custody now," Tray says with a calming squeeze of Katie's shoulders. "We're on it, 'Katie-did.' Try not to worry, and tell Gav I'll pick him up tomorrow morning so we can go to Prince Street."

"I got a new rental car," Katie says, "so he can drive there himself. Oh, and I have some contractors coming to the building in the morning—NSTAR, and a guy to install new doors and windows. Can you deal with them, please? And keep my husband out of trouble?"

"Yes, ma'am!" Tray laughs and plants a kiss on her forehead.

"May what I do flow from me like a river,
no forcing and no holding back,
the way it is with children."
—*Rainer Maria Rilke*

34

DESPITE GAVIN'S USUAL RESTLESS TOSSING AND turning, and a couple nightmares, he snored most of the night. But Katie couldn't sleep. The tension in the house—from inside as well as outside—has been accelerating at a pace that defies sleep and implies danger lurking beyond nightmares. She is more than exhausted. She's emotionally depleted.

Katie has been up since four-thirty working at her desk, remotely managing her Kauai art gallery and the restaurant via email and text, as well as making phone calls to find contractors for jobs on Gavin's to-do list. All in the den at the rear of the house—which her mother had used as a bedroom before she died, but now this has become *her* room, her "command central." Well, hers and Maggie's. After Destiny delivered art supplies yesterday morning before Katie went to get Gavin from the hospital, she rolled up the carpet and put it, along with the television and big pieces of den furniture, into the garage. She pulled down the drapes from the sliding glass doors to maximize the northern light, then set out the acrylic paints, canvases and brushes in what is now her office *and* studio.

While Gavin was with Tray yesterday afternoon, Katie brought Maggie into the room and briefly experimented with the paints. Making a note to buy easels for both of them, Katie now surveys her space, breathes deeply and smiles, feeling a glimmer of light piercing the darkness gripping her family.

It's six-thirty and the sun won't be lighting the morning sky for another half-hour, but Katie hears Maggie waking. She closes her computer and runs upstairs.

Two hours later, Maggie is a tornado of unrestrained energy. She's had her breakfast, insists on dressing herself to go to the Child Study Center, and now she and Patches are chasing each other all through the house while she sings "Kool, kool, kool!"

"We'll start walking to school in a minute, sweetie," Katie says as Gavin comes downstairs. "And Daddy is going to meet Tray," she smiles, buttoning Maggie's sweater.

Maggie grabs Daddy's hand excitedly and pulls him proudly into her and Mommy's "studio," picks up a brush and beams as she declares, "Paint!"

Katie's grateful that Gavin agreed to go see Dr. Skokou on Monday. She wishes it was sooner, and hopes he'll make it a regular thing. But now Gavin grumbles, "So it wasn't enough to manage a gallery of other people's art, now you think *you're* an artist?" He laughs, but it doesn't conceal the mocking tone in his voice.

"Oh, it's just a nice diversion for Maggie and me," she says, instantly chiding herself for downplaying what gives her joy in order to avoid Gavin's displeasure. Or one of his many triggers.

"Diverting you from your to-do list," he growls.

Katie stiffens against her anger, refusing to be sucked into that very un-Gavin-like jab, which has been happening more often recently. Now she's anxious to get him out of the house and on his way. She hands him his jacket, walks him to the door and opens it for him. "See you later, Gav. Give Tray my love." No kiss goodbye.

After Gavin's car is gone up the street, Katie puts Maggie into her stroller and the leash on Patches for the walk to the

Child Study Center. She jogs along the several blocks, the run feeling like an escape from tension for a moment, clearing her head. It occurs to her now that Gavin—the guy who thinks he has to save everyone—may have felt his role was compromised by asking Katie for her help with his to-do list. Then demeaning her ability to do it would re-assert himself in that role. But demeaning family members was always something that ran in the DiMasi family, wasn't it? *Oh, shit, I'm so tired of standing on my head trying to figure him out and second-guess him, avoid triggering him, reassuring him. It depletes me, drains me of me. Whoever that is.*

When Katie and Maggie arrive at the Child Study Center, she ties Patches to the bike rack outside then greets Mrs. Anders. "Thank you so much for your work with Maggie, Mrs. Anders. What have you and your research team observed so far?"

"Well, you obviously know she's a very bright, advanced, precocious child. She's outgoing and seems to 'manage' her interactions with everyone, adults and children, like she's the director of her own movie. But we are occasionally seeing some indications of stress—likely due to your recent move here. Adjustment to new circumstances takes time, of course. Is there anything else going on in the home?"

Katie hesitates. "Is Dr. Malone here? I'd like to talk for a minute with both of you."

While Maggie plays with her favorite trucks, Mrs. Anders takes Katie to the director's office.

"Hello, Dr. Malone," Katie begins, extending her hand to the woman who looks like she could have been a linebacker in a former life. "Thank you so much for welcoming Maggie into your Child Study Center."

"Oh, everyone conducting research here thinks they've found a pot of gold in your little girl," she laughs. "How can I help you? Would you like to sit?"

"Thank you, Doctor. I don't want to take too much of your

time, so I'll be brief," Katie smiles in a near-grimace. "Mrs. Anders asked whether there is anything going on in our home, beyond the fact of our recent move here. There is. My husband is currently struggling with Complex PTSD, so certain things can trigger him in unpredictable ways. And we are also vigilant regarding the potential appearance of undesirable associates of my husband's deceased family."

Dr. Malone and Mrs. Anders seem a bit shell-shocked while they try to process what Katie just rattled off. As the implication of it all sinks in, the women are speechless, failing to mask their surprise and concern. Here, in an austere academic research setting, an incursion from the dark side of real life.

Dr. Malone opens her mouth first. "Well, Mrs. DiMasi, I'm not sure..."

"So your researchers may find useful data by observing our daughter," Katie interrupts her, fearing the director will say that Maggie is not welcome here due to the risk. Then without skipping a beat, she goes on before Dr. Malone can speak, "And it is very important that she is *never* released to anyone except me, her father Gavin DiMasi, or Dean O'Malley and her husband," she concludes with a sweet smile glued below her direct gaze. "Would you like me to provide a written statement to that effect?" Again, the innocent smile.

"Well, uh..." the director sputters.

"Of course." Katie pulls a paper from her backpack. "It's all clearly stated here, and if you need anything else, just let me know," she smiles brightly. "Now I need to hurry over to Pendleton, and I'll pick up Maggie at eleven-fifteen. Thank you both so much!"

Leaving the women frozen with *"What just happened?"* expressions, Katie walks away, gets Patches, and jogs around the science center into campus. Her face hurts from all the forced smiles. If only those facial muscles could penetrate inside her, wipe away the stress, the fear, the anger.

As she enters Pendleton West, a brightness, a glowing brilliance in the far distance, appears in her imagination like an exit from darkness. She wishes she could paint that vision. And in fact, realize such a vision. Her spirits lift when she sees Destiny, who turns to embrace her.

"Katie, my dear!" Destiny pulls back to scrutinize Katie's face. "How are you today?"

"That's a loaded question, girl!" Katie laughs. "I'm hanging in. I could use some wisdom and instruction on technique, so my painting can show what's in my mind."

"We can start there, but ultimately your art will reflect your heart, your soul."

"I'm not sure I've ever had the right contact info for heart or soul," Katie smirks, getting Patches settled on his makeshift doggy-bed.

"You mustn't deflect and sell yourself short, darling," Destiny says, with all seriousness. "Don't worry, it will come. Now, what is in your mind?"

"I've seen paintings that use light and dark in such a way that the light absolutely glows, as if it's alive, breathing and beckoning you to enter into another realm...a world of *release*. How can I achieve that in my painting? Can you teach me some techniques?"

"Come, dear. Let's experiment with color and texture..."

Later, Katie stands back to inspect her canvas. Dense writhing masses of brown, black and blood-red alien forms snake in portentous earth below dark roiling storm clouds. Near the right side of the canvas, there's a break along the horizon, like an eyelid opening to reveal a miasma of luminous yellow, white, peach and gold glistening like a sunrise-lit sky above the threatening firmament. She had attempted to create that opening to reveal escape, freedom, rescue and joy, to transport the viewer. Her. But its shimmering light now feels deceptive, a compelling entrapment to danger, as if its entrance leads to fires below.

She hopes that isn't a reflection of what's in her heart, or her soul.

Destiny comes to stand behind her. "Your instincts are showing, Katie."

"Instincts for painting?" Katie looks at her, hopeful.

"That's already evident, dear. I mean your instinct for where the light leads. You know the saying 'All that glitters is not gold,' yes?"

"I wanted to paint a path to escape, out of the chaos."

"Yet something told you that you might be pulled down into a different kind of chaos."

Katie is still somewhat shaken when she enters the room where spouses of people with PTSD are meeting. As each member sitting around the circle takes a turn to describe their status, when it is Katie's turn, she can only whisper, "I'm so exhausted. I never know what my husband will do or be, from one moment to the next, or how to respond, how to help him. I feel trapped. Erased. As if there's no more me."

The women on either side of her reach out to embrace her.

"Let the dead bury the dead."
—*Harper Lee*

35

WHEN GAVIN GETS TO THE NORTH END AROUND nine-thirty, he has to drive around to find a parking lot with an available space. He can't wait to hear what Tray found out from the stuff he took back to the FBI office in Chelsea. As he turns the corner to walk up Prince Street, he sees a truck outside the building, and a couple guys doing something at the front. Are they trying to break in?

He flies into a rage, runs toward them, fists swinging. "What're you doing?" he shouts, then sees the plywood door of the building is open.

Tray comes out and tackles him. "Hey man, stop," he orders.

Gavin continues to struggle, then finally realizes who he's fighting with. "How the hell did you get in?" he shrieks.

"You forget what skills come with my job, man," Tray smiles, slowly releasing his captive.

"Who are these guys?"

"The contractor Katie arranged to replace the windows, doors and locks —say hello to Francisco Rodriguez, and to the NSTAR guys installing your electric feed. Oh, and the security system is coming this afternoon. Katie just needed me to be here to get them started."

Now Gavin is embarrassed for his freak-out, and feels like a shit for the way he treated Katie this morning. "Oh, jeez..."

"So come on in and show me around. I got my guys to help me bring some industrial-size floodlights and long extension cords, so we can hook up as soon as NSTAR is done."

The guy in the NSTAR uniform interjects, "You guys are all set now. You're in business."

"Great, thanks." Tray slips the guy a twenty, then turns to Rodriguez. "Frank, we'll be inside if you need anything."

Once Tray and Gavin are inside, Gavin says in a low voice, "Isn't that risky, having those guys working outside where they can be seen? And how's the Italian mob gonna react to a Latino guy working here?"

"Well, Latinos will *not* play on the mob's team. Ever. That's why Katie got him. And I have two guys watching from across the street in case of 'outside interference.' So chill, man." Tray claps his hand on Gavin's back. "And plug this cord into the electric panel they installed. Temporary, but good for now."

Gavin lugs over the heavy-duty line and plugs it in. "How long is this?"

"A hundred feet, but I have another one if we need to daisy-chain 'em." He scans the interior. "This place doesn't look like it's gonna fall down or anything. Fire must not've burnt too long."

"Yeah, like I said. Someone obviously wants it for other reasons."

"Where we goin'?"

"Basement, then up to that secret place."

"Oh here we go with the cloak 'n' dagger, goin' down to go up," Tray grins. "You told me there's a dirt floor in the basement, so I brought a shovel from my dad's house. Never know if there's a secret passageway to China or something."

"I have flashlights and Solomon's headlamp too," Gavin says, then hauls the heavy roll of hundred-foot cord over to the basement door he took off its hinges. "You can bring the other roll of cord. And your shovel. Then we'll have to carry those floodlights down when we need 'em, too."

"Gettin' my workout today, huh?" Tray grunts. "Oh, so this goes down the stairs to the basement?"

"Right, genius," Gavin drawls. As they go down the stairs, Gavin shines his flashlight all around. "Like I told you, it's old, complete with junk, trash, and dirt floor. And rats." He flashes his light toward movement in a pile of trash on the right. "In the back there's a brass plaque from the 1700s, and a very special closet," he says, like announcing an important archaeological discovery.

"So let's see it, Sherlock."

Gavin leads the way to the back, opens the door of the closet and turns on Solomon's lantern.

"This is it?"

"This is the special closet that has an entry into a secret storage area," Gavin says with a chortle. "So, last time I was here I pulled out all these wooden boxes of liquor bottles and noticed the difference in the wood up here," he says, pulling down the top box and pointing his flashlight. "It's a hatch up to the first floor. I put all the boxes back before I left, to conceal the hatch, so we'll have to pull some out now and stand on two of them to open the hatch."

"You ever hear of this new invention called a ladder?"

"Solomon left one, a huge heavy extension ladder, but it's pretty unwieldy to drag down here. And if our friendly neighborhood intruders saw it down here, it could tip them off to the fact of something important here, y'know."

"All right, let's do this," Tray says, pointing Gavin to the boxes.

"Gee, thanks, man. How gallant of you." Gavin starts pulling out wooden boxes and handing them to Tray to stack on the dirt floor.

After sufficient boxes have cleared the way to the area below the hatch, Tray lets out one of his deep-chested laughs and ushers Gavin in with a flourish. "Go ahead; I'll bring up the rear. Yours."

Gavin dons Solomon's headlamp, climbs up on two boxes

and shines the light on the ceiling—the underside of the first floor—to locate the exact spot to push up. "Uumph—got it!" He pushes up the hatch, throws his flashlight inside onto the floor of the space, and hoists himself up.

"Good thing Hannah put me on a diet," Tray says as he climbs up into the space, which Gavin had illuminated with his headlamp and flashlight. "This isn't very big. Just wide enough for single stacks of boxes, and long. How'd you know it was here?"

"On the first floor, I noticed that the left wall of Devon's VIP room, where he set up card tables and club chairs for his 'special customers,' didn't line up with the left wall of the main store. Just maybe three feet difference, not something too many people would notice, with the shelves of alcohol ordinarily against the left wall of the store. At first I wondered if this is something Devon built, or my dad. The construction looks too new for grandpa's time here. My brother's handwriting isn't in that notebook. And the money I found in the wall," he points to the torn-away plaster, "was from 1991 and no way would Devon have left that untouched if he knew about it. So my dad must've put it there."

"Did you ever find out how or why, specifically, Devon got crosswise with the mob?"

"Nothing specific. Other than him being his usual asshole self."

"So what's in these other boxes?"

"I haven't opened them all, but one of them is stuffed with small firearms." He moves some boxes around. "Yeah, this is the box."

"We'll want to take all these boxes back to HQ. Never know what we'll find. Checking the serial numbers on those guns against the national database and running ballistics tests might reveal something."

"Have you figured out what the notebook, jewelry and ledger mean, if anything?"

"We're still working on it. So far it looks like every name in that notebook went missing around the time of those dates next to their names. And we've matched up some of the jewelry and IDs to some of those names, and also to some of the names in the who-owes-who ledger."

"So we have the names and jewelry. Wonder where the actual people are?"

"Who the hell knows? I'll get someone to lug this shit out. Someone skinny."

"Good. And look up there," Gavin points to the ceiling above the hatch they just came up. "That's another hatch, for access to and from the floors above. It opens into an upstairs closet."

"Have you gone up there?"

"Yeah. No one was living up there at the time of the fire, and the only thing of interest there now is evidence of homeless people camping out, and clear evidence that the fire never even reached the second floor, let alone the third. But the fire department sure as shit dumped a ton of water and foam into the building, almost immediately after the minor gas blast. More like a gas fart."

Tray lets out a guffaw and backhands Gavin in his ribs. "Okay, we got our work."

When they go back down to the basement, they return all the boxes to the closet and close the door. Gavin screws the hasp with its lock back on the door, then gestures to the dirt floor. "I poked my shovel into this dirt once, thinking there might be something of interest buried here, but it's packed pretty hard in most places, like it could use a backhoe."

"Don't think they make 'em small enough to fit down those stairs," Tray says, stabbing his father's shovel into the dirt. "That part isn't too hard."

"Okay, go get one of your floodlights, and we can have a contest to see which one of us finds gold first," Gavin laughs. That thought takes him back to their high school friendship, always challenging each other in friendly competition, seeing who can run the fastest, go the farthest.

"You serious, man?" Tray hoots. "Just because you beat my ass on that NaPali hike, don't think you can beat me to some mob loot here." He turns to go up the stairs, shaking his head and chuckling, then comes back down with a floodlight. "Wanna flip for left side or right side?"

"Starting at the back or front?" Gavin pulls a quarter out of his pocket.

"Back. Heads I take the right."

Gavin flips. "It's tails, so *I* get the right!"

They start digging in unison. Lots of grunting, groaning, and dirt tossing. Five minutes later, each has dug a foot-deep hole when they both yell in unison, "Got something!"

"Well, I didn't hit metal," Gavin says. "There's a little give to it."

"Same here," Tray grunts with another stab. "Guess I'll have to dig around it before I can get under it to lift whatever it is."

Five minutes later, Gavin says, "It's some sort of heavy canvas, with something inside. I've dug mostly all around, and it's big."

"Same here," Tray grunts again. "Maybe more money? Winner is the first one who pulls something out of the ground!"

Gavin resumes digging, and now flashes back to his nightmare, in which skeletons crawl out of the dirt. He stops, freezes.

Tray notices his friend is immobile, not digging, not moving. Then it hits him. "Oh, shit. Now we know..."

"Their bodies," Gavin whispers, his voice hoarse.

"Yeah. What we're digging up..." Tray nods, grim.

"All those missing guys in the notebook," Gavin mutters. His brain has finally connected the dots, at the same time his FBI friend gets it. Now he sits, curled in a ball, rocking, while his mind has escaped down a hole of its own.

Tray turns back to the hole he's been digging. He stares at

it and hesitates, then cautiously angles in his shovel, managing to get under one end of what's buried, and levers up the shovel, exposing a bundle wrapped in heavy canvas. Something is inside. He pulls out a pocket knife and slits the canvas. A skull. "Okay, Gav. Let's get outta here. I'll call in a team."

Later that day, the building—now protected with new windows, doors, locks, and a security system—is also adorned with yellow tape and barriers blocking off the sidewalk. A large team from FBI has descended on the building, the majority equipped with shovels and assigned to the basement.

When Gavin gets home that evening, he doesn't notice the unmarked FBI car with two agents positioned across the street from Katie's house. He has nightmares all that night, but hasn't told Katie why. In the morning, Tray and two other FBI agents come to visit.

"Oh, hi Tray!" Katie is surprised to see him when she opens the door. "I didn't know you were coming. The house is a mess."

"That's okay, Katie," Tray smiles. "I've brought a couple of my friends from work to meet Gavin. Maybe you and Maggie might want to take a walk? It's such a nice day that one of my colleagues across the street wants to take a walk too."

Katie instantly understands that something serious has happened, and that Tray's suggestion is more than just a recommendation. She scoops up Maggie from where she's playing in the kitchen, calls out to Patches, and heads for the door. "Don't trip on Maggie's toys," she smirks to Tray as she leaves.

"Hey, Gav, how you doin'?" Tray claps him on the back. "This is official business, man. These two agents, Zimmer and Gottfried, just need to take your statement. That okay?"

"What do you want to know?"

One guy extends his hand to Gavin. "Agent Zimmer, sir.

We just need your statement describing how you found all the things you gave to Agent Harris, and describe the chain of custody of the building and its contents. We'll be recording it all, just for the record."

"Am I under arrest for anything?" Gavin is nervous.

"Of course not, Gavin," Tray says. "Not even a suspicion. We just need to have all the information in our records."

"What you tell us may help us understand what crimes may have been committed, identify who's responsible, and whether and how we can charge them," Zimmer adds.

They all sit down in the living room, Gavin in one chair, Tray in the other, and Zimmer and Gottfried on the sofa. At one point during the questions and Gavin's answers, Gottfried asks, "Do you know whose handwriting is in the notebook and the ledger?"

"Well, I know that anything dated after 1976 was my father's handwriting," Gavin says. "He died in July 2002. Before 1976, I'm guessing it's my grandfather DiMasi's handwriting—he bought the building in 1950—but I don't recall ever seeing his handwriting so I can't be sure. He's in the nursing home in the North End; you could go check with him there."

"We did try to pay him a visit. He's currently incapacitated."

Gavin's eyes pop wide. He's heard that euphemistic word before. He knows what it implies. And another truth dawns on him. He turns to Tray. "We just talked with him last week. Someone must have tried to get information from him about what I was doing in the building."

"And that's probably the reason no one notified you about your grandfather's 'accident,' and why whoever's responsible amped up their stalking on you," Tray nods.

That prompts Gavin to tell the agents about the black SUV and car that have been following him, sitting outside his parents' house and Katie's. Tray adds the license plate number and who it's registered to. The agents take that information down. Finally Gavin walks the agents to the door. Zimmer turns before leaving and asks, "Do you have a security system here?"

"Uh, as a matter of fact, my wife had one installed yesterday afternoon," Gavin says.

"That's good," the agent says.

Tray goes out with the two men, but tells Gavin, "Official business is over, man, so I'll be back in a minute for a cup of coffee."

When Tray returns, Gavin has lots of questions. "So what was all that about?"

"Coffee, my friend. Nothing 'til I have a cup of your great coffee." Then with a hot mug in his hand, Tray says, "You guessed right. Twenty-one names in the notebook. Twenty-one body bags. Forensics has their job cut out for them, identifying all of them. Then there's one more that doesn't need much effort. Mark Solomon."

"So that's where he went."

"Yeah. Planted."

"What I'm trying to figure out is, who was responsible for killing, and who was responsible for planting?" Gavin wonders.

"It all happened over many years, so it's gonna be a lot of different people, some of the earlier ones most likely already dead," Tray notes. "Solomon's a different matter."

"The last entry in the notebook was March 2001, in my dad's handwriting," Gavin continues. "Devon had taken over the business in late 2000, but he was in rehab in March 2001."

"And no more bodies or entries in the notebook after that, or in the ledger," Tray says. "We have to wait for final ID from forensics, but if the number of names matches the number of body bags, I'm guessing there were no more bodies during your brother's time."

"Could it be?" Gavin asks. "No, it couldn't be! That Devon was a target because he discovered the bodies and refused to plant any more?"

"If so, it's probably the only redeeming deed he ever did."

"That sounds like a country-western song," Gavin snorts.

"So what're you gonna do with that building?"

"If I try to sell it, I'd have to declare that bodies were found in it, which could bollix the sale altogether."

"Nah, anyone who wants that location won't blink an eye at that news," Tray laughs. "They might even pay more for it!"

> "What's called a difficult decision
> is a difficult decision because
> either way you go there are penalties."
> —Elia Kazan

36

WHILE TRAY AND HIS "FRIENDS" ARE WITH GAVIN, Katie calls a woman who lives nearby, whom she met in her PTSD spouse group. "Hi, Miriam, this is Katie from group. You suggested we might get together sometime. Is now a good time?"

During the walk a few blocks away, Katie keeps an eye on the woman across the street, who nonchalantly parallels her, Maggie and Patches. Of course Patches notices too, periodically turning his head to track the stranger. Katie doesn't want Maggie to become fearful, so they sing songs together all along the way, moving their feet to the beat. *Itsy-bitsy spider, Row-row-row your boat,* all the easy favorites. Then Maggie begins chanting, *"Seb-un Ma-shul Steet, Seb-un Ma-shul Steet—"*

"Very good, Maggie! And what is your name?"

"Mag-gie! Ma-gret Cah-yeen Dee-Masi."

"Perfect!" Katie claps. "Now that you know what street we live on, do you know what *town* we live in?"

Maggie sticks out her lower lip, something she does when she's thinking. "No."

"Do you want me to tell you?"

"Yes."

Katie bends over so that her mouth is in front of Maggie.

"Wellz-lee," she enunciates clearly. "Can you say 'Wellz-lee'?"

"Wellz-lee!" Maggie sings.

"So where do you live, Mags?"

"Seb-un Ma-shul Steet, Wellz-lee!" Maggie sings, bobbing her head and stomping her feet with each syllable while Patches jumps along.

"You're so smart, my sweet big-girl Maggie."

When they get to Miriam's house, Katie casts a glance toward her shadow across the street as she rings the doorbell with Maggie in her arms.

"Welcome, Katie!" Miriam says, and gives her, with Maggie, a hug. "So this is Maggie. What a beautiful little girl."

"Big girl," Maggie says, stretching her arms up.

"Oh, you're right," Miriam laughs. "I can see that now." Miriam looks haggard and tired, like someone struggling to keep her head above water, almost ready to give up. "Would you like to come into my house, big girl Maggie?"

"Pat-us," Maggie points to her dog sitting at the foot of the steps.

"Is that your dog, Maggie? Would you like him to come in with you?"

Katie breaks in, "Oh, Patches doesn't have to. He's well-trained, and will just sit there."

"Nonsense. My kids love dogs. Their father took our Golden, Sadie, when he moved out, and they really miss her."

"Oh, what a lovely house you have, Miriam," Katie says, glancing around at the artwork on the walls, the sculptures, and the needlepoint pillows on the sofa.

"Thank you. Sit down, and would you like some tea?" Miriam calls upstairs to her children, "Jenny and Bobby, come meet our guests!"

In a matter of minutes, Maggie is happily playing with eight-year-old Jenny and six-year-old Bobby—she's thrilled with his trucks!—and Patches is loving it all.

"Your Maggie plays very well with other children," Miriam

nods. "How old is she?"

"Twenty-three months going on fourteen years," Katie laughs and sips hot green tea in the sunny living room. "She seems to have mastered the art of being charming to get what she wants, but we're wise to her tricks."

"That's a survival skill," Miriam smiles. "Never too young to learn that. How's she doing with potty-training? Bobby took forever, but Jenny was about Maggie's age."

"She's doing pretty well in her training pants, which she calls her 'big-girl' pants."

"And how are you getting on, Katie?" Miriam asks. "I've been worried about you."

"Oh, things are up and down." Katie looks into her cup. "It's hard to accommodate every up and down when you don't know what's coming or when, and what's the best, safest way to deal with it."

"Yes," Katie says with a grimace. "When did your husband move out? If you don't mind my asking."

"It's okay," Miriam says, then sits back, lifts her chin and pulls a deep inhale. "Three weeks ago."

"How did it come to that?" Katie asks. "Again, sorry if it's too painful to talk about."

"It just became too hard. On me, on the kids. And he wasn't going to therapy like he promised. So his down times became more frequent, lasting longer, more intense and more frightening. Dangerous. Our house was like we were under siege, our own private war zone."

"Is he a veteran?"

"Yes, Nick spent two years in Iraq and came home in April of this year. He's been back for six months and it just keeps getting worse, not better. And he has an addiction. So I told him we need to separate until he actually does the work with a therapist. It just breaks my heart." Miriam seems near tears, shaking her head and looking down at her hands. "I love him so much."

"That must have been such a hard decision to make, Miriam," Katie says, and reaches out to touch her new friend's hand. "But if his disorder is endangering you and your children, you had to make a choice."

"At the end of the day, we all must make a choice, regardless of how hard it is. In the past three weeks, I've been able to sleep nights without medication, and the kids are so much happier, like they've been let out of jail," Miriam says. "I do hope he will do the work so we can be together again."

"I hope so too, Miriam, for you and your kids," Katie says. "If things don't start turning around with Gavin soon, I may have to consider my choices too." She fights back the frustration and hopelessness that have increasingly been crippling her recently.

"We're all here to support you, Katie," Miriam says.

"I really appreciate that, more than you know," Katie murmurs, then tries to shake off the weight of it. "By the way, I love your art and sculptures—is it your work?"

"Why thank you! Yes, it is. Do you paint?"

"I had an art gallery supporting local artists in Hawaii, and when we came back here, I discovered in my late mother's house pictures of nine-year-old me with my prize-winning art," Katie says, with a combination of wonder and embarrassment. "My father died right after that, and I became caregiver for my disabled mother. I shut away all my artistic passions then, and now I'm trying to resurrect it."

"Does your husband feel threatened by that?"

"Yes! His reaction seems so unlike him."

"Our spouses want to both own us and disown us, rely on us and distrust us, love us and fear us," Miriam says with her arm around Katie.

Katie gets it. She's living it. "Whiplash."

"Exactly." Miriam squeezes Katie's shoulder.

It's small comfort for Katie to know that she's not alone in these experiences, that someone understands what she's going through. "Thank you so much for welcoming us into your home, and for talking with me. And for the tea!"

"Come by any time, Katie, and never hesitate to call if you need help, or just need a break to chat. Or go shopping!" she says with a conspiratorial smile.

"Thank you, Miriam, and the same to you." Katie squeezes her hand. "Oh, by the way, can you recommend an OB-GYN?" she asks, patting her belly. "Looks like we won't be returning to Kauai anytime soon." She rolls her eyes with a grimace.

"Absolutely! I'll text you her contact info."

"Perfect. Well, I'm guessing Gavin's meeting is over now, so we should be getting back home," Katie says. "Maggie, Patches! Time to go!"

Thoughts churn in Katie's head as she begins walking home. What will it cost her and Maggie to stay? Maggie traumatized by Daddy's unpredictable volatility? Vicarious PTSD in both of them? Potential for physical danger or injury? What sacrifices would they make to Gavin's disorder? Katie burying her passion and talent for art once again, this time forever? Relegating herself to a support function? Maggie losing her innocence, her joy? Sacrifices on the pyre of his PTSD, at the altar to the multiple generations of his family's dysfunction. How can she know when the sacrifices are too much, when the water gets too hot and the frog boils to death? What would it cost her and Maggie to leave? Very little compared to what it may cost to stay...

She doesn't turn the corner back to her mother's house. She continues walking with Maggie and Patches. Morse's Pond is probably brilliant today.

———

When Katie comes home with a very tired Maggie and a wet sandy Patches, Gavin is gone. He hadn't locked the house or set the alarm. Which tells Katie he was either very stressed, distracted, or triggered. Although he did leave a note—rather terse—on the kitchen table:

Gone to Dad's house.

That's all. No signature, no indication of when or whether he'll return. Maybe he's feeling distrustful. Katie hopes he'll at least guess the code for the security system at the DiMasi house is the same as the one here. She checks her phone to see if he sent her a message, and sees a text from Tray:

Nice seeing you this morning. The Prince Street building is now closed for investigation by FBI, so Gavin won't be spending more time there.

She wonders what's behind that, and why Gavin hadn't told her anything. She doesn't know which uncertainty is more worrisome—his family's mob history or his distrust. She hopes the mob won't be a threat now that FBI has taken over, but Gavin's distrust is a symptom of his disorder, which certainly is *not* a "closed" issue.

There's still much to worry about. Now that the mysteries Gavin has been investigating in Prince Street are seemingly under control, the analytic diversion that minimized the number and severity of his triggers no longer has that effect. Which leaves his family dysfunction and consequent C-PTSD wide open, a free-range disorder that he resists addressing. How, and whether, he can eventually conquer his disorder—without damaging people around him—is unknowable. Time will tell. But the story it tells could be either triumphant or tragic.

Katie is becoming worn down by trying to understand the incomprehensible, anticipate the unimaginable, and maneuver around all the unpredictable complexities of Gavin's disorder.

Maggie is falling asleep in her high chair over a half-eaten lunch. Feeling guilty for ignoring her daughter, Katie gently lifts Mags and takes her upstairs for her nap.

Afterward, she sits down in the living room. Puts her feet up and thinks, around in circles. Without the distraction of the Prince Street puzzle, Gavin's triggers may now occur with greater frequency and unpredictable intensity. Unless he can begin to make progress in therapy. On which she doubts his sincere commitment. Which circles her back to the questions plaguing her. The ultimate costs of staying versus leaving.

Junior kicks her belly.

Katie goes into her mother's old room—now her office and art room—and starts to check emails from Kauai. Instead, she turns to a canvas she put on her easel yesterday, ready to receive what's in her mind. Her heart. A vision of what she saw at Morse's Pond, how she felt, comes to her. The light...

She pulls out her paint, and then sees the Bristol board she gave Maggie to paint on yesterday. It is covered with crisscrossed slashes and corkscrews of dark red and black, frenetic, aggressive, angry and disturbed. It's as if an anonymous demented person or animal had attacked the blank board. Not her sweet little girl. This is the most blatant, overt indication she's seen of Maggie's tension and stress. Katie makes a note to probe for more details on her daughter's stress behavior at the Child Study Center. Although Mags has mostly hidden it from her family, it has now become evident in paint.

Stress hidden and buried is more damaging than if it is expressed. That's costly. And Katie's not the only one paying.

> "Sometimes the past needed to stay buried;
> it was the only way you could move on.
> And sometimes you had to dig it up,
> because that too was the only way."
> —Ana Aguirre

37

AFTER COMING BACK TO HIS PARENTS' HOUSE A few times—and especially after facing mob-associated intruders two days ago with Tray—the house itself no longer grips Gavin in angst and paranoia. He isn't sure if that means he's put the pain of all those childhood memories behind him, or he has accepted it. Embraced it. Like, if you can't beat 'em, join 'em.

He sits on the sofa in the family room with his feet up on the coffee table, where he has gathered from the attic his mother's Filene's Basement bag full of memorabilia, his brother's journal, all his mother's journals, and the banker's box from the library that holds research on domestic abuse. He intends to unearth the mysteries of his family, like he did in Prince Street. Would the collection of history in front of him now mirror what he found in that building? Keys to whatever it was that made his family so dangerously toxic, strewn with landmines, some of them fatal?

Next to all that is the journal Skokou gave him. He's been avoiding it, fearful that recounting the many trigger episodes he's had since leaving her might re-trigger him.

Gavin is realizing a vague sense of continuity throughout

his family's history. Will the story he records of his flashbacks and triggers mirror the distorted stories of bullying, manipulation and abuse in the family records in front of him? As well as the fatal stories he uncovered in Prince Street, left by his DiMasi grandfather and father? Toxic manipulation replicating throughout generations, like down a hall of mirrors. Now Gavin is the last man standing, the one left to bear the brunt of damage from that chain of dysfunction. To finally bare the truth and break the chain.

It would be tolerable if that damage simply left scars in its wake. He could deal with scars, the ghostly relics of healed-over past injuries. But no, those assaults throughout his childhood are deeply embedded in the fiber of his being, self-perpetuating, self-replicating. He doubts the band-aid of therapy can stop its relentless attacks, so he's reluctant to begin dissecting his triggers. That exercise will surely open the entire Pandora's box of his memories, his victimization in that cascade of history.

Instead, he picks up Devon's journal. He'd read a few snippets a couple weeks ago, and now he reads from further pages. More of typical Devon—claiming superiority, railing against those who doubt it—but there are several pages that had been punctured, either with Devon's pen or some other sharp object. The frenetically scrawled words on these pages—at least the ones Gavin can make out—reveal his twin's discovery, realization, and admission that he is not superior...he's *"tired of pretending ... but Dad expects it ... disappointing Dad would be a death sentence."* Following one of those pages is a pockmarked page of secondary dents, where Devon had written carefully in almost artistic script, adorned with flowers and hearts, about Gavin:

> he's so beautiful, I love his mind, and oh that body!
> he's the best in everything,
> I love him so much, if only he loved me,
> he can't ever leave me.

This is sick, and crazy! Gavin's head falls back on the sofa, staring up at the ceiling, mouth agape, unbelieving. The room spins like a carousel. His entire life, as far back as he can remember, from diapers to finding his brother hanging in his tower, Devon had doubled up on Dad's taunts and put-downs. Wimp, loser, nerd, a nothing, baby. Not just to Gavin, but in public—he'd broadcasted his twin's inferiority to schoolmates and friends.

Now this. Was this one of Devon's fantasies, or another form of his narcissistic manipulation? Even Devon's final words, written in his own blood and scrawled on the wall behind his suspended body—"*YOU CAN'T LIVE WITHOUT ME, TWINKIE!*"—were meant to retain control over him. Forever. Devon's demeaning insults didn't just stick with Gavin at the time. They defined him. Permanently.

Gavin slams Devon's journal down, where it flops open to the last page. In contrast to some of the earlier frenzied scrawls, the writing seems sane and controlled:

> *I found their secret storage and list of victims, and uncovered one of them in the basement. Now they think they have the right to keep doing it. NFW. I said if they do, I'm going to the police. Now they're after me.*

Reading this just piles more guilt on Gavin. In addition to failing to save Devon, he's also guilty for blaming his brother's trouble with the mob on an undefined range of Devon's typical smart-ass moves, cheating them or otherwise being a fuck-up. But seeing this now, Gavin realizes Tray was right, and here is evidence of probably "the only redeeming deed Devon ever did." Despite himself, he chuckles at that tongue-twister alliteration.

Now Gavin notices he hasn't had a trigger yet, even in this house of horrors. He goes into the kitchen and gets a glass of water, then remembers the leftover pizza and puts the last two slices in the microwave. Not so good two days old, but it fills a hole.

He looks in his mother's Filene's Basement bag. Three of his cross-country trophies. Every report card he's ever received, each with top marks and glowing teacher comments. Pictures of him and Katie in their dance finery from Junior and Senior Proms. Team photos, his Senior yearbook, pages crowded with classmates' wishes and signatures. His triple honors from the Culinary Institute. Gavin suspects why Mom had put these things away in the attic. Devon would have resented them, possibly even defaced them. But that meant they were out of sight for Gavin, too, not displayed as reminders of his worth and accomplishments. Nor visible to Dad, as evidence of how wrong he was about Gavin.

He picks up the earliest of his mother's journals, written in her beautiful script, while she was pregnant with him and Devon. She was sixteen at the time, and turned seventeen before he and Devon were born. So there's fear, worry, naïveté, morning sickness, discomfort, baby kicks—all of which is familiar to Gavin from Katie's pregnancy. His mother wrote of her love of Tony, and also her fear of him, his angry outbursts.

Gavin continues through her later journals, reading about Dad's anger at her working on her college degree and doctorate, his heavy drinking, his verbal and physical assaults on her. Yet through it all, she still loved him. She understood that his feelings of inferiority from being bullied in the macho culture of the North End had driven his bad behavior, and she wrote of her determination to save him, their twins, and their marriage from his abuse. But she couldn't save herself.

Sadness and anger vie for prominence within Gavin as he realizes that his mother knew all along—even early in her relationship with Dad—that he could be dangerous and corrosive to others, including his sons. She knew! Yet she chose to stay! It cost his mother her life, and damaged her sons. Devon. And him.

Gavin's breathing comes faster now and he stiffens, his fists clenched. He stands as his father's rage echoes in his ears, and again sees his mother sailing down the stairs, landing with a sickening crack at his feet. He starts swinging. At anything, everything, knocking over a lamp, crashing it down, kicking the contents of cabinets the intruders had left strewn on the floor, picking up bottles of liquor and throwing them into the kitchen, against the wall, punching the wall, his knuckles bloody. His rage overcomes him, he can't catch his breath, he coughs and chokes. Sobs grip his chest. He collapses on the floor.

When Gavin comes to, he remembers what had upset him, what had triggered him. His parents failed him. His mother knew the damage Tony's temperament would inflict on her and the family, but stayed. Gavin recognizes the irony that decades of his mother's love, understanding, patience, and forgiveness hadn't stopped the inevitable. Nor could he.

That makes him think of Katie. She loves him. She understands and supports him. Will that be enough to save them both? The pizza churns foul in his gut as he realizes that unlike his mother, Katie must save herself. Which engulfs him with hot stabbing pain all the way to his lungs and up his spine, a fatal foreboding of rejection and abandonment...

His back is stiff like an old man's when he opens his eyes to one more of his mother's journals lying in front of him. The one that promised he would know who he is when he reads it. He opens it with the same sort of caution as opening a box with something inside that might pop out and get you.

It's sort of a smaller version of a baby book, like the one a neighbor gave Katie when Mags was born, with places to record birth date and time, weight, length, first tooth, first haircut, first words, and so on. His mother had recorded variations on that theme, including every report card, accomplishment, award and honor he'd received. And because Mom was a psychiatrist, she also reflected on his "personality," occasionally underlining certain points. As he reads page after page, it seems to provide a map to who he is. His Self.

> Even at thirteen months, our twins are so different. Devon is carelessly adventurous and impulsive. Clearly alpha, barging ahead, asserting dominance. <u>Gavin is analytic and deliberate, intensely observant and considerate. He isn't always first, but he's usually correct and effective.</u> Yet Devon is quick to claim victory in everything, while Gavin follows him around like a shadow.

Gavin ponders this. He and Devon were identical twins, but that's DNA, not personality or temperament. They *were* reverse physically, as mirror twins, and certainly also in attitudes. But his mother seemed to have concluded that their personalities were inherently different from the very beginning, as babies. He had been probing, digging deep to understand and get things right. Devon was impulsive, skimming the surface to get there first and claim victory. Gavin recognizes that was the case all their lives. Devon's approach to life fooled a lot of people, including their father, until everyone realized there was nothing inside his narcissistic charade.

So his mother is telling him now, *in absentia*, that he should embrace who he is, despite what his father and brother always told him. In many of her entries, she contrasted Gavin with his brother, and reported on Tony's approach to fatherhood.

> Tony has picked Devon as "the winner, the best; tough," and Gavin as "the loser, the wimp." They're not even five years old! Devon's demeanor and Tony's labeling him could lead to trouble, and <u>labeling Gavin could distort his sense of self. Tony insists that Gavin's job is to take care of</u>

his brother, save him from trouble! He has to stop that, let the boys decide who they are; he'll ruin them!

As Gavin reads this, his breaths become shallow, gaining speed, getting away from him, as his body ricochets from fleeing and hiding to swinging and punching. The internal battle depletes him.

Gavin opens his eyes and looks at his watch. Where did the time go? Where did *he* go? His mother's journal lies open beside him.

> I always told Gavin how special and valuable he is. I tried to protect him from his father's and brother's bullying. I told him repeatedly he is NOT responsible for saving everyone – not his brother, not me, or anyone. But I fear he internalized the labels and role foist on him during childhood, allowing that to define him, and it may severely handicap him in the future. Gavin is such a remarkable person; I hope he can actualize his worth.

He sees the date of this entry. Christmas Eve, 2001. The night before Tony killed her. Almost like she knew what was going to happen, that her resistance would soon take its final toll.

Gavin breaks down, helplessly sobbing.

After Gavin sets the security system and locks up the house, he sees a large industrial dumpster sitting in the driveway. And there's no black SUV.

As he drives back to Katie's house, he wonders how much longer she will tolerate his C-PTSD behaviors or if she will give up to protect herself and Maggie.

When he gets home, the smell of Katie's paint nauseates him as soon as he walks in. He is emotionally drained from his "trip down memory lane," pours himself a tumbler of bourbon, and makes plans for Sunday that have nothing to do with remembering.

> "There is always light.
> If only we're brave enough to see it.
> If only we're brave enough to be it."
> —*Amanda Gorman*

38

HALLOWEEN THIS YEAR FALLS ON MONDAY. KATIE has put together an ingenious princess outfit for Maggie from parts of old dresses of hers and her mother's, with Mags asserting her opinions and directives on the design at every step of the process. Sequins, lace, chiffon, and a tiara from one of Katie's mother's old hats. Maggie is so excited, and insists on wearing her costume as they walk to the Child Study Center this morning. Luca waves to her, as do several strangers along the way.

There is no spouse meeting today, so Katie can stay longer in Pendleton working on her painting techniques, which she has been experimenting with at home. During her run into campus after leaving Maggie, she passes a lot of young Wellesley women who, like Maggie, have donned their Halloween costumes for all-day enjoyment. She smiles, some part of her wishing she had stayed at Wellesley, in this close-knit community of strong women, to focus on art as she had originally intended, rather than transferring to BU's Questrom School of Business.

Perhaps now she can make up for lost time.

When she walks into Pendleton, she swoons in the intoxicating fragrance of oil paint.

Destiny calls out to her. "Katie, darling! How is my dear artist friend?"

Katie smiles at the idea of being called an artist; she isn't sure she qualifies for that title. Not now, perhaps not ever. "I'm good, Destiny, thanks. Finding my way. How was your weekend?"

"I have some exciting news!" Destiny beams, virtually hopping. "I went to an art opening Saturday in the South End, and met the owners. They want to discuss my having a show there in the spring!"

"That's fantastic, Destiny! Was it an artist's opening at a gallery, or an opening of a new gallery?"

"Both. The owners have taken over and combined two spaces, so it's quite large. That's one reason they're interested in my large canvases. The artist I went to see knows me, and told them all about my work. I'll take you there—it's amazing! And right in the middle of the most vibrant hip art scene, much better than Newbury Street!"

"I'm so happy for you, Destiny, and I'd love to go see it." Katie turns toward the well-lit corner Destiny partitioned for her. "I can stay longer this morning, so I'm going to get to work!"

"That's perfect! So you can meet the owners when they come, around ten-thirty," Destiny calls out.

Katie wastes no time getting into her groove. With earbuds piping old tunes to her brain, she's in another world. Ma Rainey, Bessie Smith, Joni Mitchell, Traveling Wilburys, Traffic, Robert Johnson, John Lee Hooker. She's in the zone, moving and swaying, brush in hand. Soon she has traveled into the light within her canvas, the dimension she's been working to perfect, with a dynamic multi-layered composition of color, brush strokes, texture and glossy reflection. She has created the enticing realm of shelter she has sought. It beckons and pulls her into its arms as if it's alive, breathing warmth and comfort, escape from the turmoil and darkness she's painted all around it. All around her.

"May I join you in there?" a smooth male voice rolls out behind her. But Eric Clapton's duo with BB King in her ears drowns everything else out, so when the man steps around beside her, she startles and the brush she's holding out to the side as if she were dancing with her partner lands its yellow paint directly in the middle of his chest.

"Oh, no!" Katie shrieks. "I'm so sorry, sir! I'm afraid that's oil paint, so..."

He smiles. "I know. That's okay, it just makes this shirt very special." When he laughs, his eyes crinkle at the corners.

Just then, Destiny comes to join them. "Peter Thompson, this is my friend Katie DiMasi. She's in the process of resurrecting her innate talent that's been hidden away since childhood."

"Well, that's the best resurrection since Achilles," Thompson nods toward her canvas.

"No thanks to Thetis in this case," Katie grins, extending her hand to greet the man, then notices it's covered in paint and pulls back.

"But Thetis would be a great name for a blues performer anyway," he shrugs with a wry grin. "I like your choice of music."

Katie is somewhat embarrassed, not realizing she had amped up her tunes so loud.

Now Thompson turns to a woman approaching. "Katie and Destiny, this is my partner Felicia Hooper. We opened the Critical Eye last week in the South End and we're lining up kick-ass artists like Destiny to exhibit. Looks like we need to recruit you too, Katie."

Katie scoffs and shakes her head. "In my dreams."

"So we're agreed!" Destiny suddenly stands inches taller. "I'll plan on exhibiting in the spring, with Katie's help," she smiles at her friend. "And if she's ready, she can exhibit too."

Katie looks at Destiny in disbelief.

"Can you both join us for lunch today?" Thompson asks, looking at Katie with his beguiling smile.

"That would be lovely, Peter," Destiny gleams.

Now Thompson peers closely at Katie. "Wait! Didn't you formerly own a gallery in Kauai?"

Katie stiffens, surprised and flustered. "I still own it. But I can't join you for lunch. I have a daughter to pick up from the Child Study Center." She shrugs and smiles with resignation. "Enjoy." She has real life to deal with.

> "The truth will set you free.
> But not until it is finished with you."
> —David Foster Wallace

39

THE TWO MOB GUYS WHO BROKE INTO HIS HOUSE are in Wellesley Police custody, so Gavin figures the threat from his mob stalkers is over, and now has restless energy to burn, without the lure of the Prince Street mystery to occupy him. His long run with Tray yesterday, the gourmet meal he prepared for Grandma and Grandpa last night, and working out with Pedersen this morning were all diversions to avoid the work in his parents' house. And the *other* work.

On this Monday morning, he's still sweaty from his workout as he sits on his parents' family room sofa, eyeing the journal Skokou gave him as if it's a trap. He stares at its blank white pages, where he's supposed to record his trigger episodes. He thinks back over the last few days. It seems to him that he hasn't had as many flashbacks and triggers recently. Maybe he just needs more time to get over stuff. Time heals all wounds, right? But what if he's too fucked up to be fixed? Then he remembers what Pedersen said at the gym: *"You're never so broken that you can't be fixed."* But what's actually broken? Something that's causing those episodes, or something that's messing with his ability to deal with them? Are his episodes the only problem, or part of something bigger?

Gavin realizes he's just screwing himself into a hole with his overthinking. He's the one who's always helping people, fixing things. Other people's problems. Maybe he's not so good at fixing himself. *Sure, just cut out your own cancer, dude.* He knows he's probably avoiding, and missing the point altogether. Whatever the point is.

He eyes the mess he created when he freaked out Saturday. He needs to finish sorting stuff in this house, fill up Katie's dumpster, and get the hell out of here.

But that blank journal nags him.

He tries to re-create the last episodes he had, remember what happened right before, what his reaction was, what he felt. The little trick Skokou gave him—*"Focus your thoughts on connecting to the good of the here and now, not the memories, the illusions, or even the real threat in front of you"*—will effectively silence what he's trying to retrieve. Maybe he should have done that trick when he was first triggered. Stopped it before he freaked out.

So now he concentrates on his breath as he re-winds his tapes... Slow, deep, measured breaths...

The fear. The anger. The rage. The urge to hurt, fight, obliterate, pulverize, get revenge. All those feelings flood him now as he struggles to keep his head above water, as he remembers all he's uncovered in the past few days...the family he grew up with in this house, who failed him, hurt him, the same people he needed to care for him, love him, protect him. Dad's demeaning put-downs, derision, debasement, labeling him as hopeless. Devon's duplication of all that while claiming to love him, a duplicitous double-edged knife in his heart. Mom's abdication of duty, of blame, knowing all that was damaging everyone but refusing to leave, to grant shelter and reprieve to her sons and to herself.

Now they're all dead, yet that same uncontrollable helpless rage engulfs him when he is threatened or demeaned by anyone else, or even by the possibility of it, the hint or *idea* of it. So it all repeats, stays with him even now, beyond the original childhood injuries.

Gavin doubles over, choking, coughing and vomiting bile, as if expelling poison. He staggers to the kitchen sink to get water, to purge. Then he remembers other episodes. He takes a deep breath, attempting to get ahead of his out-of-control reaction.

A different kind of fear. Shame, failure, self-loathing. The urge to run away, hide, disappear, obliterate *himself*... Whenever he makes a mistake, loses control. Whenever anyone gets hurt or in danger. He didn't protect them, take care of them! Dad insisted he was responsible for taking care of his brother; that was his only purpose in life, his reason for being. He had taken that responsibility as a universal charge. He had to save everyone. And when he didn't...Mom, Dad, Devon...all his fault. So now any real or perceived threat to anyone he cares about thrashes him between the urge to fight the threat and the urge to flee, hide from the shame of failing to save.

It's that continuity he suspected. His self-talk takes over, as he realizes it's not so much related to what he discovered in Prince Street. That's in the past, in the hands of the FBI now. There's no *direct* relationship from that to his current family. It's the attitudes inherent in the mob culture that drove how he was raised. The patterns he experienced in childhood replicating in his life, like indelible ink. Like the tattoo of Devon on his bicep. It's why he's so fucked up, freaking out, hurting Katie and Maggie, driving them away. It's why he can't control or change his sensitivity and reactions to the things that trigger him. The patterns from childhood take over. They're in charge. Maybe Pedersen is right. It isn't the deaths he witnessed, it's how his family treated him when he was a kid, as if his whole childhood was a lie. Dad just repeated all the expectations he got from his father, who probably got them from *his* father. So will he ever kick this C-PTSD shit? Be in control of himself, or be controlled by it? Who says DNA is limited to genes?

> "You can't fix something until
> you admit it's broken."
> —Mark Goulston

40

A CRIPPLING WEIGHT OF SHAME BEARS DOWN ON Gavin as he passes the damaged tree on the left, before he turns into Dr. Skokou's driveway. He berates himself for repeating the same crazy stunt his brother had pulled so long ago. He wasn't on booze or drugs, like Devon had been on their sixteenth birthday, but he was high with out-of-control rage. He had long ago pledged to break the chain of dysfunction that seems to have cascaded from one generation of his family to the next. But he has failed.

Basketball boy isn't here today, shooting hoops. Gavin was looking forward to the familiar relaxing rhythms of dribbling, dunking and rebounding. But he also realizes he would feel shame facing the kid who pulled him out of his wreck.

He sits in his car in the driveway, trying to find the courage to go to the door. He promised Katie. But what can anyone do about his condition? How can anyone fix it, make it go away? Besides, what can Katie do if he doesn't go to therapy? He could just *say* he went. How would she know he didn't? But can he take care of Katie and Maggie if he doesn't get some sort of help? And what if this therapy process itself triggers him?

Gavin is having trouble quieting his mind, which is skipping all around the universe this afternoon. Well, a lot lately.

Maybe it's related to the hyperarousal Pedersen told him about. Visually, bodily, in his mind, his amygdala. From scary dangerous crazy shit to funny stuff. And all of that together. Simultaneously.

All that fragmented thinking, and all the questions, doubts and fears bombard him when he sits down in Dr. Skokou's black leather chair.

After the usual polite greetings, Dr. Skokou begins. "Gavin, you must have concerns and fears about what we're going to do here."

"Yes." *Well, duh. You got that right, lady.*

"Are those concerns and fears greater than your worries that you might be triggered by something at any time, and react dangerously, toward yourself or others?"

"Uh...maybe about equal." *Well, now that you put your finger on it, how I might hurt someone does totally scare the shit out of me...*

"Do you want to avoid reacting badly to triggers?"

"Well, yeah. Sure. But I'd rather not have triggers at all."

"There are things that can occur all around you every day, that might be a trigger for you now. But by working here, the triggering *effect* of those things will diminish, and can eventually be eliminated altogether. Your reactions to triggers will become manageable."

"So be specific about the 'work.' And how long do I have to do it?"

"As with everything," the doctor smiles, "it depends. But if you are determined to work honestly, without holding back or resisting, you'll make significant progress."

Gavin smirks. Doubt, or fear, or both, clouding his mind.

"You're worried that things we discuss here may trigger you, or bring up bad memories."

No shit, Sherlock. "Yes."

"If at any time you feel yourself in danger of being triggered, or feel very uncomfortable, just hold up your finger. Or your hand, and we'll stop."

"Okay..." *Wish that could work for the rest of the world.*

"That similar 'pause' technique holds true for your life outside our work," Skokou says. "Like when you feel unsafe, pausing to focus your thoughts on the good of the here and now, as we discussed last time."

Gavin thinks of Katie. She's the most important thing in his life. He's determined to honor and protect her at all costs. He can't understand why he's been hurting her so often recently. Demeaning her, being dismissive, snapping at her. *Like Dad always did to me...*

"And that pause technique works for me too, Gavin. If you begin exhibiting threatening or injurious behavior, I will immediately stop the session and protect myself if necessary."

Gavin understands the doctor's implication, and tries to picture how she might "protect" herself. He laughs internally, envisioning scrawny little Skokou defending herself with martial arts, a taser, or something else equally unlikely. He knows he's had violent reactions to triggers a few times, but he doesn't actually remember what he did. Only how it felt in his body. Surreal sensations for which no words exist. But he never knows what might trigger him.

Now he abruptly announces, "I need to be home by five o'clock to take Maggie trick-or-treating, Dr. Skokou." He fidgets in the chair.

"Well, that's lovely. Is this her first Halloween?" Skokou smiles.

"We put a costume on her last year for the Halloween party at our restaurant," Gavin chuckles, "but she was only eleven months old. She probably doesn't remember it. But she's really excited this year."

"Have you had any thoughts about our last meeting?" she asks, peering over her steepled fingers.

"I've had thoughts." *Of course. Those thoughts won't ever stop.* "Maybe not much specific about our meeting." He leans back in his chair, both hands firmly on the armrests, and looks at her with a direct gaze that's almost defiant.

"I imagine you'll share those thoughts if you believe they're relevant to the work we're doing here," Skokou nods with a coy smile. "The work to repair and heal from your trauma."

Dr. Skokou has just derailed Gavin's intended cat-and-mouse game. His contumacious defense visibly withers, like an inflatable bopper toy losing its air. "Trauma," he repeats, as if it's the first time he's considered the term.

"Yes, Gavin," she confirms. "That's the 'T' in PTSD."

He rebounds. "What does that have to do with all the triggers I have? The stuff you wanted me to record in this thing?" He pulls up the journal and waves it at her.

"Your triggers are rooted in, and associated with, your past traumas." Two slow nods.

Gavin stares off into space, unmoving.

"Did you record your trigger episodes in the journal?"

"Some of them."

"Do you recall what occurred to initiate your reaction, and how you responded?"

Gavin opens the journal. "Nothing very interesting," he mumbles, leafing through pages. "I was just going through stuff in my dad's house."

"Things from childhood?"

"Journals my mother wrote. Notes my brother wrote."

"What did they write about?"

Gavin is reluctant to share what he found in those journals, especially how it made him feel. His reactions. There's something holding him back, as if telling it will somehow trap him, corner him. "Like I said, nothing very interesting. Just the usual family stuff."

"What is it about uninteresting, 'usual stuff' that would trigger you?" Skokou asks. "Something traumatic?"

He again diverts. "Trauma happened later, not during childhood. Y'know, deaths in the family."

"Mmm-hmm," Skokou nods. "Often what we experience in childhood is both a predictor of, and colors our response to, trauma in later life."

Gavin is silent. He might agree with Skokou's first assertion, but he hasn't considered the latter. Those violent deaths were the logical inevitable conclusion of all that was fucked up in his family. But would those deaths have affected him differently if he'd grown up in a normal family? It would have been a terrible unexpected shock if his family had always been—well, *close*, in which case he may have felt great loss, instead of the debilitating guilt, shame, and...*anger—rage!* overwhelming him now. For having failed to save them.

"Tell me about your father. Were you close?"

Gavin laughs internally at the irony of her question, which seems to have picked a keyword from the self-talk of his mind. That adjective would never have been applied to his father; it was something Tony was incapable of, with anyone. A foreign concept. "Well, 'close' isn't something that anyone would normally associate with my dad." *Closeness in our family was limited to Devon sucking the life out of me, and Mom excusing and intellectualizing it.*

"Did he treat you and your twin the same?"

"Like I said, he didn't *do* 'close' with anyone."

"So he treated you and Devon exactly the same?"

"Of course not. We may have been identical twins, but we were different."

"So your father's treatment of each of you was the cause of, or the reaction to your differences?"

That question pokes at him. Was Dad's treatment of Devon and him cause or effect? A twist on nature versus nurture. He shakes it off and abruptly looks at his watch. "Oh, y'know, I need to get going. Traffic was already building up when I came, and I don't want to disappoint Maggie and Katie." He stands and begins to walk toward the door.

"When will you be willing to do the work, Gavin?"

Dr. Skokou asks. "When will you be willing to trust the process, trust me to help you with the work?"

Gavin is several steps ahead of her, and now stops. "I'll see you Friday," he mutters with his back to her. "Four o'clock." He resumes walking.

"I hope Maggie enjoys Halloween," she says. "And I'm pleased you're ready to do the work."

Gavin couldn't wait to get out of there. But it isn't lost on him that his reluctance to open up and be truthful exemplifies the distrust Pedersen warned him of.

He doesn't notice the silver sedan pulling out behind him when he turns onto the road, following him closely. At the same time, a text from Tray comes in on Gavin's pocketed phone:

> Local police released the two guys who broke into your dad's house before FBI could get custody. So they're loose.

> "It's not the moment that it happens,
> It's the moment right before,
> It's not the rain or crashing thunder,
> It's the calm before the storm."
> —Katherine Humpert

41

"DA-DEE!" PRINCESS MAGGIE RUNS TO GREET GAVIN as he walks in the door.

"Oh, my goodness!" Gavin exclaims. "Who is this beautiful princess?"

"Mag-gie! Ma-gret Cah-yeen Dee-Masi!" Maggie insists, extending her arms out and turning like a model. "Go Howween!" she squeals, clapping her hands and jumping.

Katie walks in looking like Van Gogh, complete with paint mimicking his *Starry Night* covering her long white nightgown, wearing a hat with a bandaged left ear, and a paintbrush tucked behind the other ear.

Gavin seems taken aback when he sees her costume. "Oh, wow! I guess I should have a costume."

"I got you a mask, babe," Katie grins, handing him a rubber Darth Vader mask. "You're already wearing black pants and black sweater, so you're good to go."

"Cool," Gavin mumbles. "So we're gonna do this?"

"I'm going to take a picture of you and Maggie first," Katie says. Gavin dons his mask, feeling more like Dopey than the powerful Darth Vader, then crouches down next to his little princess, along with Patches. "Perfect!" Katie cheers as she snaps the photo.

"Yay!" Maggie claps, and Patches wags his tail, dancing around the family as they go out the door.

Gavin smiles, thinking everything will be okay with his family. Hoping he isn't kidding himself.

Standard Time returned Sunday, the day before, so it is already dark at five o'clock, and families are out with their children, knocking on doors. Cars from other neighborhoods—rural areas where trick-or-treating presents logistical challenges, and poor or unsafe urban neighborhoods—cruise the street, delivering their children to enjoy Halloween. There is a lively party atmosphere buzzing the street, with kids high on excitement, chocolate and sugar.

"Katie!" a woman calls out.

Katie turns to see Miriam on the sidewalk, and rushes to give her friend a hug. "Maggie, do you remember Miriam and her kids Jenny and Bobby?"

Maggie beams with her little dance and holds up her goodie bag. "Tick o Teet!"

"Miriam, this is my husband Gavin," Katie gestures toward him.

Gavin turns to Katie, his mask obscuring his puzzled expression, then mumbles "Hello," with a nod to Miriam.

"Have you gone down the street yet?" Katie asks Miriam, pointing to the houses beyond Number Seven.

"No, we just got started." Miriam restrains her children from rushing ahead.

"Then let's walk together! Bobby and Jenny can show Maggie how it's done."

The sidewalks and street are crowded, with some unaccompanied older kids darting from one side of the street to the other, dodging cars. Katie and Miriam chat together when not calling out to their children, and Patches herds them all as if he were a border collie.

It's a beautiful night, wonderfully free of tension and fear.

Then, multiple events occur near-simultaneously in a surreal blur, making even a slow-motion replay or sequencing impossible...

"Are you Maggie's mother?" A woman approaches Katie. "I saw your little girl at the Child Study Center." — A silver sedan slows alongside them. — Gavin checks his messages on his cell phone. — Maggie sees Luca. "Loo-kah!" she squeals, running to hug his leg. — The woman grabs Maggie. — Patches clamps his jaws onto the woman's leg. — Luca whips out his knife on its chain. — The knife pierces the woman's butt. — She keeps running with Maggie. — Luca hits the ground, yanked by the woman impaled with his knife. — A man jumps out of the silver car and shoots at Patches. — His bullet misses the dog but hits Luca. — Gavin sees Tray's message, looks up, tears off his mask and runs toward Maggie. — The man shoots Gavin. — Man and woman-with-Maggie jump in the silver car. — It peels out instantly with its doors still open. — The car speeds up the street with Gavin and Patches in pursuit.

Gavin's legs churn faster than they've ever run, flying over the pavement, burning with psychotic rage and fear, oblivious to pedestrians, passing cars, his bleeding arm, disregarding the reality of increasing distance between him and the car holding his daughter. He's in a fight for Maggie's life. And his own.

Katie rushes into the street behind her daughter, the speeding car, her husband, screaming helplessly, collapsing in neighbors' arms, the nightmarish fears she's been resisting now fully unleashed as a heinous reality.

"Mrs. DiMasi," the doctor says, while pings and beeps of monitors echo in the ICU. "Your husband is going to recover. We removed a bullet from his arm. We have him under sedation because he was hysterical when he came in. I'm sure he will be all right when he awakens. We checked his records here, and we recommend keeping him overnight."

Katie is shivering, surrounded by the O'Malley grandparents and Dr. Pedersen, and now manages to stammer, "So should I pick him up in the morning? And how is Luca, our neighbor?"

"Yes, you can pick up your husband in the morning. And Mr. Benedetti will be okay," the doctor nods. "We're trying to locate his next of kin to let them know."

"Can I see him? I want to thank him."

"He's recovering from surgery now, but we will tell him you asked about him," the doctor dismisses her.

When Katie and her group go out into the waiting area, she is surrounded and embraced by many people. Destiny with Peter Thompson, Dr. Ted with Miriam and two other members of the spouse group, Dr. Skokou, and Tray.

When all the hugs, concern and comforting have been proffered, Tray pulls Katie aside. "Hey, girl, we're on it. We'll get her back. Do you have a recent picture of Maggie?"

Katie pulls out her phone and sends the photo of Princess Maggie to Tray; he immediately sends it out with identification and a directive.

"Did anyone in the crowd get the license number of the car?" Katie's voice shakes.

"Luca did. Tough, sharp old guy he is," Tray shakes his head in amazement. "Injured, on the ground, still had the presence of mind to get the number. But the plates were stolen."

Katie breaks down, sobbing. Thompson rushes over with a chair and eases her into it.

"You are *not* going to be alone tonight," Tray says with firm commitment. "I'll be camping out at your place, along with one of my guys manning your phones, and I think there's a whole tribe of your friends," he gestures to the crowd, "who want to keep you company, too."

Now Pedersen and Skokou are at her side.

"Katie, we've ordered a drip of anti-anxiety medication for Gavin, to start as soon as the sedative begins to wear off," Pedersen says. "And my dear, Gavin may *not* be okay in the morning."

> "People cry, not because they're weak.
> It's because they've been strong for too long."
> —Johnny Depp

42

WITH THE HELP OF THE DOXYLAMINE PEDERSEN GAVE her, Katie manages to get a little sleep, although it isn't restful. Tray sleeps on the sofa and Destiny keeps Katie company by occupying the empty spot where Gavin should have been.

Accompanied by the O'Malley grandparents and Tray, Katie arrives at the hospital the next morning to take Gavin home. She's beginning to hate this hospital, which by this point should have an entire wing dedicated to the fucked-up DiMasi family. Her hair is disheveled and her reddened eyes bleed despair.

Pedersen pulls her aside. "Katie, I'm so sorry about Maggie. And for what it's doing to you." For the first time, the doctor breaks protocol—and character—to envelop her in a long hug.

Her body implodes in hopeless sobs. "What are we going to do, Jim?"

Pedersen releases his hug and holds Katie's shoulders out at arm's length, peering into her face, understanding the scope of her question. "Tray will get Maggie back. We'll do whatever is necessary to repair her trauma." He drops his hold. "And you will need to make the hard decisions to protect her, and yourself, from further damage."

Katie's lips tighten as her eyes narrow and jaw sets in determination. With a grim nod, she asks, "And now? Today?"

"Although hospitalization may not provide the most effective treatment, it would keep him out of his own danger zone for a while so treatment can at least begin. But he won't accept voluntary hospitalization, and there's insufficient evidence at this point to have him involuntarily committed. He hasn't been charged with a crime, and hasn't directly endangered anyone's life," Pedersen sighs. "But he was given an IV drip of medication for anxiety and panic attacks overnight, and he needs to continue dosing orally after release. Maybe that will level out his behavior for now."

"Ha. I'll be surprised if he's willing to take the meds."

"See if you can persuade him," Pedersen urges. "And I think your emotional state during this stress may benefit from taking a low dose of diazepam. It's safe during pregnancy." He hands her two prescription bottles.

"What then?" Katie pleads.

"Keep a close watch on him, and when he goes off the rails, call police."

Katie notes that Jim didn't say "*if*" Gavin goes off the rails…

Once they have Gavin home from the hospital, they all gather in Katie's living room. Grandma and Grandpa, Pedersen and Tray, who briefs them on what is being done to recover Maggie. Gavin doesn't sit. He paces, occasionally punching. The air, the wall, a table, a chair.

"We're assuming they've taken Maggie in order to get something, such as cash," Tray begins, all official business, not quite the laid-back best friend Gavin and Katie love. "The man we installed in your home last night, who was replaced by Agent Broderick this morning," he waves to a woman sitting near the phone in the kitchen, "put a tap on your land line and cell phones. When anyone calls and you're not available to answer, the caller's voice, phone number and other information will be recorded. Agent Broderick will load a tap on your computer, your email and socials as soon as we're done here, and coach you on how to respond to callers and messages in a broad range of possible scenarios."

"If they want money, FBI can give 'em the three and a half mil from the building, right?" Gavin snaps, wishing he'd never taken the money out of the building, and just let them find it instead.

"Possibly, but the handoff and getting Maggie is tricky. It's a precarious undertaking, nothing you should try to do yourself."

"What if they just want revenge, and none of this matters?" Gavin shouts, throwing his arms up.

Pedersen watches Gavin warily.

"That's unlikely," Tray says, his voice calm and reassuring. "They always want something. We got warrants to search the homes of the two guys who broke into your dad's house. That didn't turn up anything. We questioned them and searched their computers and cell phones. We could have taken them into custody, but there's more value in following them. We're monitoring chatter, on the street and online. We need to get a sketch of whoever took Maggie—"

Katie's head pops up. "I can help with that! A woman came up to me and said something right before she took Maggie!"

"That's their first mistake." Tray barely suppresses a smug grin. "Shows they're careless. Or stupid. It's not the last mistake they're going to make, and that's how we'll get 'em." He pulls out his phone and sends a message. "Okay, a sketch artist will be here around eleven, Katie. I need to get back to HQ, but you have the agent here, and me on speed-dial at any time."

After Tray leaves, Grandpa excuses himself to go to an appointment. "I'll stay here with Katie," Grandma says. "Keep her company, make sure she eats something and gets some rest."

Pedersen stands and intercepts Gavin's pacing. "Gavin, this is a terrible thing to have happened. How are you going to deal with it?"

"Whaddya mean, deal with it?" Gavin growls. "What the hell can I do? I can't even protect my own kid!" He turns away.

Pedersen moves to remain in front of him, determined to not let Gavin avoid the important questions. "I'm asking how are you going to deal with your anger and stress? Your worry about Maggie's safety, your guilt over her being taken?"

"Guilt? I had nothing to do with my daughter's kidnapping!" Gavin yells.

"You continued poking the bear in Prince Street, messing with the mob when you were warned, Gavin. By both your grandfathers, by Katie, me, and Tray," Pedersen asserts firmly, without raising his voice. "But you loved the challenge, the mystery, thought you could outsmart them."

"I'm getting out of here," Gavin spits.

"You need to take your medication, son, to help you deal with the anxiety over this situation," Pedersen pleads.

"I need air," Gavin yells. "The smell of Katie's damn paint is suffocating me!"

Katie interjects, "But your arm, Gavin. And you just got out of the hospital." She speaks in a calm emotionless tone, ending in full-stop, performing her tiptoe-on-eggshells dance.

"Don't be stupid! It's just my left arm, and I don't need your damn drugs!" Gavin's emotions and focus ricochet against the walls like ping-pong between madmen, bouncing off and denting everyone in the room.

Now Gavin recalls in a flash the dream that woke him in the hospital pre-dawn this morning. The same faces he saw last evening. He knows what he must do. He runs out the door.

After everyone has gone, leaving only Grandma, the agent, and Katie, she drops onto the sofa, utterly drained.

"Have you eaten anything yet today, Katie?" Grandma asks. She picks up a throw Mrs. Goodwin had crocheted and lays it over Katie.

"I don't think so," Katie murmurs. "I can't remember. But my stomach isn't too happy with me right now."

"How about a cup of tea and a piece of toast?" Grandma says. "That should settle pretty easily on your stomach."

"Thank you so much, Grandma," Katie says as she sips her tea and nibbles on her toast. The air in the house feels so empty, so quiet, like a funeral parlor. The hollow vacuum is so dense she can't breathe. "This is all so hard, and I can't imagine how I could get through it all without your help, and Tray, and Grandpa. But I worry about Dr. Pedersen," she mutters through a bite of toast. "He seems really down. Is he okay?"

"Oh, Katie dear," Grandma says, squeezing her hand. "That's so like you, worrying about other people when you have so much to worry about for yourself and your family." She pours Katie more tea from the pot. "Jim had a sad anniversary a couple weeks ago. Fifteen years since his wife and son died tragically. And I believe he has come to see Gavin as sort of his substitute son, trying to help him in a way he was never able to help his son. So he could be feeling a bit depressed."

"And now his efforts seem to be verging on hopeless," Katie shakes her head. "That's so sad. How did they die?"

"Jim's son Brad had been struggling with mental illness for quite some time, and in a suicidal rage drove his car off an overpass, with his mother inside."

"Oh, how awful," Katie moans. "I can't imagine." From her readings and discussions in her spouse group, she knows that suicidal inclinations often occur in victims of PTSD, and worries once again about Maggie's safety. And her own.

"I need to get some air for a few minutes," she stands abruptly, trying to inhale and expel tension. "And I should check on Luca."

Grandma lifts Katie's jacket off the hook by the door and helps her into it. "Would you like me to walk with you?"

"Thanks, but no. I'll only be a few minutes. And I'm expecting the sketch artist Tray sent."

Katie calls out for Patches, but there's no response. She figures he's probably hiding under the bed, and goes out the front door. She notices Gavin has taken the car.

She breathes deeply in the autumn air, trying to expel the toxins of the last eighteen hours, but the air feels thick and leaden today. Her imagination runs in a dozen directions at once. Envisioning Maggie, where she is, whether she's hurt, how badly she must be traumatized, how are they going to rescue her... Thinking of Gavin, where is he, what's he doing now, what's his state of mind, what will it take for him to accept therapeutic help, will they ever return to a normal happy life... And what is *she* going to decide once they get Maggie back?

Luca comes to the door using crutches when Katie rings the bell. His face falls in sorrow when he sees her. "Katie, my dear. Come in. I must sit."

Katie helps Luca negotiate his crutches over to his recliner chair and raises the foot section for him. "I'm so sorry you were hurt last night, Luca," Katie says, "and thank you so much for trying to save our daughter. You'd already left the hospital this morning when we picked up Gavin, or we would have driven you home."

"I called someone I know, Katie. Don't you worry about me." Luca waves his hand, dismissing her concern as unimportant. "Now, I want to know who is doing what, in order to bring little Maggie home," he asks, leaning forward with an intensity that might signal danger if it came from a much younger uninjured man.

Katie takes another deep breath. "FBI is involved, because it's likely the kidnappers are associated with recent discoveries in the North End building that belonged to my husband's grandfather," Katie says, as Luca nods. "FBI is coordinating with police both here and in Boston. The usual, circulating Maggie's picture, wiretaps on our phones, what they call 'chatter,' lots of things."

Again, Luca nods knowingly. "Um-humm..."

"Do you have a first-floor bedroom and bathroom, Luca?" Katie asks. "I don't think you should be using your stairs for a while."

"Yes, yes, I do," Luca says, somewhat impatiently, as if he has more important things to consider. "Age-in-place arrangements, you know."

"That's good. Is there anything I can get you, anything you need?" Katie asks.

"No, but thank you. Don't worry about me," Luca says again, seemingly eager to rush Katie out. "And try not to worry about Maggie. She'll be coming home soon. Real soon. You can see yourself out," he nods toward the door.

As Katie walks back home, she thinks about Luca, curious about his absolute certainty that Maggie will "be coming home soon." And then she realizes that amid all the traumatic events, she hasn't seen Patches since last night.

> "The caged bird sings
> with a fearful trill
> of things unknown
> but longed for still
> and his tune is heard
> on the distant hill
> for the caged bird
> sings of freedom."
> —Maya Angelou

43

REPETITIVE ROUNDS OF "ITSY BITSY SPIDER" AND "ROW, row, row your boat" come from behind the locked closet door. Over and over again.

Then, "Find Mag-gie! Ma-gret Cah-yeen Dee-Masi!" Over and over again. Interspersed with "Seb-un Ma-shul Steet!" Over and over again.

A boy's voice complains, "Ma! Doesn't that kid ever shut up?"

A woman's voice replies, "She'll finally get tired and stop. Just don't unlock that door. She's been fed, watered and pee'ed, so she's okay."

"But my stuff is in there! My trucks!"

"I'm sure a little girl doesn't give a shit about yer damn trucks."

"Who is she, and why's she in there?"

"Ask yer uncle. Just stop yer whinin'. Go outside and play."

"But it's rainin', Ma!"

A girl's voice teases, "Yeah, baby, baby, baby wants his toys."

"Shut up, fatso!"

"Ma, he called me fat!"

"You two are a pain in my ass! Like my ass isn't already killin' me."

"Ma, what's for lunch?"

"Make it yerself, girl. And don't eat all your candy from last night in one sitting. You'll get sick. I hafta go to work now, and do NOT unlock that door!"

The outside door slams shut behind the woman.

Strains of the A-B-C song emanate from the closet, over and over. Then another sound, one of distress. "Go poo-poo, go poo-poo..."

The boy wails, "Oh no! Now she's gonna shit on my trucks!"

The girl says, "They're nothin' but shit anyway, fart-boy."

"Shut up! Whadda you know?"

"Well, I feel sorry for the kid. I'm gonna let her use the toilet, then we'll stick her back in there."

"Ma said not to unlock the door!"

"Who's gonna tell her, some little fink-boy?"

The girl goes to the closet, lifts the latch and cautiously cracks open the door.

"YAY! Find Mag-gie!" Princess Maggie stands there in her Halloween finery—minus her tiara—grinning with a red truck in her hands. "Go poo-poo!" She rushes past the girl, looking for a bathroom.

"Hold up, kid," the girl says. "I'll take you to the bathroom."

"Hey, what's she doin' with my truck?"

Maggie squeals "Wed twuck!" as she is dragged to the bathroom.

When she's finished, the girl grabs her arm.

"Big girl pants!" Maggie says proudly.

The girl looks at Maggie like she's an odd specimen and pulls her back to the closet. Before the girl can open the door, Maggie drops to the floor and begins zooming the truck along the soiled beige carpet, complete with sound effects, toward the boy. "Dumper!" she squeals, showing off the moveable dumpster bed.

"Ma said little girls don't like trucks," the boy says, baffled. "Can we let her stay out for a few minutes? I'll watch her. We can put her back in the closet before Ma gets home."

"Oh, fart-boy wants to play with girls!"

The girl turns on the television, too loud, and becomes immersed in her cell phone.

The boy is distracted by a cartoon on the screen.

"Go pee-pee!" Maggie says. But no one is paying attention to her. She toddles toward the bathroom, passing another door along the way. There's a scratching sound outside it, along with high-pitched whining and sporadic huffs. Maggie reaches up and pulls the lever handle down, opening the door.

"Pat-us!" Maggie whispers, putting her finger to her lips like Mommy often does for quiet. Patches clamps his jaws onto Maggie's princess dress, pulling her outside and on up the sidewalk.

As the boy and girl watch television, a Public Service Announcement comes on the screen with two pictures.

Boy yells, "That's the little girl in our closet! And that's Ma!"

Girl screams, "Kidnapped? Ma kidnapped her? They say to call the police! What if Ma goes to jail? We have to get rid of that kid, get her outta here!"

But Maggie is already gone.

> "Whoever fights monsters should see to it
> that in the process he does not become a monster.
> And if you gaze long enough into an abyss,
> the abyss will gaze back into you."
> —Friedrich Nietzsche

44

GAVIN PULLS THE CAR INTO THE GARAGE A LITTLE after two o'clock. He's jumpy and jittering all over, like he's plugged into a high-voltage current. He closes the garage door then opens the car trunk and pulls out a long rectangular black case. He closes the trunk, lays the case on the trunk lid and opens it, inspecting its contents.

He goes into the house and yells out, "Has anyone called?"

Grandma rouses from lying on the sofa. "So far, there've only been calls from people offering concern and comfort. Katie's upstairs taking a prescribed nap." Grandma stands and puts her hands on her hips, assuming her sternest grandmother look. "You could probably use a nap, too. And take your damn medication!"

Gavin recoils. He's never heard his grandmother speak this way. It's very unlike the O'Malleys, and he feels like a kid being scolded by the principal. He turns and slinks away.

She shouts after him, "I won't let you do to Katie what your father did to our daughter!"

He trudges up the stairs and peeks into the bedroom. Katie is lying on the bed, turned away from the door, breathing softly. He closes the door and goes back down the stairs, avoiding eye contact with Grandma and the FBI operative sitting by the phone in the kitchen, then out into the garage.

He loads cartridges into his M21 and his Glock. Just as he begins to close the case, Katie screams behind him, "What the hell are you doing?"

Gavin whips around, quickly closing the case. "I'm going to save Maggie."

"Not with guns, you aren't!" She stands on the doorstep, juddering violently like a volcano erupting. "And how the hell did you get those? You couldn't have gotten a license so quickly!"

"There's a place, some guys, in Littleton…" Gavin mutters like a kid caught with his hand in the cookie jar.

"Well, I'm going to call the police. You're carrying firearms without a license, and you're sure as hell not bringing that shit into this house!" She turns to go back in the house, but Gavin tries to stop her from behind, knocking her over. Katie screams long and loud.

Gavin throws open the garage door, stuffs the case into the back seat and powers the car out of the garage just as Agent Broderick rushes out and Katie screams, "And don't bother coming back here!"

Katie almost trips over Gavin's cell phone on the step as she runs into the house and frantically tries to find the paperwork for the car she rented; she can't remember where she put it, much less the make, model and license number. The FBI agent notifies headquarters that Gavin is traveling with firearms, destination unknown. Katie texts Tray that Gavin is off the rails with an unlicensed rifle and handgun, insisting he's going to save Maggie, but she doesn't know details about the car.

Although Tray knows those details, he wonders whether Gavin accidentally or deliberately left his cell phone behind, which is now pinging its location in Katie's house. FBI can no longer track him.

Gavin drives slowly down the narrow one-way Elm Street in Charlestown until he sees the number he's looking for, then glides on past, goes around the block and back again, pulling his car into a space two doors down on the left. On a street where most of the old multistory buildings sitting directly on the edge of sidewalks have been renovated with fresh siding and paint, fairly well maintained, this house is an orphan with old siding that's missing in places, peeling paint, a broken window and trash beside it. It's where Gavin's internet search revealed that Rick Salvatti's only sister lives. His memory, the flash image of the guy who shot him last night, came back to him in his early-morning nightmare in the hospital. He's pretty sure it was Salvatti. Tray says FBI searched the homes of all suspects; Salvatti was on that list, but they didn't find Maggie or any trace of her at his house. Gavin suspects the woman who grabbed Mags may be Salvatti's sister; in the blur of his memory, he thinks he saw a family resemblance.

He sits, waiting and watching, trying to regulate his breaths, focusing on a tenacious clump of dandelions growing out of a crack in the sidewalk. Gathering his courage. And his Glock, which he sticks under his belt, under his jacket. He gets out of the car and opens the rear door to pull out his case, then runs to the house. He looks in a window and sees the television on, through threadbare curtains. *Family Guy* reruns. A girl, maybe ten or eleven, sits on the sofa.

He goes to the door and knocks. Inside, a young boy yells, "You gonna get that, fatso?"

"I'm telling Ma, fart-face!" Her voice comes closer as she walks to the door. She opens it a crack and peeks out.

Gavin slams his shoulder into the door, knocking the girl to the floor, and rushes into the house. Before she can catch her breath to scream, he shuts the door and points the Glock at her. "Where's my daughter!"

The girl stammers, blubbering, then catches her breath and stands, channeling her mother's tough-talk. "I don't know what you're talkin' about, and you'd better get the fuck out of here before I call the police!"

Boy pipes up, "You mean the little princess they're looking for?"

Girl yells, "Shut up, stupid!"

"I saw her walkin' out on the sidewalk," boy fibs.

"Yeah, that's it!" girl says. "You better go get her!"

"I don't believe you. Where's your mother?"

Girl pokes boy in the ribs with a *"keep your mouth shut"* glower, then says, "Oh, she went out to get some milk and stuff. She should be back any minute."

"I thought Ruby Salvatti tends bar at the Warren Tavern."

Boy catches on to his sister's ruse. "Yeah, but not on Tuesdays."

"Well, I need to keep you two in one place while I check the house for my daughter." When Gavin pulls rope from his case, the girl gasps upon seeing the long gun. Gavin ties each child to the stair railing leading up to the second floor. "Now just be quiet and I'll untie you as soon as I've looked around."

"Wonder how far your little girl will go while you're doing that?" The girl says in a sing-song taunt.

Gavin rushes, frantically storming from room to room, opening cabinets and doors, then spots a sequin he thinks came from Maggie's princess costume on the floor of the closet. He picks it up and holds it out to the girl. "This came from Maggie's dress," he shouts. "You're lying! Where is she?" He shoves the Glock in her face.

The girl juts out her jaw defiantly. "She left. We were watching TV and she snuck out when we weren't looking. We don't know where she is, and our Ma is gonna be mad!"

The boy mumbles, "Uncle is gonna be even madder."

"Your Uncle Rick?" Gavin asks, then sees the flashing blue lights outside.

The door breaks open and two police officers rush in with guns drawn. "Drop the gun! You're under arrest!"

Gavin is dragged to the squad car by three policemen. He's handcuffed but still struggles, swinging at the officers, kicking, screaming. He shouts, "Where's Maggie? Salvatti, I'm gonna kill you son of a bitch!"

He loses consciousness.

> "There are wounds that never show on the body that are deeper and more hurtful than anything that bleeds."
> —Laurell K. Hamilton

45

IT'S BEEN TWENTY-FOUR HOURS SINCE MAGGIE WAS taken. It feels like several lifetimes to Katie. It's around five o'clock when her cell phone rings. She looks at Broderick to be sure the agent is ready to monitor the call. Then she answers, "Hello."

A deep male voice speaks in an official manner. "Hello. This is Officer Michael Paliotta from Boston Police Department, calling you from Charlestown."

Katie glances over to Broderick, who nods confirmation on the source of the call.

"We have a dog here with the name of Patches and your phone number on his tag. Is this your dog?"

"Why, yes! Yes it is, and he went missing!" She's incredulous that Patches has somehow gotten himself all the way to Charlestown—what's that, fifteen miles? Losing him has been just one part of her trifecta of tragedy today. "When can we pick him up?"

"May I ask your name, ma'am, and where you live?"

Katie is puzzled by that question. "Uh, I'm Katie DiMasi, sir. We live in Wellesley. Seven Marshall Street."

"Then we also have your little girl Maggie here."

Katie wobbles and drops, nearly fainting, joyful sob-coughs

of relief emptying her chest.

The officer's voice softens. "It's going to be okay, ma'am. Someone found them walking down School Street here and we need to transfer them downtown to Boston headquarters. But your little Maggie refuses to get into our squad car, and definitely not without her dog. Child Protection Services is waiting for us downtown, where you can pick her up. And your dog too. Can you talk to your daughter to convince her to come with us?"

Agent Broderick gets on the line, identifying herself as FBI, verifying the officer's identification, and making sure BPD has notified FBI headquarters. She then nods for Katie to continue with the call.

Katie tries to calm her excitement, which feels like the gates of heaven have opened. "Thank you so much, sir. This is such a relief!" Her voice comes out as half cheer, half cry. "May I talk with Maggie now for a minute?"

When Maggie's voice comes on the line, Katie nearly collapses all over again. "Oh, sweetie, I'm so happy you and Patches are safe. I can't wait to hold you and hug you!"

"Bad lady taked me. An' a bad man."

"Yes, sweetie, but you don't need to worry about them anymore."

"But nice boy gots lotsa twucks!"

"Well, I can't wait to hear all about it, sweetie. We'll talk about it as soon as Grandpa can drive me to get you. You and Patches need to get in the nice policeman's car now, so he can take you to where we can get you and bring you home."

"Okay, Mommy," Maggie says. "Quick!"

Katie ends the call reluctantly, wanting to reach through the phone and pull her daughter to her.

Grandma calls her husband while Agent Broderick talks to Katie. "I talked to your friend Agent Harris. He says he'll meet you at BPD headquarters."

"Oh, that's good," Katie sighs. "Maggie and Tray have a real love thing together. She'll feel safe with him."

"We aren't sure your danger is completely over," the agent adds, "so FBI will keep someone here for at least the next few days."

While they're *en route* to Boston in Grandpa's car, Katie texts Tray that they're on their way. He replies that she should call him when they arrive, so he can come out to the lobby to meet her. It's fully dark when Grandpa pulls up to the police station, a massive bulwark of a brick building nearly a block long. There's no parking here; he drops off an über-anxious Katie with Grandma, while he parks in the Government Center parking garage.

Inside the building, the crowded lobby reverberates in the cacophonous buzz of a full-moon night with multiple interactions among different parties, several pulsating with high tension. If Katie didn't know that Tray would be coming out to escort her, she could easily be overwhelmed. She exhales when she sees him, just as Grandpa enters the lobby after parking the car. She runs to the strength of Tray's embrace.

"You okay, girl?" he asks, looking down into her face.

"I'll be better when I can get my arms around my daughter," Katie murmurs.

"Then let's go get her." Tray nods to the front desk clerk and leads Katie and the grandparents down the hall to the elevator. Once they reach the third floor, Tray leads them down another hall to a door with a small window. When Tray opens the door to usher the family in, there are just two adults, a man and a woman. "Katie, please sit," Tray says. "Someone from CPS is taking Maggie to the bathroom. Before she joins us, we want to share with you everything we know about her ordeal. This is Officer Paliotta, who was the first policeman on the scene to respond after a citizen called 911 about Maggie, and Ms. Helen O'Dougherty, from CPS."

"Ma'am," Paliotta speaks first. "I can't imagine what you've been going through, and what your daughter has experienced. I responded to a 911 call about a little girl who seemed lost, who was telling everyone her name and where she lives. The local citizen who made the call remembered seeing the PSA on TV with her picture. It was your dog that found Maggie first, and wouldn't let anyone near her. That's how I got your cell number to call you."

"What did you learn about her captivity and how she escaped?" Katie asks.

Ms. O'Dougherty's face droops sorrowfully as she explains what she was able to piece together by talking with Maggie.

Tray interjects, "Your neighbor Luca Benedetti has some old connections in the Italian 'community,'" he says with air quotes. "He sent us a tip on where to look for Maggie. That's how we found where she *had been* kept, like Ms. O'Dougherty just explained. We all know how clever Mags can be, so it's no surprise she managed to escape."

"But despite her positive attitude," Ms. O'Dougherty adds, "Maggie *is* traumatized. It's important to get psychological help to get her past this without lasting damage."

"I completely agree. Of course she's traumatized! And I know exactly where we can get the best help for her," Katie says, thinking of the extensive professional resources at the Child Study Center. She looks over to Grandma O'Malley, who responds with a determined nod. "Now let's bring her home."

"A couple more things I need to tell you, Katie," Tray says. "Luca's tip is also how we arrested the people who took her."

Katie struggles between feeling relief and revenge. "The woman and man who grabbed Maggie?" she asks, at the same time wondering about the other thing Tray wants to tell her.

"Yes, the woman is the sister of Richard Salvatti. He had convinced his sister to take Maggie and keep her at her house in Charlestown."

Katie remembers that name and nods her head, waiting. "What was the other thing you wanted to tell me?" Her imagination goes wild with fears...Maggie might be injured, or might have been abused...

"Luca's tip is also how we managed to go there in time to intercept Gavin with his guns," Tray says.

Katie's heart crashes against her chest and the room spins. "He's in custody now."

Tray and Grandpa both catch her as she falls.

> "Unexpressed emotions will never die.
> They are buried alive and will come forth
> later in uglier ways."
> —Sigmund Freud

46

KATIE NEVER WANTS TO LET MAGGIE OUT OF HER arms. She holds her daughter, still warm and damp from her bath, wanting to siphon out every bit of trauma her baby has experienced, erase it all, the cruel injustice of such a young child being caught in the crosshairs of her father's perverted history.

"Mommy," Maggie murmurs into Katie's chest. "Wuv you."

"And Mommy loves you, *so* much."

Maggie leans back and spreads both arms out, singing, "*Thi-i-s-s much!*"

"And more," Katie whispers, nuzzling her face into Maggie's tummy, recalling how her father used to do that, and the funny blubbering sound he made that always tickled her skin and made her giggle.

"Seepy, Mommy," Maggie mumbles, putting her arms around Katie's neck.

"Would you like to sleep in Mommy's bed tonight?" Katie asks, peering into her daughter's face. "I need to talk with Tray and everyone downstairs for a few minutes, but then I'll come to bed and be with you, because I'm sleepy too. Is that okay?"

"Uh-huh," Maggie exhales, collapsing into Katie's shoulder.

Katie lays Maggie on the side of the bed where Gavin

should be, tucking her beloved stuffed dragon beside her, and the covers over her. She kisses her head and closes the bedroom door, leaving it slightly ajar so she can hear if Mags cries out.

Despite the joy and relief of having Maggie back, everyone gathered in the living room sits mournfully as if someone has died. Grandma has made a pot of tea and pours a cup for Katie.

"Is she okay, Katie?" Grandpa asks.

"For now. But more than anything, she's exhausted," Katie sighs, sitting down in the upholstered armchair. "We'll know more tomorrow. Or even later tonight. It won't be surprising if she has bad dreams or nightmares."

"It's going to take time," Pedersen agrees, regret weighing his voice.

"Yes," Grandma says, hugging her arms around herself and rocking forward, her face contorted in grief. "Such a tragic thing to happen to a sweet young child."

Pedersen reaches over to touch Grandma's arm. "Carla, can you inquire at the Child Study Center for a therapist who can work with Maggie on this?"

"Of course," Grandma says, her mouth grim. "She'll need a play therapy approach, obviously. I know exactly who can deal with this."

"Thank you, Grandma." Katie takes a deep breath. "So let's address the elephant in the room," she says, chewing her lower lip and gripping both arms of her chair. "Tray, when and how did Gavin get arrested, what are the charges, and have they set bond?"

Tray glances over to Pedersen. "It was around five o'clock—"

"How did they find him?" Katie interjects.

"When we gave your neighbor Luca's tip to local police on where Maggie might be, she was already gone when they got there—they had no idea she was over on the next block with Patches—but Gavin was inside the house threatening the kids." Tray hesitates. "Then when the officers took him into custody, he was, uh, not really himself..."

"You mean he was crazy violent." Katie moans, slumping over and shaking her head slowly. Hopeless despair grips her, sensing that Gavin is falling off a cliff, with no bottom in sight. Grandma rushes over and perches on the arm of Katie's chair, hugging her shoulder.

"Right now he's in pre-trial detention," Tray goes on. "Bail wasn't set, due to his state of mind and the seriousness of the charges—"

Katie's head pops up, fear draining her face. "What *are* the charges?" She dreads the answer.

Grandma looks to Pedersen, telegraphing an appeal for help. He nods, grim.

"It's not good." Tray's sorrowful eyes betray his professionalism in favor of friendship. And human kindness. "FBI had no hand in it; BPD has the case. He had two unlicensed guns, threatening two kids he'd just tied up, after breaking into their house. Add resisting arrest to that, and..."

Katie breaks down, sobbing uncontrollably into Grandma's arms.

Pedersen speaks up. "Then we need to make sure he's remanded to a mental hospital for evaluation, rather than being held in a cell where he's untreated, and in greater danger."

Tray nods, then looks to Grandpa, whose eyes narrow with understanding. "There could be a risk of revenge from mob-affiliated fellow inmates," Grandpa says low.

"I've asked the officer in charge to expedite scheduling the arraignment," Tray says. "If Dr. Pedersen testifies regarding Gavin's condition and the need for evaluation, we might be able to pull him out of there to somewhere he can get the help he needs."

"I'll be there, with documentation," Pedersen says. "Just tell me where and when."

Tray looks at his phone. "I know a lawyer who's handled a

similar case; I texted her a couple hours ago. She just got back to me. I'll coordinate everything that needs to happen, for as soon as the court will allow."

"So when will we be able to bring him home?" The crease between Katie's eyebrows deepens in a battle between her desire to have him home and the unpredictable tension his disorder brings with him.

Grandpa interjects, "Katie, no! One damaged victim is enough for you to deal with now."

Tray reacts to Grandpa with a solemn eyelid-drop of agreement and a nearly indiscernible nod, then turns to Katie with loving kindness threading his voice. "This whole process will take time, 'Katie-did.'" He reaches his hand over to touch her arm. "We'll all be working on this from multiple angles to do what's best for Gavin. And for you."

Katie lifts her head. "He needs medication and therapy, which he has so far resisted. He promised me to do the work, but I'm not sure I can trust him to do it if he just returns home," she sighs. "I mean, I love him and want him to get back to his former good and wonderful self, but things have been getting worse, not better."

"His former self buried all his trauma," Pedersen cautions, "under that veneer of 'good and wonderful' you love, Katie. So until he confronts all he's buried—which is now coming to the surface in a dangerous way—and rebuilds himself, you won't see much that's reliably 'wonderful' from him."

Katie hadn't thought of Gavin's disorder in this way. That his good, kind and caring nature she fell in love with may have been a "veneer" he used to keep his resentment and anger over his childhood abuse in control. Under wraps. And now will that protective veil fall away, releasing all Gavin's pent-up anger? He has had violent displays of anger in reaction to some of his triggers. She sets that concern, that fear, aside for now, where it sits on a shelf, keeping watch.

Pedersen turns to Tray. "Could the attorney you know petition the court to commit Gavin to hospitalization in a secure facility?"

"I'll talk to her," Tray says. "Honora Kaplan knows the system and all the players. Tough old bird with a heart of gold."

Pedersen cracks a knowing grin. "You're right," he chuckles. "Honora's a pain, but always right."

Tray smiles, then adds, "The earliest point when commitment is normally argued is at arraignment, so Honora will have to scramble to get up to speed."

Grandpa asks, "Should you slow-roll the arraignment, to give her more time?"

"That's a risk," Pedersen's head shakes a vigorous "no."

"I agree," Tray nods to Pedersen. "Honora can do this." He pulls out his phone and begins texting.

Pedersen frowns. "If the court agrees, they'll automatically send him to Bridgewater, which would be the absolute worst thing for him. Dr. Skokou and I can serve as witnesses to the current condition of his disorder and get him into McLean, where they have a couple locked wards. She and I both have privileges there, so we can collaborate in treatment." He pulls out his phone. "I'm contacting the chief there now. I hope they can be ready by arraignment, day after tomorrow."

"Poor Gavin," Katie shakes her head, looking down at her trembling hands. "I want to see him, Tray."

"It's too late at night now, but in the morning..."

Grandpa interjects, with an intense, almost fierce look. "Why do you want to see him, Katie? He's ruined your life, and Maggie's too! Our daughter did the same thing, making excuses for her husband, insisting he wasn't a bad person, and—"

Katie slaps her palm on her thigh and stands. "I am *not* prepared to abandon the man I love, who I know loves me and Maggie! We may have to be separated while he does the hard work he needs to do, but he's still my husband and I will support and encourage him as best I can!"

Katie immediately runs as the first screams come from upstairs.

"Your nightmares follow you like a shadow, forever."
—*Aleksandar Hemon*, The Lazarus Project

47

GAVIN LIES BACK ON THE HARD MAT OF HIS CELL. He closes his eyes, trying to breathe. The focused, measured breaths he'd practiced—the conscious, deliberate in and out process that has pulled him back into reality many times during the past months—isn't working now. After Maggie was taken.

Now he's in this place, this nightmare. Bars silhouette against the dim light of the hallway. Hollow sounds from unknown sources. Cold hard floor and walls trap him in darkness. No way out.

But he's been here before. In his nightmare so long ago. And now it's happening, for real. *Déjà vu all over again,* as Yogi Berra used to say.

How did it come to this?

He feels like he's falling. Plummeting, out of control, a bottomless descent, drowning in his own madness. He should have known it was coming, that it was waiting for him. He was warned. That night, nine years ago.

There's no way to stop it now. He spirals helplessly down a long dark tunnel, like a drunken man losing consciousness, the same nightmare from the past, now replaying in his current reality...

In blackness, he is surrounded by bars spaced a few inches apart. Walls of bars enclose him. Bars above. Bars underfoot, resting on rough cement, cold and clammy to his touch. How did he get here? How can he get out? He shouts. No sound comes out. He grabs the bars and shakes. Nary a rattle. Deadbolts clang shut all around him. No way out. He shouts again. Still no sound. The cage vibrates. It moves. Then plummets. Icy water engulfs him. He and the cage plunge deeper. He cannot breathe. His chest tightens. He struggles, pulls on the bars. Can't breathe...

> "Damaged people are dangerous.
> They know they can survive."
> —Josephine Hart

48

"WHERE'S TRAY?" GAVIN ASKS, HIS FIRST WORDS TO Katie as he sits across from her at the cracked Formica-top table Wednesday morning. Two guards in the cold, cavernous room observe inmates and visitors. Gavin's left leg vibrates, jiggling up and down at a furious pace. His eyes narrow in concentration, focused beyond Katie on something or nothing in the distance, as he takes slow deliberate breaths.

She hopes his concentrated breathing is an indication he's doing his calming routine. She speaks softly, cautiously. "Well, sweetheart, at this point, they only allow one visit by a family member and one from your lawyer each day," Katie says. "And no children under the age of twelve. I hope someone told you they found Maggie, and she's back home."

"Yeah, that's good." He fidgets. "But I need Tray to tell me if Salvatti and his sister are locked up for good. And whether FBI is going to charge anyone for the bodies in the basement."

Katie winces. The Gavin she always knew would be anxious to know how they found their daughter, how Maggie's doing, and how *she* is. What has happened to her husband? "Well, I can ask Tray about that," she says, scrutinizing him for any indication of his state of mind. She manages to catch his gaze for a brief moment. "But Salvatti and what's buried in that basement should be the least of your concerns right now.

How your daughter is going to recover from the trauma of being kidnapped is much more important." She loses the lock on his eyes, and now tries to jolt him back. "Also, the charges against you for your little stunt, and how you're going to avoid going off unhinged again should be your real worries."

Gavin blinks and returns his gaze toward her, but shows no reaction to anything she just said. "So when am I getting out of here?" His vibrations increase.

"You're being arraigned tomorrow. Thursday." She doesn't elaborate. The lawyer will do that, and she hopes Gavin can hold it together then.

"Finally, I can get back to my own bed!"

Katie knows that won't happen, and shudders to imagine how he'll react when he has to be hospitalized. "Were you able to sleep last night?"

Gavin pulls back with a look of disgust. "You've got to be shitting me, Katie."

She feels like she's talking with a stranger, not the sweet considerate man she loves. She wonders if something happened to him during confinement last night. "You want to tell me about it?"

"Nothing to tell," he snaps. "Just get me the hell out of here."

"Well, in case you're interested, your daughter didn't sleep well last night." Katie eyes him, hoping that information might elicit a glimpse of the old Gavin. "She had nightmares and screamed sporadically all night." Nothing but a flicker of impatience from him. "And I haven't had a good night's sleep in weeks, so last night was no exception. In case you're interested."

"Well, now you know what it's like for me. And when I get outta here, I know some people who're gonna get a real surprise from me."

"That won't help your case, Gavin." Katie's fists clench tightly, oozing red in her palms. She takes a deep breath.

"Sweetheart, I love you and can't wait for the old Gavin to come back to us. But that Gavin is being suffocated by PTSD. Your past traumas. If you ever want to salvage your life, your marriage and your family, you need to do the work. Like you promised."

Gavin juts his jaw forward. He doesn't look at her. "The *'work'* can't help me." His head stiffens like a man determined to fight all the way to the gallows.

"You haven't *let* it help you," Katie murmurs, then stands. "Your lawyer is waiting to see you, Gavin. She's the one person who can get you out of here, so try to cooperate."

When Katie leaves through the waiting area, she walks over to the woman Tray described as the lawyer. "Ms. Kaplan? I'm Katie DiMasi, Gavin's wife. Thank you for being here, and for helping us at this awful time."

A wiry little sixty-something woman, Honora Kaplan stands to face Katie. "I'm here because Trayvon Harris asked me to. No other reason."

Katie thinks Tray's description of Kaplan as a "tough old bird" may have been an understatement. "I understand. Tray has been Gavin's best friend since high school. What has Tray told you about Gavin's mental health?"

"Enough." Kaplan sits back down on the bench and motions Katie to sit. "And I had a phone conversation with Jim Pedersen this morning. I've known him since undergrad at Harvard. You have good people on your side. My question is, what do *you* want for Gavin? Jail, hospital, home? Separation, divorce?"

Katie is dumbstruck by Kaplan's direct questions. Straight to the core of what Katie has been reluctant to grapple with. What she's afraid to confront. Because there are no good answers. Now she realizes her jaw is hanging open. "I don't know. Yet. I wish I could have my husband, our life, back the way it was. The way he was. Before…"

"Of course. But I'm sure Pedersen has explained that the genie is already out of the bottle and there's no putting it back any time soon."

Katie makes a mental note to tell Tray his description of Kaplan falls far short of the mark. This "tough old bird" is as no-nonsense and blunt as they come. But spot on. "I wanted to warn you, Ms. Kaplan." Katie hesitates. "This morning Gavin seems to have the most detached and aggressive attitude I've ever seen in him. It's totally contrary to his nature, which has always been extremely considerate and kind. I don't know what's happened to him, but I'm hoping he can get the help he needs in the hospital..."

Kaplan's lined face relaxes, and her voice softens. "For your sake, I hope you're right."

But Katie hears the doubt and skepticism in the tough old bird's voice.

> "Art enables us to find ourselves and
> lose ourselves at the same time."
> —*Thomas Merton*

49

ALMOST IMMEDIATELY UPON KATIE'S RETURN HOME from visiting Gavin that morning, Grandma serves her a hot cup of tea and a cranberry scone. As if she had been anxiously awaiting Katie's arrival.

An unnatural quiet hangs in the house like a palsied breath. Maggie sits in the corner of the kitchen floor, with Patches's head resting on her leg. Her upper body rocks slightly forward and back, as if she is hearing a soothing lullaby. She is sucking her thumb—something she's never done before—and has a book on her lap, moving a finger of her other hand along each line as if she's reading the words, murmured as nonsense syllables in a sing-song manner and muffled behind her thumb. She doesn't look up to greet Katie.

"She's been there for a long time," Grandma says with pursed lips and a worried frown.

"She had a rough night," Katie despairs. "Even though I assured her each time she cried out, that she's safe now and everything will be all right, none of that can erase her trauma."

Grandma nods. "After you left, she wet her 'big-girl pants' and brought her Pampers to me. Then she took all her trucks and threw each, one by one, out the door to the garage."

"What did she say?" Katie asks.

"Nothing I could understand. It's like your highly verbal

little girl has regressed."

"Has she eaten anything?" Katie's words are heavy with sorrow.

"She put a few Cheerios in her mouth, one at a time, then spit each one out like it didn't taste right. She did drink her juice from her sippy cup, though. Oh, by the way, I arranged for Anita Forsberg, the child psychotherapist, to be here in the morning."

"Good. Thank you," Katie says, then takes her tea and scone to the corner and sits on the floor beside Maggie. Patches remains unmoving on the other side of his charge. "What are you reading, Mags?"

Maggie doesn't stop what she's doing or look at her mother.

"After I finish the tea and scone Grandma gave me, I'm going to our art studio to paint what I feel inside, Maggie." She bends her head to peer into her daughter's face, which remains implacable. "Some terrible things have happened in the past few days that make me feel so many awful ways." She puts her hand to her heart and shows the anguish in her face to Maggie. "I need to get those feelings out of me, talk about them, but saying the words doesn't always help very much. So maybe if I can *show* how I feel, paint it all, it might not hurt so bad. It might not be so scary. What do you think?"

Maggie looks up to Katie and nods slowly, her eyes wide and wet.

"Would you like to share my scone, then join me in our art studio?"

Maggie eats most of Katie's scone without spitting it out, while Patches snarfs up the crumbs. Then she wordlessly grabs her mommy's hand and leads her into their art room. She immediately begins pulling out pots of acrylic paint and brushes.

"We have one piece of unpainted Bristol board left for you, Mags, and one blank canvas for me!"

"Feel," Maggie says, thrusting a brush toward Katie.

Katie nearly dissolves. Her daughter, her child, giving her permission to feel. To breathe. To realize, to understand. To know. She crouches down to her level, places her hand on Maggie's heart and whispers, "You too, Mags. You feel, too," then kisses her angel gently and accepts the brush.

Patches settles on the floor in front of the sliding doors that lead to the back patio. The two easels—one normal size and the other small, customized for Maggie—are positioned back-to-back, perpendicular to the doors, where afternoon light confers an inviolable aura to the mother-daughter drama.

Unlike her previous bold attacks on the board, Maggie paints cautiously today, constraining her strokes in miniature studied detail, beginning in the lower left corner of her board. She chooses each color carefully after due deliberation.

As Katie stands in front of her wide canvas, the brush in her hand becomes an extension of her fingers, an agent of her body and soul. Dark, tight, constricted, knotted forms writhe in agony all across the bottom of her canvas. Then her strokes gradually open and flow upward on one side, like pulsing energy, adding more and brighter colors, vibrant and light, glowing, expanding, rising toward the top of the canvas like a golden phoenix.

Katie stands back for a moment to feel the untethered freedom of that mythical being, then is struck by the unpainted area on the left side of her canvas. She ponders its void, unsure why it is there, why she so neglected that space, whether there is reason or meaning in having done so. She picks up a wider brush and grips it with both hands as if she might receive inspiration, revelation, or a coded message through it. She cautiously dabs its full width into the black paint, then begins making wide arcs on the blank canvas, starting where the writhing forms end on the left side, sweeping up and around, then with a smaller brush blending white into those arcs, growing more arcs above that, and continuing to the top of her canvas. After blending more white and a hint of blue into the black, a mass of angry roiling storm clouds appear, alive and rising above the dark earth, encroaching into the brilliant gold on the right, threatening its joy, its life.

"Mommy..." Maggie's voice is petulant.

Katie rushes over to Mags and kneels beside her. "What is it, sweetie?" She looks over Maggie's head at the painting she has done. There are several apparent objects that have a big red X or frantic scribbles over them. Although at almost two years old, Maggie hasn't mastered drawing, a couple of those X'ed-over objects seem to represent people.

"Make go 'way." Maggie mumbles.

"Make someone go away?"

"Maggie maked bad people go." Maggie points to her painting. "Now make feels go 'way."

"You want those bad scary feelings, those memories of what happened, to go away."

Maggie is solemn as she nods her head, her lower lip quivering.

"Would you like to tell me about what's in your painting?" Katie asks. "Sometimes it helps if we can name what we want to go away, *tell* it to go away, and take its awful feelings away with it."

Maggie takes Katie's hand and begins to point to elements of her painting—most of which don't resemble what she says they are, of course. Bad woman has a big red X over it, bad man has an X. Luca has a yellow circle around him. Mean girl has scribbles. Nice boy has a yellow circle around him. A red shape is "nice boy's wed twuck." A yellow squarish shape is beside a white shape with brown spots that represents Patches, with a yellow circle around him.

Katie points to the yellow square. "Is that the door where you went out of that house?"

Maggie nods soberly.

"You're so smart, so brave."

Maggie points to one more object. A black squarish space

harbors a tiny little creature inside its lower right corner. "Maggie," she states, very seriously. There are furious red scribbles over the blackness of the square.

"That's such a good painting, Maggie. I can see you must have felt alone and scared in that dark closet. Are you still having some alone and scared feelings now?" Katie touches her fingers lightly to Maggie's cheek.

Maggie nods solemnly.

"Do you think we should tell those bad feelings *really loudly* to go away?"

Maggie props her fists onto her sides like Mommy does when she's serious, then stomps her foot and shouts at her painting, "Go 'way!" Then she does what can only be described as a war dance, complete with screeching noises that could chase away the most dangerous demons.

Katie is overcome, laughing and crying all at the same time. She scoops up Maggie in her arms and dances with her, joining their noises. It feels good, a cathartic exorcism. But she knows it isn't over. The purging of Maggie's trauma will take more time, and more war dances.

As their dance subsides, Katie asks, "Do you think we should put away our paints, clean our brushes in the basement sink, and then have lunch?"

"Yes, Mommy," Maggie says, and begins gathering their supplies. When she sees Katie's painting, she points to the right side, the golden phoenix, and says, "Mommy's woom."

Katie smiles. Apparently Maggie thinks all paintings should represent people in some way, and that Mommy should be in that golden space, that room. "You're so smart, Magsy-Wagsy! Yes, that's where Mommy belongs." She takes up black paint with her palette knife and quickly cuts a narrow impasto silhouette of a woman with untamed curls against the golden atmospheric glow. And then cuts a small silhouette beside it, with outstretched hands joined with the woman's.

"Maggie!" her daughter squeals in delight, clapping her hands.

"That's right, my smart big girl!"

Then Maggie looks at the other side of Katie's painting and frowns. She points, her lower lip protruding. "Daddy."

Katie freezes mid-stride, startled by her toddler's perception. "Daddy is sick right now, Maggie. It may take some time until he's well enough to come home to us."

Maggie nods soberly, still pointing. "Daddy," she repeats.

"So yes, Daddy is in a dark place right now," Katie murmurs as she knifes a gray shadow outline of a bearded man into the dark left side of the painting. "But he will someday return to us in our bright place."

Just as they are finishing cleaning their brushes, the doorbell rings. It's Destiny, lugging several pre-primed canvases of various sizes, Bristol board, and a great deal more paint. Katie squeals, "Destiny! I can't believe you—this is so generous! Maggie, look what my friend Destiny brought for you!"

Maggie hasn't met Destiny before, so holds back, hiding behind her mother, then runs into the kitchen, where Grandma is making lunch.

"This whole terrible experience has made her so...skittish. Afraid, actually," Katie says.

"Well of course it has, my dear," Destiny says, hugging her friend.

Katie calls out to the kitchen, "Grandma, come meet my friend Destiny, who is teaching me how to paint!"

Destiny laughs, "Katie darling, you already know more about painting than you realize—it's intuitive. Your talent just drips from your fingers."

Katie dismisses this with a laugh. "Destiny, this is Gavin's maternal grandmother Dr. Carla O'Malley. She's been a lifesaver ever since we came back here from Kauai."

Grandma wipes her hands on her apron. "Will you stay for lunch, Destiny?"

"I came to give Katie and her little Maggie my support and love, and now you want to give *me* sustenance?" Destiny laughs. "Let me ask Maggie if it's okay for me to stay a little while during her lunch."

In no time at all, Destiny has won the trust of both Grandma and Maggie.

After lunch, as the three women sit around the kitchen table with Maggie falling asleep in her mommy's arms, Katie feels a warm comfort all over, like being safely snuggled in a favorite old blanket. "Thank you for coming over, Destiny, and for encouraging my painting."

"Thank *you* for giving me the courage to open an art gallery, Katie dear." Destiny looks intently into Katie's eyes. "And I'm encouraging you to give yourself permission to become who you really are, Katie—not *just* a caretaker of unwell people. Embrace that remarkable, brilliant individual inside you."

Permission to feel. And now permission to be...

> "Face the demons of my inner being and tell them that you love me, that you are here to stay. Tell them they don't scare you and promise me you'll never walk away."
> —Anita Krizzan

50

ON A SPRAWLING MODERN BRICK MULTI-STORY campus occupying an oversized city block, where the waters of Boston Harbor lap its rounded outer perimeter, with broad muscular arches and a beefy cylindrical tower whose top reminds Katie of San Francisco's Coit, she paces the marble halls of the District Court. It is Thursday morning and she is not alone; Tray and Pedersen are there too, but she feels alone, tension braiding fear throughout her body, twisting dark scenarios in her mind as she waits for Honora Kaplan, who is supposed to have met with the District Court Clerk this morning, before Gavin's arraignment.

The hallway outside the courtroom writhes with people in throbbing clusters moving in diverse directions, like a disturbed ant colony, the merged sounds of voices, footsteps, doors opening and closing, summing out as cacophonous anxiety. It is less than fifteen minutes before their assigned court appearance, and Katie is near panic.

Soon the distinctive slam of strident heels penetrates the hallway noise as Kaplan weaves through the crowd toward them. With no greeting aside from a curt nod, the attorney gets right to the point. "I talked with the District Court Clerk, who told me that because of Gavin's demeanor during arrest and subsequently in confinement, the judge asked the on-staff Court Evaluator to conduct an assessment prior to arraignment. That's for the purpose of assessing whether a competency hearing is required to determine Gavin's fitness to stand trial. Then I talked with the Court Evaluator, whom I know quite well. He skirted a bit outside protocol by sharing with me that Gavin is basically a train wreck this morning. Freezing, almost catatonic, occasionally panicking and attempting to flee, then failing to do so, ducking under the table with his head tucked under his arms." She catches her breath and scans the stricken faces in front of her. "Incidentally, variations on that theme were apparent to me when I met with him yesterday."

Katie's breath stalls and she feels light-headed, but she manages to find words. "How will that affect his position in court today?"

"It isn't clear to the Evaluator that Gavin is currently able to fully understand the charges against him and assist rationally in his own defense. So he's going to recommend that Gavin be hospitalized for further evaluation by psychiatric professionals and treatment, until such time that competency can be restored. That would put proceedings on hold until competency is achieved. *If* the judge agrees with the Evaluator's recommendation."

Katie notices Pedersen standing off to the side, looking more tired than she's ever seen him. Pale, wan, withdrawn. Is he ill? She worries that this ordeal with Gavin, who seems to have become Jim's surrogate son over the years, has taken a lot out of Pedersen. She hopes he hasn't lost hope. For Gavin or for himself.

Pedersen speaks up now. "Honora, if there's a moment the judge seems reluctant to agree, can you call me to testify? Is that allowed in an arraignment?"

Kaplan cocks her head, weighing Pedersen's request. "It's a bit unusual, but not prohibited..."

"And then can we influence which hospital he's remanded to?" Pedersen prods. "I have a signed document here from Dr. Kulkarni at McLean stating that they will reserve a bed in a locked ward there for Gavin." He hands it to her.

She takes the document and looks at it. "The State won't pay McLean's rates, Jim," Kaplan scoffs, stuffing the document into a folder in her briefcase. "And all the supervision and reports that would ordinarily be done at Bridgewater will be required. I assume you'll be involved in his treatment?"

"Yes of course," Pedersen confirms. "And Kulkarni has agreed to the reporting requirements, as detailed in that document. It won't be the first time McLean has performed this service, and the State won't be required to pay any more than they would for Bridgewater."

Katie studies Pedersen and wonders whether McLean is making special arrangements because of his relationship with Kulkarni, the institution, or his relationship with the patient. As Kaplan said yesterday, Gavin does have good people on his side. Katie is grateful and feels a glimmer of hope, lessening the weight of her fears. Tray puts his arm around her shoulders and squeezes.

Kaplan checks her watch. "We should go in now and get settled."

When they enter the small courtroom—not one used for jury trials—Katie, Tray and Dr. Pedersen sit directly behind Kaplan, where Gavin will be seated. Pedersen is on the end for easy access if he needs to testify. Grandpa, Dr. Skokou and Dr. Ted from the spouse group are in the row behind.

Katie feels weak, beyond nervous. Her mouth is as dry as sandpaper and tastes foul, as if her stomach bile is belching toxic chemicals. She worries about Maggie, whether she's feeling abandoned while Mommy is gone—although Katie did explain to her where she's going and when she'll return. She hopes Mags will be okay with Destiny and Grandma this morning.

The court seems to be behind schedule. While they wait for Gavin to be brought in, Katie turns to Tray, speaking low. "Thanks for being here, Tray. It means so much to me. And Gavin will really appreciate it."

"We're like family, girl," Tray whispers and pats her hand. "Of course I'm here for you. You're going through a tough time."

"Yeah. So are Gavin and Maggie." Katie's head sinks low. "By the way, what's happening to the people who took Maggie?"

"They're being held without bail. Don't worry; I don't think Rick Salvatti will get out any time soon, although his sister might get a short sentence or be put on probation. She doesn't have a prior record, and she was coerced by her brother to do it. And she has two kids, who are in foster care now."

Katie feels sorry for those kids—especially Maggie's "nice boy" with the red truck. "Oh, and what about the stuff Gavin found in the Prince Street building? He seems anxious to know."

"Well, that's a more complicated story—lots of bodies over several decades," Tray shakes his head. "We have someone in custody for Solomon's death but there's still so much we don't know on all the bodies—who killed 'em, who buried them. We're still investigating, but a lot of people who were responsible over the years might be dead, or 'incapacitated,'" he air-quotes. "Linskey is trying to get his brother's lottery winnings, but that's a long shot, given his B&E at Gavin's house."

"Sounds like Gavin won't get much satisfaction out of that treasure hunt. He wants revenge."

"That's what Salvatti wanted. So now that's the PTSD version of Gavin talking." Tray turns a sorrowful face to her, seeming to commiserate, or apologize, for what may lie ahead.

Katie looks over at Pedersen, recalling what he said about Gavin's veneer of "good and wonderful" being blown, now that his past trauma is coming to the surface. She cringes to think about what Gavin 2.0 will be like.

They stop their whispering and turn their heads toward the side door as two guards usher Gavin in. He's wearing the clean proper clothes Katie left with the jail foreman yesterday, and his hands are cuffed. There's a vacant look on his face as he stares straight ahead, focusing on nothing, like he may be in one of his "freeze" reactions. He doesn't look at anyone. Not Katie, Tray, or Pedersen.

The bailiff calls out "All rise" before Gavin has sat, and everyone stands while the judge comes in. Katie looks around the room and wonders who all the people filling the benches are. Do they have anything to do with this case? With Gavin, or with the people who took Maggie? Should she be worried?

Kaplan whispers to Gavin to sit. He has the look of someone with dementia. Disoriented, confused, fearful. Katie desperately wants to embrace him, inject vitality into him, reignite his strength and goodness. Remind him of who he is. Was.

The proceedings happen so quickly Katie can't keep up with them. Everything goes by in a flash, much of it in formal obtuse legal-speak. The offenses are cited by the prosecutor, the judge asks for the plea, Kaplan replies "Defendant pleads 'not guilty,'" the judge calls on the Evaluator to present his findings and recommendation, Kaplan cites the kidnapping as trigger for the defendant's offenses and calls Pedersen to speak, he briefly cites Gavin's history and current diagnosis, Kaplan presents the document from McLean to the judge, and the judge remands Gavin to that facility for thirty days or until such time as treatment can restore competency for trial. The gavel drops with a resounding finality.

Gavin doesn't seem to comprehend what just happened. Kaplan tells him to say something to his wife before the guards escort him away for transfer.

He looks dazed and bewildered, but turns around. "Tray, old buddy!" He laughs, then seems shocked as he reaches out to Tray and realizes his hands are cuffed. "Wha—?"

Katie tries to help him focus. "Gavin, you're going to get

help in a good place, and I'll come see you there, and—"

The guards begin pulling him away. A visceral fear, one of horror, overcomes him—

Katie panics, hoping he won't react violently—

"Don't let them do this, Katie! Don't give up on me! I need you! You have to save me—!"

His shouts fade as he is dragged down the hall.

Katie dissolves under the overwhelming weight of loss.

> "A friend is someone who helps you up
> when you're down, and if they can't,
> they lay down beside you and listen."
> —*A.A. Milne*, Winnie the Pooh

51

KATIE NEEDS THE WORLD TO GRANT PERMISSION for another five hours in every day.

Between visiting Gavin at McLean every day, taking Maggie to therapy, managing two businesses thousands of miles away, tying off all the loose ends on the DiMasi properties, going to spouse group, constant engagement with people who've suddenly decided they're her best friend, dealing with doctors and the courts on Gavin's treatment, and keeping up with FBI's investigation of crimes uncovered in the Prince Street building, Katie has little time or energy to paint, feel, or be whatever it is she's supposed to be. Other than a one-armed juggler.

There's the doorbell now. Patches runs to stand guard. Katie looks through the peephole, then opens the door to greet Honora Kaplan, who proffers a quick hug. Katie smiles inwardly, noting the tough old bird's progress.

"Good morning, Honora! Thanks so much for meeting me here." Katie gestures to the sofa. "Maggie, say *hi* to Ms. Kaplan."

Maggie looks up from the dining room table, where she is "writing" an illustrated book.

"I understand your life is very hectic these days," Kaplan says, waving to Maggie. "So I'm happy to come to Wellesley for our meeting. I have another appointment in Needham today, so it's sort of convenient. But I'm afraid I'm going to make your life a little more hectic."

"Hold on," Katie smiles. "I think I'm going to need some coffee for this. You want some?"

"Definitely, thanks."

"Black, no sugar, right?"

Kaplan gives a thumbs up.

Katie places Kaplan's cup on the coffee table, then sits with her own cup in a side chair opposite her attorney. "Is there something new?" Katie had consolidated several legal issues with Kaplan's firm in order to simplify her life. Spare her sanity. Any one of those issues could drag her down into tangled weeds at any time, so having help from the various specialties in Kaplan's firm has been a life saver.

"We have a lot to cover," Kaplan pulls out her iPad, "so I apologize if I'm direct."

Katie smiles, thinking *Why should today be any different with Honora?*

"First of all, the court has become impatient with Gavin's progress. Three weeks in, and they say he's worse than when he went in."

Katie nods. "That's for sure. I see that every time I visit him."

"So unless he makes a turnaround in the next week, we're hearing they may propose a plea of 'not guilty by reason of insanity,' which would put him in a psychiatric institution—not McLean—for the length of time the judge declares."

"But the circumstances...and he's a first-time offender."

"Which will reduce the recommended length of sentence, but if he doesn't get a manageable diagnosis even at the end of that period, he won't be released." Kaplan watches as Katie crumbles. "Katie, you may want to consider visiting Gavin only once a week. It isn't helping him or you."

Katie sniffs. "Yes, you're probably right."

"Well, on to some good news, *Kathryn Angela Goodwin DiMasi*," Kaplan says like announcing an award. "We got Gavin's signature on the documents giving you Power of Attorney over all his assets as well as your joint assets. Which means you're free to sell your restaurant, his house, his building in the North End—"

"Oh, that's both good and scary," Katie mumbles. "Like, it would be good to get all that stuff from the past out of our lives, but he could also recover at some point and really resent me for doing it." She remembers Pedersen explaining that when Gavin begins to seriously do the work of rebuilding who he is from a clean slate—not the manipulated unreality of his youth, he may emerge as a different person than the "good and wonderful" man she married. How can she know who her husband will be, months or years from now?

"That's possible. But at least you now have the option," Kaplan says. "Which brings us to the other piece of good news. FBI's evidence collection in Gavin's Prince Street building is complete, and now you've got a clean offer on the building."

"From whom?" Katie doesn't want to support more mob involvement in the North End.

"It's a home goods chain out of Ohio, a rising competitor to Crate & Barrel," Kaplan grins. "We've vetted them. They're squeaky clean."

"Okay, I'll look at it. And *try* to discuss with Gavin," Katie shrugs. "I'm making progress on cleaning out his parents' house across town. I've put the stuff I think he'd like to save in a storage locker I've rented, hired an estate sale company to sell and give away what's left, and hired a cleaning and painting crew. But I'm not sure this time of year is good for putting it on the market."

"You could place it with Coldwell Banker under the condition that it be shown only to serious buyers, then make it public on MLS in the spring season if it hasn't been sold."

"That sounds like a good idea," Katie nods, thinking.

"By the way, just yesterday I got an email from a restaurant chain based in California, saying they're interested in buying '*Ono Kūloko*.'"

"Oh, really?" Kaplan asks. "Are you open to that? When are you going back home to Kauai?"

"I'm not sure I *am* going back," Katie shakes her head. "I need to be near Gavin. And besides, I've made some friends here, a new life. This feels like home,..." She shrugs. "I'm going to ask Anakoni, Gavin's sous chef, if he wants to buy it before I make a decision. And also, interestingly, Kalea wants to buy my art gallery."

"Can either of them afford to do that?" Kaplan is skeptical.

"I'm thinking a price that's equivalent to the current value of inventory and any outstanding debts, plus whatever legal costs are involved."

"You're way too generous, Katie." Kaplan peers at her over her half-glasses.

"I'll run everything by you, Honora."

"Okay," Kaplan shrugs. "The other piece of good news is that Rick Salvatti was sentenced to ten years with no chance of parole for abducting your daughter. His sister got five years, but she'll probably get early parole because she doesn't have a prior record."

"I feel sorry for her kids," Katie mumbles.

"Oh, and Linskey was sentenced to three years for breaking into Gavin's house, but he's appealing. And insisting that the money Gavin found in the building belongs to him."

"It probably does, but FBI will have the final say on that," Katie shrugs.

"By the way," Kaplan brightens, "did Trayvon tell you he's being promoted, and transferred to Boston?"

"Yes, he said 'the guys upstairs' are impressed with what he's doing on the mob cases, based on the evidence from Prince Street. So he owes us, I guess," Katie jokes.

Just then, the doorbell rings again.

"Oh, Honora, I think that's my friend Destiny Abara, coming to take Maggie for a walk. She's become Maggie's BFF," Katie grins.

"That's fine," Kaplan says, getting up. "We've covered everything for now, and I have to get over to Needham anyway." As she walks toward the door, she turns to Katie. "Thanks for the coffee, dear. You're one of the strongest women I've ever known. You can do this. And more."

Katie and Destiny walk arm-in-arm behind Maggie, who is dancing up the sidewalk singing the ABC song.

"Thanks for all your business advice, Katie darling." Destiny smiles and squeezes her friend's arm. "You had a really successful gallery in Hawaii. I'd love it if you could partner with me in our own art gallery?"

"Wow, Destiny, I didn't know my advice was for a joint venture with you!" Katie laughs.

"Well, I have my eye on a space that just opened up in the South End, and I could really use both your business as well as artistic expertise in making sure it succeeds."

"That's intriguing, Destiny," Katie smiles. "Would you be competing with Peter?"

"Oh, not at all. I want to focus on indigenous art—American and African."

"Well, I'm happy to give you my opinions, but I'm not sure about 'partnership.' Like, what investment of both time and capital would be required? And is this even a good time for you to be making this change?"

Destiny smiles like she has a secret. "Tray is now officially separated, and we're dating, so I guess it's time for change." Destiny looks at Katie with raised eyebrows, as if seeking approval.

"Tray's job in the FBI takes him all over the world for

extended periods of time, so I guess it's not surprising that his marriage has taken a hit," Katie frowns. "I never had the chance to get to know Hannah very well, though."

"Tray says he found out she was cheating on him."

"Well then, he may have to do some remodeling on the tattoo he got the day before their wedding," Katie grins.

"Yeah... I'm waiting for that." Destiny chuckles. "By the way, how's Maggie's therapy progressing?"

"Pretty well. Her therapist says the painting Maggie has been doing has made a significant difference, and she's returning to the Child Study Center next week. And she rarely wakes up with bad dreams these days."

Up ahead, Maggie stops short where a moving truck is blocking the sidewalk in front of Luca's house. "Luca?" She frowns.

Katie recalls seeing high-tech security installation on Luca's house a few weeks ago, and now sees him outside, barking orders to the movers. She takes Maggie's hand and walks over to greet him. "Hi Luca, I see you're getting around pretty well on that leg of yours!"

He's not in a good mood. "Yeah, yeah," he mutters gruffly. "These guys don't know what they're doing. Amateurs."

"You aren't moving, are you, Luca?"

"Yeah. Arizona."

"Is that for your health?"

"Yeah. My health. Not safe now, after..." He turns away, his shoulders slumped like a man approaching the gallows, and goes back into his house.

> "Life isn't about finding yourself.
> Life is about creating yourself."
> —George Bernard Shaw

52

"HAPPY BIRTHDAY TO YOU, HAPPY BIRTHDAY, DEAR Maggie," they all sing, with Maggie clapping her hands and eyeing the two glowing candles on the cake.

"Okay, Mags, now you blow out the candles," Katie says, taking pictures with her phone. "Would you like me to help you huff and puff?"

"Desty!" Maggie points, giggling.

"You want me to help blow out your candles?" Destiny asks, and Maggie nods emphatically.

"Make a wish first, Mags," Katie says. "But don't say what it is—keep it your secret."

"I'm going to need your help to blow them out, big girl!" Destiny says with all seriousness. "Okay now, One! Two! Three!" Maggie and Destiny blow together.

"Yay!" Everyone cheers when the candles go out. Miriam's little Bobby, who has grown quite fond of Maggie and seems to think he's her protector, gives her a slobbery kiss.

The dining room is crowded with celebrants gathered around the birthday girl. There's Katie, Grandma and Grandpa, Tray, Pedersen, Destiny, Peter Thompson, Dr. Ted, Luca, Miriam and her two children, and Dr. Forsberg, Maggie's therapist. Gifts and cards clutter the room and overflow into the living room—from those in the room and others who are absent. Mrs. Anders and Dr. Malone from the Child Study Center, several members of the spouse group. Even Officer Paliotta, who brought Maggie from Charlestown to Boston, and Ms. O'Dougherty from Child Protection Services, who sent along a chicken-scratched note from Maggie's "nice boy" saying happy birthday and that she can keep his red truck. Maggie has won the hearts of many people.

"What did you wish?" Miriam's daughter Jenny asks Maggie.

Mags hesitates, then murmurs, "I wished Daddy will be not-sick. An' he comed home."

Everyone holds their breath for a moment, then Katie says, "Yes, sweetie, we all wish that. Would you like some of that yummy cake now? And we can save a piece for Daddy in the fridge."

Maggie closes her eyes and puts her hand on her heart. It's a gesture she has learned during her twice-weekly "play" sessions with Dr. Forsberg. It's a grounding technique to help remind her that she is okay, that whatever is upsetting her in the moment cannot destroy her.

It's the Tuesday after Thanksgiving. Katie's thoughts turn to Gavin, missing his daughter's second birthday. Just as he also missed what had become their own special traditions on Thanksgiving. The holiday this year was different. And difficult. Katie took Maggie to visit Gavin in the morning—the first date the locked ward permitted children to visit. But Gavin's demeanor upset Maggie. A lot. After which neither Maggie nor Mommy had stomach for "holiday" when they joined the grandparents for turkey dinner. The mood was depressed, with moments of forced cheerfulness, and lacked the spirit of thankfulness. Both Katie and Maggie simply toyed with their food.

So much has changed in the four weeks since Maggie was taken. But change had already been set in motion months ago, on July 15, when Devon performed his final act of gaslighting on his twin. That triggered a cascade of upheaval that has affected the entire family, every condition of their lives, and will certainly continue to do so in the coming months. Likely years.

But as Katie now looks around the room, she realizes that life for nearly everyone here has been altered in some way, ranging from cataclysmic to trivial.

Maggie will miss Luca when he moves to Arizona at Christmas. Katie worries about his safety and has asked Tray to investigate whether there has been blow-back in the Italian "community" after his cooperation with FBI.

Dr. Ted is deep in discussion with Miriam, who has taken a new job in town and initiated a divorce from her husband. Ted has always seemed particularly fond of Miriam.

Both Grandma and Grandpa have announced their respective retirements—he from his professorship at Harvard and she from her position at Wellesley College—both at the end of this academic year. And they've booked extensive travel well into the future.

Pedersen seems to have aged tremendously in the past month. Katie's concerned about his health, and has urged him to get a complete checkup. He also seems morose, perhaps mourning the apparent futility of saving Gavin, his substitute son.

Of course the man who is not in the room is the one who has changed the most. She has cut back on her visits to him; now only twice per week. She never knows what she will find each time. His disorder is consuming him. He refuses to trust Dr. Skokou, and he's noncompliant with Pedersen's efforts as well. The medication helps only marginally better than its side effects. It will be a long process of steps forward, steps backward, but slowly, Gavin 2.0 is revealing himself as an angry uncaring person. A one-eighty from the former sweet Gavin who cared too much, thinking he was responsible for everyone's welfare. Katie hopes this version isn't permanent, that there will eventually be a Gavin 2.1.

Tray has become "involved" with Destiny. Perhaps his elevated position in the FBI will spare him so much travel, bringing more stability to a relationship. Katie smiles now, watching him whisper with Destiny in the way of lovers.

Thompson's "Critical Eye" gallery is reportedly booming despite having had a falling-out with his partner. He's been frequenting Pendleton a great deal recently, seeking Katie's opinions and advice about his business, praising her talent and begging her to have a solo show at his gallery. Today he hovers around her, trying to help with Maggie's party, cleaning up and generally fussing.

Katie feels like her entire world is changing. All around her, and inside her. Some of those changes are out of her control, while in other cases it is she making the changes. And she's changing within herself. Some of that seems like a good thing, when she's energized and inspired, and other times she's overwhelmed and uncertain, mourning what has been lost, wanting to turn back time to when everything seemed more certain.

Yet getting rid of some parts of the past has given her more freedom to embrace new dimensions of life she'd never experienced before. She's now becoming unburdened from managing multiple balls in the air at once. Having power of attorney over her and Gavin's joint assets has enabled her to sell their little house on Kauai quickly and profitably. The Prince Street property, as well as their restaurant and her gallery on Kauai, are all under contract now.

And Katie has been painting daily in Pendleton, with greater confidence and intensity, often with Maggie and Patches in their own little corner of the expanded studio area Destiny arranged for her. She's amassed a broad range of deeply inspired paintings, venturing into new techniques and themes, as doors open to unexplored corners of her heart.

At four and a half months pregnant, she is beginning to show. Everyone she knows wants to lay their hand on her belly, as if to encourage his health and growth. Or to experience the mystical energy emanating from the life within her, as if touching that extraordinary glow will confer the same power to them.

The way so many people are repeatedly drawn to her and her baby bump now triggers a memory in her: Pre-pubescent Katie meeting with a school counselor long ago. It was during a phase in which she had begun hanging out with the "in crowd," occasionally "acting out"—flirting and dressing inappropriately. She can't remember why she was meeting with the counselor, or the woman's name, although she can picture her clearly now. She can see her expression, the tilt of her head, the way she leaned forward, and hear the impassioned tone of the woman's voice when she said, "Be careful, Katie. You don't realize how powerful you are. When you walk into a room or crowd, your strengths, your confidence, your power, all emanate from you, making you a magnet for weak people who will try to steal your power and use it to control you."

That was after her father died, when she began burying it all. Ambition, talent, and dreams. Why is she remembering that now?

"I wanted a perfect ending. Now I've learned, the hard way, that some poems don't rhyme, and some stories don't have a clear beginning, middle, and end. Life is about not knowing, having to change, taking the moment and making the best of it, without knowing what's going to happen next."
—Gilda Radner

Epilogue

PETER THOMPSON'S "CRITICAL EYE" GALLERY IS PACKED with people on opening night, Friday, February 10. Just in time for Valentine's Day gifting, Peter insisted. And the red dots are going up on painting tags all around the room. Katie can't imagine why anyone would want to buy any of her emotional paintings—which Peter has branded as **Transformational**—for a Valentine's Day present. But people are buying, nevertheless.

Peter issued press releases to his mailing list as well as to newspapers, art publications and art critics throughout New England and New York City, touting the talents of Katie Goodwin, her professional name (although she signs each piece simply "KatieG"), as the new artist to emerge on the scene, the one to watch. The adjectives and comparisons to great artists he claimed in the press release seem pretentious to her.

At seven months pregnant, she survived a scare when a little spotting occurred back around Christmastime, but she's okay now. She just needs to avoid being on her feet too much, so she paints while resting on a stool with a special footrest Ted made for her. And everyone babies her. Grandma, Destiny,

Peter, Tray and many other friends.

Now Peter has pulled up a fancy designer stool for her in front of her largest canvas, one of the first to get that red dot, so she can field questions from the crowd. His voice booms out to get everyone's attention. He drapes his arm over her shoulder and pulls her close with a squeeze.

"This," he begins, "as many of you know, is the incredible Katie Goodwin, the artist who has created all this *transformational* art!"

There is applause and vocal affirmation from the guests.

Peter goes on, "I first became aware of Katie's brilliance when I went to Hawaii last year and read an interview of her in *Hawaii Magazine*, in which she declared that artists must have something meaningful to say, to make others *feel*. And clearly many of you have been moved by the power and emotion in her paintings—she certainly makes us feel! And she is doing all this while growing a new life within her," he looks down at her with a smile.

Katie is relieved he doesn't place his hand on her belly the way he frequently does, as if rubbing a magic lamp to make a genie appear.

"So imagine what she will create next!" Peter pronounces with his arms out like a game show host. "She's here to answer your questions and discuss her inspiration for her work. She tells me she may entertain commission requests as well."

Katie and Peter have never discussed doing paintings on commission, but she maintains a sanguine demeanor as people begin asking questions. Her voice is soft with no microphone, so people come closer. She certainly isn't going to divulge the true "inspiration" for the pieces she's been creating over the past several months, for the same reason she isn't using DiMasi as her professional name.

As people pepper her with questions—about her background, training, her future plans, the meanings behind specific paintings or titles—a reporter from the *Boston Globe* begins asking personal questions regarding her family life. She deflects and stands, suggesting the session is over.

Then a movement in the back of the crowd catches her eye.

Bushy red hair atop a tall bearded man.

Gavin...glowering in her direction.

No one informed her he was released. She stiffens, unsure whether to be happy to see him, or worried.

"Is everything okay?" Peter grips her arm. "You're not smiling."

If you or anyone you know is having difficulty managing their emotions, is a trauma survivor, has been diagnosed with PTSD, or is feeling suicidal, please reach out for help:

- PTSD Foundation of America: (877) 717-PTSD (7873). http://ptsdusa.org/get-help/national-outreach/
- NAMI (National Alliance on Mental Illness) HelpLine: Call 1-800-950-NAMI (6264), or text "friend" to 62640 or email helpline@nami.org or go to https://www.nami.org/help
- National Suicide Prevention Lifeline: (800) 273-TALK (8255) https://suicidepreventionlifeline.org/
- Crisis Text Line: Text HOME to 741741 http://www.crisistextline.org/how-it-works/

BOOK CLUB DISCUSSION QUESTIONS

1. In the first chapter of this story, Katie seems calm, logical, in control, almost detached. What does that tell us about her and her relationship with Gavin? What lies behind her composure?

2. What has happened to Gavin before the story begins? What was his life like before that happened, and how is he different now?

3. When Gavin learns he must return to Boston to settle his father's estate, what is he afraid of?

4. How does the mob figure in Gavin's worries? Regarding his family history? Regarding his safety and that of his current family? Regarding his PTSD triggers?

5. What sort of person has Katie been for most of her life? What has been her career? Why or how is that different from what she discovers in the boxes in her childhood room?

6. Why do you think Gavin is able, for the most part, to avoid falling apart while he's investigating the puzzling mysteries in the Prince Street building?

7. What are Gavin's primary triggers, what in his past are they based on, and how does he respond to them?

8. How did Gavin develop PTSD? How is Complex PTSD (C-PTSD) different than PTSD, in etiology as well as symptoms? How/why did Gavin get C-PTSD?

9. How is Gavin's attitude toward Katie changing, and why?

10. In your opinion, why does Gavin resist therapeutic help?

11. What do you think Katie feels is missing, incomplete, or unfulfilled within her? How can she resolve that?

12. One theme in *Secrets In The Mirror* was "the imperative to save others versus the struggle to save oneself." How is that repeating in *What Lies Buried*?

13. The other theme in *Secrets In The Mirror* was multigenerational patterns of dysfunction and abuse—something Katie feared, and what Gavin vowed to break in that book. Do you think he has succeeded in breaking those multigenerational patterns? If so, how? If not, why?

14. What do you think will happen to the characters going forward?

    - How will Maggie be impacted, long-term, by what's happening in her family?
    - How will Katie find and fulfill her true self? What will be her biggest challenges?
    - Will Gavin finally "do the work" and heal? Will he be different—Gavin 2.1? If so, what will Gavin 2.1 be? Will he and Katie reunite?
    - How will Dr. Pedersen, Tray, and Destiny figure in Katie's and Gavin's lives?

ACKNOWLEDGMENTS

There are so many people who've had a hand in making this story possible, I don't know where to start!

To all of you who have read *What Lies Buried*—thank you so much for joining me in Gavin and Katie's story! I hope you've enjoyed it, and/or found it thought-provoking. If you have questions about the story, or want to find out what happens to Katie and Gavin next, you can find me at https://lesliekain-psychfiction.com/. I encourage you to leave your comments about the book here: http://www.Amazon.com/review/create-review?&asin=B0CSWW8CFL.

To those readers who appreciated *Secrets In The Mirror*, I thank you. Many of you wondered how Gavin could recover from his ordeal in that story. Let me assure you that Gavin wondered about that too, and nagged me into hearing him out when I didn't think there needed to be a sequel. I was so wrong! He—and Katie—told me their stories for *What Lies Buried*, so I thank them as well.

To my critique partners Nancie Abuhaidar, Tonya Bervaldi, Annie Ginn—I love you, and I couldn't have gotten through this without your critical perspective and inspired comments!

To all the wonderfully encouraging fellow writers of the WFWA—Women's Fiction Writers Association—thank you for your community and support! I live in Mexico, so can't meet with many of you in person, so your virtual online support has been invaluable. Specific gratitude for *so* many of you, that enumerating would require an entire page!

To my many friends in San Miguel de Allende—both locals

and expats—your love and loyalty has kept me going, and I apologize for often being unavailable while giving birth to my latest literary "baby"! Special love to the two expat psychotherapists who have advised on the C-PTSD aspects of this novel!

To Atmosphere Press, thank you Cameron Finch for being my advocate. It is because of your understanding, insight, wisdom, and flexibility that I've returned to Atmosphere for this sequel. To my developmental editor Jonathan Smith, you are awesome and have helped me make this novel even better than I imagined! Please stick with me for the next book! And the next one!

To my husband Ron Nicodemus for putting up with me and my preoccupation: thank you, dear. I owe you. Please hang in there with me, because I'm not done yet. And to our seventeen-year-old blind cat Sheba, thank you for keeping me company in "our" writing chair.

To the many ARC readers, reviewers, and podcasters who have applauded my first novel and have continued to encourage my work, this sequel is my repayment for your loyalty. Katie and Gavin say, "See you in the next book!"

ABOUT ATMOSPHERE PRESS

Founded in 2015, Atmosphere Press was built on the principles of Honesty, Transparency, Professionalism, Kindness, and Making Your Book Awesome. As an ethical and author-friendly hybrid press, we stay true to that founding mission today.

If you're a reader, enter our giveaway for a free book here:

SCAN TO ENTER
BOOK GIVEAWAY

If you're a writer, submit your manuscript for consideration here:

SCAN TO SUBMIT
MANUSCRIPT

And always feel free to visit Atmosphere Press and our authors online at atmospherepress.com. See you there soon!

ABOUT THE AUTHOR

LESLIE KAIN writes "Psychological Fiction With Heart"
Stories about messed-up people whose greatest obstacles to happiness lie within them.

Leslie Kain was always writing something when she was a kid—fantasies, poems, secret plans—culminating in running away across country at fifteen, never looking back. In her careers (psychology, Government Intelligence, nonprofits), her writing was limited to nonfiction: professional and research. Finally dabbling in fiction during spare moments above the clouds, her short stories found their way into literary journals and anthologies. She developed personal relationships with her characters, who relentlessly nagged her into longer stories. Her debut novel, *Secrets In The Mirror,* published in 2022 by Atmosphere Press, has been honored with many awards; its sequel, *What Lies Buried,* was released May 2024 by Atmosphere. A member of WFWA, Kain also recently contributed to the anthology *A Million Ways: Stories of Motherhood.* She leverages her education, training, and experience in psychology to write stories of inner conflict and emotional transformation. She earned degrees from Wellesley College and Boston University. She now lives in Mexico with her husband and cat Sheba. Follow her on her website https://lesliekain-psychfiction.com.